for my dear Talented artist
a good friend with speed

Thanks & gratitude for your
valuable participation in this
project. Thank you George

with best

Henry

Dec 11-2001

The Surgeon

✳✳✳

Anatomy of a Conspiracy

✳✳✳

Hormoz Mansouri

Trafford
PUBLISHING™

Order this book online at www.trafford.com/08-0754
or email orders@trafford.com

Most Trafford titles are also available at major online book retailers.

Note for Librarians: A cataloguing record for this book is available from Library
and Archives Canada at www.collectionscanada.ca/amicus/index-e.html

Printed in Victoria, BC, Canada.

ISBN: 978-1-4251-8063-8

*We at Trafford believe that it is the responsibility of us all, as both individuals
and corporations, to make choices that are environmentally and socially sound.
You, in turn, are supporting this responsible conduct each time you purchase a
Trafford book, or make use of our publishing services. To find out how you are
helping, please visit www.trafford.com/responsiblepublishing.html*

*Our mission is to efficiently provide the world's finest, most comprehensive
book publishing service, enabling every author to experience success.
To find out how to publish your book, your way, and have it available
worldwide, visit us online at www.trafford.com/10510*

 www.trafford.com

North America & international
toll-free: 1 888 232 4444 (USA & Canada)
phone: 250 383 6864 ♦ fax: 250 383 6804 ♦ email: info@trafford.com

The United Kingdom & Europe
phone: +44 (0)1865 487 395 ♦ local rate: 0845 230 9601
facsimile: +44 (0)1865 481 507 ♦ email: info.uk@trafford.com

10 9 8 7 6 5 4 3 2

In Loving Memory

of

My First and Foremost Teacher

My Father

Mansour Mansouri

Educator, Author, Poet, Musician, Artist

1911 – 1990

ACKNOWLEDGEMENT

You would not be reading this book without the unconditional love, sacrifice, emotional support and professional advice from the people who have shaped my life for years, let alone the novel you're about to read.

To my lovely wife, Vida, for affording me the "space" to complete this work.

To my darling daughter, Behnaz, for her superb editing and polishing of my manuscript.

To my wonderful sons, Behzad and Farshad, whose success in their respective professions of Finance and Medicine, despite adversities and hardships, has inspired me in creating the main character of this novel.

To my gifted niece, Shahrzad Marvasti, and my talented friend **Serge Alahverdian** for their artwork and design of the front cover of this book

To the "Author Friendly" professionals at **Trafford Publishing,** for their expertise, patience and cooperation.

From the bottom of my heart.
Thank You

ONE

The large automatic door swung open. Down the hall, people in green scrub suits, hats and masks were moving in and out of the rooms. Far back in the rotunda there was a flurry of activity. Nurses were crisscrossing the halls and carrying material into the rooms. Phones rang incessantly and orders were flying out for instruments, IV bottles, medications and blood. The place was sizzling with serious professional activities but nothing out of ordinary for the usually busy operating room at the prestigious Manhattan Medical Center (MMC).

A few stretchers were lined up against the walls ready to carry patients to the Recovery Room. A crib on wheels was rolled out of OR3 into the hall. Two nurses and an anesthesiologist were pushing and chatting loudly. The baby was screaming for attention. *What did you do to me; it hurts.*

He was too young to verbalize his pain.

"Did you call for the next patient, Susie?" The anesthesiologist asked the nurse.

Susan Flynn did not seem to hear him. She was in no mood for casual conversation. She appeared upset at something, deep in thought, shaking her head and looking angry.

"Susie, did you call for the next patient?" He repeated loudly.

"Yes Jim, on the way"
"Gotta leave early today"

"Not before you talk to your friend Dr. Brinkley and ask him to behave." Susan looked unusually annoyed.

"Susie … It was all a joke, he does this all the time. You shouldn't take it personally."

"Oh Yeah? What happened to decency? What happened to professional ethics? He clearly went over the line with this and he's going to pay for it." Susan raised her voice a notch.

"What's the matter with you today, Susie?" the anesthesiologist looked baffled. *She's nuts today.*

"You don't think he insulted me?" Susan scowled.

"I don't mean to be disrespectful, Susie, but you are overreacting."

"Oh, you men. You're all the same." She muttered.

The crib rolled through the automatic door, into the next hall and entered the Recovery Room.

He was the youngest surgeon on the staff, a little over three years out of training. His ID tag read "Brian Brinkley, M.D., Dept of Surgery." He would add **F.A.C.S.** to the end of his title in another year or two, when he becomes a **F**ellow of the **A**merican **C**ollege of **S**urgeons.

Dr. Brinkley picked up the patient's chart, pulled down his mask, and flashed a bright smile as he walked out of OR 3.

This was his first pediatric hernia repair as a practicing surgeon, and he was happy about it. *Another successful case.* He patted himself on the back.

Three years into his young and flourishing surgical practice, Brian was just beginning to feel comfortable with his work. Confident of his diagnostic and technical abilities, he yearned to move beyond routine and repetitive cases and mustered courage to test himself in the fringes of his specialty training. Surgery on newborn and infants challenged him.

The painful memories of his residency training years were still vividly with him. There was not a single case Brian would do without somebody, be it his Chief resident, his Attending surgeon or Chief of surgery watching over his shoulder and ready to bark if he made the slightest error.

Here, he was his own man now. He was the one who would make sensitive decisions, give the orders and demand action. It felt so good.

The first three years in private practice was hectic. Business was slow and competition was formidable. Brian struggled to survive, but he was a quick study. He learned the tricks of the trade and gradually broke ground in a highly competitive environment.

Brian realized early on that he could not simply show off his credentials as a newly trained, cutting edge surgeon and expect a flock of patients to rush into his office. He also couldn't expect that his medical colleagues would break their ties and alliances with their own surgeon friends and refer their patients to him instead. It would take more than academic credentials to build and secure his practice and he understood this early on.

Now, in his fourth year in practice, he was beginning to feel comfortable. His office was swarmed with new patients and his competitors were nervous.

Brian walked into the doctor's lounge and sat by the telephone, dialed a special number and dictated an operative report. He described the surgical procedure and patient's condition and ended with the usual and customary final sentence: patient tolerated the procedure well and was transferred to Recovery Room in satisfactory condition.

"Satisfactory." He repeated the word, just to make sure.

He then opened the patient's chart and wrote an operative note.

The name plate on the patient's chart read: Elliot Silverman. Age: 2
Diagnosis: Right Inguinal Hernia.
Procedures: Right Inguinal Hernia repair. Exploration of left inguinal canal.
Outcome: Uneventful.
He underlined the word… Uneventful.
He then wrote the orders: Patient could be discharged home in the evening.

"Dr. Brinkley 2234." The overhead page announced.

Brian picked up the phone and dialed 2234. The Recovery Room nurse wanted to know if he would stop by to talk to the baby's parents.

"They can wait" He hung up the phone abruptly.

A nurse stuck her head through the door and looked around. She spotted him at the dictation station.

"Dr. Brinkley. You have a call on line 2"

"Thank you" he said as he picked up the phone.

"Dr. Brinkley here..."

"Hello baby, it's me"

"Hi darling. So good to hear your beautiful voice. What's up?"

"Just anxious to know how your first baby hernia surgery went?"

"Perfect. Perfect. The nurse could hardly keep pace with me!"

"What was the rush for?"

"You don't waste time when you have a two year old under anesthesia. Gotta be quick,"

"Oh wow! I thought this surgeon was only fast and quick in bed" she chuckled.

"Hey … you naughty... naughty girl"

"Sorry I didn't mean it" she said playfully.

"Dr. Brinkley 2234" It was the hospital operator again.

"Hold on a minute babe" he pushed the Hold button and dialed 2234 on the other line.

"Recovery"

"Dr. Brinkley here"

"Sorry to bother you Doctor, but Elliot Silverman's parents are very anxious to …"

"I said they can wait. If they want to talk to me they should wait. Understand?" He fired angrily. Back to the other line.

"Sorry baby, these stupid nurses. Listen Jenny, I have no surgery tomorrow. Let's take the boat out. It should be a nice day." He said, fully expecting an affirmative response. And he got it.

"What are you doing tonight?" She asked

"I'm speaking at the annual meeting of the nursing and paramedical staff of the hospital."

"Wow ... Excuse me! What is all that about?"

"I've been invited as the guest speaker to update the hospital staff on advances of medical and surgical sciences."

"OK, professor Brinkley, enjoy the limelight."

"I'll do my best baby, let me go now, this kid's parents are going bananas."

The OR supervisor was in her early sixties. A no-nonsense, old-timer nurse whose mere presence in the OR theatre would demand discipline, responsibility and respect.

Across the desk from her, Susan Flynn, the charge nurse for OR 3, was collecting her thoughts and preparing a report on the behavior of the young surgeon.

"What's the matter Susan? You look angry." The supervisor asked.

"I am, Mary, Very much so." Tears welled up in her eyes.

"Here ... take a tissue ... Calm down and talk to me."

Susan swallowed the big lump in her throat and managed a brief smile.

"I'm sorry." Then she talked.

The verbal report was distressing enough for the supervisor to recommend filing a formal complaint, but she paused for a moment.

"Susan ..." She fixed her gaze onto Susan's wet eyes. "Are you sure of this? It's a very serious accusation. You're talking sexual harassment, Susan."

"Call it whatever you want." She replied. "He humiliated me, insulted me, made me feel violated, Mary." She sniffed and blew her nose into a tissue.

"Ok, Susan. I want you to sleep on it tonight. Think it over and if you still feel the same way by tomorrow morning, file a formal complaint. It will be dealt with at Medical Staff Committees later on."

Mary wanted the report on her desk by the next morning.

"I'll be happy to do that" Susan replied. Her eyes sparkled with a glare of satisfaction.

The Recovery Room was relatively quiet. It was still early in the morning and most of the customers were under the knives at that time. It would be a few more hours before things would get really hectic.

Baby Elliot Silverman was sound asleep now in his crib, surrounded by his parents and nurses.

Dr. Brinkley strutted in triumphantly and made his presence known by loudly asking who the nurse in charge of the baby was.

He then moved towards the parents with a fake smile.

Mrs. Silverman rushed forward "How did it go Doctor?"

"Very nice and easy" replied the surgeon as he put his arm around her shoulder in a condescending gesture.

Mr. Silverman joined them as they all walked towards the crib.

"You mean that painful lump above his right groin is gone now?" asked the mother.

"Gone for good" said the Doctor.

"Why is it that he has bandages on both sides? The lump was only on the right side." The father asked.

Dr. Brinkley paused for a moment, as if preparing an answer for a lay person.

"Infant hernias are often bilateral; I mean they exist on both sides, even if the lump is only on one side. So, we make an incision on the other side to see if there is a hernia there"

Fishing expedition, the father thought. *Two incisions, twice as much money.*

"And did you find another hernia on his left side, Doctor?" He asked

The answer came in a very low tone, "No" as if *it should be just between me and you.* And he very quickly followed "Take him home this evening. I'll see him in my office next week. The nurse will give you an instruction sheet for do's and don'ts"

He waved good bye and went back to OR.

The lecture hall was packed with hospital nurses and other paramedical staff, anxiously awaiting the appearance of the guest speaker.

Brian was the rising star of the institution and his popularity was soaring among the hospital employees and medical staff, much to the chagrin of the rival surgeons whose livelihoods were being threatened by the rising popularity of this relatively inexperienced newcomer.

Brian was young, energetic, populist and aggressive. He rode on the high tides of being the most recently educated and up-to-date surgeon and had a claim on having brought into this hospital the most recent advances of surgical science and techniques. He had energized a dormant and inactive department of surgery that was falling behind from the rapidly advancing surgical sciences.

It was obvious to some, but not to all, that a great deal of Brian's notoriety had nothing to do with his surgical knowledge and skills, although those could not be denied. He was charming, amiable and charismatic. His very presence would generate excitement and pleasure.
His friendly smile and mild manners would hide his underlying toughness. Deep down he was shrewd, determined and unrelenting to crush the competition and march forward.

The applause was thunderous when the director of nursing introduced the guest speaker, Dr. Brian Brinkley.
The introduction was loaded with praise and commendations of the young surgeon's credentials, skills and personality.
Brian strode across the stage and raised both arms in acknowledgement of the enthusiastic audience, as he positioned himself behind the podium.

"Thank you, thank you … thank you."
The applause slowed down and the cheers faded slowly.

"Thank you for inviting me to address this gathering of the most dedicated, enthusiastic and hard working health care professionals ever put together in one place."

The hall exploded again in cheers and applause. He sure knew how to conquer the heart of his audience.

Brian went on to describe an overview of the health care delivery system of the country and outlined its deficiencies and problems.

He projected a gloomy view of the rapidly deteriorating quality of health care as the private practitioners were being stranded and trapped by the newly rising corporate predators called HMO's or Health Maintenance Organizations.

Brian spoke about the economic ills of the medical organizations as they struggled to survive in a very hostile environment of governmental regulations and liability restrictions. He complained about the ever increasing cost of medical equipment, advanced technologies and modern diagnostic modalities.

"Who are the true victims of the deteriorating health care system? You may all say the patients, the general public, the children, the pregnant mothers, the indigents, the elderly, the disabled, the chronically ill, and you are all correct. But, what about the healthcare workers, the nurses, the technicians, the secretaries, and yes ... the doctors."

Another round of applause.

He explained how the doctors in private practice have had to cope with the rising cost of keeping the office door open, and, how the nurses and paramedical workers have had to deal with low wages and salaries. And, yes, how the doctors have had to subsidize their low income by other ventures such as real-estate, investing, moonlighting, and down sizing their practice.

The speech went on for nearly an hour. Brian spoke of the good and bad of the medical profession, skillfully keeping the audience alert and focused, by mixing the depressing projections with cheerful anecdotes.

Brian reiterated a crowd favorite. "The old lady complained to her plumber about his large bill. One hundred and seventy five dollars? She said. I go to my doctor, he spends an hour examining me and his bill is only thirty five dollars. And the plumber responded: Lady, when I was a Doctor, I also charged thirty five dollars, and that's why I am a plumber now."

Laughter broke out loudly and was mixed with long applause.

Towards the end, he instilled hope and optimism based on the emergence of advanced medical research, modern surgical techniques and more educated and sophisticated health care practitioners. He stressed upon the medical ethics, and reminded everyone that the medical profession is a noble humanitarian endeavor which demands sacrifice and hard work.

The speech ended just as it started, among thunderous applause and cheers. He mingled with the crowd for a while and said good bye.

* * * * *

TWO

The Long Island Expressway has a reputation as being the longest parking lot in the world, especially during the summer week-ends when people escape the city and rush to the beautiful resorts, beaches, State parks, historical sites and sweeping ocean views of eastern Long Island. The world famous towns and villages collectively known as The Hamptons along the south shore of eastern Long Island boast the finest restaurants, shopping and historical attractions. The beaches are swarmed with vacationers soaking up the warm summer sun and dipping into the cool, crisp waters of the Atlantic Ocean. The swimmers challenge the waves and the surfers brave the rolling taller waves away from the shoreline. The boatyards and marina are rushed by sailing enthusiasts to take the boats out. By the evening people squeeze into the crowded side walks and browse the colorful shops, jewelry stores and antique outlets.

On that late summer day the traffic was relatively light.

The Mercedes Benz convertible was cruising at 80 Miles per hour, going east. Speed limit: 55 Miles per hour.

The sky was spotless, and a nice cool breeze was coming in from the south shore. The air was clean and the atmosphere was romantic.

The girl sunk low into the passenger seat, stretched her legs and playfully raised her arms, holding her hands against the rushing wind through the open roof. Her beautiful eyes were hidden behind the sunglasses, her long blonde hair floating and twisting with the sharp breeze rolling in. The radio was blasting pop music and she was lip singing along.

Brian pushed a button on the steering wheel and the display screen on the dash board changed to the telephone mode. A list of saved telephone numbers from his Bluetooth- enabled cell phone appeared on the screen. He called his service and the radio volume was automatically lowered.

"Hi, Dr. Brinkley here ... I'm not going to the hospital today. Page me if you need me ... I mean only emergency calls please ... any messages today?"
"No Sir, it's nice and quiet"
Nice and quiet, wonderful. That's what I need today.
"Keep it that way please, thanks, bye."

The girl cheered.
As the phone clicked off, the volume on the radio automatically rose again and she started singing along.

Exit 68 offered a shortcut to Montauk Highway heading east to the Hamptons.
Brian's boat was docked at the East Hampton Point Marina. While his GPS was programmed to get him there he could find his way to the marina with his eyes closed.

The facility included a restaurant with an outdoor deck, private changing lockers and bath house. The customers were mostly celebrities and the affluent.

The Mercedes pulled in behind the "Stop Here" sign and Brian closed the roof and stepped out. Jenny moved out lazily and stretched before walking. The trip had taken over two hours from Manhattan.
The car was whisked away by valet parking attendants. It was 1:30 p.m.
Brian and Jenny stopped at the bar for a couple of cold beers and a snack of shrimp and lobster rolls.
Brian went to the phone and ordered the boat to be readied.
They separated for a change of clothes and then headed for the boatyard.

The ocean was calm with a soft breeze. The motor boat, a 33-foot sport cruiser with sleek hull and luxury interior raced towards the open sea until the shoreline was barely visible and then dropped anchor. Seagulls flew by back and forth and chirped.

They had brought snacks, fruits, and liquor for the day. Brian had dinner reservations at his favorite steakhouse in East Hampton and, just in case his secretary Helen could cancel his 8:00 a.m. surgery the next morning, he reserved a $1400 a night luxury suite at The 1770 House East Hampton Inn. The place had been built over 200 years ago as a private New York residence, now it accommodates the elite and the high class vacationers.

Brian went below deck and placed a bottle of whiskey, a **Macallan 21 Yr Single Malt Scotch,** on the bar and a bottle of wine, his favorite Brunello di Montalcino 1999, in the fridge. He changed into his bathing suit, ran up on the deck and jumped right off the bow for a dip. Jenny bared it all and dove in. The water was cool and crisp. She was hot and inviting.

They fell into each other's arms and rolled, pulling and pushing in and out of water, laughing loudly.

They hugged and kissed and caressed. Their legs wrapped around each other, pushing up in harmony to keep their heads out of the water. They swam around the boat a few rounds, racing each other, and then floated motionless to regain their strength.

Back on the boat, Jenny had the bikini on again.

They placed the lounge chairs side by side and stretched their tired bodies under the glow of the sharp afternoon sunshine and started soaking in the sun. The conversation was joyful and amusing. They told each other sweet stories, jokes and anecdotes. No serious stuff. He puffed on a king size Dunhill International as two more cold beers went down.

Brian felt the flow of warm blood under his skin as the cool breeze gently rubbed his body. His eyes closed and he fell asleep.

When he woke up the sun had moved on towards the horizon. The world was so quiet and peaceful. The boat rocking gently. The seagulls dancing above.

Next to his lounge chair he found a dish of fruit, some nuts and a glass of his favorite drink, Scotch on the rocks, neatly arranged on a small table waiting for him.

"Thank you Jenny." He muttered.

He could hear soft music coming from below deck. He raised his head looking around for Jenny. She was nowhere to be seen. He stared at her empty lounge chair and noted her bikini hanging on the edge. His imagination went wild. He gulped his drink, jumped off the chair and rushed downstairs.

The room was dark and cozy. Soft lights from the ceiling reflected off the walls. A hint of expensive French perfume lingered in the air. He recognized the aroma of the perfume he'd given her a week earlier as a spur of the moment gift. Music was soft and romantic. Barry White's deep baritone voice attracted him further into the room.

Reflecting off the shiny surface of the satin bed sheet, he could make out her curvy silhouette, stretched on the bed, gently rolling from side to side, and as he approached the bed, she pushed the sheet away and exposed the beauty of her nude body. Her skin was soft and silky, her face flushed and her sinful smile betrayed the glow of passion reflecting off her inviting gaze. Her eyes an endless sea of boiling desire.

She winked.

His knees trembled. His heart pounding. He felt dizzy as the boat was rocking slowly with the gentle waves.

"Hello my Angel."

They lunged at each other and embraced fiercely. The kiss was fiery, passionate and endless, until … just moments after he felt the warmth and softness of her breasts on his chest his ultimate pleasure was shattered by the harsh beep of his pager.

She pulled back and he grabbed her tighter. *Ignore the damn thing.*

"Could be urgent honey, answer it."

"Fuck it … not now."

But there was no ignoring a persistent page.

He reached the phone and called his service.

"Hi … Hello … here … it's me … Dr. Brinkley. What's up?"

"Sorry to bother you Doctor, but they are calling for you from the hospital"

"It should be a mistake. I am off and I don't have patients in the hospital today"

"Yes, but the call is from the Department of Pathology. A doctor Gonzalez insisting that he should talk to you today"

"Oh, Dr. Gonzalez, OK, I'll call him now"

"You want the number, Doctor?"

"No'.

He got hold of himself and kissed Jenny on the cheek. "I'm sorry babe."

He picked up the phone and went back on the deck. The secretary took the call and put Brian on hold. Dr. Gonzalez was reading slides but it would be just a minute. A call from Carlos Gonzalez usually meant some kind of trouble. A routine call for a routine report would not come from the Chief himself.

Brian ran to the mini-bar and fixed himself a quick drink. Scotch on the rocks. He gulped it down quickly and made a second one while the phone was being held between his ear and right shoulder.

"Hold on Doctor, he is picking up"

"OK"

"Hello Brian, sorry to bother you at this time, but I am extremely concerned about what I saw today in this hernia specimen. What's his name, the two year old baby you did yesterday?"

"Elliot Silverman, What's wrong?"

"That's right, Elliot Silverman. You repaired his hernia and removed some tissue".

Was this a question or just a statement? What's he trying to get at?

"He had a hernia on the right side. I also explored the left side." Brian explained.

"Was there a hernia on the left side also?"

"No, we didn't find a hernia on the left side"

"But you did remove some tissue from the left side as well, correct?" The chief inquired.

"I think so. Looked like some fatty tissue". Brian said cautiously.

"Um ... I wish you had not ..." His voice trailed off as if he was puzzled or something.

"But you haven't told me what the problem is, Dr. Gonzalez." Brian's voice trembling.

There was a long pause. Brian waited anxiously.

A soft warm hand touched his shoulder and a hot deep kiss landed on his left cheek.

He almost jumped off the chair. He pushed her back and waved his left arm as if telling her to get lost.

"You know what, Dr. Brinkley, this is a bit complicated to discuss on the phone, why don't you come here early in the morning. We can sit behind the microscope together and look at this specimen. Then I can explain to you why I am so concerned about this case."

"If that's what you want Sir, I'll be there first thing in the morning"

"That'll be the best. I'll have the coffee ready for you at seven a.m. Adios"

Brian dropped the phone and cursed under his breath. He was now angry and restless.

"What's the matter darling?" Jennifer looked worried.

Brian evaded the question, picked up his glass and went back to the bar.

Jennifer realized something serious had happened.

"Get dressed, Jenny. We're going home." He hollered from downstairs.

"But we had plans for tonight, honey. Why should we go back now?"

"Because I have to. I've got to get to the hospital at seven a.m."

"You better explain this to me." Jennifer sounded quite upset.

"Let's go Jenny. I've got no time to explain."

"You never have enough time for me. At least tell me what happened"

"Come down here; let's pack this stuff and go."

He turned the engine on and the boat roared.

"What are we doing with dinner reservation and hotel?"

"I'll call them from the car and cancel them."

"Why can't we have dinner here?"

"Jenny … Jenny, stop getting on my nerves. It's getting dark, we've got two hours drive to get back to the city and there is tremendous traffic on the way."

The trip back home was anticlimactic. The longest parking lot in the world was endless. The mood in the car was somber. Brian was visibly nervous and short tempered; Jennifer remained quiet and kept to herself. No music. No conversation.

* * * * *

THREE

**The sign on the door read: Michael Sloan, M.D., F.A.C.S.
Chairman, Department of Surgery.**

The office was spacious and elegant. A huge mahogany desk and an executive leather chair highlighted the view from the entrance. Comfortable couches and arm chairs were lined up against the sidewalls and numerous frames, laminated certificates of achievements, degrees, diplomas and recognition awards decorated the walls.

At 9 a.m. the door opened and the Chairman and his entourage entered the room. He had just finished his first case of the day. He was still in his scrubs, with a mask hanging below his chin, and, of course, he was wearing a white lab coat. Staff were not allowed to leave the OR suite in their scrubs unless they had a lab coat on. He made the rules.

With him, came in his secretary, Joanne, the OR supervisor Mary Dorsa, and two surgical residents.

Michael Sloan was an old-timer type of Chairman. The hands-on surgeon who liked to spend most of his time teaching the residents in OR. He hated administrative work, meetings, seminars and most of all politics. Nevertheless his 6′ 4″ large frame, sharp eyes and serious features, at the age of 66 were quite imposing and authoritative.

Dr. Sloan removed his mask, took off his coat and walked behind his desk. The entourage lined up in front of the desk awaiting orders.

He asked the surgical residents to discharge the patient on B2 and check on the lab results of his afternoon cases. They nodded and left.

His secretary, Joanne, read his meeting schedule for that day: Operating room committee at 12, luncheon served, and Morbidity and Mortality (M&M) conference at 5 p.m. He sent her for coffee.

"You wanted to see me Mary, what's up?" he asked the OR supervisor as he sunk into his leather chair.

"Yes Sir, I want to talk to you about an incident report, filed by one of the nurses against Dr. Brinkley".

"Sit down Mary, but make it brief. I have to go back to the OR"

The supervisor placed the report on his desk and asked if he wanted to read it later on and take the appropriate action.

"I shall read it in detail, but give me a brief summary now" He said.

The brief summary took 20 minutes, at the end of which the chief looked angry and disturbed. No such behavior in his operating rooms was ever acceptable, and yet it was most unexpected from somebody like Brian Brinkley. *Something's fishy here* He thought.

"Do you believe this, Mary? You work with these guys all the time."

"It's a serious accusation, Dr. Sloan, but we can't ignore it. Dr. Brinkley makes dirty jokes quite often, who knows, he might have gone a little too far this time."

"How about the nurse Susan? Is she emotionally stable? You're sure she's not making this up?"

"Don't think so. She might have misunderstood him but that's all. She's been deeply disturbed by this, crying all the time.

"Maybe we should talk to her first. This damn thing is serious and may destroy the poor guy's career."

Mary frowned and resisted the notion.

"Dr. Sloan, if we don't deal with these matters seriously the nurses will leave. The place will fall apart. Let the chips fall where they may. The Ethics committee will deal with this."

"I'm gonna hold this for a day or two. I'll talk to Dr. Brinkley. Something doesn't look right here."

"You talk to him, Dr. Sloan, but the complaint has already gone to the Medical Director's office."

"Oh Christ" The chief growled in anger "why did you send this without my permission, Mary?"

"This has to do with the nursing department, Doctor. I sent it to the Director of Nursing; she passed it on to the Medical Director."

Something' fishy alright. The chief thought.

Joanne walked in with coffee.

"Call Dr. Brinkley and ask him to meet me here at 11:30"

"Yes sir"

The phone rang. Joanne answered it and turned to the Chief:

"They're waiting for you in OR".

* * * * *

Earlier that day, at 7 a.m. Dr. Carlos Gonzalez was getting ready for a full day of work, in the Pathology Department.

He prepared the microscope and lined up the slides of hernia specimens marked Case # 2202.

The secretary buzzed and the speakerphone blasted: "Dr. Brinkley is here."

"Send him in". *And have a shot of Morphine ready for him. He's gonna need it.*

A knock at the door. The young surgeon entered.

"Morning Dr. Gonzalez"

"Morning Brian. Please call me Carlos".

"I was up all night. Cannot imagine what could be so serious about a kiddy hernia specimen"

"Sorry I dragged you here. I thought it was best if we both looked at it together" He said calmly.

"I should be in the OR by 8" Brian said, hoping this would minimize the problem.

Gonzalez frowned. *Bet you can't get off this one so easy. You don't even belong to OR.*

"I'll get you out of here fast" the Chief walked towards the microscope.

"You told me you explored the opposite side as well" He asked.

"It's more or less standard procedure" Brian said, struggling to sound sure of himself.

"And you removed some tissue from the opposite side, although there was no hernia"

"Sure, looked like a lump of fatty tissue".

"Did you ask the nurses to send the specimens of each side separately?" He looked directly into Brian's eyes.

"Don't remember. Don't they do this routinely? What's the policy?" Brian's voice trembled.

"The policy is common sense. They may do this routinely if there is cancer"

"Who expects cancer in a kiddy's hernia sack?" Brian asked.

"There was no cancer. There was another structure you normally don't want to see in a hernia specimen. Let's look".

He sat behind the microscope and focused the view over the first slide.

The microscope had two viewing portals opposite each other. A teaching microscope. And Dr. Brinkley was about to learn the most important lesson of his professional life.

Brian sat on the other side and slowly peeked into the tube. At first there was no reaction. He wasn't sure what he was looking at. Then he frowned and suddenly his jaw dropped.

Gonzalez's eyes were off the microscope and fixed onto Brian, analyzing his reaction.

"Is this my patient's specimen?" Brian asked, in denial.

"Yes ... Yes it is". *Not so easy kiddo. Keep looking.*

"You understand what those tubular structures are?" Carlos asked.

"I think so, Vas Deferens. They shouldn't be there. Are you sure you didn't have another hernia specimen yesterday?" *Could this be a mix-up?*

"Not another kiddy hernia." Gonzalez answered emphatically.

"Now let me tell you what my problems are"

"PROBLEMS?" ... *You mean this is not enough of a problem. You have more?*

"First and foremost, I want you to know that by the hospital policies

I am obligated to report this case to the Quality Assurance (QA) committee. In due time you will be called to explain the circumstances. I will be there and do my best to cool things off; hopefully this case will not be reported to higher authorities outside the hospital"

"Department of Health, you mean?" Brian asked, as if he didn't know.
"Sure". *You may have to eat your license if proven negligent.*

"Second" … Dr. Gonzalez gazed at the microscope and paused for a moment.
Brian waited anxiously.

"The specimens of both sides have been mixed up, there is no way to know that the mishap has NOT occurred on both sides, in which case, you understand Brian, that you have permanently damaged this kid with serious consequences for his future life"

Brian was frozen. Eyes fixed on the floor, no motion, no response. His ego badly bruised. His knees weakened.

"Did you say you have an 8 o'clock case? It's time." Carlos said.
Brian jumped off the chair, and sat down again.
"I'll delay the case, if you don't mind. I need to talk to you more about this mess"

"Why don't you call the OR from here? There's the phone". He offered, pointing to his desk.
Brian called the OR and asked that his case be pushed back to later on in the morning.

"I'm sorry Dr. Brinkley, I have to get you the OR supervisor. I'll put you on hold for a minute". The loud music came on.

He looked at his watch. 8:05 a.m. He hoped it wasn't too late.
"This is the OR supervisor, can I help you." Mary Dorsa's voice was harsh and angry.
"Hi … Dr. Brinkley here. I want to push my case back a couple of hours"

"Wish you'd called a bit earlier Dr. Brinkley. The patient was just moved into the room and anesthesia is ready to put him under." Mary had him by the ropes. The incident report of yesterday was still fresh in her mind. *Squeeze his balls as hard as you can.*

"Mrs. Dorsa I have an emergency. They just have to wait"

"Are you in the Emergency Room, Doctor?"

Brian lost his cool.

"No I am not; I'll call you when I am ready, just tell the anesthesiologist to hold off". He hung up.

Mary Dorsa put the phone down, opened a drawer and pulled out an incident report sheet.

The OR committee was extremely harsh on the late arrivals. Some lazy surgeons come half an hour late for their 8 a.m. cases and all the cases of the room would then fall behind the schedule.

Dr. Gonzalez called the secretary for another coffee for himself, and one for Brian. *Bring him a strong one. He needs it badly.*

"We'll look at all these slides together, and then I'll get the anatomy book and review the components of the Inguinal Canal, then you can describe to me the course of the events in OR, as this case progressed. We both shall learn something from this case." He did not wait for a response.

Shortly after 9:30 a.m. the secretary buzzed:

"Dr. Brinkley, there is a call for you on line 2. It's from the Chairman of the Department of Surgery.

Brian was puzzled. What else was going on? *Damn the supervisor, she could hardly wait a minute to report me.*

He picked up the phone and pressed the button on line 2.

"This is Dr. Brinkley"

"Hi Dr. Brinkley, the Chairman wants to see you in his office at 11:30."

"What's happened? I am in Pathology. Can I see him later on?"

"11:30 Dr. Brinkley. The Chief's schedule is tight."

"Why can't I see him later on?" he sounded irritated.

"Do you want to ask him yourself!?

"I'll be there at 11:30." The phone dropped down.

Brian looked at Dr. Gonzalez inquisitively.

"Have you reported this to the Chairman already?" His mouth remained open, his heart was pounding and his face was pale and frightened.

"No ... No ... No, Only you and I know about this. He probably wants you for something else now. He'll find out about this case later on at the OR, or QA committee". Gonzalez did his best to sound reassuring, for now at least.

Dr. Brinkley gathered his strength, stood up and said thank you.

He thought of calling OR and pushing his case back further, may be early afternoon.
Who wants to talk to that bitch, the supervisor, again?
He decided to walk to OR and find a more friendly nurse. *Certainly not Susan Flynn.*

* * * * *

The meeting with the Chairman topped his disastrous morning. His case was delayed further but not before he had to deal with a hostile OR staff and angry patient and his family.

Brian entered the Chairman's office with his heart in his throat.

"Brian, Susan Flynn has filed a complaint against you, a very serious one indeed. What happened in the OR yesterday?" The chief asked.

Brian couldn't believe his ears. *What the hell is going on here?*

"What kind of complaint, Chief? I don't think we had any problems yesterday."

"Apparently you made one joke too many and she took it seriously."

"Since when is making jokes reported to higher authorities?" Brian asked sarcastically.

"When it implies sexual harassment."

"Sexual harassment? For crying out loud what's she talking about?"

"She claims you made sexual advances or something like that and she was offended." The Chief calmly replied.

"It's a damn lie."

"Well, you'll have your chances to defend yourself."

"Are you serious Chief? You're going to send this to Ethics committee?"

"I wouldn't have, but the nursing department already sent it to the Medical Director. I have a copy of the complaint here, would you like to look at it?"

Brian exhaled. "Sure."

Brian read the report and dropped the papers on the desk.

He was outraged and insulted, couldn't believe such despicable accusations, wanted to ask the Chief to call his accuser in right then and confront her, but he knew better, the complaint had been filed and had to be addressed in the appropriate forum. For now, he just wanted to go home and cry. *Jenny, where are you?*

Suddenly he remembered, he had surgery to do.

Back to the OR.

* * * * *

FOUR

Susan Flynn correctly expected his phone call as she got off the elevator. She turned the key and entered her apartment. The phone was ringing incessantly. She rushed in, dropped her purse on the couch and reached for the phone.

"Hello" Catching her breath.

"Hi, Susan it's me, Peter, How did it go yesterday?"

"Exactly as we planned. He's in deep shit"

"I wanna hear every detail"

"Listen, I just got through the door, give me a minute to change. I'll call you back"

"I tell you what; let's go out for a drink and chat."

"How about dinner?" Susan asked playfully.

"Dinner is fine if my service leave me alone. This damn beeper has been going off all day."

"What time and where" She asked.

"How about seven thirty at the Botanica?"

"Just fine."

"Love you."

Susan jumped in the shower. She was excited and exhausted. A significant drama was being played around her and she was part of it. She had nothing personal against Brian Brinkley, but she would do anything and everything for the love of her life, Dr. Peter Molano. She was also supersensitive towards surgeons who treated nurses as inferior and servants. Attitudes touching on arrogance. No guilty feelings here.

The hot shower relaxed her. She was enjoying the unexpected power she had gained over the young, aggressive and apparently successful surgeon. She trapped him into playing her game. She first irritated him by responding harshly to his gentle and often innocent sexual remarks, forcing him to make denigrating comments on feminism and female inferiority, all in a joking mood, and finally dragging him into a sexual harassment trap. All this, while a hernia repair was being done. She got under his skin and got the worst out of him. He now had to face an Ethics committee and respond to her flaming Incident Report.

Susan walked into the crowded bar and looked around. She was upbeat, jolly and in a festive mood. She was radiant and beautiful. The music was loud. She found him in the corner with two drinks on his table. Vodka on the rocks and her favorite, a Cosmopolitan.

The glasses clinked. They kissed and sipped with cheers.

"You look so beautiful darling." Peter said.
"Hard to believe, since you made me do ugly things."
"What did you do?"
"I trapped him into saying things he shouldn't have said, and I reported him. You take it from there."
"Let me tell you what he's done to all of us. Then you wouldn't feel so guilty."

Peter went on to explain to her that since Brian joined the surgical staff over three years ago he had broken every unwritten rule of conduct that had existed between the practicing surgeons for years. These guys were a number of surgeons in private practice. They received no salaries, no bonuses, and no benefits of any kind. Their system was fee- for-service and their resources were their referring physicians, the doctors who sent them patients in need of surgery. Since Brian came on board, he had tried every trick to break into this system.

"New competition scared you guys, yeah?" Susan asked.
"You bet. However, it was obvious from the beginning that he was not playing fair and square."
"How so?"

"Peter tilted his head back and swallowed, "I'll tell you over our next drink."

Peter ordered another round. He went on to describe for Susan that when Dr. Brian Brinkley joined the staff he was newly trained, enthusiastic and hungry. He aggressively broke into other surgeons' territory. He tried to befriend their referring physicians by wining and dining them, socializing and bribing. He stole their patients when he could. He eroded their income and made them all truly worried.

"Scared for our survival and upset with Brian's unorthodox behavior, we gathered together and started brainstorming." Peter continued. "What Brian was doing was not illegal or against the rules of the department. It was, however, unethical. There was no rule against taking your colleagues out to dinner. There was no policy against socializing with your medical colleagues, taking them out on your boat, sharing a weekend at your summer house. We concluded that the only way we could stop him was to play his own game. Do something a bit unethical but not illegal. So my friends appealed to me to seek your help, and you played the game so fantastically well. I am so proud of you baby."

"What's going to happen to him now?" Susan asked worried that she might have done Brian more harm than she intended.
"He will be investigated by hospital authorities, not for his practice of surgery but for his conduct. That will bring him down to earth." Peter replied.

"I heard he was called to the Chairman's office today and he spent a lot of time in Pathology." Susan wondered what that was all about.

"Pathology, I wonder why?" Peter pondered.
"Did his case go alright yesterday?" He asked. Susan shrugged.
"Hope he knew what he was doing in the middle of all that back and forth bickering" she said.
"I passed him in the hall today: he looked terrible." Peter said.
"Which hall?" Susan asked.
"Coming out of the pathology department" he said.
Susan was deep in thought. *Oh … shit, the kiddy's specimen*

"Had to be the specimen. I didn't think it mattered." Susan mumbled.

"What about the specimen? Talk to me Susan" Peter said anxiously.

"I neglected to send out the right and left side specimens separately. Does it really matter Peter?"

"Um … for a hernia? Maybe not." Peter responded.

"He never told me what to do with the specimens anyhow." Susan worried she'd done something awfully wrong.

Peter glanced at his empty glass and called for another round. He'd just warmed up to his successfully executed plot. Susan's anguish was deepening.

"Are we having dinner tonight?" Susan asked after the last drink.

Peter looked at his beeper.

"It's been quiet. Let's go for it." He asked for the bill.

* * * * *

The silver Jaguar snaked through the heavy 5th avenue traffic. Jennifer Bradley was deeply concerned about the unexpected call from Brian pleading her to meet him at Hyatt Regency for drinks and talk. *He had to talk to somebody.* She already had a dinner engagement with her friends, her co-workers at the New York University Medical Center, where she worked as Manager of the Business Office. At age 27, she had gained the distinction and respect as a superb manager on account of her educational background, her personality and discipline.

He better have a good reason. She was not happy about missing the dinner with her friends.

Jennifer had met Dr. Brian Brinkley about four years earlier when he was a chief surgical resident. He was handsome, young and flirtatious. He would walk into the cafeteria and young ladies would stop eating, mouths agape, and eyes rolling in his direction. Nurses were falling for him right and left.

Jennifer happened to be having lunch alone when Brian approached her table with a full tray of food in his hand.

"Hi, may I join you?"

"Of course Dr. Brinkley"

"Oh … you know my name?"

"Who doesn't know your name around here?

"Thanks." He appreciated the complement.

Brian put his tray down next to hers, and stared with amazement.

"How nice, we're eating the same food"

"It's the best you can get in a hospital" she said sarcastically.

"I'm lucky to get a chance to have lunch at all, whatever it is." *Don't you see I am chief surgical resident? Very important.*

She sensed the narcissistic tone in his voice but let it pass. His charm prevailed.

"What's a gorgeous looking girl like you doing in this place?"

"I manage the business office." *I run the business that pays your salary.* She meant to say.

"You mean am I looking at the future CEO?" He asked jokingly. *Flattery worked sometimes.*

"By the time you are chairman of the department, I'll be CEO." She laughed.

"Hopefully you'll get there first and then hire me on, in case no one else wants me." They both laughed loudly.

He took a big bite of grilled chicken and gulped the Diet Coke down and looked at his watch.

"How many lives have you saved today, Dr. Brinkley?"

"Call me Brian, please. I count them by the end of the day." He said playfully.

"I want an answer by this evening." She smiled.

"How about over some decent dinner? I'm off this evening.

"No chance." *You can't rush it.*

The dinner was on a few days later, and again and again.

Brian and Jennifer started dating seriously. Soon they were in love.

Marriage had not been discussed as yet. Brian had some growing up to do. He was smart, ambitious and egotistical, but quite insecure.

He lost his mother at the tender age of eight. He was raised by an authoritative and disciplinarian father who was in military and failed to reach the ranks higher than Lieutenant colonel. A jealous and vindictive stepmother didn't help either. As Brian grew up, he was under intense pressure and discipline by his father to perform well, and in fact he did.

Brian first attended Columbia University and then the College of Physicians and Surgeons. Later he completed his surgical residency training at the New York University Medical Center.

All along he yearned for his lost childhood and stolen adolescence. He never dated seriously in college or medical school. His life was his books, his studies, his academic performance and dreams of future accomplishments.

Brian's relationship with his father was strained. Hardly anything he did would satisfy the old man, and yet he was overwhelmed by his authority and would thrive to reach higher goals just to make his father happy.

After his specialty training, Brian had multiple offers for academic positions, however he didn't find them challenging enough. He preferred private practice. He wanted to face competition and fight for survival. He was constantly in need of proving something to somebody, and in the highly competitive world of private practice the sky was the limit, and the boundaries of professional conduct were blurry enough for him to push and test his limits.

He chose to set up practice in uptown Manhattan and was appointed to the surgical staff of Manhattan Medical Center (MMC).

In Jennifer, he found a sanctuary from the pressures of life. Beyond love and sexual attraction he found meaningful companionship. He could open his heart to her and enjoy the pleasures of intimacy. At times she was his lover, and at other times she was a good mother for him. She knew how to tame this restless child. In reality she was his best adviser and confidant.

For Brian notoriety came sooner than expected. He was newly trained, up-to-date and aggressive. Five years had passed since the last time a new surgeon had joined the surgical staff of the hospital. That was a very long time considering the rapid advances of science and technology, modern surgical techniques and equipments.

He showed off his skills, in a variety of diagnostic modalities and bold surgical approaches, in the lecture halls, conference rooms, at the patient's bedside, in the coffee shop, and even restrooms, hoping that he would impress the members of the medical staff, the ones who would hopefully refer patients to him.

They did, and in a very short time he was on top of his world.

His practice boomed and his ego inflated. While this was what he always wanted, rapid success and fame harmed him. His manners and behavior became tinged with indifference and arrogance. Complaints started pouring in from patients and their relatives, nurses and even his office staff for his lack of caring and attention.

Gradually his tolerance for spending enough time with his patients, holding their hands, feeling their pains, and showing care and compassion waned. He became oblivious to the human aspect of his profession.

And two days ago, following the events surrounding the kiddy hernia repair his world began to crumble.

* * * * *

FIVE

The silver Jaguar parked at the curbside in front of the Hyatt Regency on 42nd Street.

Jenny left the key in for the valet and got her ticket from the attendant. She rushed through the revolving door into the front lobby, up the Escalator and onto the main lobby. The newly renovated Bar and Lounge covered the full length of the lobby on the street side with large windows facing the 42nd Street. A row of round cocktail tables lined up alongside the windows.

It was around 8 p.m. The place was swarmed with patrons, around the bar and at the tables. The atmosphere was abuzz with music, and humming with conversation, cheers, laughs and clinking glasses.

All the way down the narrow hall, at the very end, she found him at the last table, facing the window and watching the street traffic. Brian was holding his nearly empty glass with his left hand and a cigarette in his right hand. Almost half the length of the cigarette had burned into ashes, still hanging on to the rest. His last puff was a long time ago, he was deep in thought.

She approached the table cautiously, worried and anxious to find out what was so important that he had to call for such an urgent get-together.

The kiss was not the usual one. Just a peck on the cheek.

"What are you having?" He asked, trying to hide his anxiety.

"White wine's good. You ok?"

"Yeah, I wanna go back to Hamptons right now, get on the boat and sail miles away from the shore. I wanna hear the waves and feel the cool and crisp wind going through my body, calm down and cleanse my soul. I need to clear my mind and try to understand what went on today and why.

He waved to the waitress.

"One more of this and a glass of white wine" he said, holding his glass up in the air.

"Chardonnay ok?" The waitress asked.

"Yeah".

"What happened today, Brian?" Jenny asked nervously.

He took a long drag and crushed his cigarette in the ash tray, and lit another one. A king size Dunhill International.

"What the hell are you doing Brian? You stopped smoking two months ago. A couple on the boat OK, but now you're at it again?" she raised her voice one notch.

"Two months ago? Ah … you may as well say two days ago. I was living in a different universe. Today, my whole world crashed down on me".

She put her soft hand on his, and squeezed.

"You poor baby, tell me who ruined your day?"

He shrugged. "Don't know. Can't figure it out. A lot went on today and somehow I can't put the pieces together. It has to be some kind of conspiracy, a well planned one". He was gazing at the floor as he talked.

"OK, let's start from the beginning, the very first thing in the morning. How did your day start?"

"Remember the call I received from the Pathology department, the other day on the boat?"

"Yeah. Sure I do. Put you in a bad mood as we rushed back to the city".

"Right, that one. I had to see the Chief of Pathology, and go over the specimen of that kid's hernia. Apparently he's found something in the specimen that shouldn't be there.

"Something important?" she asked.

"They make it look serious, and yet it could turn out to be completely inconsequential."

"So what's the big deal?" Her voice rose again, impatiently.

"The big deal is that they are trying to make a big deal out of this"

"And who are they?" She asked.

"All of them, from the OR nurse to the OR supervisor to the Chief of Surgery to the Chief of Pathology. They all ganged up on me today. A well orchestrated assault"

"I think you are being a bit paranoid" she said in a calm voice.

Brian erupted "What the hell are you talking about; it's my ass on the line"

"OK ... Ok ... let's take it one step at a time, what's with the OR nurse and supervisor?"

"That fuckin' whore, Susan, has filed a formal complaint against me and the other bitch, the supervisor, passed it right on to the Medical Director and Chairman of the department"

"For cryin' out loud, what is this about?"

"Sexual harassment. Can you believe that?"

"Say what? Sexual harassment? How did that happen?"

"It didn't Jenny. I am telling you. This is a planned conspiracy." He sipped the last drop of his drink and burned a third of the cigarette by a long drag, and blew it into the air.

Jennifer pulled a notebook out of her purse, clicked the top of her pen and gave Brian an angry, suspicious look.

"What's her name again?"

"Susan something ... Flynn, I guess ... its Flynn ... Susan Flynn."

Jenny jotted the name down and closed the notebook.

"Why do you think she would make such a serious accusation against you?" She asked.

Brian rested his forehead on the palm of his right hand, holding the cigarette at the very tip of his fingers away from his hair. He was deep in thought. Jennifer can not know the language and the course of conversation that went on between him and Susan Flynn.

"Are you with me Brian?" Jennifer asked loudly.

"She mixed up the two specimens and I chewed her up. That must be it. She was shaken and upset" Brian made up the story quickly and was very happy about it. He actually went on to explain to Jennifer how serious a matter this thing was and how much trouble it had caused for him.

A few minutes of badly needed silence followed.

Brian called the waitress and asked for another round. He looked washed out.

Jenny was not finished yet.

"Did you see the chairman?"

"Yeah, he called me to his office and took me to the woodshed." Another lie.

"He had no right to do that. Those bitches ought to prove their accusations first"

"That'll be later on when they call me to appear before the Ethics committee"

"And if their accusations stick?"

"I'll be kicked off the staff"

Jennifer thought for few seconds and asked "Did the chairman know about the specimen problem?"

"Not when I was there. I'm sure he'll soon have his chance to take a second shot at me"

"And when is that?"

"When they call me to appear before the OR committee and most certainly the QA Committee. Quality Assurance that is"

"And if the problem is real and you are found negligent?"

"Thanks for your confidence. I guess you believe all this shit is true". He was frustrated.

"Brian, just answer the damn question." She snapped.

He moaned and groaned, quite restless and agitated.

"Who knows, I'll lose my job, will be barred from practicing surgery in the State of New York, a malpractice lawsuit will follow, and then I'll lose my assets, and likely my girlfriend. Are you happy to know this now?" He was drunk and almost incoherent.

Jennifer picked up the napkin and wiped a teardrop rolling down her cheek. She tried to control herself and forced a fake smile.

"Of course I don't believe this entire nonsense, darling. It all came down on you unexpectedly and kind of knocked you off balance. Tomorrow will be a different day".

"Let's get something to eat" she suggested.
"I wanna go home now. I have no appetite."
"I'll drive you home." She paid the bill.

He fell asleep in the car. She had to drag him into his apartment, put him in bed and tuck him in. She kissed him, turned off the lights and tiptoed back to the door and left.

There was a nice cool breeze in the air. She realized the gravity of the situation and felt her legs were heavy and knees shaking. She sank deep in her car seat and sped away.

* * * * *

SIX

*

The phone rang before her alarm clock was set to buzz at 6 a.m.

Jennifer could hardly open her eyes and struggled with the weight of her arm as she tried to reach for the phone. Her whole body was still weak and limp. The room was dark, the air was heavy and her mind was still hazy and confused. She might as well have stayed up all night. No rest. No relaxation.

She gathered her strength, pushed the sheet back and with her eyes closed and her head hanging down from the edge of the bed she reached and picked up the phone.

"Hello"

"My car is missing Jenny, what happened last night?" Brian's voice was shaky and slurred.

"I drove you home darling. You ok?"

"Guess so. I couldn't remember. Where is my car now?"

"Wherever you left it when you went to the Hyatt last night."

"Left it with the valet. Gotta find the ticket" his voice trailed.

"What time do you have to be in the hospital?"

"Have an 8 o'clock case. Gotta be there by 7:30" He said.

"You don't have time to go after the car now. I'll pick you up at seven and take you to the hospital. See if you can find the ticket"

"Thanks baby. See you soon"

Jennifer dragged her tired body to the shower and soaked herself in hot water.

Brian had no idea that she had planned to go to the hospital anyway.

At exactly 7:30 a.m. she kissed him good bye and dropped him off at the main entrance.

As he was walking away she pulled the passenger side window down and called him.

"What time do you want me pick you up?" she hollered.

"Call me around 4. I've got to get my car"

He walked back to the car, leaned over the open window and said "I'll take you to your favorite restaurant tonight."

The outdoor visitor parking was around the corner, where there was a separate entrance for employees. She parked and walked in among the crowd rushing in to report to work.

Down the hall, people fanned out, heading for their respective departments. There was a directory on the wall showing the general layout of the hospital. The Operating Room was on the second floor. The Business Office, Nursing Department, Admitting Office, coffee shop and dining hall on the first floor, Pathology and Medical Records were in the basement.

She took the hallway on the left and followed through and entered the spacious main lobby. The ceiling was four stories high, the floor divided in separate sections each elegantly decorated with seating arrangements, armchairs, coffee tables and numerous plants, for visitors. The lobby was fresh from the pages of Architectural Digest; hardly the usual hospital décor. The information desk was staffed with few uniformed receptionists directing the visitors to their destinations. There was a large stack of brochures, newsletters and information pamphlets on the counter.

Jennifer approached the desk and introduced herself as a very close friend of Susan Flynn, the OR Nurse, and wanted to know if she was at work today.

"I've been trying to contact her for the last two days. She's not answering her phone calls" She sounded quite worried.

The receptionist asked if she could wait a minute.

She picked up the phone and dialed the OR and talked to somebody for few minutes.

"Ma'am she is up there but she's scrubbed and cannot come to the phone. Would you like to leave a message?"

"Oh no, please don't interrupt her. I'm glad she is here and she's OK. I'll call her later on. Thanks." She picked up a newsletter, and walked away.

The elevators were busy running up and down at the peak of the morning activity. Jennifer took the stairs up to the second floor. There was a sign on the wall with arrows pointing to the left for the OR, to the right for the ICU and Recovery Room. She turned left and went down the hall where a large automatic door led to the main OR area, but the door was closed. The sign on the door read Authorized Personnel Only. To the left of the door there was a large waiting room for the patients' families. A nurse behind a desk in the corner was talking on the phone in a hushed voice. There were few relatives in the room, some seated and some pacing anxiously. The clock on the wall was ticking at 8:35 a.m.

Jennifer strolled over to the desk as the nurse hung up the phone.

"Hi, I'm Janet Reilly, from the Pathology Department. I need to talk to Susan Flynn. I understand she's scrubbed, but do you know what time she takes her break?"

"Usually around 10." The nurse answered nonchalantly.

"Good, that's when I take my break. Can you pass on a message to her please?"

"Sure."

"Would you tell her to meet me in the coffee shop at 10:05?"

"OK, 10:05." She scribbled a note.

"What was the name again?" She asked.

"Janet Reilly, from Pathology."

"Thank you, I'll let her know."

Jennifer took a few steps towards the door and suddenly turned back

"Oh, I'm sorry. I'm not sure she knows me. Could you describe me to her, you know … blonde, red jacket, etc?"

"I'll do my best"

"Thank you so much, you're very nice."

The coffee shop was coming alive with a flurry of morning activities. The customers at this hour were not employees. Those people will swarm the place at around 10 a.m. and later on at about 3 p.m. This hour belonged to visitors, reps, some physicians and the like. Soft jazz music and the aroma of fresh brewed Columbian coffee filled the air.

The clock showed 9:05.

Jennifer walked in and surveyed the room. There was an empty table in the corner away from the crowd. She left her newsletter on the table and went to the counter. Her stomach was growling. She didn't have dinner last night; she recalled sadly, her friends had to do without her, and no breakfast this morning.

She ordered a toasted plain bagel with cream cheese, honey and an extra croissant, an orange juice and a medium size coffee with room for milk and sugar.

Back at her table she set the breakfast items neatly, sank in the chair and hid her face behind the newsletter. She had forty five minutes to kill.

At about 10 she noticed the change of crowd in the coffee shop. Uniformed employees were coming in groups. Nurses, with different color uniforms rushed in, for a quick coffee and pastry. She spotted a few OR nurses with their distinctive scrub suits, under the long white coats. *The rules applied everywhere.* The clock ran to 10:15. She began to wonder if Susan Flynn ever received her message.

Her gaze was fixed on the entrance to the coffee shop when she spotted him walking in, escorted by two young nurses, one on each side. *Very young and bubbly indeed.*

She quickly hid her face behind the newsletter.

Brian and his entourage sat at the counter and ordered coffee and pastries. Their conversation was loud and playful. Jennifer wondered if he was the same Brian she met last night at the Hyatt Regency. Here, he was clearly in his favorite turf. The eminent surgeon trying to control and impress people around him. *Son of a gun is fooling around.*

The phone at the other end of the counter rang.

"Is there a Dr. Brinkley here?" The waitress asked loudly. Brian answered and went to the phone. He was called back to OR.

"Excuse me Ma'am; are you by chance Miss Janet Reilly?"

Jennifer heard the voice from the other side of the newsletter, and almost ignored it. Suddenly she remembered who she was supposed to be. Quickly, she lowered the paper and saw her. Susan Flynn was looking down, frowning at her.

"Oh yes. Are you Susan?"

"Yes, but I don't know you"

Out of the corner of her eye Jennifer saw Brian leaving the coffee shop in a hurry. She felt relieved, stood up and offered a hand shake.

"Of course you don't know me; they have me tucked in the back rooms of Pathology in the basement. Would you sit down please?"

Susan sat down across the table from Jennifer and looked at her watch.

"I know you are on your break and probably have very little time. I am actually off today. I'll be very brief for now. We can talk more later on." Jennifer said.

Susan remained quiet and very curious as to what this was all about.

"I am one of many secretaries back in pathology." Jennifer continued. "You should have done something bad or unusual in the OR, they've been talking about you in pathology."

Susan froze. She got the message immediately. *The damn kiddy hernia specimen.*

"Were you in the same room with Dr. Brinkley when he operated on a two year old kid?"

"Yeah, and what did I do wrong?" Susan asked, hoping that this was a different issue altogether.

"I overheard the conversation between our Chairman and Dr. Brinkley. The Chairman was very upset that the specimens had been mixed up. I don't know what it meant, but ..." Jennifer gazed sharply into Susan's eyes and continued. "Dr. Brinkley said you had ignored his specific orders to send the two specimens separately. He said he was going to ask the Operating Room Committee to look into this matter and take disciplinary action against you." Jennifer paused for a moment, gauging Susan's reaction.

"That's a lie. I was never told what to do with the specimen." Susan snapped.

"Hold your fire Susan. I'm not judging you. All I know is that Dr. Brinkley said he was going to make sure that you'd be fired."

"Fired? You mean I'll lose my job?"

"Listen Susan, these surgeons hold a lot of power in this hospital. They are the bread and butter of this institution. They perform hundreds of procedures annually and bring in considerable revenue. You won't have a chance against his power when it comes to a choice between you and him."

"And why are you telling me all these things, you don't even know me" Susan asked. "How much time do you have" Jennifer asked quietly. Susan jumped.

"Oh my God. I've got to go"

"OK. I'll explain the rest to you later on. It hurts me that these powerful people impose their will on us. You are being made a scapegoat for what he's done wrong. The chief was questioning him about his surgical technique. Sounded like he had removed some wrong tissues. I will contact you again. Do not call for me downstairs. I need to keep my job."

"Thank you very much Janet. Can I call you at home or on your cell phone?"

"No. I will call you. We can't get too casual about this. We both have a job to keep. I'm sure some type of written report will be generated about their conversations. The matter will be formally referred to the OR Committee. It's almost a certainty that a law suit will be filed on behalf of this kid. The hospital has to protect itself. You may be named."

"Can you find out about this report, when it's filed?" Susan asked anxiously.

"I'm the one who will type it. You'll hear from me, promise."

"Thank you Janet. Please talk to me soon" Susan said as she stepped away from the corner,

"Sure." Jennifer couldn't hold back a faint smile, as she nodded farewell.

* * * * *

The Sign of the Dove, a trendy restaurant, up in northeast Manhattan was bustling with hungry patrons at 8 p.m. The atmosphere was jovial and music was refreshing. It was a good place to be at the end of a day full of hustle and bustle. Most certainly very fitting, for Jennifer and Brian who arrived together. Shortly after 8 PM.

They followed the maitre d' through the front room, down a few steps into the larger and elegantly decorated area and were offered a table near the end of the hall.

Jennifer looked tired, pensive and unaffected by her surroundings as yet. Brian appeared happy and relaxed, quite opposite from the distraught and tormented soul he was, just the night before.

"How was your day darling?" Jennifer asked.

"Better than I thought. No problems in the OR, no complaints against me, no reprimand. Just like a regular day and my cases went like a breeze, nice and easy."

"So what happened to all the problems you had yesterday?"

"It's as if they didn't exist" Brian shrugged.

"I think you're in denial." Jennifer said

Brian paused and looked around the room "I need a drink" he said as he waved the waiter in.

He ordered Gray Goose on the rocks and looked at Jennifer.

"A glass of white wine is fine" she said.

He opened the menu and ignored the conversation. Jennifer was waiting for an answer.

"Brian, you should think this matter through a bit more seriously" she said calmly.

"I did all the thinking I could do, I got nowhere. What happened two days ago was clearly the result of some conspiracy. It is not going to work." He said

"So you decided to ignore it. Forget about it. It didn't happen.

Yeah?"

"I decided to show them they couldn't bring me down. I went to work, showed my face, mingled with friends, and ignored the bitches."

"I have done my own thinking too, Brian."

"And?"

"And I see three major problems you have to deal with."

"And?"

"And before I tell you what they are, you should answer a few questions."

"Shoot." He said

The drinks arrived and the waiter asked if they were ready to order

"Few more minutes please."

Glasses clinked and the hot tasty contents were gulped down quickly.

"What exactly did you do wrong at surgery? You can't hide it forever."

She waited for an answer. Brian was staring at the candle. A few long seconds passed. She looked sharply into his eyes awaiting a response.

"It can happen in the most experienced hands. I removed things more than I should have."

"Things?"

"Yeah, certain structures that are intimately attached to a hernia sac"

"And how important is that? Is the kid damaged?"

"I would have known better if the bitch had not mixed up the specimens."

"I am not asking for detailed anatomy. Is the kid possibly damaged?"

"Possibly." He muttered.

"For how long?"

"Permanently."

"Permanently? Now I want to know the anatomy." Jennifer asked curiously.

The waiter arrived to take their orders. She ordered a mescaline salad and broiled salmon.

Brian was hungry and ordered a Caesar salad and black angus, medium well with baked potato. A second round of drinks was also ordered.

The conversation was on hold until the drinks arrived and consumed.

"Listen Jenny, I can't teach you anatomy here. Maybe later on in bed" He chuckled.
"Shut up." She yelled angrily.
"I truly believe whatever happened is completely inconsequential to the kid." Brian said emphatically.
"I am now completely lost. You admit that something went wrong, something that could happen to the most experienced surgeons and possibly cause permanent damage. Sounds serious enough, and yet you believe it is inconsequential. Which one Brian?"
"I would have known which one if the bitch had not mixed up the specimens."
"You are dancing around the question again. Let me ask you a different question. Assuming the damage is real; let's say the worst case scenario, what exactly is going to happen to this kid?"
Brian glanced at his surroundings, as if he was afraid of somebody hearing this, and frowned. He gathered his strength, clasped his hands and locked his fingers together, rested his elbows on the edge of the table and placed his chin on his hands and kept his eyes focused on his empty glass of vodka. Jennifer waited patiently. She would take no nonsense this time.

"The worst case scenario is that he may never ever be able to have kids of his own" Brian quickly covered his mouth by his hands. His jaw clenched.

Dinner arrived. He had lost his appetite.
Jennifer fired the next serious question ignoring the third person standing by the table serving dinner.
"Have you informed his parents?"
"No. And I am not so sure I should do that, at least until the final report of pathology is available" he said.

Jennifer was deep in thought, contemplating the ramifications of this event. She slowly picked up her knife and fork and broke the salmon into smaller pieces and squeezed a piece of lemon over the fish. Jennifer nibbled while Brian just looked at his dish, as if waiting for instructions what to do. He called the waiter and ordered another round of drinks. His head was warming up while his steak was cooling off.

"Let's eat now. We'll talk more later on" Jennifer said.
"How is the fish?" He asked.
"Dead" She said. A loud burst of laughter broke the ice.
"I love the way you keep your sense of humor." Brian said.
"I hate the way you've destroyed it lately. Dig in now."

Brian went to work on the steak as his next drink was placed on the table.

The ritual went on in the usual manner until the knives and spoons were placed at 4 o'clock position on the empty plates, signaling the waiter to take them away.

Jennifer gathered her thoughts and resumed the conversation.

"Now, let's go back to the three problems I believe you have to deal with, and very seriously"
"And what are they?"
"First and foremost, you've been accused of sexual harassment. I would like to know the exact exchange that took place between you and Susan, the nurse, but I leave the details for later on. The accusation has been made and you will have to fight it off."
"She cannot prove anything." He said angrily.
"She may not have to prove anything Brian. In this day and age of political correctness, the appearance of wrong doing is as bad and damaging as the actual act. Once the word gets around, you're toast." Jennifer continued, "Imagine people's reaction when word gets around about the eminent Dr. Brinkley sexually harassing the nurses. You are young and attractive, you are single, you are popular, people tend to believe these rumors readily, and before you get a chance to prove your innocence you'll lose your referring physicians, your patients, your friends, everybody. It'll be devastating to your practice. You should counter this immediately, before it becomes an official investigation.

"How can I do that?"

"I think I can help you with this. Please listen to me and do it." She paused for a moment to make sure Brian was paying attention.

"Counter attack" She said forcefully, waving her fist in the air. "First thing in the morning you write a letter to the chairman of the operating room committee accusing Susan Flynn of negligence in handling the specimen and mixing up the tissues of two separate sites. You describe how significant and serious this error was and recommend that she be fired."

"Wow. You think they will fire her?"

"Sure they will. The hospital cannot afford to lose a lucrative surgeon. The nurse can be replaced easily. Remember, I run the business office of another gigantic hospital. I know the inner workings of the system. You write the letter as forcefully as you can and give it to me. I'll make sure Susan will get wind of it. You may find her at your doorstep begging for forgiveness."

"Sweet ... baby." Brian uttered elatedly.

"Second." Jennifer paused for attention.

"You have committed a technical error in surgery with adverse consequences for the patient. This matter will be taken up at the OR committee or QA committee or both and you will have to appear there and explain. If you believe such an error can happen in the hands of the most experienced surgeons then you better do some research and gather some statistics and be prepared. Once this matter becomes known to the kid's parents, it is almost a certainty that a lawsuit will follow. You should be prepared to defend yourself."

Brian was trying to swallow his pride. This issue was the hardest for him. He had established a reputation as a well trained, state-of-the-art, successful surgeon. His young age and lack of experience, however, forbade him from the realization that even in the best of circumstances things can go wrong. Certain mishaps are not totally preventable. He had heard of Murphy's Law, but not experienced it firsthand. "If it CAN go wrong, it WILL go wrong."

He had forcefully popularized his image as "Dr. Perfect". Nothing would go seriously wrong under his care. He was holding to this image as being a notch above others who, through their longer careers, had encountered complications and, on occasions, less than satisfactory results.

This was the first eye opener for him and he had a hard time of it. Denial. Denial.

Brian's first reaction was that there was a mix-up with another patient's specimen. *Sorry, no other kiddy hernia specimen existed on that day.* Then he wanted to get another opinion from an outside pathologist. That required notification of patient's parents. Now he is trying to minimize the seriousness of the matter by implying that this can happen to any surgeon, even the best of them.

"Are you with me Brian?" She realized he was drifting away.
Brian shook his head "Yeah … Yeah, I follow you"

"Last but not the least." She paused again, staring directly into his eyes. "Are you going to inform the kid's parents?"
"I have thought a lot about this, and I am not sure what I should do. Again, if the bitch had not mixed up the specimens it would've been easier to decide what's best to do."
"Explain it to me" Jennifer said
"There is a big difference if the damage happened on one side or both sides."
"Meaning what?"
"The beauty of human anatomy is that there is a lot of redundancy in the system. You lose one eye; you have another one to see things. You lose one lung; you have another one to breathe with. In a man's body, sperms are made in the testicles. The tubes that carry the sperms from the testicles are called vas deferens. The vas deferens travel through the area above the groin where hernias develop, and they can be accidentally cut off while the hernia sac is being removed. If one side is damaged, the other one still works. No problem. If both sides are cut off, the person cannot deliver sperm and can never have natural offspring of his own."
"You mean if you had done the surgery on one side only, and had removed the tube by mistake, the kid would never know what happened to him and would have no problem having children?" Jennifer asked

curiously.

"Exactly. And in that case why should his poor parents be told of this and be subjected to many years of anxiety, guilty feelings, sadness, and fear of never having grandchildren for their golden years."

"Now, with the specimens mixed-up, you cannot tell if the damage was done on one side or both." Jennifer was beginning to realize the complexity of this ordeal. She was deep in thought and almost didn't notice when the waiters cleaned the table. Her train of thought was broken when she was handed the dessert menu.

"A hot cup of coffee would be just fine." She told the waiter.

Brian asked for an after dinner liquor. A Remy Martin, please. He was suddenly in a better mood, realizing that his sweetheart was beginning to understand his dilemma and leaning to take his side.

"You remember Dr. David Friedman?" She asked.

"Yep. The chief of Pediatric Surgery at NYU."

"Did you know him personally?"

"Sure. I rotated through his service several months during my residency"

"I think you should talk to him. He is experienced and surely has faced similar problems during his long career." *It can happen in the hands of the best surgeons*, she remembered.

"My impression of him was that he was cocky and conceited. After all, he was the top man in his department. I almost sensed that he would enjoy finding fault with junior attendings or residents. I'm not sure if he would give me an unbiased advice, but I will talk to him." Brian was anxious to end this conversation.

A young, cute waitress approached the table with the Remy Martin and a steaming cup of coffee. Brian flashed a quick smile and asked for the check.

* * * * *

SEVEN

Manhattan Medical Center, in uptown Manhattan, New York, has been known as one of the largest private hospitals in the city, mostly serving the affluent, the celebrities and the political elite. With a 650 bed capacity, the hospital had a claim on being one of the most sophisticated, best equipped, technologically advanced medical institutions, with impeccable safety records, lowest morbidity and mortality rates, highest patient satisfaction records and one of the most efficiently run medical centers.

To maintain such a level of proficiency and financial health, the Board of Directors was extremely sensitive to any measure of incompetence and misbehavior committed by the staff and would not tolerate adverse publicity of any kind. Reports of wrongdoings moved quickly through the appropriate committees and reached the higher echelon of decision making authorities. Lower level employees could not live through the scrutiny of poor performance and the department heads bore the responsibility for undue developments under their watch. The heads would roll at the drop of a hat.

Susan Flynn was fully aware of her tenuous situation. She knew she was walking on thin ice and could not afford to allow the accusation of negligence in handling the hernia specimens stick. She sincerely believed she had done nothing wrong. The specimens are handled at the discretion of the surgeons and she had received no specific instructions in this case. Alas, it was her words against his and she knew that he had the upper hand.

Her encounter with Janet Reilly shook her up and raised a few complicated issues. She realized that she was about to lose her job on this matter, and yet, she had filed a most serious accusation of sexual harassment against her accuser, Dr. Brinkley, who was about to send a recommendation to the OR committee asking for her dismissal. Well, it was only hearsay at this time. She wasn't sure if it was true. All she had heard was from Janet Reilly's eavesdropping. *Who was Janet Reilly anyhow?* She could not call her, contact her, or discuss anything with her. Everything was shrouded in mystery.

She heard from Janet that there was a technical error in surgery which made her specimen mix-up relevant and extremely important. Susan had no idea what the technical error was, how serious it was and how the higher authorities were dealing with that.

Was Dr. Brinkley himself standing on thin ice?

Would she be able to use her sexual harassment report as a bargaining chip? *I withdraw this, you withdraw that.* Nah ... She wasn't about to destroy the grand plans of her beloved Dr. Peter Molano and his co-conspirators.

Susan spotted her coming out of the coffee shop as she turned the corner past the front lobby reception desk heading for the cafeteria. Janet Reilly was among a group of employees going back to work. They came face to face with each other just past the corner.

"Hello Susan, I was hoping to see you" Jennifer said as she reached inside her purse and pulled out an envelope.

"Take this and read it later on. I am in rush back to work. Will talk to you soon."

"I need to talk to you now, Janet. Could you come to Cafeteria with me?" Susan said anxiously.

"No ... no. I have tons of reports to type. You read the letter; we'll talk about it later. Enjoy your lunch" she rushed past Susan and disappeared in the crowd.

Susan walked slowly towards the cafeteria, flipping the envelope in her hand. It was blank front and back.

The in-house phone was on the wall, at the entrance to the cafeteria. She picked up the receiver and dialed zero.

"Operator. Can I help you?"

"Yes, could you page Dr. Molano for me please?"

"OK, I'll try the OR for you"

"He's not in the OR. Please page him"

"Hold on please"

Holding the phone to her ear, she opened the envelope, pulled out the paper and unfolded it. The letterhead read Brian Brinkley, M.D. General Surgery.

She noted that it was a photocopy of a letter addressed to the Chairman of the Operating Room Committee. She broke out in a cold sweat and felt weak.

"Dr. Molano." The line came alive.

"Hi Peter, where are you honey?"

"Oh ... Susan. What's up darling?"

"I need to see you. I've got to talk to you now."

"Something happened? You sound panicky"

"I am Peter, extremely worried. Can you come to the cafeteria?"

"Sure, but I'm in a meeting now. I'll get out in twenty minutes. See you there."

She hung up and walked in. By now she'd lost her appetite for lunch. She picked up a cup of coffee, paid for it and found herself a small table away from the crowd. Sunk in the seat and opened the letter.

She read the letterhead again. Brian had written a harsh, critical letter to the committee describing the circumstances in the OR when he was doing a bilateral hernia repair on a two year old boy named Elliot Silverman. He complained that the circulating nurse, Susan Flynn, was totally inattentive to the case, constantly going in and out of the room, spending some time on the phone and handing in wrong suture material to the scrub nurse. Her mind was somewhere else and at times looked like she did not want to be there at all. She caused considerable distraction and contributed to some tension and confusion during the case. *Son of a bitch is covering his ass for his technical error,* she thought.

He went on to write that he was appalled to find out, the following day, that she had mixed-up the specimens obtained from the right and left side surgery, a horrendous error that could have long term consequences for the patient. *What a pathological liar this guy is.* Susan was enraged.

The letter continued, in harsh tone, that with incompetent nurses, such as Susan Flynn, working in the operating room, he could no longer trust the institution and may have no choice but to take his patients somewhere else. He demanded that Susan Flynn be placed on suspension immediately and, preferably dismissed.

Susan could not take her eyes off the letter; she was frozen, numb and motionless. She could hear her rapid heartbeat and was gasping for fresh air.

A hot kiss on the cheek and a warm hello from Peter Molano woke her up from a bad dream. He noticed the tears rolling down her face.

"What is going on darling?"

"I did this for you Peter, you've got to protect me" Susan said while holding back the tears.

"Would you calm down please and tell me what's upsetting you?"

She handed the letter to Dr. Molano and said, "He is taking revenge now. I reported him and he's trying to have me fired. I can't lose my job Peter."

Peter was deep into reading the letter. Susan took a sip of her cold coffee while staring intently at Peter and his reaction.

"Nonsense" he grunted and threw the letter on the table. "No way can he get you fired. I'll make darn sure everybody on the committee knows he has a sexual harassment complaint against him. This is an obvious act of revenge. It doesn't wash." Peter was visibly angry.

"It is going to be his word against mine, Peter."

"Let me investigate this further Susan. I'll discuss this with our group and take care of it. Don't panic, don't worry, nobody's going to fire you." Peter tried hard to reassure Susan.

"Who's in the group? I think I have the right to know. I did this on behalf of you all"

"True, but we can't play this loose. The slightest hint of collective action against a practicing physician is going to be considered a conspiracy. We have sworn each other to keep this secret." Peter was anxious to change the subject.

"Is anybody from this group on the OR committee?" she asked.

"I don't know, I'll find out"

Susan folded the letter and placed it in her pocket.
Peter stood up and looked at his watch.

"I gotta go to the OR now. I will find out more about this and call you tomorrow."

"Please find out when the OR committee meets and who is on it." Susan asked anxiously.

"Will do, bye now." He left.

* * * * *

The secretary opened the door and stuck her head into the prestigious office of the Chief of Pediatric Surgery, at New York University Medical Center.

Dr. David Friedman, a petite figure in his late sixties had himself almost buried under mounds of papers, articles and medical journals piled up on his desk.

He had finished his morning surgeries, a quick lunch and a few dictations, and now was preparing for afternoon rounds with residents and fellows.

"Excuse me sir, there is a doctor Brinkley here to see you."

"Oh yes, he called yesterday, bring him in."

The door swung open and Brian walked in.

"Good afternoon sir."

"Hello my boy, how are you. Come in please." The Chief lifted himself up halfway off the chair and pointed across the desk as he stretched his right arm for a handshake.

"How is life in private practice, Brian?" He asked.

"Full of ups and downs sir. A lot of hassle and struggle, and yet, a great deal of satisfaction. Overall it's worth it."

"You've been in practice for how long now?"

"Little over three years"

"You should be feeling comfortable by now, yeah?"

"Almost. The problem is that during training you have so much support around you. Your senior residents, your attending surgeons, your chiefs, they are all around you, watching you like a hawk. If you have a problem, they solve it for you. If you have questions, they are there to answer them." Brian was trying to set the stage for discussing his own predicament.

"And then" he paused for a few seconds "you are thrown into this vast ocean of private practice, in a small boat, drifting away, and a huge wave is heading towards you."

The chief began to realize why Brian was there.

"Is there a wave heading towards you now?" The chief asked.

"I'm afraid so, a big one. I need advice." Brian had never been so humbled.

"What happened?"

"I cut the Vas Deferens fixing a kiddy hernia."

The chief felt like smashing a book on Brian's head. *You stupid asshole, how many times I've told you to watch out for that damn tiny little tube?* He suddenly realized Brian is not a resident anymore. He should treat him differently.

"You can't do anything about it now" he said, trying to remain calm.

"I realize that"

"How old is the kid?"

"Two years old"

"The hernia was on one side or both sides?"

"Only the right side." Brian chose not to get into explaining why he explored the other side, and how the specimens were mixed up.

The chief shifted his position on the chair, tilted backward and placed his feet on the edge of the desk.

"Some researchers have attempted to repair the transected Vas Deferens in an infant, like microvascular surgeons repairing transected small vessels under the microscope, but only if you realize the problem at the time of surgery and even then, you never know if it works."

"I know chief." Brian wanted to end this technical discussion, but the chief was just warming up.

"When you sew the two ends of a broken vessel back together, the blood flow will keep the tube open. At age two, nothing flows through the Vas and the hook up will shrink and clog. This has been researched in animals."

Brian remained silent and appeared distant to the discussion. *For crying out loud, leave me alone chief. This is not a classroom.*

"I appreciate the information chief, but my dilemma is with an ethical question rather than a technical one" he tried to change the subject again.

"And what is the question?" the chief asked.

"The question is whether I should inform his parents of this mishap, or just let it go"

The chief jumped off the chair, stomped his feet on the floor and said "Just let it go? Are you kidding me?" He managed a broad smile to camouflage his scornful sneer.

"One way or another they'll find out, and then you'll be toast" he said.

Brian prepared himself for presenting his strongest argument. Something he had thought of a lot, day and night, since the accident.

These academic guys don't live in the real world, they are protected by the system, they don't pay a big chunk of their income towards malpractice insurance premium, they don't worry about losing their license, they don't face the patients and their families on a day by day basis, their interns and residents do. I am not going to dig my own grave.

"Here is my point of view chief. If I tell his parents now, these poor people will have to live in constant anxiety and anguish for next twenty, twenty five, thirty years or more to find out if their son can have children of his own. It's cruel. Also, once they know about this, it's almost a certainty that those vultures, the lawyers, will be knocking at my door to devour my corpse. I'll be digging my own grave. Why not let them go on believing that their son's operation went well. He will grow up in a happy family and one day he will have a child of his own, a little cute grand child for his parents. What's wrong with that?"

"It could be logically correct, but ethically wrong. They have every right to know what happened at surgery. If they find out from another source, you will be sued for hiding this from them as well, a double jeopardy." He paused and went on "now, let me offer you a solution that gives you the best, of both worlds"

Brian kept looking at him with anticipation.

"You tell the kid's parents what happened, then give them a lot of hope and assurance that he will have no problem having children in the future and then send them here, I will sit down with them and reassure them. One side is damaged; the other side is OK, what's to worry about?"

Brian was drenched in a cold sweat. How he wished he had not touched the other side or that stupid bitch had not mixed the specimens. He felt more than ever that this gigantic problem was only his own. No help from the chief.

"Thank you for your advice chief. I'll keep you informed"
"Have a good day my boy. Life is full of surprises, deal with it."
Brian shook his hand and left.

* * * * *

EIGHT

Central Park was swarmed with late afternoon crowds, joggers, walkers, strollers, wanderers; love birds, white collars, blue collars, multi-collars, and all other symbols of New York's multi-ethnic society who loved to escape the civilization and find temporary refuge in this semblance of a natural habitat.

A brief passing shower had cooled off the air and a nice soft breeze was quite refreshing.

The Great Lawn was crowded with evening settlers, stretching their tired bodies and relaxing on a soft blanket, contemplating another day of the hectic New York life.

There was to be a live performance by the New York Philharmonic later on in the evening.

The ballfields were active. Adjacent to the Heckscher Ballfield the hungry spectators were rushing to the Ballfields Café for a quick meal.

Farther south and to the west, another New York landmark, Tavern on the Green, Central Park's largest and most flamboyant restaurant was getting ready to serve sumptuous dinners to the rich and the elite.

They met at the main entrance but had no intention of eating there; instead they decided to go for a walk, alongside the Sheep Meadow, one of Central Park's most famous and favorite green fields. People were sunbathing, tossing Frisbees and picnicking.

Susan Flynn showed no enthusiasm for sightseeing and was oblivious to her surroundings. She was anxiously focused on what she could get out of this meeting with Janet Reilly.

Jennifer Bradley on the other hand appeared to be enjoying the scenery and intended to drag the prelude on as long as she could before she would smash her prey with another piece of bad news.

"You come here often, Janet?" Susan asked.

"As often as I can. I love it. The park rejuvenates me. I'm sick and tired of those crammed basement back offices of the pathology department. I come here to get a new lease on life."

"Wonderful. You work everyday?" Susan asked.

"Pretty much. I take a few days off once in a while."

"I read Dr. Brinkley's letter, asking for my dismissal. I'm worried."

"You should be. These guys are powerful. I hope the committee members are more understanding and fair. Do you know who sits on that committee, Susan?"

"I don't, but I'll find out soon. I have my own sources." Susan paused and stopped walking for a second, then turned to Jennifer and frowned.

"What is it?" Jennifer asked

"By the way Janet, how did you get your hand on that letter? Do you know Dr. Brinkley or his office staff?"

"No. I didn't get a chance to explain this to you the other day, in the coffee shop. Myself and a few other secretaries have formed a small network to alert each other of what's going on in the hospital, mainly to protect our jobs. Employees are being fired right and left for no good reason at all. We have to protect ourselves. I overheard Dr. Brinkley's conversation with our chief, Gonzalez, when he said he was going to ask the OR committee to look into your performance. I alerted the secretary who is in charge of the OR committee that such letter was forthcoming, and she passed on a copy of the letter to me when she received it."

"Oh good, then you should be able to find out who sits on the OR committee."

"I certainly can, but, listen; this is all to remain strictly between me and you."

"Sure, I appreciate your trying to help me out. I just hope he will have to face the Ethics committee before the OR committee."

"Why is that?"

"I reported him to my supervisor for bad behavior in the OR." Susan sounded revengeful.

"Bad behavior? What did he do?" Jennifer asked as if this was news to her.

"Started with some sexual remarks and then became a bit personal and I didn't appreciate that. I beefed up my report to indicate sexual harassment."

"Wow ... sexual harassment is a very serious charge. Can you prove it?"

"Dammit ... it'll be my words against his."

"Not exactly." Jennifer said in a supportive tone. "Did you have witnesses?"

"There were others in the OR; anesthesiologist and other nurses, but I'm not sure they will support my claim of sexual harassment."

"They won't." Jennifer paused for a minute, and went on: "A prominent and popular surgeon's whole career will be on the line. They could take his license away. It's a very heavy burden to carry for any witness. Bet you they won't go that far. At the most he will be asked to apologize for the verbal insult, if that was the case."

"What options do you think I have to fight the dismissal?" Susan asked with a pale face.

It's time to hit her hard right now. Jennifer spotted a bench under a tree. She walked towards it. "Let's sit down here for a while; I have to explain something to you." She jumped up to catch a Frisbee passing by. She couldn't reach.

"There is more bad news I have to give you before you check on your options." Jennifer said as they sat down on the bench.

"What now?" Susan asked. Her voice, terse and defiant.

"I typed Dr. Gonzalez's report of his meeting with Dr. Brinkley. He is extremely critical of your handling the specimens and speaks of dire consequences of such errors and now he is asking for your dismissal as well."

Susan bent and covered her face with her hands and started crying. Jennifer remained quiet for a while until Susan calmed down. She pulled a Kleenex tissue from her purse and handed it to Susan.

"Where is he sending this report to?" Susan asked, fighting a big lump in her throat.

"To the OR committee, but it is sitting on my desk as we speak."

"Are you going to send it over soon?"

"I can hold it back for a few days, but fairly soon it has to go there. I don't quite know when the next meeting is scheduled"

"What's going to happen to me, Janet?" Susan asked, holding back tears.

"You'll be fired. With two strong recommendations for your dismissal, the OR committee has no choice but to act. It will certainly happen, Susan … unless …" Jennifer paused for Susan's full attention "unless you withdraw your claim of sexual harassment and apologize to Dr. Brinkley before this whole mess finds its way to the OR committee."

"I don't kiss anybody's ass, Janet. This is unfair." Susan cried louder.

"Let's be realistic Susan. You cannot prove sexual harassment against Dr. Brinkley. You have a serious problem on your hand with this specimen mishap. That, by itself, can knock you out. C'mon lady, eat your pride a little bit and save your job."

"Apologize to that jerk? No way." Susan was obviously struggling with herself.

"OK, don't apologize, but make it look like this whole thing was a misunderstanding. Tell him you were overburdened with work and personal problems and you had a short fuse on that day and you did not appreciate his innocent sexual remarks. This is not an apology, it's just a clarification. No doubt he will take back his request for your dismissal, and he may even share the blame of mishandling the specimens with you. After all, he was the surgeon and ultimately responsible for what went on in the OR"

Susan was deep in thought by now. The idea appealed to her, only if she could keep it from Dr. Peter Molano, who would most definitely be opposed to withdrawing her accusation. He was counting on her help to knock out a formidable competitor. No way would he go along with this.

"Thank you Janet. I'll think about it." She said, as she stopped sniffling and dried her eyes by a tissue.

"I think this matter can be resolved easily and your job will be safe, if you think about what I just told you." Jennifer patted Susan on the back.

"Can I just withdraw my accusations without apologizing to Dr. Brinkley?"

"Sure you can. Write a note to the OR supervisor, and act like a magnanimous, forgiving soul, and ask her not to forward your incident report to the OR committee. Take it back. You didn't mean it to be so harsh. You misunderstood Dr. Brinkley's remarks and don't want him to get into trouble. But, remember, if you want his cooperation in the issue of specimen mishandling you should approach him directly. Write to him and explain to him that you did not receive any specific instructions from him, and, very politely express sadness that this incident had caused any inconvenience for him and his patient. He would love it, Susan. He is a macho, self-centered, narcissist. These people like to be praised, admired, adorned, and loved every minute of their lives. You praise him and he would love to have people like you around him all the time. He will save your job."

"You want me to kiss his ass, yeah?"

"If you want to save your own ass." Jennifer responded harshly.

"I guess I have to. When is this God-damn committee meeting?"

"I think in a few days. I can find out"

"I'll talk to the OR supervisor tomorrow."

* * * * *

His office was in the basement, administration section, opposite Pathology and the laboratory. The sign on the door read: Joseph Brown, M.D. Medical Director.

Inside, the walls were covered with bookshelves, and the shelves were filled with numerous medical reference books, binders, thick and thin, labeled "Rules and Regulations" and "policy manuals" for each department.

His desk, a large mahogany colored piece of art was neat and impeccably organized, a reflection of the man himself, a well disciplined professional with a knack for punctuality, precision and orderliness. His job would demand no less than that.

As the Medical Director of the Manhattan Medical Center, he was ultimately responsible for the medical affairs of the hospital. Every department, in-patient or out-patient, was under his constant scrutiny. Slightest deviation from the accepted norms of medical practice would raise a flag and initiate an investigation through numerous committees for which he would set the schedules and agendas.

Attached to his office, there was another large room, the file room, with wall-to-wall secure cabinets containing files for every member of the medical staff. Every physician's file contained records of his or her performance, results, complications and level of activity, number of malpractice lawsuits against them and the conclusion of each.

At 7 a.m. Nancy Robertson, the staff secretary, entered the room and checked the desk. Everything was in order. She left Dr. Brown's schedule of the day on the desk. A full day of work summarized on one piece of paper. Medical Records Committee at 9 a.m. followed by the credentials committee, meetings with the director of residency training program, working lunch with a couple of department chairmen, Ad-Hoc committee for selection of Medical staff officers, president, vice president, treasurer and secretary, for the following year. Later on in the day, he should work on setting the agendas for the upcoming OR and QA committees.

At precisely 7:30 a.m. he entered his office and placed his attaché case next to his desk.

He took a glance at his schedule and sunk into the plush executive leather chair. On hot summer days he would take off his jacket and roll up his sleeves, but he was attached to his principles and discipline. The bow tie would stay fastened. His gray hair and neatly trimmed goatee softened the sharpness of his gaze and the glare of his seriousness. He put his reading glasses on and picked up a stack of papers, reports coming from different departments as Nancy placed his first cup of coffee on the desk, always on the right hand side.

"Morning Nancy." He said without taking his eyes off the reports.

"Morning Sir. You have Medical Records Committee at 9."

"I noted that on the schedule. Would you go to Medical Records and get me the chart of a patient named Elliot Silverman. He is a 2 year old boy who had hernia surgery few days ago."

"Elliot Silverman. Yes sir."

She walked out and he kept reading the reports. Statistics from the Admission office. The hospital was maintaining ninety eight percent occupancy rates. That was good. Medical Records reported a sharp increase in incomplete charts, and that he didn't like. He dictated a harsh memo to the medical staff. Complete your charts within two weeks or face disciplinary actions.

He reviewed the incident reports and the one that caught his eye quickly was a sexual harassment claim made by an OR nurse against a Dr. Brian Brinkley. He did not know the surgeon personally. *Should be a new one on the staff.*

He sipped his coffee and went through the rest of the reports. Nosocomial infection rate was stable. Few applicants for staff appointments were waiting to be called in for an interview.

He finished the reports and picked up another file, titled Administration Directives. This was another area of his responsibilities that had to do with hospital administration and not the medical staff. He would often find himself between a rock and a hard place. As a physician, and Medical Director, his allegiance and loyalty was with the medical staff. On the other hand he was employed by the hospital, to protect the institution against unacceptable or sub-optimal medical practice. He was often hated and despised by both sides. The administration constantly pressed him to come down hard on the physicians who did not perform well.

Nancy returned from Medical Records and handed him the requested chart.

He glanced through the admission information. The operative report: "Bilateral inguinal hernia repair", and then the discharge summary: "Patient's hospital stay was uneventful. He tolerated the surgery very well and discharged home in satisfactory condition." He turned the page and looked at the pathology report: "Several slides show fragments of

Vas Deferens." *Son of a gun is hiding a major complication.*

He noted the surgeon's name: Dr. Brian Brinkley. He quickly fingered through the reports he had reviewed earlier and pulled out the incident reports and matched the names. They were the same. *Umm … interesting. He screwed the patient and the nurse at the same time!* He thought.

Nancy buzzed him from her desk.

"Dr. Sloan, Chief of surgery, on line 2. He wants to talk to you now. He is in a rush to the OR.

"I'll take it now." He said as he picked up the receiver and pressed line 2.

"Morning Mike, what's up?"

"Hi Joe, How are you?"

"I'm fine, what's on your mind?"

"We have a problem with one of our surgeons; I wanted to talk to you"

"Would that happen to be Dr. Brinkley?"

"Oh, you know about him already?"

"Dr. Gonzalez asked me to look into a case he did a few days ago. So I am reviewing the patient's chart as we speak."

"On the surface looks like he practically castrated the kid, however, there are serious doubts about that. What're you gonna do with him?"

"For sure he will be called to appear in the OR Committee. What about this bizarre sexual harassment accusation against him? You know about that?"

"I saw the incident report. I am not so sure how legitimate this claim is. How should we handle it Joe?"

"I have no choice but to convene the Ethics committee, and come up with a decision. It is serious."

"Sure it is. I agree with you."

"Gotta go now. Have a good day, Joe."

"Bye."

* * * * *

NINE

The waiting room of the surgeon's office was filled with patients. A grumpy old man in the corner was visibly annoyed with the constant howling of a baby boy sitting on his mother's lap. The boy's father was reading a magazine, totally ignoring the scene of the generational conflicts. People had been waiting for almost an hour, and most of them appeared edgy and restless. Finally, the receptionist stuck her head through the window and called for attention. "I have good news now. The doctor had been delayed at surgery but he just finished and left the operating room. He'll be here in twenty minutes."

Thirty more minutes of moaning and groaning went by. The receptionist kept apologizing and the grumpy old man kept scowling at the boy, further frightening him. *Who is this ugly old creature? I'm afraid he'll eat me!* The boy shrieked and punched his mom in the face.

Dr. Brinkley entered through a private entrance and went into his office. The secretary rushed in and handed him three messages. "They've been waiting a long time. Should I bring in the first patient?" She asked.

Brian looked at his messages. Two calls from Jennifer Bradley. *Must be urgent.*

"Put the first patient in. I have to return this call. It'll be quick."

The nurse left. He took off his jacket and put his white lab coat on and sat at the edge of his desk and dialed.

"Hi darling. What's up?"

"How is my most favorite surgeon doing today?"

"I'm fine and I'm late getting in the office. They're going to kill me."

"Have you decided to tell the boy's parents what happened in the OR?"

"Yep … I have decided not to tell them anything."

"How could you Brian? They have the right to know. Did you talk to Dr. Friedman?" She asked anxiously.

"I did. Actually I went and visited him in his office and had a long conversation with him"

"And …"

"And he said I should tell them the truth, but, I have decided against it. I'll tell you my reasons later on. Let me go now, a patient is waiting"

"Before you go, have you seen your mail today?"

"No. I just came in. Why?"

"I think you will get an interesting letter from your accuser, Susan Flynn, today or tomorrow"

"Wow … that is interesting. How do you know?"

"I'll tell you later. Go see your patient. Talk to the kid's parents, Brian."

"Love you baby. Call me this evening"

"OK. Bye now"

He noticed that the waiting room was suddenly quiet. The boy was not crying anymore. The old man had been taken into the examination room. *Smart move.*

Brian picked up his chart from the door pocket and entered the room.

His first few patients were post-ops. Their first or second visit after surgery.

The boy was brought into the exam room along with his parents. He was quiet and playful. The nurse handed him a lollypop while glancing at his parents for approval.

Brian entered the room with a big smile. The nurse followed.

"Hello Elliot. How are you?"

Mr. and Mrs. Silverman greeted the doctor with respect. The mother was holding the baby in her arms. The nurse reached and took the baby and placed him on the examination table. The boy shrieked loudly and struggled to jump off the table, as the doctor put his hand on the baby's belly and exposed the incisions.

"Very nice, he is healing well" he said, looking at the parents.

"The left side incision looks a little red and swollen, Doctor." The mother said, looking quite worried. The father followed "This is the side that had no hernia. Is it infected?"

"No Mr. Silverman. There is no infection. It is normal for a fresh incision to be slightly red and swollen. It's only a week since his operation. It'll be alright." He said, as he checked the baby's testicles.

Hey, it hurts; take your hands off me. The baby screamed.

Brian pointed to the mother to pick the baby up. She did and he was quiet again.

"Do you want to see him again?" The mother asked.

"Not unless he has problems"

"Dr. Brinkley, I know you are busy, I wonder if I can have a few minutes with you" the father asked.

"Of course, come into my office." He walked out and Mr. Silverman followed him into his office. The mother took the baby to the waiting room.

Brian sat in his chair behind his desk, not knowing what to expect.

"Please sit down" he pointed to a chair near his desk.

"Thank you." Mr. Silverman sat down and leaned over the edge of the desk, resting on his elbows.

"I asked you this question in the Recovery Room, Doctor. I'm not sure I understood your answer. What made you cut him on the other side, where he did not have a hernia?"

"Mr. Silverman, I told you it is more or less a routine procedure. Some kiddy hernias are bilateral, meaning they occur on both sides, even though the hernia does not show itself as bulging above the groin."

"But you did not mention this to us before surgery"

"It was on the consent form and you signed it." Brian said as he raised his voice a notch. *Was it really written on the consent?* He thought so, but was not one hundred percent sure.

"Probably so, I don't remember seeing it. I thought maybe something unexpected happened at surgery that made you cut him on the other side."

"Nothin' happened. Why are you so worried about this?

"I'm sorry Doctor. I don't know if you have children. Parents worry about everything. I suppose he is alright now. Is there anything we should be concerned about him in the future?"

Brian struggled with himself and was extremely tempted to break the silence and explain to him what happened in the OR. Dr. Friedman, Jennifer and his own conscience were bugging him to talk. He just couldn't muster enough courage to do so. He had an easy way out. Why should he subject these poor people to many years of anxiety and uncertainty? No, he just couldn't do it.

"Absolutely nothin'." He said "he'll be fine. He's a good healthy kid." Brian stood up, as if telling Mr. Silverman to get lost.

"God bless you Doctor. We cannot thank you enough."
"Thank you. Mr. Silverman. Call me if you have any questions." He shook hands and directed Mr. Silverman towards the waiting room.

Three hours later Brian sunk into his chair, exhausted and yearning for a Scotch on the rocks and a cigarette. He finished dictating his office notes, and went through his mail of the day. There was a letter from the office of the Medical Director, Manhattan Medical Center. He opened the letter. It was a Memo from Dr. Brown, requesting him to attend the next OR committee meeting, to be held the following week, Tuesday morning, 9 a.m. in the Staff Room. A discussion will be held on the case of his patient Elliot Silverman.

He put the letter aside and looked through the rest of his mail.

He spotted it instantly. A letter from Susan Flynn. He opened the envelope, and pulled out two pieces of paper. The one on the top was addressed "Dear Dr. Brinkley". The other one was a photocopy of a letter addressed to Ms. Mary Dorsa, the Operating Room supervisor.

In her letter to Dr. Brinkley, Susan started with greetings and expression of deep regret of what had happened a week ago in the Operating Room. She was so sorry that she had misunderstood Dr. Brinkley's friendly conversations, jokes and anecdotes, and because of her emotional preoccupation with numerous family problems, lack of sleep and pure exhaustion, she had felt personally insulted by his sexually tainted references. She apologized for her overreaction which was unfair and uncalled for. She sincerely apologized for having reported him and accusing him of sexual harassment.

This, she considered the most inexcusable action she had ever undertaken in her life and now she was begging for his forgiveness. She went on to praise him as a true gentleman, and a superb surgeon. She asked him to read the enclosed photocopy of a letter she had written to the OR supervisor retracting her claim of sexual harassment against him, and requested that the letter be forwarded to the OR Committee as soon as possible.

At the end she took full responsibility for the mix up of the hernia specimens, although she gingerly inserted a reminder that he had not given her specific instructions.

Brian took a quick glance through the other letter, totally overjoyed with both letters and wondered what had caused Susan's change of heart which took a tremendous load off his shoulder. And how in the world did Jennifer know about this?

He called his secretary and asked her to copy both letters and mail a copy to Dr. Joseph Brown, Medical Director of Manhattan Medical Center, whom, he had assumed, would investigate Susan's accusation through the OR or Ethics committee and a copy to Dr. Michael Sloan, Chairman, Department of Surgery.

He then picked up the phone and called Jennifer, begging her to have dinner with him. He had a lot to talk about.

* * * * *

The phone rang in the OR main office and the secretary picked up the receiver.

"OR, can I help you"

"Mornin'. This is Dr. Molano. I wonder if Susan Flynn is available."

"She's scrubbed Doctor. Can I take a message for her?"

"Would you happen to know how long she'll be tied up?"

"Just a minute please" She put him on hold and pushed the intercom button for OR3.

"Hello, this is the OR secretary. Is Susan Flynn still scrubbed?"

A distant voice echoed in the room "Yes. I am. What's up?"

"Hi, Susan. There is a call from Dr. Molano for you. He wants to know how long you'll be tied up"

"About forty minutes. Ask him where I can reach him."

"OK, I'll take his number and give it to you later on"

Susan struggled to remain focused on her work. One mistake had gotten her into enough trouble ten days earlier. She couldn't help it. *Why the hell he is calling me now? Did he find out about the letters I sent few days ago? Is he mad that I withdrew my claim against Dr. Brinkley?*

She had decided not to tell him anything about the letters. She had been tormented between her anxiety to keep her job and her loyalty to the man she loved so much. On the other hand, how long could she keep this from him? He and his secret group had their own sources within the system. Wouldn't it be better if she told him herself and explained things personally? Ah … he would be furious, yelling and shouting and throwing things around, and then she would be crying and begging for his understanding.

She was anguished because she had to break her promise and could not be party to this plan any longer. She was going to lose him for sure. Which would be worse? Losing her job or her love?

A loud angry voice shook her up "Susan … Are you here? Three times I've asked for the larger clamp. Come on now" The surgeon yelled.

She handed the instrument and tried to control her shaking knees "I'm sorry Sir."

An hour later she ran out of the OR3 and went right into the main office. The secretary handed her a note. Call Dr. Molano at his office, he'll be there for a while.

She ran into the nurse's locker room. Nobody was there. She leaned on the wall, took a deep breath and dialed.

"Dr. Molano's office. How may I help you?"

"Hi this is Susan Flynn. Is he there?"

"I'm sorry. He just left. He was expecting your call. You can reach him on his cell phone"

"Thank you so much". She hung up and dialed Peter's cell phone.

"Dr. Molano"

"Hello darling, were you looking for me?" She braced herself for the worst.

"Susan dear, something has puzzled me." *Oh god, he is in good mood.* "Do you have that letter from Dr. Brinkley to the OR committee?"

"Of course. You read it. Why are you asking?"

"The secretary who handles the OR committee knows nothing about it"

What?! Could that be true? She thought.

"You sure? The letter was dated few days ago, and the secretary gave a copy to a friend of mine"

"Friend? Who?"

"Janet Reilly. She works in Pathology. She also told me about the report Dr. Gonzalez had sent to the OR committee criticizing me for mishandling the specimen and asking for my dismissal, Peter. Do you know about that?"

"No, Susan. I'm sure she would have told me about it. Hey, what's going on here?"

"Peter, the letters are there, I'm sure. Go back and talk to her again. When is the OR committee meeting?

"Next Tuesday"

"Did the secretary tell you about any other letters she might have received?" Susan hesitantly asked.

"No, what letters?" *Thank goodness, he doesn't know.* Susan was happy. "How do I know ... looks like these days everybody wants to fire me"

"Nobody can fire you, Susan. Don't be paranoid."

"Peter, I cannot afford to lose my job. You understand? Right now there are two powerful people in this institution after me. They are going to get me fired." Susan raised her voice sharply, as if laying the grounds for telling Peter about her letters, but she wasn't quite sure yet.

"Don't you worry, Susan. Your sexual harassment report is going to knock Brinkley down." Peter said, trying hard to keep Susan in line for his plans.

"You don't understand Peter, this guy is wounded. He was chastised by the Chief of Pathology for some kind of technical error. He is going to use me as a scapegoat. I am no match against him."

"Calm down Susan. Believe me, I know the OR Committee secretary very well. I am very suspicious about Dr. Brinkley's letter. Where and how Janet Reilly did get her hand on this letter? Why don't you go to pathology and ask her. This is an urgent matter."

"Are you sure the secretary did not get the letter from the Chief of Pathology either?" Susan was now puzzled and a bit suspicious.

"No. She would have told me about it. Why don't you question your friend, Janet something, about that letter also."

"OK. I'll see her at lunchtime."

"I'll be in the hospital by then. Page me please after you see Janet."

"Will do. Bye now."

Susan was tempted to call Janet in pathology right away, but decided instead to go there at lunch time. Things were beginning to look strange. Janet had repeatedly warned her against making phone calls to pathology. She had often wondered why. Was it possible that all the phone calls in the hospital were being recorded for security purposes? *Naah ... not likely.*

Perhaps she did not want to be overheard by her colleagues. And why was she hiding in the back offices of pathology? Why was she so secretive? All this tempted Susan to go to pathology but she was called back to OR3, for her next case.

At her lunch break she zoomed out of the OR, down the stairway, into the main lobby, passed by the coffee shop and down another stairway to the basement. She had never been there. The halls were crowded by people coming out of offices going for lunch. She looked at the signs on the wall. Administration offices to the left. Pathology and laboratory to the right.

Susan rushed down the hall and found the main entrance to the pathology department.

A receptionist was on the phone at the front desk. She looked around and waited.

"May I help you?"

"Yes, I need to talk to Janet Reilly. She is somewhere in the back offices."

"Janet Reilly? I'm not sure we have a Janet Reilly here"

"Oh yes, you do. She is a friend of mine. She works here."

"Wait a minute please. I am kind of new here. Maybe I don't know everybody. This is a big place here." She picked up the phone and called somebody"

How could she not know Janet Reilly? The chief's private secretary? Susan wondered.

Before the receptionist hung up the phone Susan said "She is Dr. Gonzalez' private secretary"

The receptionist put the phone down. "Oh ... The chief's private secretary? She is here. I just saw her a few minutes ago. I thought her name was Janice. I'll call her for you."

"Thank you ... Thank you, I'll wait"

Susan anxiously paced the room as she glanced at the people coming in and out of the department.

A robust, heavy set, middle aged woman came out and went to reception desk. The girl pointed towards Susan and she approached her.

"Hi, I'm Janice. Are you looking for me?"

"I'm so sorry. I'm actually looking for Janet ... Janet Reilly."

"Who is Janet Reilly?"

"She works here, Dr. Gonzalez' secretary."

Janice frowned. *What the heck is she talking about?*

"I don't think so. *I am* his secretary"

Susan was now perplexed. Janice noticed and tried to be helpful.

"Are you sure she works here in pathology?"

"Yes I am. She is my friend. I've seen her here."

"You have actually seen her here? In this department?"

"Not exactly, we usually see each other at coffee breaks in the coffee shop."

"Perhaps she works in administration, the other side of the basement." Janice said.

"No ... no. She works here. She types Dr. Gonzalez' reports."

"Oh … no Ma'am, nobody types the chief's reports but me. That's for sure."

Susan was agitated and lost. Still unbelieving. *Why are they hiding her from me?*

The receptionist punched quickly into the computer and pulled out a page out of the printer and took a long glance at it.

"Excuse me ma'am. This is a list of our employees here at pathology. There is no Janet Reilly here."

Janice asked her to check the hospital wide employee list and she did.

"There is no Janet Reilly in this hospital ma'am."

Susan was mumbling "I don't understand. She was here a few days ago. Was she fired?"

"Nobody has been fired from this department recently." Janice said.

Susan leaned on the wall, her knees trembling. A filmy layer of perspiration was building up on her forehead. She was dizzy. She struggled to pull herself together and managed a faint smile as she said "thank you" and left the room. *Where are you Janet Reilly? What the hell is going on?* She ran back in the hall, up the stairs, onto the first floor and stopped at the coffee shop. Hopelessly, she looked inside, back in the corner where she had first met her. No sign of her. She sat at a table and leaned over the edge, rested her elbows on the table and held her throbbing head in her hands. She was beginning to realize what had happened. Janet never gave her a phone number. Did not want her to call or go to pathology. She was an imposter. *Oh my God. What has she done to me?*

She jerked her back as she felt a warm hand on her shoulder.

"Susan, are you OK?" Dr. Molano frowned as he looked down at her face.

"I don't know Peter. I don't know."

"You look so pale and sweaty. What happened? Did you talk to Janet Reilly?" He asked as he sat down at the table.

"No, she's not here"

"She's off today? Why don't you call her?"

"She's not here. She does not exist. She's vanished. Nobody knows her. They are denying she ever worked here. She never gave me her phone number. She's gone."

"Didn't you say she was your friend? How long did you know her?" Peter asked curiously.

"She wasn't my friend. I've actually met her here twice. Right there on that corner and once in the hall. She said she worked in the Pathology department. She gave me Dr. Brinkley's letter and told me about Dr. Gonzalez' report. Oh … I'm sorry, that was at Central Park. I did not see the report in writing." Tears were now rolling down her face.

"Central Park?"

"Yeah, we went for a walk the other day."

"Listen, Susan." Peter said, with a calm and reassuring voice. "We'll figure this out later on. I promise you I'll get to the bottom of this. I'll find out who this shadowy figure was."

Peter was in deep thought for a moment, his gaze fixed on the floor. "Obviously this person was acting on behalf of Brinkley. This is fraud. He is trying to derail the OR committee proceedings before your sexual harassment accusation comes up.

Susan was now crying out of control. People passing by were curious, some couldn't help stop and look.

"Get hold of yourself, Susan." Peter said, trying to hold her hand. "No harm has been done to us. You have not been fired yet. Our plans are on track. Why are you so upset now? Why are you crying so much?"

"Because I've been had. She scared me to death that I'll lose my job soon, unless I did something about it."

"And you …"

"And I did. I withdrew my sexual harassment claims against him and wrote him a letter of apology."

"You did what?" Peter's voice rose sharply as he scowled at her.

"I just told you. I did that to save my job."

Peter looked furious and pounded the table with his fist. "You better get me Brinkley's letter. I bet he never sent it to OR committee. He only used it to intimidate you. I shall kick his ass big time." He stood up and looked down at Susan and said "You better find out if Dr. Gonzalez ever wrote a report to OR Committee" and left.

Susan gathered her strength, went to the phone on the wall and dialed OR.

She told the supervisor that she had an emergency and asked if she could leave.

Mary Dorsa said it was OK. She would find a replacement for her.

* * * * *

The receptionist at the front desk of the Pathology Department was surprised to see Susan Flynn in front of her again. She cut her phone conversation short and hung up. She gave Susan a strange look, shook her head and said "There is no Janet Reilly here, believe me"

"I need to see Janice. Dr. Gonzalez' secretary, please."

"She's busy back there; may I take a message for her?"

"No. Please call her and ask if I can see her for few minutes"

The girl reluctantly picked up the phone and dialed.

"Sorry Ms. Turowsky. She is back."

"Who is back?"

The girl looked at Susan and asked her name.

"Susan Flynn"

"Susan Flynn, ma'am. The lady who was looking for Janet Reilly. "

She heard a click. The line was cut off. She looked into the receiver and frowned.

Susan moved her head close to her and whispered "What's her last name?"

"Turowsky."

"Turowsky? Thank you.

Moments later Janice's massive body came thunderously through the back door and charged towards Susan. Her face red and angry. Susan winced and took a step back.

"I am very busy back there, I told you ..." Susan cut her off "I'm awfully sorry. I understand there is no Janet Reilly here. I need to talk to you for few minutes. It's extremely important for me and for you"

Janice backed off, and asked with a calmer voice "Are you a nurse?"
"Yes I am, I work in OR"
"Follow me please" She turned around and went in. Susan followed.

They went through a long hall, passing by several rooms filled with microscopes, computers and cabinets with narrow drawers. Doctors in white coats, peering into the microscopes and dictating into a hand held recorders. Further down in the hall, the smell of Formaldehyde filled the air; the technicians were cutting the specimens and preparing the slides. Susan thought of the hernia specimen.

Wonder how much confusion that specimen had caused for these poor people? She thought.

They entered Janice's office. A small room, crammed with tons of papers, a Dictaphone and a Computer.
"Please sit down ... Coffee?" Janice asked.
"No thanks. I'm really sorry for the trouble I caused you."
"It's alright. What's on your mind?"
"Few days ago a lady with the name of Janet Reilly came to OR and asked if I could meet her in the coffee Shop. I did. She claimed to be the private secretary of Dr. Gonzalez, typing his dictations, reports, whatever. She told me of a meeting that took place here between Dr. Gonzalez and Dr. Brinkley, one of our surgeons."
Susan paused, looked intensely at Janice and asked "Are you aware of such meeting?"

"Yeah, Dr. Brinkley was here few days ago." *How the hell did Janet know of this meeting?* Susan wondered.
"Janet Reilly told me of a report that Dr. Gonzalez had prepared for OR Committee." She paused again, hesitated first and asked if she knew of such report.
"Yes I do. A report has been prepared but I cannot discuss the details with you" Janice grunted.
"I understand, ma'am. I have been told Dr. Gonzalez is recommend-

ing that the committee ask the administration for my dismissal. Is that true?" She wiped her wet eyes with the back of her hand.

Janice handed her a tissue and said "I'm not allowed to disclose the contents of the report. I'm sorry." *Oh … God. That could be true.* Susan feared.

"That's OK, I understand." Susan said, as her voice trailed.

"What are you worried about Susan? Why should Dr. Gonzalez ask for your dismissal?

"I made a bad mistake in handling a kiddy hernia specimen."

Janice's eyes opened wide. "Oh, that was you? They've been talking about this case here last few days. I'm sorry."

"Yes, I guess I committed the crime of the century!" Susan said sarcastically.

"Let me tell you something. I know the chief was extremely upset about this, but I'm not sure it was all directed at you. Maybe I shouldn't say this, but apparently there was a technical error at surgery as well, and that made the mixing up of the specimens so much more important."

"I guess I should be happy that I had an accomplice in this crime."

"I have told you more than I should have. Take it easy, hopefully everything will be alright." Janice tried to calm Susan.

"I hope so. You better watch out for this Janet Reilly. Whoever she is, she knows a lot about what's going on here."

"I'll talk to the chief about this. Thank you for the information."

"Thank you for seeing me."

Susan shook hands and left.

* * * * *

TEN

Nancy Robertson, the Staff Secretary, walked into Medical Records, and waved hello to the rows of office workers as she strolled through the main secretarial area.

The room was huge, housing two dozen people, almost all women, each one with their own cubicles, desks, file cabinets and computers. The walls were lined with shelves and cabinets, containing thousands of patient medical records.

Orderlies, almost all men, were pushing carts stacked with files and records, moving them from one section to another.

Management of Medical Records, in a large medical institution such as Manhattan Medical Center is a complicated and daunting task.

Each record is initiated at the time of patient's admission to the hospital and adopts its own life throughout the patient's hospital stay. In the Admitting Office a Face Sheet is prepared with the patient's personal information, including name, address, phone, occupation, next of kin, insurance information, and the like. A Name Plate is prepared for each patient, by which a basic piece of information such as name, and medical records number is stamped on every piece of paper which becomes part of the record.

As patients are transported to their assigned room and floor, the newly created record, now traditionally referred to as a patient's chart, will follow them. An Intern or Resident or attending physician writes a History and Physical. This adds a few more pages to the chart before many more pages of lab reports, x-ray reports, day-by-day progress notes written by the doctors and nurses, make the chart increasingly voluminous. Every event surrounding the patient's hospital stay, every test, every surgical intervention, report of surgery, consent forms, pathology report, treatment plans, medication, nursing care, physical therapy, progress notes, discharge planning and doctors day-to-day orders are recorded in the patient's charts, not to mention a summary of every conversation between the physicians, nurses, patients and family members.

After patients leave the hospital, one way or another, the chart arrives at the Medical Records Department, often many inches thick. At this time, the chart, or medical record, is a messy, disorganized bundle of numerous, multicolored papers, held together by paper clips, clamps, etc. The record now begins its journey through the cubicles staffed by specialized medical records personnel who will take it apart and organize it in a chronological order. Several different sections are created for related material. Order sheets together, progress notes together, likewise surgical reports, pathology, lab reports, radiology reports and so on. Physicians are obligated to dictate a final summary, either a discharge or death summary, when a patient leaves the hospital.

Once the medical record is organized, another group of personnel will comb through the pages, looking for deficiencies such as missing reports, summaries and signatures. Each physician's order or progress report, each nurses' entries are required to be signed with time and date recorded.

The chart now moves to its temporary housing in the Incomplete Records section of the shelves, the pages with missing signatures and dates now color coded for appropriate physicians and nurses. Notices are generated and sent to the doctors to complete their charts usually within two weeks. Total number of incomplete charts of Medical Records Department is the best indicator of the discipline and efficiency of the staff and the institution as a whole.

As Nancy Robertson walked towards the office of Judy Jackson, the Director of Medical Records, she passed by another room which was locked and double locked and guarded like a major bank vault. The room contained special cabinets with security locks, holding a special category of medical records. These records belonged to patients with potential or factual litigation issues. Malpractice suits against the physicians invariably involved the hospital as well since hospital had deep pockets. Claims against the hospital for equipment malfunctioning, Nosocomial infections, poor patient care and lack of protection such as patients falling and breaking bones are abundant.

The room was informally known as the Litigation Room.

The Director had just finished a phone conversation when Nancy walked in.

"Mornin' Judy"

"Hi Nancy, What can I do for you?"

Nancy approached the desk and placed a list of patient names in front of Judy.

"What's that?" she said.

"The Medical Director wants to see these charts today."

"Today? It takes quite a few hours to locate these charts." Judy frowned.

"He wants to review these records for the OR committee meeting tomorrow. Can you get somebody on it right away?"

"I'll try, but ..." her voice trailed off as she was looking through the list.

"I think a few of them are locked in" Judy said without taking her eyes off the list.

"You mean in that litigation room?" Nancy asked.

"Yep, right there. I need authorization from upstairs"

"Get it Judy, it's urgent."

"I'll see what I can do."

"For goodness sake, Judy, he's gonna bug me all day until he gets them"

Nancy stepped back and turned around to leave. She then paused and turned back as Judy was entering the names in her computer to locate the records.

"By the way, Judy, all these patients belonged to one specific surgeon. How many law suits does he have against him?"

"You mean this guy?" Judy pointed to her screen and said "Maybe too many. People upstairs are not very happy with this. He's been in practice only three years or so. He has a bunch of these charts in there." Judy nodded in the direction of litigation room.

"When can I expect the records?" Nancy asked
"I'll call you when I have them."
"Thanks." She left.

Judy waited until the door was completely shut. She picked up the phone and dialed zero.
"Operator, can I help you?'
"Hi, this is Judy in record room. Can you get me Dr. Molano?"
"Just a minute please"
"Dr. Molano's office. May I help you?"
"Hi, this is Judy Jackson. Is he in?"
"Yes. I'll put him on right away. Hold on please"

Seconds later he was on the phone
"Hi Judy, what's up?"
"Things are rolling. Looks like tomorrow's the day"
"I was hopeful, but some complication has developed. Susan has flipped. She's scared to death. She withdrew her claim against him, so we have no case at this time"
"Oh yes you do. That issue was for the Ethics committee. Brown is reviewing few of his cases. Apparently he's had a bad complication in the OR recently. Brown just asked for several of his patients' records"
"Give him as many as you can."
"I actually called to thank you again, Peter. It looks beautiful. It literally shines around my wrist" Judy said as she was staring at her beautiful diamond bracelet.

* * * * *

Peter Molano, MD., F.A.C.S.

The name plate on his desk was polished and decorative. He stared at it while reminiscing about the agony, jealousy, anxiety and mental tortures he suffered for a few years before he could finally add, F.A.C.S. (Fellow, American College of Surgeons) to his title.

He had been denied the title when he first applied and interviewed for it.

His application included a summary of his educational background, a list of his surgical experience and the number of surgical procedures he had performed during previous two years.

The interviewers questioned the unusually large numbers Peter reported during the first two years of his private practice when he worked in a small upstate New York community hospital.

The hospital had not been able to substantiate those numbers, due to inadequate staffing and disorganized Medical Records Department, and the questions had lingered on for months.

Peter was struggling to get on the surgical staff of the Manhattan Medical Center, and move to New York City, however, a prestigious organization such as MMC would not accept him, unless he became a Fellow of the American College of Surgeons.

Four years after his graduating from the surgical residency training program at the State University of New York, Downstate Medical Center in Brooklyn, two unrelated events turned the table in his favor and he took advantage of them.

The community hospital he used to practice in, hired an ambitious young lady, fresh out of an MBA program, to run their Medical Records department, and on the day she stepped into her new office, a large bouquet of red roses from Dr. Peter Molano awaited her. It was of no interest to the hospital authorities that she had been dating the young surgeon for a few months.

Two months later, the American College of Surgeons received a detailed letter confirming Dr. Molano's surgical activities and the number of cases he had reported on his application.

The letter was signed by one Judy Jackson, MBA. Director of Medical Records.

Meanwhile at MMC, the Board of Directors welcomed their newly elected member, an influential, multimillionaire community business-man, who had donated generously to the hospital for many years.

His name was Edward Molano, and at the time the Board had no knowledge or interest that his nephew, Dr. Peter Molano had applied and been denied appointment to the surgical staff.

Within the ensuing few months, Edward Molano gained consider-able power in the events of the hospital. He brought in a new Medical Director by the name of Joseph Brown, MD and Dr. Peter Molano, now with F.A.C.S. title, was accepted on the staff of the Department of Surgery. Shortly after, Ms. Judy Jackson was rewarded with a transfer to MMC as the Director of the Medical Records Department.

Peter's intercom buzzed.
"Suzan Flynn on line 1, Doctor"
"Thank you. I'll take it"

"Hello Susan. What's up?"
"Are you still mad at me darling?"
"I am disappointed. You shouldn't have written those letters. We had a plan together and you ruined it."
"If they fire me will you hire me as your office manager?" Susan said jokingly.
"I already have an office manager and the hospital will not fire you"
"I admit I fell into a trap by this imposter, Janet Reilly, but my job is still in jeopardy."
"How so?"
"The Chief of Pathology will report to the OR Committee about the hernia specimen debacle and most likely will put all the blame on me. Who is there to defend me?"
"You are represented by the nurse's union; you cannot be fired with-out just cause. Somewhere along the line you will have an opportunity to defend yourself. I am a surgeon, Susan. It is my responsibility to tell the nurse how a surgical specimen should be handled"
"Did you hear what I said, Peter? Who is there to defend me? You said you would check with your group and find out who sits on the OR Committee."
"Stop defending yourself before you are accused of anything"

Susan realized Peter was evasive. He would not talk about his secret group. She almost sensed that Peter didn't care if she was fired. He was too consumed with his own agenda. *Knock out Brian Brinkley at all cost.*

"Any chance you can take your letter back, Susan?" he asked.

"No chance. Mary Dorsa passed it on to higher authorities. It is in the hands of the OR Committee now. Who sits on the OR Committee, Peter? I need to know." Susan was raising her voice a bit impatiently now.

"I will find out today. I promise." Peter was calm and conciliatory.

"You better find out and get to those guys before something bad happens."

"Calm down Susan. You are so hysterical you are threatening me." Peter said half jokingly.

"This is not a laughing matter, Peter, you don't want them to know who got me into this trouble to begin with. Do you?" Susan dropped the ball skillfully.

A long pause. Peter was a bit shook up. It dawned on him that Susan could do some serious damage. He controlled his anger and swallowed his words.

"Peter? Are you still there?"

"Yes, I'm sorry sweetheart. I'll take care of everything if you stick with me."

"I love you my dear. I am always with you."

"OK. I'll talk to you soon."

"Bye."

Peter dropped the receiver on the phone with a bang, tilted his chair back and placed his feet on the edge of the desk. He was nervous and agitated. He stretched his arms and placed his hands behind his neck, fingers interlocked. He closed his eyes.

He was second guessing himself for trusting and choosing Susan Flynn to carry out his plot against Brian Brinkley. Susan had become increasingly unstable and unreliable, and now she was a liability.

He would have preferred to see her found negligent and fired. If she named him as the conspirator of a plot against Dr. Brinkley, he could rebut by calling this an act of desperation for saving her job.

Oh my God. Things can get really messy. He thought.

He better try to keep Susan on his side.

Peter thought he still had a good chance of accomplishing what he initially set out to do. *Get rid of the competition. Kick Brian off the staff.*

He dropped his legs off the desk and opened the drawer and pulled out a letter. This was Brian's letter to the OR Committee, which Susan had received from Janet Reilly.

He was almost certain the OR committee's secretary had not received such a letter.

Janet Reilly. He had thought a lot about Janet Reilly. *Who was this mystery woman?*

Obviously she was working on behalf of Brian, and certainly she succeeded in having Susan withdraw her sexual harassment claim against Brian.

Peter smiled. He could use this whole event against Brian. And the letter in his hand, written on Brian's office stationary and signed by him was the best evidence of his tampering with the OR Committee's investigation of him.

Peter buzzed his secretary

"Yes Sir."

"Get me Dr. Joseph Brown, Medical Director at MMC"

"OK"

Moments later she buzzed back

"Dr. Brown is in a meeting. He is expected back in his office by two p.m."

"Thank you."

He decided to go and see Dr. Brown personally. He went to the copy machine and made a copy of the letter.

"Cancel my hours this afternoon" he told his secretary as he left the office.

* * * * *

The living room was warm and cozy. The lights were dimmed and few decorative candles were burning. Smooth jazz music filled the air. Jennifer was seductively dressed in a body hugging black silk dress and stiletto heels. A drop dead sexy outfit…perfect for the romantic evening she had planned.

She opened the blinds and looked out through the window, expecting Brian's car to park any minute.

The evening temperature was unusually cool for early September. It was only two weeks ago that they were boating in the Hamptons. But, this was New York. It never remains too hot or too cold for too long.

The cool weather outside was of no consequence. Brian was coming for dinner and Jennifer expected that it would get pretty hot indoors.

The dining table was set with an exquisite Wedgwood china pattern which Jennifer inherited from her late grandmother. Tall tapered candles reflected light off the gold rimmed plates. Waterford wine goblets would later be filled with Stag's Leap 2003 Cabernet Sauvignon; Brian's favorite Napa Valley cabernet.

Jennifer was acutely aware of Brian's anxiety and restlessness this evening with expectations of being grilled, criticized, insulted, and kicked around in the OR Committee meeting the next morning. She had to calm him down, build up his morale, and pamper him with love and affection, and, very carefully, give him a few words of advice. He was proud of his accomplishments and would not tolerate criticism and adversity. His ego was large yet fragile.

In the kitchen, the aroma of broiled salmon, sautéed mushroom and mixed vegetables filled the air. Brian's favorite ice cream, Butter Pecan Häagen-Dazs was chilling in the freezer.

The Mercedes parked across the street. Brian stepped out, locked the doors and headed towards Jenny's apartment.

Jenny was at the door, waiting.

As soon as he entered, they kissed passionately, holding on to each other so tight as if this was their last good bye.

She hung over his shoulder and stepped up on her tiptoes. He clinched his arms around her waist and pressed her tender, lithe body against his.

She opened his tie, pulled his jacket off and pushed him onto the couch.

"You're mine tonight, baby."

She whispered into his ears and took a gentle bite of his earlobe. The erotic move was irresistible; he unbuttoned her blouse and exposed her soft, trembling breasts.

Another passionate long kiss, followed with endless caressing and embracing. The fire was burning hot in them and the gleam of ultimate desire flashed in their eyes.

They dragged their half naked bodies into the bedroom, dropping clothing along the way. In the intimate moments of lovemaking, the world was a distant place as if it didn't exist.

They took a hot shower together and decided to have dinner in their bathrobes.

Jenny poured the wine and their glasses clinked.

After dinner the mood gradually changed from the fantasy of romance and lovemaking to harsh realities of life.

They were both dressed up now, relaxing on the couch and contemplating the day that was coming next. Brian lit a cigarette and took a long puff.

"What time is the OR Committee meeting?" she asked.

"8 a.m."

"Are you worried about anything?"

"I was worried about two serious issues, but now there is only one."

"You mean the complication from the hernia surgery?"

"Yep ... which is the less serious of the two."

Brian was in deep thought for a moment. He took another drag and blew up towards the ceiling.

"You know Jenny; I never understood what made Susan withdraw her complaint."

Jennifer paused for a moment, flashed a cute look at Brian and said:

"Let's say ... I took care of it."

"You did what?"

"I took care of it."

"How?"

"I visited her at the hospital, pretending I was a secretary working in pathology, and knew about her mixing the specimens, causing serious problems for your patient. I told her that you were going to have her fired."

"I can't believe this." Brian was amazed. A deep puff again.

"But she *did* believe *me*, and became extremely concerned about losing her job. I pointed out that if she apologized to you, you might forgive her."

"I may not forgive her outrageous accusation, but I never intended to have her fired."

"Brian, you have already forgiven her. She withdrew her complaint and the issue is moot now. You make sure this is not brought up or discussed at the meeting. You have her letter of apology."

"They may still bring it up, 'cause I strongly suspect there is some kind of conspiracy going on against me. They are jealous of my success and popularity."

"If they do, you should immediately object and refuse to discuss the matter" Jenny adamantly replied.

"I am going to kick ass, you just wait and see"

"Be careful my dear, they are powerful people."

"Is there anything else you've done?" Brian cautiously inquired.

"No. I just didn't want this sexual harassment accusation stick to you. True or false it could destroy your career, perhaps your life."

"Understood. And I appreciate what you've done. Next time please let me in on it ahead of time."

"Ah-hah, is there going to be a next time too?"

"Hope not."

He kissed her hard and playfully spanked her butt.
She loved it.

* * * * *

ELEVEN

The Chairman called the meeting to order and counted the members present to make sure there was a quorum. There was.

In fact, the attendance was unusually high this time. Perhaps some of them had gotten wind of an extraordinary meeting.

The OR Committee meeting was now in session.

The Staff Room was a large, neatly decorated meeting place for the medical staff.

Many lectures, journal clubs, monthly departmental meetings and committee meetings as well as Medical Board meetings took place in this room. It was in fact much larger than a regular room. It was a lecture hall with the main area filled with rows of seats, a podium and audio-visual facilities.

Adjacent to the lecture area, there was another section with a very large, rectangular table and comfortable chairs used during committee meetings.

The OR Committee was chaired by the Chairman of the Department of Surgery, Dr. Michael Sloan. Each section of the department such as general surgery, peripheral vascular surgery and pediatric surgery was represented by the chief of that section. In addition to that, other depart-ments such as OB-GYN, orthopedics, neurosurgery, and pathology were represented by their respective chairmen. Also, the Director of Nursing, the OR supervisor, and the hospital's Medical Director were members of the committee.

The staff secretary was in charge of keeping the minutes and preparing paperwork. There was a folder for each member, containing a copy of the agenda, a copy of the last meeting's minutes and other memoranda.

Coffee was prepared on a separate table in the corner. Food was not allowed while the meeting was in session.

The meeting was generally open ended. That meant it would go on until every item on the agenda was discussed and proper decisions were made. On average the meeting lasted one and a half to two hours, although three to four hours sessions were not unheard of.

The secretary passed out an attendance sheet to be signed by the members.

The Chairman asked if all the members had read the minutes of the last meeting and if there were any corrections or changes to be made. A few minor items were discussed and resolved quickly.

The Chairman asked the OR supervisor to report the number of surgical procedures, in-patient and out-patient, performed in the previous month. The numbers were in line with expectations for this season.

Requests for new equipment, presented by different department or section chiefs, were discussed and sent to administration of consideration.

Medical Director, Dr. Joseph Brown arrived a few minutes late apologizing. He was completing a detailed report for the committee on Dr. Brian Brinkley.

The Chairman explained to the members that there had been a serious complication on a pediatric hernia case, performed by Dr. Brinkley, along with an error in preparing the specimen, which has serious consequences. Additionally there is an ethical issue involving this surgeon and all of this made it necessary to call Dr. Brinkley to come to this meeting for questioning.

The secretary said Dr. Brinkley is in the Medical Directors office, waiting to be called in.

The Chairman nodded and she picked up the phone and called the office.

Minutes later, Dr. Brian Brinkley entered, and was seated at the table. Perfunctory greetings were exchanged.

Brian appeared nervous. He looked around the table and was not sure whether he had a single friend and supporter among the physicians present. He was suspicious that this whole event was planned and orchestrated to knock him out. He was not aware who was a true adversary and who was merely a silent observer. He knew he would soon find out.

Dr. Sloan thanked Brian for coming to the meeting. Formalities and civil behavior, as short lived and ephemeral as they may be, had to be afforded their dues.

They would have kicked my ass off the staff if I didn't show up. Brian thought.

"We are going to discuss three main issues with you, Dr. Brinkley." Dr. Sloan said.

"And maybe a few other related matters, if that's OK with the Chairman" Dr. Brown jumped in with a sneer.

The Chairman frowned and flashed an angry look at Dr. Brown.

"The three issues are the surgical complication, the specimen mix up, and an accusation of ethical nature against you by an OR nurse. I trust you are aware of these matters, Brian. Are you not?"

"I am fully aware of them and am happy to explain."

The Chairman continued "The case at hand is that of a 2 year old boy …" He paused and turned to the secretary taking notes "Medical record number AP236559."

"I have it Sir." She said.

"The boy underwent a bilateral inguinal hernia repair. Is that right, Dr. Brinkley?"

"The repair was done on the right side only. The left side was explored and no hernia found." Brian attempted to correct the record.

"OK, I will now ask Dr. Gonzalez to take it from here and tell us what the pathology showed."

"Thank you, Mr. Chairman. We received the specimen in a single jar, and initially had no knowledge that the case was bilateral, until the paper work arrived later. The slides were prepared by our staff. In a hernia specimen you expect to see the hernia sac, may be some fatty tissue we call 'lipoma of the cord' and that's it. In this kid's specimen we saw abundant tubular structures, characteristic of vas deferens or, in layman's term, the sperm duct."

The Chairman interjected "Dr. Brinkley, do you agree that you have accidentally removed a section of this kid's sperm duct?"

"I do, unfortunately. I have looked at the slides with Dr. Gonzalez."

"Dr. Brinkley, for the record, could you describe what the vas deferens is or does."

"I'm glad you said "for the record", otherwise I would think I am taking my anatomy exam here." A burst of laughter by the members made Brian slightly more relaxed and comfortable.

"I'll be glad to tell you" Brian continued "vas deferens is a tubular structure that carries the sperm from the testicle to seminal vesicles, a storage space, inside the pelvis. These tubes are adjacent to the hernia sac." He looked around to see if the explanation was adequate.

Heads nodded around the table.

"And would you say that if you accidentally remove a section of this tube along with the hernia sac, the sperm has no other way to get out of the testicle?" The Chairman asked.

"That's my understanding" Brian said, looking at the pathologist for approval.

The Chairman turned to Dr. Gonzalez and said "Carlos, could you tell us what the ramifications of such accidental complications are?"

"Well, this will bring us to the second issue you were going to discuss, and that is the way the specimen was sent to our lab."

"What do you mean by that?" Dr. Sloan asked.

"If surgery had been performed on one side only, well, there is always a second side, I mean a second vas deferens to carry the sperm and the kid would be OK. The problem here is that the specimens from both sides have been mixed up. So it is *possible* that both tubes have been cut …"

He was abruptly cut off by the Medical Director "And it means, Dr. Brinkley, that you have permanently damaged this kid. He can never have children of his own."

Brian raised his hand, looking for a chance to speak.

"We will give you a chance to respond" Dr. Sloan said. "But let me first ask Dr. Gonzalez if there is a way of having a reasonable idea whether the damage was on one side or both?"

"No, the tubes are exactly identical in shape and form, but an educated guess on my part, considering the abundance of the tubular structures seen, is that the damage was on both sides."

Brian could not hold off anymore and jumped in.

"I respectfully disagree with this conclusion and some other things mentioned here." He raised his voice a notch and a heavy silence fell upon the members. Brian glanced around the table.

"You may continue" the Chairman said.

"This patient had a definite hernia on the right side, and yes, unfortunately his right Vas was cut. It should not have happened, but certain percentages of complications in surgery are unavoidable. This is a fact known to every surgeon. And, Dr. Gonzalez, how could you come to such conclusion that damage has occurred on both sides? I only *explored* the opposite side because there is a high incidence of bilaterality in pediatric hernias. I would have saved this kid another operation. He did *not* have a hernia on the other side. There *was* no hernia sac. I only removed some fatty tissue. In fact, it is quite *unlikely* that the damage has occurred on both sides."

He glanced around the table again, looking for signs of approval of his rather strong rebuttal. A hand had been raised at the end of the table. It was Dr. Gerard Navarro, Chief of Pediatric Surgery section.

"Brian" he said "you spoke of percentages of accepted complications. You are a general surgeon and not a pediatric surgeon. May I ask you how many pediatric hernias have you done within last two years?"

"Gerry" Brian responded "every general surgeon is trained and qualified to repair a kiddy hernia. It is not a congenital hole in the heart. It is just a simple hernia repair"

A simple hernia repair! Dr. Brown scribbled on his note pad and shook his head.

"How many, Brian?" Dr. Navarro repeated the question.

Brian tried to get out of this jam again. "The numbers don't mean anything. I have been adequately trained" he replied.

"How many, Doctor?" This time the question had a harsh tone.

Brian paused. The question was relevant. The committee was silent as the members held their breaths. The eyes fixed in Brian's direction.

"One." Brian muttered in a low, barely audible tone.
"Figures!" Dr. Navarro said with a sneer and sarcastic tone.

Brian looked at him with disgust. He could not tolerate being put down like this.

"Dr. Navarro, should I assume you have never had any complications? Wonderful. Certainly there was a time that you did your very first surgical procedure of any kind. Does that mean you were not qualified and should've never done it?"

"I'm not being investigated here, Brian. You are"

"Gentlemen … gentlemen." The Chairman called for calm.
"Let me go back to Dr. Gonzalez" He looked straight into his eyes. "Carlos. On a scale of one to ten, where do you think the likelihood of bilateral damage lies?"
"Nine and a half." Gonzalez responded and continued "Again, I refer to the abundance of tubular structures in this specimen. Too many for one sided damage. Too many."

The Chairman scratched his head and rubbed the back of his neck with the palm of his hand.
He then turned to the OR supervisor.
"Mary, why did the nurse mix the specimens? Aren't they in-serviced and trained to handle specimens correctly?
"Sure they are, Dr. Sloan." Mary Dorsa responded. "Susan Flynn is one of our best nurses. This was obviously an error. She claims she was

never told by Dr. Brinkley what to do with the specimen. She was also totally disturbed by Dr. Brinkley's conversations while the surgery was in progress."

"What conversations, Mary?" the Chairman asked.

"According to the nurse, he was constantly joking and making sexually offensive references to the nurse."

"That is an absolute lie" Brian exploded "our conversation was nothing more than the usual, every day type of friendly, casual chat. I am appalled at Ms. Flynn's reaction. I agree she is a good nurse. I suspect there is more to this than meets the eye."

The Chairman interrupted "let me now go to the third issue, which could explain why errors occurred by both the surgeon and the nurse." He paused. The committee was silent in expectation.

"Dr. Brinkley, are you aware that Ms. Flynn filed an incident report after this case was over."

"Yes Sir. I am."

"You probably know that she has accused you of sexual harassment. A very serious claim indeed."

There was a gasp by the committee, and Brian felt blood rushing into his face. He was livid.

"With all due respect, Mr. Chairman, you should also know, and you do, that she has already withdrawn her complaint with explanation, and she has apologized to me. You should not have raised this issue here, unless I am to believe that you are not impartial."

Brian did not give the Chairman a chance to respond. He opened his folder and pulled out copies of Susan's letter and passed them on to the members.

Everybody reached for one and started reading.

"Hold on a minute, Gentlemen." Dr. Brown, the Medical Director jumped in. "It is my turn to talk." He opened his folder and fingered through the papers.

"Dr. Brinkley. I'm afraid you are wrong. There are very good reasons why this issue should be raised here, despite the fact that the nurse has allegedly withdrawn her complaint. I shall explain that to you fully, but first, let me clear a few other questions that exist."

He looked at the Chairman.

"Let's have a ten minutes recess." Dr. Sloan announced and stood up, stretching his back.

The meeting broke up and members started chatting with each other in small groups. Brian left the room without saying a word.

He went to the lobby, sank in a plush couch in a quiet area and called Jennifer on her cell phone.

"How is it going darling?"

"Not so good. The wolves are growling and attacking me from every direction."

"Is the meeting over?"

"No, we're on a break. I am puzzled at something. I strongly objected to the Chairman raising the issue of sexual harassment, and he almost backed off, but that sonofabitch Medical Director said he has other reasons why this issue should be discussed, and he is going to do that after the break. He pulled out a paper from his folder. I don't know what it is. Do you have any idea what he is up to?"

"Not really. He could concoct anything he wants. Stand firm against him."

"Could this have anything to do with your contacting Susan Flynn?"

"Seriously doubt it. Nobody knows me in the hospital"

"OK. Gotta go now. Talk to you later."

"Good luck honey."

The meeting was called to order again. Everybody was back.

"Dr. Brown. You have the floor." The Chairman said.

"Thank you, Mr. Chairman." With his glasses sitting almost at the tip of his nose, he glanced above the rim in Brian's direction.

"How is the patient doing, by the way?" he asked Brian.

"Doing very well. I saw him in my office one week after surgery. His incisions were healed and he was a happy little boy."

"Good. How about his parents? Were they happy too?"

"Certainly."

"Does this mean you did not inform them of this complication?"

"No Sir. I did not."

"Don't you think you have an obligation to do so?"

"Obligation to whom?"

"To his parents and to this institution. The hospital is liable as much as you are."

"I am not going to destroy his parents' peace of mind, happiness, aspirations and desires of someday, in their golden years, being able to play with their grandchildren. Who knows what will happen twenty years from now. There is still a possibility that he has a normal vas deferens on the other side. It is cruel to put them through such a heart wrenching anxiety for so many years. I am looking at the human aspect of this issue and not the legal aspect."

"And, what about our hospital's liability?"

"Well, Dr. Brown, if it pleases you go ahead and call the hospital attorney and Mr. Silverman and wait for plaintiff's attorney to knock at your door. Those vultures drool at such opportunities. Go ahead and inform the parents so that *you* will have peace of mind and not *them*. As usual, we always dig our own graves, don't we?"

Everybody was in deep thought. A long silence ensued. The conversation was most unusual in this environment. Matters being looked at from a humanitarian angle and not the institutional view. Sympathy and support was being built up for Brian's arguments. Alas they were short lived.

"Dr. Brinkley" the Medical Director broke the silence "Who is Janet Reilly?"

"Who?"

"Janet Reilly."

"Never heard of her. Who is she?" Brian felt sick to his stomach.

"Apparently an agent of yours, roaming through this hospital and threatening Susan Flynn, the OR nurse we've been talking about, to withdraw her complaints against you, otherwise you, with all your powers in this hospital will make sure that she will be terminated. Who is she Dr. Brinkley?" the Medical Director's pretentiously angry voice echoed in the room.

"Hold on just a minute" Brian fired back. "I have no knowledge of such person. You better call Susan Flynn in here right now. I want to confront her." Brian's voice was trembling in anger, and perspiration was building up on his forehead.

Dr. Brown pulled out several copies of a letter written on Dr. Brian Brinkley's letterhead, and threw them on the table, spreading them all the way to the other end.

Hands shot out seizing a copy.

Brian picked up one and took a long look. He frowned; he wanted to throw up but struggled to keep his composure. He wiped his forehead, raised his head and looked around the table. The eyes were off the papers and focused on him.

The letter was addressed to the Chairman of the OR Committee, describing the behavior of Nurse Susan Flynn, on the day he was operating on a 2 year old boy, named Elliot Silverman. He blamed her for lack of attention to her duties, spending time on the phone and leaving the room frequently and finally making the serious error of mixing the specimens. He called her unreliable and asked that she be suspended and preferably dismissed.

"Mr. Chairman" Dr. Brown called "have you received such a letter from Dr. Brinkley?"

"I have not, and I don't understand how you got it?"

"So it is a fact that the committee has never received this letter from Dr. Brinkley" Dr. Brown looked at the secretary.

"That is true, Sir. I've never seen this letter before." She said.

"Dr. Brinkley, did you send this letter to the OR Committee?"

"Not only did I did not send this letter, I have never written nor seen this letter. This is a fabrication."

"You really did not intend to send this letter to the OR Committee, did you? You only used it to intimidate Susan Flynn to withdraw her sexual harassment claim. Isn't that true, Dr. Brinkley?"

Brian jumped off his chair and stood up. He was fuming and outraged. He stretched his arm, pointing to Dr. Brown while holding the letter in his other hand. "You should be ashamed of yourself, Dr. Brown" he screamed. "I already told you I knew nothing about this letter. It is on my letterhead OK, but it was NOT written by me." He tapped on the bottom of the letter by his index finger and hollered "THAT is not my signature."

He then turned to Dr. Sloan.

"Mr. Chairman, I demand an apology from this man, right now."

"Sit down please, Dr. Brinkley" he demanded.

"An apology, Mr. Chairman. Right now."

"Brian. Sit down please."

"He has shamelessly insulted me and I demand an apology."

"Brian."

"I shall hold this committee responsible for insulting my professional integrity. Shame on you all."

He picked up his papers and folder, turned around and walked away from the table.

The Chairman stood up and yelled "Dr. Brinkley, nobody has ever walked away from this table like you are doing. Please come back and sit down."

"When I receive Dr. Brown's apology, in writing, I'll come back. He has my letterhead. The address is there."

Brian walked out of the room and slammed the door shut.

The Chairman dropped his pen on the table in frustration and announced a ten minutes recess. He then turned to Dr. Brown and said "you better stay, we have work to do."

The members milled about drinking coffee, taking a much needed stretch and making personal phone calls before gathering around the table again.

The meeting was called to order again.

A hand was raised from the other end of the table. It was the chairman of the OB-GYN Department, Dr. Stanley Kaplan.

"Dr. Brown, with all due respect, you raised some very serious accusations against Dr. Brinkley. You accused him of sending an undercover agent here with a fictitious letter, to intimidate one of our nurses and in a sense tampering with the legal proceedings of this institution. I think you owe this committee an explanation. When and how did you obtain this letter and what evidence do you have that this is an authentic letter and not a forgery?"

The heads turned towards Dr. Brown, who was fixing his spectacles on his nose and looking through his file. He shrugged.

"The letter is authentic, I assure you" he said without turning his head.

"And where did you get it? Who gave it to you? And how do you know Janet Reilly?"

The Medical Director frowned and glanced at the other end of the table.

"Dr. Kaplan" he said "I cannot answer those questions here. You just have to believe me."

"Excuse me, Sir. We respect you as our Medical Director, not as a prosecutor. You have insulted one of our colleagues and potentially opened the door for a defamation claim. You better explain."

The Chairman interrupted.

"Hold on gentlemen. We are getting drifted away from the scope of this committee's responsibilities and we have to bring our deliberations to some conclusion."

He continued "Dr. Brown, I have to agree with Dr. Kaplan. If you don't want to back up your accusations against Dr. Brinkley with solid evidence, you should not have made them to begin with. We'll let the minutes of this meeting reflect that the committee did not receive satisfactory answers from you."

He glanced at the secretary and Dr. Kaplan and they nodded.

"Mr. Chairman" Dr. Brown spoke "I'll back up my statements at an appropriate forum in the near future. At this time I would like to inform the committee that this is not the first time that Dr. Brinkley's patients have had significant complications. He's been under observation by us for quite some time, and here I have a summary of nine other problematic cases he's had. We investigate these cases because our institution cannot afford too many mishaps. We are a first rate medical facility and we take pride in our exceptionally low complication rates."

"Excuse me, Dr. Brown" the Chairman jumped in "If I may interrupt you for a second.

If these nine cases have had serious complications, why is this the first time we are hearing about them?"

"Mr. Chairman, you should know better what is going on in your department. These cases will be sent to the Quality Assurance Committee, and we'll add the pediatric hernia complication to that list. The QA committee will decide if Dr. Brinkley should be suspended or placed under your observation or whatever."

Dr. Sloan asked members of the committee if they would recommend any action against Dr. Brinkley at this time. The consensus was that they should wait for the results of the QA committee investigation.

"How about the nurse who mishandled the specimen? Should she be fired?" Dr. Sloan asked.

"No" answered the OR supervisor, as she looked around the table for support. "Susan Flynn is an excellent nurse. We cannot afford to lose her. Moreover, it is still unclear who was at fault, the nurse or the surgeon."

The committee agreed.

The chairman asked if there were any other issues for discussion. A unanimous "no" was the answer. Members were tired and anxious to get out of the stuffy room to clear their heads.

"Thank you. This meeting is adjourned."

* * * * *

TWELVE

The following day witnessed a flurry of activities in relation to the OR Committee events.

Susan Flynn was on pins and needles when she received a call from the OR supervisor. She, *Mary Dorsa*, had forcefully defended her against *several* calls for her dismissal and had convinced the committee that she was indispensable. In short, Susan was not fired. But, Mary Dorsa would not settle for the short version. She wanted Susan to remember how indebted she should be to her and not forget her great favor when Mary is up for promotion.

Susan called Dr. Peter Molano to give him the good news, however, for reasons unknown to her, Dr. Molano knew exactly what had transpired. The phone lines were burning between his and Dr. Brown's all night.

How could he know all this? He is not a member of the committee. Susan wondered.

He told Susan that Dr. Brinkley was grilled, chastised, reprimanded and practically kicked out of the meeting, pending his investigation by the powerful Quality Assurance Committee, of which, he, the eminent Dr. Peter Molano, had recently been named Chairman.

That'll be the end of Dr. Brian Brinkley. That's for sure. Susan thought.

Peter reminded Susan that it was absolutely critical for them to find

Janet Reilly, or the person who pretended to be Janet Reilly. Her confession of being an undercover agent for Dr. Brinkley would most definitely end his professional career.

Dr. Michael Brown, the Medical Director and Dr. Peter Molano, discussed the strategy for the upcoming QA Committee.

Peter would have liked to include the Janet Reilly issue in the agenda, for a chance to deliver the final blow himself, but he was advised that the issue was not in the purview of his committee. The Quality Assurance Committee was created to protect the quality of patient care. The Janet Reilly issue will be referred to the Medical Board, the highest deliberative body of medical staff affairs and from there it would go to the Board of Directors for a final decision. *Brian Brinkley had his work cut out for him.*

Jennifer Bradley had tried repeatedly and desperately to talk to Brian, following the OR committee, but he was nowhere to be found. After all, he was supposed to call Jennifer right after the meeting and let her know what happened. She waited all night, called Brian repeatedly, left messages, but he was not answering his cell phone. She had left several messages this morning as well. His office could not locate him and several attempts to page him at the hospital this morning failed. *Something must have gone wrong.* She was quite worried.

She called the OR and was told that Dr. Brinkley had cancelled his cases for the day and possibly for the rest of the week. *That was a shocker.*

Jennifer was smart enough to understand that this had something to do with her; otherwise Brian would run to her with any other calamity that would befall him. She just could not put her finger on it.

She was anxious to find out what went on at the OR Committee, but she had no contacts. She thought of calling Susan Flynn. She knew Susan could not have been fired and, therefore, there was something to celebrate. But, she decided against it. It was too risky. It would have been disastrous for Brian if they were to find out who Janet Reilly was.

Suddenly it dawned on her. Had Susan Flynn found out that Janet

Reilly was a phony figure? Could she have gone to Pathology asking for Janet Reilly, only to find out no such person existed? And if so, could she have informed hospital authorities? And what proof she would present. Janet Reilly had left no traces, no phone number, and no address. She thought of every contact she had with Susan. The coffee shop meeting. The Central Park walk. And … wait a minute … there was another one … in the hospital … in the hall outside the coffee shop. She gave Susan a fictitious letter she had typed on Brian's letterhead. A letter addressed to the OR Committee. *Oh God … How could this be possible?* Did this letter *really* find its way to the OR Committee? And … did the committee confront Brian with his own letter which he had never written, never sent, never knew anything about it. *This is disastrous.* Jennifer suddenly started bawling.

She cried.

Dr. Michael Sloan had a sleepless night. He was not quite sure if he should take Brian's side; an active, promising, educated surgeon or the administration's side with deep concern about the institution's reputation and viability.

He assessed the situation in his mind several times, balancing positives and negatives of each side, and more and more he suspected that the issue was driven by intentions other than the concern for the patient's safety or hospital's reputation.

Why was Brian Brinkley the target of an investigation? And, why is the Medical Director poking his nose into Brian's old cases and fishing for some evidence of wrongdoing? *There had to be more to this situation than meets the eye.*

He decided to call Brian in for a personal conversation.

At 8:30 a.m. Brian arrived at Dr. Sloan's office.

"Mornin' Chief."

"Mornin' Brian. Thank you for coming."

"I didn't think after yesterday you would want to see me again, let alone talk to me"

"You were not on your best behavior yesterday. You shouldn't have left the meeting the way you did."

"You're right. I'm sorry if I was disrespectful."

"Why did you snap like that?"

"For me there was no point staying there and taking all that crap from the hostile Medical Director."

"Why do you think he was so hostile to you?"

Brian shrugged. "No idea. I am actually puzzled. This was not about a hernia complication. Every surgeon encounters adverse results from time to time. I have had less than others. I believe I am the target of jealousy and rivalry for my success and popularity."

"You think the Medical Director is envious of your success?"

"Not him. He is not a surgeon and therefore I am not a threat to him. He is doing the dirty work for others, and I'll find out whom."

"Any idea?"

"Not a clue at this time, Chief."

The Chief leaned back on his chair and put his feet on the edge of the desk.

"Listen Brian, I have always liked you and admired your work here. I also sense they are laying a trap for you and I don't want to fall into that trap as well. After you left the meeting Dr. Brown informed the committee that at least nine other cases of yours are being investigated for complications and they will be reviewed at the next QA Committee meeting. Are you aware of that?"

"Not at all. You see … here is another reason for my suspicion. This is a fishing expedition they're doing. Why shouldn't I know that my cases are under scrutiny? And why all these cases are being brought up together? To have a greater impact? I bet. Had they informed the Department of Surgery of this investigation?"

"No, and I told him at the meeting. I believe if there were serious complications we would have known about them."

"It's a trap, Chief. A trap"

"I think it is, but first we should see which cases they are looking at. I'm willing to support you to the end only if you solve a very serious puzzle for me."

Brian frowned and looked intensely at the Chief.

"What puzzle, Chief?"

"Janet Reilly. Who is she?"

Brian felt a heat wave smack his face. He was visibly flushed.

"That's been my question since yesterday. You have to believe me. I have no idea. I did not write that letter, I did not sign it, and did not deliver it."

"But the scenario looks very fitting. Susan Flynn files a very serious complaint against you. Then your letter, excuse me *that* letter, surfaces and she panics that you will have her fired, then she apologizes to you and withdraws her complaint. Makes sense, doesn't it?"

"It does, except that I had nothing to do with it. I should also tell you that Susan's complaint against me was very surprising to me. We had some casual, friendly conversation, a few innocent jokes, the ones we repeat everyday, and suddenly she turns that into an accusation of *sexual harassment!*"

"So, what's behind it?"

"I don't know. I think she is also doing the dirty work for somebody else. There is a missing link here. I need to figure that out."

"I think you are on the right track but don't underestimate your opponent's strength. They can make you and they can break you. Be very careful."

"Where do I go from here?" Brian asked.

"Just keep doing your work as usual. When you left the meeting yesterday the question came up whether we should suspend you or put you under supervision. It was decided to wait until QA decides on your other cases. So you have another boiling pot waiting for you."

Brian felt anger rising in him again. He raised his voice a notch.

"Suspension? … For what? Nobody else has ever had a complication here?"

The Chief became a bit philosophical like a grandfather explaining some unpleasant realities of life.

"Listen, to be fair, we have to realize that this organization is extremely concerned about lawsuits. Granted, most of them are frivolous and ridiculous, nevertheless it cost the hospital a bundle to defend every one of them. The legal fees are enormous. You should understand. That's why you're paying so much for malpractice insurance premium."

"Ah … Chief … please don't remind me of that. It's killing us all."

'That's correct. On this case of yours, the hospital's concern is not so much the complication itself, which can possibly be defended, rather the way you have dealt with it so far."

"What is it that I have not done?" Brian inquired.

"Well, to begin with, it looks like you did not have consent to explore the other side. I think you did the right operation, but hostile parents, and more so their lawyers, will jump on this. Then, somehow they screwed up the preparation of specimens, and now we don't know if the damage was inflicted on one side, which would have been inconsequential, or both sides, which makes all the difference in the world for this kid. And you heard the pathologist's opinion that the damage was bilateral. You could say the nurse was responsible for the specimen mishap, but they had their kid in *your* hands and the buck stops with you."

Brian was shaking his head, and the Chief continued.

"Worst of all, you have not informed the parents of this complication."

"But Chief…" Brian jumped in; however the Chief cut him off with the universal stop sign of stretching his arm and holding the palm of his hand towards Brian.

"Ah … ah … you can argue with this as long as you want, the lawyers don't care about the emotional distress of the parents and they don't give a shit who gets hurt. The law says; *their* law I mean, that parents should be informed of what happens to their children."

Brian swallowed his frustration with this issue. He was sure he had done the right thing and was not willing to give up on it. He was more anxious to finish this conversation.

"I will deal with that issue, Chief. Thank you for your confidence and support."

"Don't forget about finding Janet Reilly."

They shook hands and Brian left.

Brian exited the hospital quickly. He went to the parking lot and sat in his car.

He was pleased with Dr. Sloan's gracious attitude, and he almost felt guilty that he lied to him. He had a very good idea who Janet Reilly was.

As soon as he saw the letter at the meeting he figured everything out. He was furious at Jennifer for going to that extreme without his knowledge. He felt she had done him more harm than Susan Flynn or whoever was behind her actions. She should have realized how serious such covert action was. He was afraid of confronting her since the possibility of losing his cool could cause serious damage to their relationship. He still loved her very much.

He thought of Susan Flynn's behavior. Who was using her against him? He had to find out soon. He realized that Susan had truly panicked. She did not want to lose her job. This was a price she was not willing to pay for doing somebody else's dirty work. So, her commitment was not unwavering. Her weakness saved him the embarrassment of going through an Ethics Committee investigation. Thanks to none other than Jennifer.

He realized that he should tap into Susan's weakness in order to find out who was behind all this.

He needed Jennifer, also known as Janet Reilly, more than ever.

He opened his cell phone and dialed.

"Hi, it's me"

"Ah, for goodness sake, is it really you? Where have you been since yesterday? Were you lost somewhere? Were you hit on the head and forgot everything? I've been dying to get a hold of you since last evening. Did you forget all about me? You said you would call me after the meeting. Have you checked your messages? What is the cell phone for? What's going on Brian?

"Are you done?"

"No, but I'm listening."

Brian paused for a minute. "You're not talking." Jennifer jumped in. "Who is Janet Reilly?" Brian asked.

No answer. Jennifer broke out in a cold sweat, her mouth closed shut, her tongue could not move.

Brian waited.

"Who is not talking now? The hospital authorities are desperately looking to find, apprehend and prosecute Janet Reilly. And I have been officially accused of sabotaging the legal proceedings of the hospital's affairs by sending in Janet Reilly as an undercover agent.

"You had nothing to do with it. That's a fact."

"Who is going to believe me? She passed on a letter from me to Susan Flynn"

"Give me a little room here to think, Brian. I can explain everything to you, and I will take care of whatever comes up. If necessary I will come out of hiding and take full responsibility for whatever Janet Reilly has done. Let's think this over together. Don't do anything irrational. Let them keep looking for Janet Reilly. You keep denying knowing her. After all she was good for you. She took a huge load of sexual harassment accusation off your shoulder. Don't you understand what that means?"

"Listen, Jenny." Brian answered, trying hard to control his anger. "I love you dearly, I adore you, but I just have this extreme desire to ring your neck. You better come up with some answers. I want to know if you left your phone number, or address or something with Susan. If they find out who Janet Reilly is, I am history."

"I have left nothing with Susan. There is no chance they can trace me, I mean … Janet Reilly.

"Don't call me for the next few days; I'm very upset at you."

"Would you want to ring my neck *tonight?*"

"Um … yes."

* * * * *

THIRTEEN

Since the day of the alleged sexual harassment, Susan Flynn had declined to work in the same operating room with Dr. Brinkley. The Nursing Department and OR supervisor had expressed understanding and accommodated her on the daily OR schedule.

Susan avoided eye contact with Brian when passing each other in the halls and had evaded unintended contact with him no matter when or where.

Then came the letter of withdrawal and apology to Dr. Brinkley, and the nursing authorities were not quite sure if they should go back to their original scheduling. There was a great deal of curiosity as to what was going on. They decided to keep Susan and Dr. Brinkley separate for a while.

After revelations about Janet Reilly, Susan battled bouts of bewilderedness, deception, frustration, anger and at times depression. She regretted having written those letters, but, on the other hand, she became increasingly suspicious of Dr. Peter Molano and began to suspect that she was being used by him. This was another bitter pill for her to swallow. She loved him dearly and had hopes of their relationship flourishing into a long term commitment.

Susan was angry at having been trapped by Janet Reilly, but, who was Janet Reilly? Where was she? Would she show up again? Would she call?

Dr. Molano was pressuring her to find Janet Reilly, but the only connection she could possibly explore was through Dr. Brinkley. After all, Janet Reilly was working on his behalf, or for his interests. Avoiding Dr. Brinkley would not be helpful. Susan was hoping they would schedule her again to work with him. That would give her an opening. However, she could not personally request that. It would raise a lot of suspicion as to the legitimacy of her original sexual harassment claim. She would jeopardize both her reputation and her job.

She requested to take night calls, when there was usually only one team of nurses, an anesthesiologist and support personnel available to handle emergency surgery after midnight. A back up team could be called in if needed. She was hoping that one of those nights Dr. Brinkley would show up for emergency surgery.

And it happened about two weeks later.

Susan received a call from the ER at about 2 a.m. They were sending a multiple trauma patient, badly injured in a car accident, up to the OR for abdominal surgery.

Susan obtained all the necessary information such as patient's name, sex, age, medical history, availability of blood for transfusion and consent for surgery.

"And who is the surgeon?" she asked.

"Dr. Brinkley."

Her hands were shaking as she wrote down the name. She felt a wave of nervousness moving through her body, her knees trembled.

Get a hold of yourself girl. She tapped her head with her knuckles. *Another mishap here, I'll be finished.*

The patient was rolled in on a special bed and Susan signed the appropriate papers and checked the chart. A young man in his late twenties was involved in a motor vehicle accident and had sustained intra-abdominal injuries. He was pale and his blood pressure was low. He was bleeding internally.

The anesthesiologist took over and started pouring fluids and blood into his veins until his blood pressure came up and he could be safely put to sleep. Shortly after induction of general anesthesia his pressure dropped again. He was in shock. He was bleeding fast.

Susan was running incessantly all around getting the OR ready, helping the scrub nurse to set her table, calling the blood bank for more blood, giving medications to the anesthesiologist, and answering phone calls.

Brian frantically changed into a scrub suit, wearing booties on his shoes, a cap on his head and a mask on his face as he entered the sterile area of the OR. He rushed to the sink, scrubbed his hands and entered the operating room ready to be gowned and gloved.

He hardly noticed Susan Flynn, as he approached the table, prepped and draped the patient and, quite skillfully made a long midline incision and entered the belly. It was full of blood. He ran his hand inside, up towards the liver and felt deep cracks. *Shit, the liver is smashed.* He grunted.

He suctioned the free blood out of the belly. Now he could see the internal organs better. Spleen was normal. Intestines were bruised but not ripped off. That was good.

"What's the pressure Jim?" he asked the anesthesiologist.

"70 Systolic. Very low"

"Keep pumping blood into him."

"Going in full force"

The long tedious work went on and on, until he finally managed to control the hemorrhage from the depth of the shattered liver tissue.

"Pressure is up to 110 Systolic, Brian." The anesthesiologist said.

"Good. You may slow down the transfusion now."

"Will do."

Three hours and twenty minutes after the incision was made the case was over.

The patient was alive and stable. The surgeon, anesthesiologist and nurses were barely alive and able to stand.

They were visibly exhausted, soaked in perspiration, drowsy and dizzy from exhaustion and deeply worried about the poor young man with smashed liver. He was not out of the woods yet.

As things calmed down and the patient was transported to a stretcher, the masks were pulled down and faces glanced at each other.

"Hello, Susan. How are you?" Brian broke the ice.

"Thank you, Dr. Brinkley. Nice to see you"

"Are you going to the Recovery Room with the patient?"

"Yes Sir."

"And then?"

"I'll come back here to clean up."

"Good. I'll write his orders and dictate the case and will come back here. Could you wait for me?"

"I'm not going anywhere."

Twenty minutes later, they met each other in the OR rotunda. They were alone.

"It's almost 6 am. I'm dying for a cup of coffee. Would you like to go to the cafeteria with me?" Brian asked.

"Sure. I'm just about to fall asleep myself."

"Good. Let's go"

A triumph for both sides. Rarely were two people so much in need of each other's company and yet so far apart. Each holding a deep secret the other one's destiny depended on.

Between the two of them, the mystery of Janet Reilly and Peter Molano could be unraveled in a fraction of a second. But neither of them would give away one iota of their deeply held knowledge so easily. A lot more communication, closeness, contact, and trust would be needed first. None was there at the time. In fact they were extremely suspicious of each other, each believing that the other side's pretension of civility and friendship was self serving, and therefore they were more resistant to give away anything.

Brian strongly believed that Susan had no personal animosity towards him. They had nothing in common. She was certainly working for somebody else, somebody who was threatened by Brian's success and popularity. Another surgeon maybe? Possibly of his own specialty. Perhaps in a position of power and influence. How about Dr. Michael Brown, the Medical Director? Nah … He had no common interest with him, but Dr. Brown most certainly knew the person Brian was looking for.

Susan knew very well that her sexual harassment complaint had infuriated Brian, and he would do anything in his power to destroy her. And powerful she believed he was.

She had no doubt that Janet Reilly, whoever she was, worked for Brian, and for him to take a risk of sending a spook into the hospital to trap Susan into withdrawing her complaint was a strong indication of his determination and resolve to knock her out definitively. And yet, he was the only one who could reveal the true identity of Janet Reilly. She needed him for now.

So much for mutual trust and confidence between them. All they had in mind was their self interest.

They walked into the cafeteria. It was very quiet, with dim lights. They poured coffee and Brian picked up a Danish pastry and glanced at Susan with a thin smile.

"One for you too?"

"No thanks. I've no appetite."

Brian paid for their coffee and his pastry. He looked around and found a remote table near a window. The soft brightness of the dawn was breaking through the window. The world was still asleep while they were up saving lives.

They sat opposite each other at the table and began drinking their coffee. A good excuse to let the other one start the conversation.

"I haven't had a chance to thank you for your beautiful letter, Susan. Your compliments are greatly appreciated." Brian took a sip of coffee and glanced at Susan for her reaction.

"I'm glad you liked it and I assume it did what it was meant to do."

"Which was what?"

"To convince you that I should not be fired."

"Fired? ... Who was going to fire you and why?"

"You were. Because I filed a complaint against you."

"That was a serious and unjust accusation indeed, but I never intended to have you fired."

"Well, I was told you did."

"Whoever said that was dead wrong. I was not only upset and disappointed but very surprised and puzzled as to why *you* would make such an accusation. I certainly did not expect that from you. This looked more like the work of somebody who had an agenda. An intentional attempt to destroy my reputation. A character assassination, if you will. To be honest to you, my feeling was that you had been coerced to do someone else's dirty work. I felt sorry for you, but I never intended to have you fired."

Susan remained quiet for a moment, deep in thought, with her cup of coffee stuck to her lips.

"With all due respect, Dr. Brinkley" she finally spoke "you're not telling me the truth. I saw the letter you wrote to the OR Committee, asking for my dismissal. Actually I have a copy of that letter. I'll show it to you if you want."

"I've heard about this letter. I didn't write it. I believe there is a conspiracy going on against me to destroy my reputation. I don't know who is behind it, but I believe you know that person."

"I work for nobody but myself, Dr. Brinkley" Susan fired back.

"I don't mean to upset you, Susan, but you are young, attractive and emotional, and people may take advantage of you."

"Nobody can take advantage of me" she replied defensively.

Brian raised his voice a notch "you know who is behind this mayhem. I think you should come clean and tell me who it is. I'll deal with him directly. At this time I am holding you responsible for all this turmoil. You initiated this by filing a false accusation against me. As you know, the OR Committee met, and I was there and I did not ask for your dismissal. I am telling you the truth, I never intended to have you fired, but I can still do that."

Susan's hands were shaking. She was visibly nervous and angry.

"You can say whatever you want, Dr. Brinkley. I am not anybody's agent like the ones who work for you."

"I beg your pardon?"

"Your spies. The ones who roam the hospital on your behalf and intimidate people like me until I get on my knees and beg for your forgiveness. Dr. Brinkley, who is Janet Reilly and where is she?"

"I don't know anybody with that name, Susan. What are you talking about?"

"Don't deny it. She is your agent and I am desperate to find her.

"I think this is getting more and more complicated. I have no agents. I need no agents. Who is feeding this garbage to you?"

"I have not been dreaming this. It was real. She found me in the coffee shop and told me about your conversation with Dr. Gonzalez. She claimed she was his secretary. She warned me that you were upset that I had mixed up the specimens and you no longer trusted me and would not work with me. She later gave me a copy of your letter."

Brian saw tears rolling down her face. He lowered his voice and changed his tone.

"Did it ever occur to you that you were being set up by whoever is behind all this in order to turn you against me and make you stand firmly behind your sexual harassment accusation?"

"No. But it worked the other way. I withdrew my complaint"

"Your conscience bothered you."

"I could not afford to lose my job."

"Your job is safe Susan. You tell me who is using you and I'll be your biggest supporter"

"OK. I'll make a deal with you. You bring me Janet Reilly and I will tell you who your enemies are."

"Enemies? Are there more than one?"

"Yes."

"I don't make deals. I don't know a Janet Reilly.

"Well, you might want to find out who she is. She's obviously working on your behalf."

Brian didn't respond. People were coming in for breakfast and the place was becoming crowded and noisy.

"Looks like we can't continue this conversation here much longer" he said "but let's not forget about it. I would like us to remain friendly and respectful of each other."

From the other end of the cafeteria a distant voice was calling "Dr. Brinkley, Dr. Brinkley"

Brian stood up, and searched for the caller. The voice became louder and closer.

"Dr. Brinkley. Dr. Brinkley."

Brian noted a movement among the crowd standing in line. Somebody cut through the line and dashed towards the rear of the cafeteria where they were sitting.

A young man, an orderly working in the OR arrived, catching his breath.

"They need you in the Recovery Room urgently. They've been calling for you all over the place for forty five minutes.

Susan jumped and ran towards the phone on the wall. Brian instinctively didn't waste time calling upstairs. He just ran as fast as he could. Out of the cafeteria, through the hall into the main lobby. People were jammed in front of the elevators. He turned around and took the stairway, up to the second floor, and into the Recovery Room and froze.

A large crowd of nurses and doctors were packed around his patient's bed, working on a cardiac resuscitation.

The charge nurse hollered. "Dr. Brinkley, where have you been? He's been in shock since shortly coming out of the OR. He has no blood pressure and no pulse now"

Brian worked his way through the resuscitation team and reached the bed. His patient was near death, cold, clammy, pale, non-responsive and had no EKG rhythm. He was intubated and on a respirator. His chest was being pumped. Five IV lines were wide open, and blood was being transfused. The anesthesiologist was running the show and was angry.

"Brian, you left him here and disappeared. Where the hell have you been?"

"Down in the cafeteria. Never heard a page."

"You know they're not allowed to use the overhead page at night. It wakes up every single patient in the hospital"

Brian hardly paid attention to that. He checked the abdomen. Dressing was soaked; abdomen was markedly distended and tense.

"He's bleeding, Jim. We've got to take him back in. Damn liver broke loose again."

"I can't give him anesthesia with no blood pressure and no pulse."

"He's not gonna make it unless we stop the hemorrhage."

The nurse at the head of the bed said "We've got a rhythm. Sinus tachycardia. Still, I've got no BP"

"Do we have enough blood for him?" Brian asked.

"We sent to the blood bank for six more units" the head nurse answered.

"I mean do we have blood available now?"

"No Sir. Not yet"

"How long ago did you request the blood?"

"Thirty five minutes."

"This patient does not have thirty five minutes to live. Get on the phone and tell them to move their ass down there."

"Pulse is stronger. BP 70 Systolic" the charge nurse announced.

"Stop pumping the chest. Give him two amps of Bicarb" Brian said. Then he turned to the anesthesiologist "Jim, let's take him in. We're gonna lose him."

"Ok, if that's what you want. Let's go."

The crowd scattered. They started rolling the bed. Susan walked in and said "I've got the room ready."

"Thanks Susie, you are a good nurse after all" Brian managed a smile.

The patient was taken back to the OR. Brian scrubbed. A surgical resident arrived to assist.

They were gowned and gloved. The patient was prepped and draped and Brian removed the stitches and belly popped open pouring blood all over the place. Brian reached for the liver and packed the bleeding area tightly with Lap-Pads to control the hemorrhage.

"I have no blood pressure again" Jim said.

"Are you pumping blood into him?" Brian asked.

"The last unit I had here is gone. More is on the way."

"Get the God damn blood here fast Susie" Brian yelled.

"Hey guys, I have no rhythm again. Let's pump his chest" Jim hollered.

The resident started external cardiac massage. Brian had one hand in the belly packing the liver. He noticed no more active bleeding. It was not necessarily good news. No blood pressure, no bleeding.

Resuscitation went on for half an hour more. No response. No blood pressure, no pulse, no sign of life. He was gone.

A deadly silence fell in the room. Brian was distraught and exhausted. Susan broke down and ran out of the room.

Brian closed the incision again. Just a few stitches on the skin to hold the guts from pouring out. The other layers didn't matter anymore.

Brian felt fatigued and washed out. He was soaked in perspiration and was weak and squeamish. He would have kicked himself in the ass if he could. He should have stayed with the patient in the Recovery Room for a while, whether it made a difference or not. He depended on the system as it had always been. Ordinarily he would get calls from the nurses immediately if there was anything wrong with his patients. What a freaky set of circumstances this morning. *Unbelievable*

Once again the Susan Flynn saga had caused him serious problems.

No point in blaming anybody. He had to regain his strength for a more daunting task ahead. He had to face the patient's family, give them the horrible news of his death and assure them that he went quickly, he did not suffer and it had been a miracle that he made it to the hospital to begin with. Nobody survives this type of liver injury, but the medical staff wanted to give him any possible chance he might have had. And they did. And he had none. He was at peace now. No pain. No suffering.

What a bunch of bullshit. He thought. The man suffered the worst kind of liver injury. *If that is not suffering what is?*

"He went quickly." *He went quickly? My ass.* He did not go quickly. He was dragged to the OR twice, poked with multiple needles, tubes, IV's. His belly was ripped open twice. His liver was squeezed, packed, sutured. His lungs were pumped with air. His chest was crushed to get his heart going, possibly cracked a couple of ribs.

All this was not done to give him *"any possible chance he might have had."* Nonsense.

He never had a chance.

Everything was done so that the people he was attempting to console wouldn't sue him for not trying. Even if they understood, somewhere along the way a lawyer would get his or her hands on the case. Brian's judgment didn't matter.

A nurse walked into the room.
"Dr. Brinkley, the family is waiting in the lobby."
"Ok. Could you have somebody bring them to the private room, up here? And I want a nurse there when I talk to them."
"Yes Sir"

Passing by the nursing station, he saw Susan curled on an armchair, holding her head in her hands, crying.
"I understand how you feel Susan. I'm sorry."
"It was all my fault. I will not forgive myself. We shouldn't have gone to the cafeteria"

Brian sat down next to her and held her hand. *Ah ... he so badly needed somebody to hold his hand.*
"He never had a chance to begin with" he tried to comfort her "you shouldn't blame yourself. After all he was my responsibility. You did your job in the OR, and you did it
remarkably well. There is only so much you can do. We all did what we could do. You can't save them all."
She wiped her eyes and blew her nose.
"What are we going to do now?"
"We should all go home now."

* * * * *

Mary Dorsa, the OR supervisor, was turning the pages in a patient's chart which was thin, and in disarray. It had not had a chance to be organized yet. Too short a time between admission and death. The admitting surgeon had dictated his admission note and operative reports. They had not been transcribed yet. The chart will be put together when it reaches Medical Records. It would eventually find its way to many committees, offices and most likely a court room.
She had a brief report from the nurses, and a death certificate that had not been signed yet.

The chart was still alive and evolving, in need of signatures, reports, reviews and filing.

The patient, however, was dead.

Her phone rang. It was the Medical Director.

"Hello Mrs. Dorsa. This is Dr. Brown."

"How are you Dr. Brown? What can I do for you?"

"I need some information about Dr. Brinkley's patient who died in the OR last night."

"I am reading the nurse's reports on this case as we speak"

"I understand it was a bad car accident injury."

"That's correct."

"And he had to be taken back to the OR."

"Yes."

"This is very confidential Mary, but the surgical resident told me that Dr. Brinkley somehow disappeared for a long time while his patient was in shock in the Recovery room. Is that correct?"

"The Recovery Room nurses' notes indicate that they were calling all over the place for him for about forty five minutes. They thought he might have left the hospital, but his service could not find him. When he came back his patient was in cardiac arrest. Brian took him back to the OR."

"I would like to have a full accounting of the events last night, minute by minute if necessary."

"OK Dr. Brown. We'll prepare a detailed report for you."

"By the way, was Susan Flynn there last night?"

"Oh yes. And she was also missing while Dr. Brinkley was gone. They were found together in the cafeteria."

"That's strange. I thought they were at odds with each other. What happened?"

"I'm not sure, Dr. Brown. It's indeed strange."

"Could you mention her in your report as well?"

"As you wish Sir."

* * * * *

The phone rang in the Medical Records Room.

The secretary answered.

"Medical Records. May I help you?"

"Good morning. This is Dr. Molano. Can I talk to Ms. Jackson?"

"Certainly, Dr. Molano. She'll be glad to talk to you. Hang on a minute."

"Hello Peter, So nice to hear your voice." Judy Jackson said cheerfully.

"Hello sweetheart. How are you?"

"I'm fine. What's up?"

"I'm tied up in the OR at the moment. I need to review a few charts for the QA Committee meeting. Could you collect them for me?"

"Only for you darling but, it'll cost you dinner."

"Oh, that's fine as long as I have my special dessert afterwards."

"I'll see to that. Whose charts do you want?"

"The same ones you gave to Dr. Brown before the OR Committee."

"You mean Dr. Brinkley's complication cases?"

"Yep, plus the hernia case. You know the name?"

"Elliot Silverman, It's a household name around here. Everybody wants his chart these days."

"And there was a trauma case here last night, didn't make it. Do you have that chart?"

"The OR supervisor has it. We will get it later on today."

"That's wonderful. I'll come down later."

"I'll be here and ready for you."

"Love you baby. Take care"

* * * * *

FOURTEEN

Susan Flynn woke up with a splitting headache. A sharp sliver of bright sunshine was poking through the curtains. She rubbed her eyes, but her mind was still hazy. The room was dark but it didn't look like her usual early morning wake up time.

She focused her eyes onto the bedside clock. 3:30 p.m.

"Ah." She remembered she had worked the night before and had arrived home sometime around 8 a.m. Everything was coming back to her now. She drove home crying loudly all the way. She was exhausted, dizzy and depressed. No appetite, no breakfast. Too tired to shower, she went right to bed, but could not fall asleep. The guilty feeling of leaving her patient to die was overwhelming.

She cried out of control, until her pillow was wet. She turned it over and continued crying. The big lump in her throat was not going away.

She thought of her conversation with Brian and, somehow, she had a good feeling about that. She needed Brian in order to find Janet Reilly, although he kept denying knowing her. She remembered that she was offered a deal. *Dr. Molano for Janet Reilly.* She wasn't ready for that yet.

Before the demise of the trauma patient overshadowed everything else, she remembered, she had started feeling good about Brian. She sensed he was nice, sincere, compassionate, and honest. The feeling was potentiated when he held her hand and consoled her. She felt guilty for what she had done to him and began to hate Peter Molano. Her mood swung again. She loved Peter and was not ready to give him up. But,

Peter was becoming increasingly rough with her. He showed no understanding of her concern for her job, as if it didn't matter to him. He was consumed with his own agenda. Perhaps if she found Janet Reilly that would turn Peter around and, Susan would get what she was desperate to have. Love, attention, support. She had to see Peter soon and tell him about what went on in the cafeteria the night before.

She got out of bed, still wobbly and unsteady on her feet. She pulled the curtains. Bright afternoon sunshine poured in. She rubbed her eyes again. She felt weak and queasy. She realized she had had no breakfast and no lunch. She was hungry. She grabbed a granola bar from the kitchen and went into the shower. The pulsating water was refreshing. Her body warmed up and relaxed but her mind was still racing. The scenes form the Recovery Room, the crowd around the patient's bed, the pumping of the chest, the pouring of fluids and blood into his veins, rushing him back to the OR and opening his belly again, blood all over the place, and the chaotic efforts to save his life paraded in her mind like scenes from a movie.

And then, she remembered ... that she had left the hospital without completing her paperwork. There were lots of papers she had to sign, and a detailed nurse's note she had to write in the patient's chart, timed and dated.

She decided she would go back to the hospital to finish her work and, perhaps, she would see Dr. Molano there. She knew it was his OR day working till late in the afternoon.

She arrived at the hospital shortly before 5 p.m. and went to the OR lounge. She asked the secretary if the patient's chart was still there.

"I gave it to Ms. Dorsa earlier today" she said.

"Oh ... is Mary still here?" she asked hoping to hear a negative. Susan was in no mood to be questioned and lectured about what went on last night.

"She had to leave earlier but she left a message for you ... it's somewhere around here." She found a piece of paper and handed it to Susan. The OR supervisor wanted her to write a report about last night's events, separate from her customary nurse's note in the patient's chart. *The hell with the report.* She didn't think that was her job to do. She would write her nurse's notes in the chart and that was it.

Come to think of it, she didn't want to be blamed for leaving the patient for forty-five minutes. The patient was out of the OR and in the Recovery Room so other nurses were in charge of him. Susan was present when the patient was taken back to the OR. She would write a brief note on the patient's condition in the OR. She would refuse to blame or incriminate anybody for wrongdoing. *I did that once and all Hell broke loose.*

"You think the chart may still be on Mary's desk?" she asked the secretary.

"Most likely it is. She did not return it to me."

"I'm going to sneak into her office. OK? I have to complete my notes from last night."

"OK with me. I don't know nothing."

"Thank you sweetie."

Susan turned the door knob slowly and pushed. The door swung open and she entered. The room was dark. She turned the lights on. *Mary has an open door policy! She just doesn't know.* Susan smiled.

She found the chart on Mary's desk with a handwritten note attached to it. She couldn't help reading the note. Mary had left a reminder for herself. *Detailed report for Dr. Brown of what went on with the trauma patient's care, and why he had to be taken back to the OR. Also remember to mention Susan Flynn's absence for forty-five minutes. The orderly found her with Dr. Brinkley in Cafeteria.*

Susan could not believe her eyes.

Jesus Christ, they are ganging up on us. Mary Dorsa and the Medical Director! What the hell are they looking for? She had done nothing wrong. Obviously they were after Dr. Brinkley. She thought they might be part of the secret group Peter Molano had talked about.

She couldn't figure things out anymore.

She sat down behind the desk, opened the chart and signed everywhere she was supposed to, and wrote the briefest nurse's note she had ever written. Only describing the patient's condition. No mention of the infamous forty-five minutes. No mention of the frantic efforts the nurses had made to find Dr. Brinkley. She did, however, emphasize that the blood bank was very slow and the patient's transfusion was delayed significantly. She knew they were ultimately going to blame Dr. Brinkley for the patient's demise. *This is for you Brian. It isn't fair what they're doing to you.* She thought she owed him one.

She left the room and went back to the secretary.

"Is Dr. Molano still working in there?"

"He finished half an hour ago. He went to Medical Records. You want me call him there?"

"Oh, no. no, I'll see him later on."

Susan thought it was a good opportunity to catch Peter in or near Medical Records.

The place was secluded in the basement, and at this time hardly anybody was around.

She needed to talk to him in private, some place hidden and quiet.

She left the OR, skipped the elevator and walked down the stairway into the lobby. On the opposite side of the lobby she spotted Dr. Molano talking to a few people. She figured they were his patient's family members. She did not approach. It wouldn't be appropriate to interrupt them. She sat down and watched him from afar. He was still in his green scrub suits with the white lab coat on. He looked so professional and handsome. Ah … she so much wanted to hug him. She loved him so dearly. She felt so happy and secure when he held her with his strong arms, caressed her and kissed her passionately.

Peter said goodbye to those people and headed for the elevator. Susan took the stairway again and entered the hallway in the basement. Going towards Medical Records Peter was ahead of her. She followed in his shadow. He was walking faster and faster. *What's the rush for Peter?*

He entered the Medical Records department and closed the door.

She decided not to enter the room just yet. She figured he was going to sign his charts, maybe dictate some discharge summaries and complete his records. She'd give him time to finish his work. That way he was more likely to be relaxed and attentive when she told him what she had to say.

She strolled around the halls while keeping an eye on the door. She expected him to finish his work and walk out. Once in a while somebody would pass by her, but nobody was coming from or going into the Medical Records. The employees were gone. The evening was quiet.

She looked at her watch. Five minutes … Fifteen minutes … Forty-five minutes, that's enough. She couldn't wait any longer.

Susan went to the door, turned the knob slowly and pushed the door open, very quietly.

Surprise! The room was dark except for two dim ceiling lights at the very end of the large room. The main lights were off. Nobody was working there. *Darn it. He snuck out.* She thought.

The cubicles were empty; the desks were piled with charts. She slowly walked farther in, hoping she would find him in a corner at the end of the room working under the dim lights.

She noted a glass window at the end of the room, with horizontal lines of soft light coming through half closed blinds from inside the adjacent room. As she approached, she could hear a female voice, laughing.

She reached the wall, and stood next to the window. She could now hear a male and a female voice, barley discernible but obviously chatting and laughing together.

Very quietly she turned, facing the window, and adjusted her eyes to narrow openings through the shades. The room was dimly lit. Only one end of the room was in her view. Nobody was there. The voices were coming from the opposite side.

She turned her head to the other side, but from where she was standing she could hardly make out another section of the room with file cabinets next to the wall, and a couple of chairs. She noted a white lab coat hanging on the arm of a chair.

The voices grew now louder, but still mostly laughing, and sounds of passion and romance like young lovers cooing to each other.

In order to see the section of the room where the sounds were coming from she had to move to the middle of the window, where she could easily be seen by the people inside. A big risk to take. But by now she was deeply concerned that the man in there could possibly be Peter Molano. *Oh … no, dear God, don't let it be Peter.*

She crouched down low, and crawled towards the center of the window and very slowly straightened her knees and lifted her body till her eyes reached the lowest space through the shades. Suddenly she heard the door to the main room open and somebody stepped in. She quickly jumped to the side and crawled under a desk, hiding.

A man's voice said "Security, anybody here?" He then turned the main lights on.

Susan noted that the light in the room she was peeking in quickly went off.

Nobody answered. The main lights went off and she heard the door close and a clicking sound followed. *He locked the door from the outside.* She feared.

The lights behind the window went on again and shortly after the voices could be heard.

Susan moved behind the window again, staying low, and tried one more time to peek through.

The view was quite clear this time but only up to the top of a desk.

The woman was sitting at the edge of the desk, leaning back, her skirt pulled up to her waste, her legs wrapped around the lower body of the man who was standing against her, naked from the waste down and moving back and forth, in a lovemaking motion.

She closed her eyes. Couldn't believe what she was seeing. But she had to look.

She tried to see the faces, but the blindes were tilted downward, blocking the view above the desk.

Her heart was pounding and her knees trembling. She felt weak and dizzy. She sat on the floor, hoping against hope that the man was not Peter.

Minutes later the lights coming through the shades intensified. Suddenly the main room also lit up. Susan jumped off to the side again, and went under the desk. She stuck her head to the front leg of the desk where she had the view to the door next to the window.

The door opened and now she could hear the voices clearly, along with sounds of kissing and cooing. They said goodbye to each other and the man stepped out into the main room, as he was putting his lab coat on. The coat momentarily blocked Susan's view to his head and he moved fast towards the main door.

The woman stepped out of the back room in a rush and hollered "Peter … Peter"

"Yes Judy"

Susan clearly heard Peter's voice and she knew who Judy was. Judy Jackson, the Director of Medical Records Department.

"Security locks the door at this time. You can't get out" Judy said.

"Good, I get to stay here with you all night"

Susan was biting the leg of the table to hold off screaming.

"Here is the key. Unlock the door from inside and leave the key on the desk near the door."

"OK love."

Peter left and the door closed. The lights went off and the room was dark and quiet. Judy went back to her office and closed the door.

Susan rushed to the main door. It was closed and locked. She could not see the desk near the door. The room was dark. The key was supposed to be there. She walked to the left side of the door, feeling the wall with her hands. No desk there. She moved to the other side. Fumbling with her hands she touched an object which slid away and crashed on the floor with a loud thumping noise.

The ceiling lights went on. Susan sat on the floor looking for a place to hide.

Judy opened the door to her office and listened. No more noise.

Susan saw that she had knocked off a few charts from the top of a desk. Now she could see the key sitting close to the edge of the desk. The lights went off again.

Susan moved quickly. Picked up the key and unlocked the door. She pulled the door open and stepped out. Then, instinctively stepped back in to leave the key on the desk, but stopped. She thought for a second and went out again and closed the door.

Let the bitch remain trapped in there.

Devastated, heartbroken, confused, sick to her stomach, with her world crashed on her head, Susan managed to reach the lobby and rush out the door onto the parking lot. She jumped into her car and drove away. Tears pouring down, blurring her vision, she almost slammed into an oncoming SUV, but veered to the right and passed by.

On her way home, she thought of the unbelievable events of her last twenty four hours, and how her world had suddenly turned upside down. She was tired, weak, washed out and needed quite a few days of rest. Maybe staying in bed forever. She had no desire to work. How could she go to work the next day and pretend nothing had changed in her life? They would certainly drag her to this and that meeting, interrogating her as harsh as they can, and possibly suspending her for a while if not firing her altogether. Her personal life was shattered; she had just lost the man she loved so dearly, her world was now empty and devoid of meaning, hope, enthusiasm, and drive. She just wanted to get away from it all. Nothing to do, nothing to plan, nothing to hang her hopes on, except that for the next day she had only one task in mind. Only one task. She would call Dr. Brinkley. She was ready to accept his deal.

Peter Molano for Janet Reilly.

* * * * *

Judy Jackson cleaned her desk, straightened her ruffled blouse and skirt, combed her hair and refreshed her make up. She turned the lights on in the main room and headed for the door. She looked for the key on the desk. It wasn't there.

She picked up the charts from the floor, and looked around, assuming that the key had fallen down as the charts crashed to the floor. She looked everywhere. No key.

She turned the door knob and pulled. The door was locked. She knew better. These special security locks could only be opened from either the outside or inside by specific keys. She had one for the nights she worked late. *Darn it, Peter. You forgot to leave the key on the desk.*

She went back to the phone and dialed the operator.

"Hi, this is Ms. Jackson. Could you see if Dr. Molano is still in the house?"

"Sure Ma'am. I'll page him for you."

"You may wanna try the OR. He was there a while ago."

"Good idea, I'll have him call you back."

"Thanks."

Minutes later the phone rang. She picked up quickly.

"This is Dr. Molano."

"Hi Peter. It's Judy. You rushed out of here so fast you forgot to leave the key on the desk. I can't get out of here without the key."

"It's right there Judy. On the desk. Near the front edge."

"It's not, honey. I have looked all over the place. I looked under the desk where you dropped a few charts on the floor"

"I dropped what?"

"The charts. Did you not realize you pushed few of them off the desk as you left?"

"No. I didn't drop anything and I most definitely left the key exactly where you asked me to."

"Well, it just disappeared. I am trapped here now."

"OK. Relax. I'm in the doctor's locker room in the OR, changing. I'll come down shortly."

"Look in the pockets of your scrub suit. The key is there."

"Judy, honey I told you I left the key on the desk. It's somewhere around there. Why don't you call security and tell them you lost your key. They'll come and open the door for you"

"I don't want the security man coming in here. I'm afraid, Peter. Please come down."

"Ok hon. I'll call security myself and come with him. You stay back in your office."

Peter came out of the locker room, passing by the front desk the secretary called him.

"Dr. Molano …"

"Yes."

"Did Susan Flynn find you in Medical Records?"

"No. Why?"

"She came here about an hour ago and asked for you."

"Did you tell her I was in Medical Records?"

"That's where you told me you were going, in case somebody was looking for you."

"I just wanted *you* to know where to find me."

"Ok, well, If you didn't see her, she didn't find you."

Peter frowned. For a moment he looked worried. He looked at the secretary, and then glanced around, as if he was lost or had forgotten where he was going next.

"I'm sorry if I upset you, Doctor. I did not send her down there. I offered to call you for her but she said it wasn't necessary"

Peter just walked out without answering her. He was visibly disturbed.

He went down to the main lobby and asked the switchboard operator to page security and ask them to open the Medical Records room for him.

They both arrived at the main entrance to the Record room simultaneously.

"Thank you Officer, I was working in there earlier and I left my papers inside." Peter said.

"Not a prob'em Doc."

He opened the door and Peter entered.

"You going to work here for a while, Doc?" the Officer asked.

"If I can, I'd like to finish my charts."

"Not a prob'em. I'll come back later on and lock the door."

"Thank you. I appreciate it."

The security officer left and Peter closed the door. He searched the top of the desk, the floor under and around the desk and found nothing. He went straight back to Judy's office. Peter was disturbed and nervous.

"I'm afraid we had a visitor here earlier. She might have taken the key" Peter said.

"You mean when we were …!"

"Yes, but I'm not sure what she's seen or heard."

"It's impossible, Peter. Security locks the door after the staff leave. Nobody can get in here."

"Well, I think she did."

"Who are you talking about?"

"One of the OR Nurses. The secretary told her where she could find me. She's been stalking me recently."

"What the hell does she want?"

"Don't know. It may be just attention. Women do a lot of things to get attention,"

"Fuck her." Judy yelled loudly. "If in fact she was here and hiding, she is going to get a lot of attention from me and the hospital authorities."

"I'll find out what she was doing here. Promise. Let's get out of here now before Security comes back and locks the door again." Peter implored.

Judy gathered her things and they left.

* * * * *

FIFTEEN

Susan Flynn woke up the next morning, still so tired and weak as if she had never made it to her bed. She sat at the edge of the bed and glanced around her bedroom. The room looked like a war zone. Everything was in total disarray. Clothes scattered on the floor, on the chair, on top of the dresser. Her phone was off the hook. A blanket was hanging off the side of the bed and two pillows lay on the other side of the floor. There was only one shoe near the door. *The other one must be still in the hall!* She thought.

There was every semblance of a shattered life around her. Unfulfilled dreams and broken promises. She found no reason to get out of bed. She fell back and wrapped the comforter around herself and closed her eyes.

A while later, she opened her eyes and glanced at her bedside clock. 7:50 a.m.

She remembered that she was on 9 to 5 shift that day. She still had time to shower, dress up and go to work. *Nah … let them struggle without me.*

She reconnected the phone, then picked up the receiver and called the hospital and asked for the OR. She talked to the secretary and called in sick.

A hot steamy shower could change everything. It did, to some extent.

She stepped out and dried herself and kept her bathrobe on. She made instant coffee and went back to bed. She thought of three people she had to deal with as early as possible.

Judy, Brian and Peter.

First and foremost, Judy Jackson.

She called the hospital and asked to be connected to Medical Records.

"Hi, may I talk to Ms. Jackson please."
"Who is this?"
"Her close friend, Susan."
"Hold on a minute please."

"This is Judy."
"Hi Judy. I heard you lost your key"
A long pause.
"Who is this?"
"I am the girlfriend of the man you fucked last night."
She heard a bang and no response.

Judy dropped the phone on the desk. Her hand was shaking and for a moment she was not sure how she should react.

"Are you still there or did you pass out?" Susan asked.
Judy finally got control of herself and picked up the receiver.

"Listen, I don't know who you are. If you have something to say to me it would be best if you made an appointment and came here."
"Oh … I should make an appointment with you? I'm sorry I barged in last night without an appointment."
"I don't know what you talking about, but …"
"You damn sure know very well what I'm talking about" Susan interrupted her with an angry tone. "You stupid bitch trapped my boyfriend and fucked him. I was there and I have pictures to prove it." She bluffed.
"Pictures? For Chrissake what are you trying to do to me?"
"I don't give a shit about you, it's about my boyfriend. I want you to tell me if this was a onetime fling or have you two been doing it for a while."

"Listen, whoever you are, I don't appreciate your accusations and I don't know who your boyfriend is. I think you are deranged and need a psychiatrist. I am going to hang up and if you call again ..."

"Ah ah ah... don't hang up. I'll tell you who my boyfriend is. The gorgeous Dr. Peter Molano. Did you know we'd been together for more than two years?"

A long pause again.

"Did you?" Susan hollered.

"I don't know Dr. Molano personally. I only know of him as a physician on the staff here."

"Judy, stop bullshitting with me, you had him all over you last night. Right on your goddamn desk. Do you wanna see the pictures?"

"If you have pictures I sure want to see them. Bring them in and we will deal with each other."

"I don't make deals. You answer my question or you will see the pictures on the bulletin boards all over the hospital."

"What is the question?"

"Have you been listening to me? I asked if you two have been doing this for a while or did you just seduce him last night when he came in to do his charts?"

Judy was in a state of panic. She thought of those pictures all over the hospital and she shuddered.

Susan put the pressure on. "You're taking too much time to answer. Let me ask the question again. Have you two been together a long time? Yes or no?"

"We've been good friends for a while."

"Don't you give me the 'good friends' bullshit. How long have you been fucking each other?"

"We've been friends since before we both came to this hospital."

"Did the sonofabitch ever tell you he had a girlfriend here?"

"No, never."

"Now you're talking. I guess both of us have the same question now, which one of us has been his side dish?"

"I guess we'll just have to ask him." Judy responded as her voice trailed off.

"I'll deal with that asshole in my own way. You figure out yours. Thanks."

"Hold on please, Susan. Don't hang up."

"What else do you have to tell me?"

"I feel as though both of us have been victimized by this guy. Could we meet and get to know each other and deal with him collectively?"

"I'll let you know."

"Fine, and maybe you can return my key."

"Do you believe me now that I was there?"

"If you really are Susan Flynn, then yes, I believe you."

"How do you know my name?"

"I'll tell you when we meet."

Susan hung up.

Judy put her head on the desk and broke down. She wanted to get a hold of Peter, grab him by the neck and choke him to death, but first, she had to tell him about this phone call and hear his explanation.

* * * * *

Dr. Brian Brinkley finished his morning surgery. He went into the locker room and changed. He was hungry and anxious to get to the cafeteria for a good lunch. He had to be in his office by 1:30 p.m.

As he walked out of the locker room the secretary called after him.

"Hi Dr. Brinkley, Dr. Sloan wants you in his office."

"Now?"

"Right now. His secretary called twice."

"OK. Thank you." *Dammit, there goes my lunch.*

He went to the Chief's office.

"Come in Brian. Could you tell me about this trauma case the night before last?"

"Yes Sir. Where do you want me to start?"

"I have reviewed the chart. I know about the patient's injuries. The OR supervisor tells me that you had disappeared for forty-five minutes while your patient was in shock. Is that correct?"

"When I left the Recovery Room he was not in shock. I went to the cafeteria. I did not hear a page. I had no idea what was going on."

"You think the outcome would have been different had you stayed with him in the Recovery Room?"

"Absolutely not. His liver was shattered into pieces. He lost too much blood. The blood bank couldn't keep up. You know chief; these types of cases don't survive."

"I believe you; however, on paper it doesn't look good that you had been incommunicado."

"Well, ask the authorities to fix the overhead paging system. How could I have known that they were looking for me?"

"OK, you make that suggestion to the QA Committee. They are going to grill you on this."

"I'll be prepared for that, Chief."

"Good luck. Dr. Brown has already inquired about the case."

"Figures."

At 1:40 p.m. Brian entered his office in bad mood. His stomach was growling. He was hungry.

His desk was covered with messages. He glanced through them. They were mostly from patients, one from Jennifer, and ... wow ... Susan Flynn had called three times.

He took his jacket off, sat behind his desk and dialed Susan's number.

"Hello?"

"Hi, this is Dr. Brinkley."

"Hi Dr. Brinkley. I wanted to thank you for your kind words, your compassion and your caring attitude the other night in the hospital. I'm sorry that I had lost it after the patient died. I was struck with a tremendously guilty feeling for having left the patient, and when you sat next to me and held my hand and comforted me I felt so relieved. I never knew you had such a big heart and I'm truly sorry I have caused so many problems for you recently and ..."

"Stop it Susan. I don't think I deserve all these compliments. As I told you, you did your job in the OR superbly and you had no further responsibility after the patient left the OR.

"Well, Dr. Brinkley, somehow I thought I shouldn't have gone to the cafeteria with you."

"I'm glad you did. I'm very happy we had a chance to talk to each other" Brian replied.

"So did I" Susan responded. I have thought a lot about our conversations and the more I think, the more I realize that you've been victimized. I have come to the conclusion that I have done a great injustice to you and I owe it to you to reveal the identity of your adversaries, the people who took advantage of me and tricked me into doing what I did to you. That reminds me of your offer, the other night in the cafeteria."

Brian began to wonder if this call was another trick by Susan. What exactly caused her change of heart? She sounded serious and innocent; nevertheless Brian was uncomfortable to give away the secret of Janet Reilly, which could give his enemies formidable ammunition. On the other hand, he needed to know who his enemies were. This was a calculated risk he had to take, but not so easily.

"OK, Susan. I understand what you are getting at. And I appreciate you accepting my offer. I need to know how sincere and serious you are. If you reveal to me the name or names of my enemies, would you be willing to stand behind it and testify, if necessary, on my behalf?"

"Absolutely"

"Would you be willing to put the names and the story behind it in writing?"

"Certainly"

"And explain what caused your change of heart and how you came to realize that you were being maliciously manipulated to participate in a conspiracy against me."

"Most definitely"

"Ok, Susan" Brian took a deep breath then continued "before you tell me anything I want you to take your time and put this whole event in writing, from the beginning to the end. Spell out how you were approached and chosen to bring sexual harassment charges against me, and what you were promised in return, and what made you change your mind and come out in my defense. Write this in the form of a letter to me and place it in an envelope, addressed to me, but do not mail it. Within the next few days you'll meet Janet Reilly and you will give her the envelope.

"Where do I meet Janet Reilly?"

"Don't worry about that. You know she can find you."

"That's for sure, she's done that before."

"I've got to see my patients now. Stay in touch."

"Thanks."

Susan hung up. Very excited to get to work on that letter. She got out of bed and dressed up.

Brian called Jennifer.

* * * * *

Susan Flynn knew that her relationship with Dr. Molano was over for good. What she was not sure of was whether Peter knew that there would be no more Susan Flynn in his twisted life. He had shattered her hopes, aspirations and her dreams that someday she could share her life, love and happiness with him.

She wanted revenge.

The letter she wrote to Dr. Brinkley explained in detail Peter's role in an elaborate conspiracy to destroy a colleague's career, and eliminate a formidable competitor. But, up to this point, it would be her word against his. Not exactly a strong position.

She thought it would be great if she could join forces with Judy Jackson and Janet Reilly.

Judy was in the same position as she was, in relation to Dr. Molano, and Janet Reilly, whoever she was, certainly acted on behalf of Dr. Brinkley.

The letter was her ticket to Janet Reilly.

Susan thought of calling Peter and confronting him about the events in Medical Records, the other night. She was sure Judy had called him already and, maybe, it would be best if she waited a while. Perhaps Peter would call her first.

And that is exactly what happened.

Late in the afternoon her phone rang.

"Hello?"

"Hi Susan, this is Peter. How are you darling?"

"I'm OK."

"That's it? You're just OK? You sound upset. What's the matter?"

Sonofabitch is pretending nothing's happened!

"Nothing,"

"I heard you were looking for me yesterday. I had gone to Medical Records."

"I know. The secretary told me."

"Did you go there looking for me?"

"I did." *I have the key to show for it.*

Peter paused for a moment, assessing Susan's reaction.

"I'm sorry I missed you."

You stupid asshole. You did not miss me.

"I don't think you missed me, Peter. You were busy fucking a woman on her desk. I decided not to intrude."

"What the hell are you talking about Susan. Are you out of your mind?"

Susan exploded.

"You know damn well what I am talking about" she screamed.

"Susan, Susan."

"You stupid sonofabitch couldn't keep your pants up."

"Susan."

"You don't even have the decency to admit it and apologize."

"Susan, please ..."

"How many more mistresses do you have?"

"Susie, listen to me."

"I'm not listening to a piece of shit like you."

"I can explain honey."

"You explain it to the hospital authorities, when I send them the pictures."

"Pictures? What pictures?"

"You were busy but I had all the time in the world to take some pictures. Didn't the bitch tell you? You two make such a nice couple fucking each other."

"Susan, please don't do anything irrational. Please give me a chance to explain."

"Needs no explanation. A picture is worth a thousand words."

"Listen darling. I am going to come over and prove to you that the person you saw was not me."

"Certainly the dick in the picture looked like you. Don't you sonofabitch dare come here. I'll have the police waiting for you."

She hung up.

For the first time today, she felt good.

* * * * *

Three days after the Medical Records event, the Manhattan Medical Center employees list was reduced by two.

Susan Flynn was informed by the OR Supervisor that she was fired because of too many mishaps under her watch. *She refused to write the report she'd been asked for. Nobody disobeys Mary Dorsa.*

Judy Jackson received a letter from Administration thanking her for her services and informing her that the hospital could no more support her employment.

In other words, she was fired.

Judy had reported the loss of her security key. The security department had informed the Administration of unusual activities they had noted inside the Medical Records office the same night the key was lost.

It was discovered later on that shortly before these two employees were fired, the chairman of the Quality Assurance Committee, Dr. Peter Molano had requested and was granted emergency meetings with the Medical Director and a member of the Board of Directors, named Mr. Edward Molano.

* * * * *

SIXTEEN

Before he saw his last few patients, Brian placed a call for Jennifer. She was still at work in the Business office at the New York University Medical Center.

"What are you doing after work today?" Brian asked.

"Had no specific plans, what's up darling?"

"I wonder if you could stop by my office. I have very good news, which is also extremely confidential. We can talk about it in the privacy of my office. By the time you're here, the staff will be gone"

"Um … will six-ish be OK?"

"Perfect. Love you."

"See you then."

His last three patients were routine post-operative follow-ups. No problems, no complications. They were happy, and Brian was elated.

The secretary and two nurses wrapped up and said good-bye.

The only thing that put a slight dent in his unexpected euphoria of the day was the reduction in the number of new patients who had made an appointment for the following week. This was still within the range of seasonal fluctuations and not so unusual, however, in the back of his mind, Brian was concerned that recent events could adversely affect his practice, if publicized and talked about too casually by the physicians who were aware of them.

Well, he decided not to worry about that now.

He took off his white coat and went to a cabinet next to the bookshelves. He opened the solid door and took out two glasses and a bottle of Chivas Regal, Premium Scotch whisky. He got ice from the fridge and prepared two drinks. He then lit a Dunhill International and sank into his leather chair behind his desk.

Moments later, Jennifer walked in.

"Wow, look at this" pointing to the glasses of whisky "what are we celebrating today?" she asked.

Brian jumped off the chair, ran around the desk and hugged her firmly.

They kissed passionately.

"Sit down and relax baby, we have a lot to talk about."
She sat down and picked up her drink and took a sip.

"I got a call from Susan Flynn, earlier this afternoon."
"And ..."
"And she praised me, adored me, worshiped me and repeatedly apologized and expressed regret for what she had done to me and offered to reveal the name of the person or persons involved in an orchestrated conspiracy against me. See, I was right."

"I had no doubt from the very beginning that you had been set up; however, what makes me extremely curious is why she is jumping ship?" she said.

Brian thought for a moment. "If she, in fact, *is* jumping ship. I hope this is not another trap."

"It's not." Jennifer said emphatically. "I know her, I've met her, and she is not lying now."

"How do you know that?"

"With the sexual harassment accusation, they already had you by the balls. That was their strongest weapon against you, and yet, she withdrew her claim. She wrote you a letter of apology, and now she is appeasing you."

"And why is she doing all this?" Brian asked as he blew out a thick cloud of smoke and took a long big sip of scotch.

"Well, I made her believe that you were going to have her fired. She didn't want to lose her job."

"Fair enough. But she was not fired. Why is she still apologizing, and why now?"

Jennifer was now warming up with her whisky and eager for an in-depth analysis.

She made herself another drink.

"My female instincts tell me something else is going on now. I think something has happened between her and whoever was pushing her to act against you, possibly a breakdown of a romantic relationship, something of that nature."

"That's interesting" Brian said "now I see why she wants to reveal some names. Sounds like a revenge." He was all smiles.

"OK. When is she going to give you some names?"

"She has a condition attached to this."

"And what is that?"

"She wants to see Janet Reilly."

"You're kidding?"

"No. I'm dead serious. Since she found out that Janet Reilly was a fake, she's been bugging me to tell her who real Janet Reilly is."

"And what can I ... I mean Janet Reilly ... do now?"

"I think it's time for you to pay her a visit."

"Ok, but I don't think it's good for you that I show my face anywhere in the hospital."

"You're right. Can you call her at home?"

"I think I have her home number."

"Remember, I have asked her to write a detailed account of who is behind this conspiracy, and why she has changed her mind and is now apologizing to me. We need this in writing, Jenny."

"That's smart. When is she going to do that?"

"Before she meets with you. That was my condition for her to see you again."

"Good. Good." She nodded.

"Make sure she'll keep her end of the bargain." Brian was firm.

"You bet."

"OK. Let's go have dinner, I'm hungry."

* * * * *

It looked as though Susan Flynn's miseries were never-ending. Just a short few weeks ago, she was on top of her world. She had a nice job, a distinguished boyfriend and for her hopes and aspirations of a bright future, the sky was the limit.

She was deeply in love with Peter, and he had made her believe that they would have a future together; not knowing that he had promised similar futures to few others not the least of whom was Judy Jackson.

When she was asked by Peter to trap Dr. Brinkley into a sexual harassment scheme, she did not realize how serious a matter that was. She had been told repeatedly by Peter that because of Brian's unprofessional behavior, his surgical practice and that of a few other surgeons were in jeopardy.

So, on the day of the kiddy hernia repair, she played her role skillfully. In fact so skillfully that she goofed on her own job and mixed up the specimens.

The appearance of Janet Reilly on the scene changed everything. Susan became deeply concerned about losing her job, and her anxiety peaked after she read Dr. Brinkley's now infamous letter and the possibility of similar recommendations for her dismissal coming from the Chief of Pathology. By then, she had also become increasingly suspicious of Peter's honesty and true intentions. He showed no concern about Susan's job and would not tell her who those other surgeons were who wanted Dr. Brinkley out. She felt she was being manipulated by him and kept out of the loop. She lost faith in Peter and withdrew her sexual harassment complaint.

The OR committee meeting came and went and her dismissal was proved to be a non-issue. There were no such recommendation and no intention to have her fired. She was ecstatic and yet, uncertain of her relationship with Peter. Perhaps he was right when he repeatedly assured her that she would not be fired.

Then, there came the disturbing realization that Janet Reilly was not who she pretended to be.

This threw Susan into a tremendous confusion with strong feelings of guilt. She didn't know who she could trust anymore. She was angry. Perhaps her fear of being fired was premature. And if in fact Janet Reilly was an agent of Brian Brinkley, he did deserve to be knocked off the staff.

She should not have withdrawn her sexual harassment complaint. And she was truly embarrassed that she did not stay all the way with her beloved Peter.

The pendulum swung again in favor of Peter. Susan made a commitment to find the real Janet Reilly. She made herself accessible to Brian at the cost of leaving her sick patient and spent time with him in the cafeteria.

Her emotional roller coaster flew off the tracks when she followed Peter into the Medical Records Department and personally observed the *real* Dr. Molano in action.

This was a devastating blow to her recently raised hopes and expectations of things finally working out in her favor. She was now furious and bitter. The man who was the object of her hopes and aspirations for a meaningful relationship had used her for his devious intentions against a surgical colleague and manipulated her into committing an immoral act of falsely accusing Dr. Brinkley of sexual harassment. Peter had just destroyed her emotionally.

Her last conversation with Dr. Brinkley and the prospect of finally finding Janet Reilly, pending her writing the whole story of Peter's conspiracy against him, temporarily saved her from the grip of depression and despair. She managed to control her emotions, organize her thoughts and write in revealing details the true identity, character and vicious nature of an immoral demon called Peter Molano. Once this letter finds its way, through Dr. Brinkley and into the hands of the hospital hierarchy, Peter will have to kiss his career good-bye.

The anticipated pleasure of revenge warmed up her heart and relieved the tightness in her chest. She could breathe easier and relax a bit. She felt warm blood flowing again through her body.

She read the letter again and again, revised a few sentences and added a few more. She made sure nothing of substance had been left out. She forced herself to instill every nuance of her feelings, every subtle shade of her emotions, anger, outrage and frustration into every word, sentence and paragraph. *Ah, she felt good. He's going to pay for his actions.*

Susan typed the final version of her manuscript, just to make sure every word and sentence is read and understood correctly. She signed and folded the letter, placed it inside an envelope and sealed it. On the back of the envelope she wrote in large letters **Brian Brinkley, MD.** She collapsed on her bed. Every bone in her body was aching from exhaustion, physically and emotionally. She kept her thoughts focused on how and when she would hear from and see Janet Reilly. Susan was not sure whether she would express happiness and delight of seeing Janet again, or utter anger and outrage at the mischievous tricks Janet had played on her.

Nevertheless, she was cognizant of her need to solicit Janet Reilly's help if she was to be successful in her efforts to destroy Peter's career.

She knew she could have two effective allies in Janet Reilly and Judy Jackson and why not arrange for the three of them to get together and coordinate their actions against Peter.

She would call Judy Jackson and arrange a meeting as soon as she was in contact with Janet Reilly.

Looks good. Very good strategy, indeed. She thought so.

Her new found sense of direction, energy and enthusiasm was, alas, short lived when her phone rang. It was Mary Dorsa, the OR supervisor, who in an unfriendly, cold and frosty voice informed her that she had been fired.

Fired ... But why? Oh no, was this a nightmare or what?
I lost my job after all. Her body was shaking all over.

She smashed the receiver on the phone and threw herself face down on the bed and started crying. She punched the mattress with her clenched fists, kicked the foot of the bed with both legs and thrashed the pillows around. Her screams could hardly escape the choking pressure of her face pushing into the mattress. Her face drenched in the pool of tears on the sheet.

Once her battered body ran out of her last quantum of energy and her tears dried out and her breathing became shallow and sporadic, she passed out.

Hours later, she never knew how long she was out; the incessant ringing of the phone forced her to open her eyes. A huge throbbing headache made her dizzy. Her mouth was dry and bitter, her chest beating with palpitation. The room was dark and the walls were moving around. The phone kept ringing, and each ring sounded like a deafening cannon fire right into her ear.

She mustered whatever strength she had left and fumbled for the phone.

"Hello"

"Hi Susan, this is your old friend Janet."

A moment of silence. She tried to sit up on the bed.

"Janet who?"

"Reilly. Janet Reilly, remember me?"

She paused again. Beginning to wake up.

"Oh. Hello stranger. Is this the invisible Janet Reilly who presumably works in pathology but nobody has ever seen her there?"

"Yes I am, and this is not the time for you to be sarcastic."

"I just wanted to know if this is the fake Janet Reilly or the real whatever your name is."

"You can still call me Janet Reilly. Fake or real I am the one who saved your job and you better remember that."

"Thanks but no thanks. I lost my job anyway."

"I'm sorry to hear that."

"I need to see you Janet. My life is in shambles. Please don't disappear again."

"If you stick with your end of the bargain I'll be happy to see you."

"Sure. The letter is ready. When do I see you?"

"Tomorrow evening at the Lenox Room, up on Seventy Third and Third Avenue. Seven p.m. OK?"

"OK, I know the place. There is only one thing I wanna ask you. Would you mind if I also ask a friend of mine to join us?"

"For what purpose?"

"We're both caught in the middle of the same nightmare and we think you can help us."

"Is she from the hospital?"

"Yes."

"You think there is a connection here between her problems and yours?"

"Most definitely, and it is clearly tied to the events I have described in my letter."

"What's her name?"

"Judy Jackson. She is in charge of Medical Records."

"Listen Susan, I am no therapist, or social worker or public advocate and most certainly I don't want to be involved in hospital affairs. This has to be only on a personal level."

"I promise it will be. I'd appreciate it if you'd only listen to us."

"OK, see you two tomorrow. Don't forget the letter. No letter, no meeting."

"Sure. See you tomorrow."

"Listen, Susan. I don't know your friend and don't like to hang around the bar or the lounge alone for too long. If you don't show up by seven fifteen p.m. I'll be gone for good. You'll never ever find me again."

"I understand. I'll be there on time."

"Bye now."

Susan rubbed her eyes repeatedly, pinched her arm and looked at her surroundings, just to make sure this was not a dream.

It was real.

She couldn't believe she had just talked to Janet Reilly. She could hardly wait to see her. Darn it, she forgot to ask for her telephone number again. Susan anxiously glanced at the readout on the phone for caller ID and was annoyed to see that Janet was calling from a blocked number. Now Susan had no way of contacting her just in case she couldn't make it to the meeting in time. Then she remembered that Janet had refused to give her telephone number in the past. Come to think of it, she thought, Janet was unusually abrupt and cool with her. This was not the Janet she knew. The nice, friendly lady who cared for her and protected her against the demonic authorities who were bound on having her fired.

What the heck, I don't care who Janet Reilly is anymore. She thought.

It was so ironic. She was initially eager to find Janet Reilly in order to help Peter and his plans against Brian Brinkley, and now she is impatiently looking for Janet Reilly in order to help Brian Brinkley and destroy Peter Molano.

Funny, how things can turn and twist in life, and Susan didn't know the worst was yet to come.

She looked at the clock. 5:05 p.m.

She was hoping she could get a hold of somebody at Medical Records and get a telephone number for Judy Jackson.

The person who answered the phone informed her that Judy Jackson was no longer employed by the hospital. And, no, they did not have her home phone number.

Now she had another problem. How could she find Judy? In fact deep down, she was happy that Judy was fired. Despite their unintentional rivalry, she was pleased that Judy did not end up having Peter all for herself. On the other hand, Judy could be a very strong ally now against Peter. She simply had to find her and bring her to the meeting with Janet Reilly.

* * * * *

Peter had not called or visited the Medical Records since his sexual encounter with Judy Jackson and, unbeknownst to him and Judy, within the view of his other girlfriend, Susan Flynn.

The sudden and totally unexpected dismissal of Judy Jackson had puzzled the staff. Naturally rumors were moving from one cubicle to another among the staff, speculating her relationship with hospital authorities and, more so the physicians, amongst whom one name stood out. Peter Molano.

The staff knew that Peter and Judy knew each other for years when they both worked in another hospital in upstate New York. Peter visited Judy here frequently and used to call almost every day.

So, when the call came in from his office, nobody questioned the authenticity of the call.

"Hi, this is Dr. Molano's office. Is Ms. Jackson there by chance?"

"No, she does not work here anymore."

"I understand. Is there a way Dr. Molano can reach her? He had asked her to compile a few charts for the QA Committee.

The secretary pondered for a while.

"I don't know anything about this. I can call her at home and ask."

"I wonder if you can give me her home number. The doctor needs to talk to her urgently."

The secretary hesitated for a while.

The caller jumped in again "Do you wanna talk to Dr. Molano yourself? He's a bit busy with a patient."

"Oh, no. Not really. I suppose Ms. Jackson wouldn't mind. Actually I know she wouldn't mind for Dr. Molano. Here's her phone number."

Susan Flynn wrote the number down and thanked her.

She snapped her fingers in a rare, joyful moment the likes of which she had not experienced recently.

She made herself a cup of coffee, relaxed on the recliner and stretched her legs. She did a mental review of her plan of action against Peter and pondered how she could bring Judy Jackson into her camp.

She picked up the phone and dialed the number in front of her.

"Hello?"

"Hi, Judy. This is Susan. How are you?"

"How dare you call me again? How the hell did you get my home number?"

"Calm down Judy. I need to talk to you, please."

"I have no interest in talking to you. You've destroyed my life. Get off my phone."

"Hey Judy ... Judy. Please listen to me for a minute. I can say the same things about you."

"What the hell are you talking about? You stole my boyfriend, invaded my privacy, stole my security key and because of you I just lost my Job." Judy broke down, sobbing loudly.

"Judy, do you realize that both you and I have been victimized by this fake and phony character, Peter Molano? I told you that I had a relationship with him for the past two years. He pretended he loved me and that I was the only woman in his life. All these times he was also with you and God knows who else."

Judy interrupted "I have a hard time believing this. Our relationship goes back several years when we were both in upstate New York."

"Judy, after I told you about this the other day, did you confront him? Did you question him? What did he tell you?"

"He totally denied that he was with you. He said you'd been stalking him recently. He trashed you and promised me to have you fired."

"Well, sonofabitch was right about that. I was fired alright. But you should know that he also had *you* fired. He is cleaning up after the big mess he's made and he doesn't give a shit about you or me. I told him that I had pictures and that scared the hell out of him. He is a dangerous man."

"What do you want from me now?"

"I want you to believe me. I want you to accept the fact that he is a monster. Let us join our efforts to expose this man and get our jobs back."

"I'll have to think about that. You need to give me some time."

"I'm meeting a friend of mine tomorrow evening. A person who knows a lot about Peter. She warned me to stay away from him and she is going to tell me a lot of things about his background. Her name is Janet Reilly. We've known each other for a long time. Why don't you come and join us tomorrow. What do you have to lose?"

Judy paused for a moment and said "I'll come only if you promise to return my key and destroy the pictures if you in fact have them."

"That's a deal." Susan answered with no hesitation and gave Judy the location and address of the meeting place."

"Seven p.m. sharp, please."

"OK."

* * * * *

SEVENTEEN

The Medical Director raised his voice on the phone impatiently,

"I don't care if it is your lunchtime, Mike. I want you in my office at 1 o'clock sharp."

"Why is this meeting so important and urgent, Joe?"

"I've asked the Chairman of the QA committee to come here to set the agenda for the upcoming meeting. The problems with Dr. Brinkley are piling up. He is a member of your department. Looks like reviewing his cases is going to take up all the time we have for one full session, if not more. We had nine cases to go over and now this trauma case of the other night makes it ten. We can't catch up with this guy's complications."

"OK, Joe. I'll keep an open mind, but let me be up front with you, I think you guys are picking on this young surgeon." Dr. Michael Sloan responded.

"It's our job to protect the reputation and integrity of the hospital, Mike. It's your job too, don't you forget it."

Michael Sloan swallowed his pride and did not respond in kind.

"I'll be there at one. Don't make it drag on forever. I'm busy" he said.

Dr. Joseph Brown, Medical Director, hung up the phone and called his secretary

"Nancy, please call Dr. Molano and ask him to be here no later than twelve thirty p.m. I need to talk to him privately before the one o'clock meeting. And, by the way, when the Chief of Surgery comes here make sure we're not interrupted for an hour or so. No calls please."

"You got it Chief." Nancy Robertson acknowledged.

"Do we have all the charts here?"

"Have them all. In fact it was easy to find them. For some reason Judy Jackson had put them all together before she was fired."

"Very nice. Thank you."

Michael Sloan walked into the Medical Directors office at one o'clock sharp, still in his scrub suit and a white lab coat.

"Hey guys. What are you up to?"

Peter Molano greeted the Chief and said "Up to the case number ten!" Pointing to the pile of charts on the desk in a sarcastic gesture.

Dr. Brown interrupted them. "Please sit down Mike. Before we go over these cases, I want to let you know that in our opinion the sexual harassment charge against Dr. Brinkley is still open and I may in fact convene the Ethics committee to investigate."

Michael Sloan frowned and could not hide his anger.

"How could you do that? Didn't the nurse withdraw her complaint?"

"She did, but we have reasons to believe that she was coerced into doing that by an imposter claiming to be Dr. Gonzalez' secretary. This is sabotage and we believe Dr. Brinkley had a hand in it and we should not let him off the hook so easily."

Dr. Sloan was deep in thought, trying to comprehend the plot behind all this.

"Can you prove that such an imposter existed?" he asked.

"Of course" Peter responded. "Susan Flynn will testify, and we already have the fictitious letter Dr. Brinkley presumably wrote to the OR Committee asking for Susan's dismissal. The letter he never sent to the committee but was used to intimidate Susan ..."

"Wait a minute" Dr. Sloan interrupted. "Susan Flynn was fired the other day, allegedly for negligence at work. She is not going to testify in support of the hospital, and even if she does, her testimony will not be credible."

"Don't worry, Mike." The Medical Director interjected "she will say whatever we want her to say when we offer her job back."

Michael Sloan looked quite disturbed.

"What ever you want her to say?" *Smells like a conspiracy to me.* "You fired her and now you are hiring her back on the condition of complicity with your plans?"

"Well I just mentioned this to you as a point of information. Let's go over these cases. We need you to prioritize these in order of seriousness, so that we can spend the appropriate amount of time on each one."

"Do you have a summary of each case? I don't have enough time for all of these charts."

Peter Molano pulled the charts nearby and opened them one by one and read a brief summary of each case. Dr. Sloan was impressed that Peter had done his homework so well. He sensed Peter's special interest in these cases. *I wonder why?* He pondered. On other occasions he had often found him aloof and uninterested in the process.

The two more serious cases worthy of investigation were the kiddy hernia repair and the trauma case. All the other ones did not appear to represent a significant deviation from the standards of surgical practice. Why these cases had been picked he did not know but for the time being he decided not to make a big deal out of it.

Dr. Molano brought up a most unusual suggestion.

"We will review all these cases at the QA Committee meeting, but I don't think it is necessary for Dr. Brinkley to be there."

The Medical Director nodded in approval, but Dr. Sloan objected strongly.

"It is against the Rules and Regulations. He should be there to explain. You cannot investigate him without his presence."

Peter Molano tried hard to hold his ground "Listen Chief, it is our job to determine if he has deviated from the standard and acceptable practice of surgery. His explanations would be invalid anyhow."

"I beg to differ with you, Peter." Dr. Sloan tried to keep his cool. "You cannot try the guy in absentia when he is available to defend himself. It is wrong and I will not stand for it."

Peter glanced at the Medical Director, looking for support.
"I'll check the By-Laws and let you know" he said.

Dr. Sloan was not satisfied.
"I think it is imperative that he should be called to attend. I also think you should write to him and give him a list of these cases so that he can prepare his response."

Dr. Sloan finally prevailed. He was reassured by the Medical Director that Dr. Brinkley will be notified and asked to attend the meeting.

After Dr. Sloan left, the Medical Director turned to Peter,
"Don't worry about him. I'll make sure Brian will not come to the meeting."
"That'll make things easier" Peter nodded.
"If we get to the Ethics Committee meeting, are you sure you can have Susan Flynn come in and testify against Brian?"
"I am, Joe. Don't worry; I'll make sure she'll come."

* * * * *

Rumors were flying fast throughout the four corners of the Manhattan Medical Center about a young surgeon who was the most popular among the nurses and hospital staff.

In the coffee shop, cafeteria, the lobby and wherever few staff members gathered together around the water coolers or coffee machines for a short break, the talk of the day was about Dr. Brian Brinkley and unconfirmed accusations of sexual harassment against him.

Granted, he was young, single, attractive and popular, nevertheless nobody perceived him as a philanderer, womanizer or a jerk. He was witty, sociable and pleasant, but those who knew him well had a very hard time to believe the accusations of sexual harassment against him. This was serious and dangerous.

For a long time Brian had been the subject of much gossip. He obviously enjoyed the company of young and attractive women. He always had female companions at the coffee shop or cafeteria. But those curious, nosy women could not tie him to any serious relationship.

There were rumors that he was hiding his personal life outside the hospital. There were talks about a gorgeous beauty who, on occasion, had been spotted dropping him off or picking him up at the main entrance.

So, where did this sexual harassment rumor come from and how did it happen, nobody knew. Nevertheless, the rumor carried with it additional bits and pieces of information that gave credence to the accuracy of the matter. The incident had happened in the OR and the nurse involved had refused to come to work the past few days. And Dr. Brinkley had been summoned to the OR Committee to be questioned about this matter.

There was also a day that he abruptly cancelled his cases. Most unusual for the most active surgeon on the staff.

Gradually the rumor worked its way from the lower level staff, employees, secretaries, nurses etc, to the Medical Staff.

In the Doctors Lounges there were whispers about Brian Brinkley to the amazement of his friends and curiosity and concern of those who had a working relationship with him, those who referred patients to him and depended on his expertise.

As to the authenticity of these rumors, most of the physicians laughed it off. Brian was a gentleman, not a jerk. This simply couldn't be true. But a few who were present at the OR Committee meeting witnessed the discussions between him and the Chairman on this issue and the explosive exchange between him and the Medical Director who accused him of intimidating the nurse to withdraw her claim. Something had happened for sure, and now rumors were spreading all over the place like a dark cloud covering a bright sun.

This was not good for Brian's future.

In this era of political correctness, even the appearance of wrongdoing was enough to tarnish one's reputation and destroy professional careers.

And this is exactly why Brian hung up the phone angrily and fumed, "I could never believe these guys would question me seriously. They've been my friends and now I cannot convince them that there is a conspiracy going on against me." He lifted his gaze from the phone to the other side of his desk, there was nobody there. He was talking to himself. For the first time he was beginning to grasp the enormity of the matter. These guys could stop sending him patients and destroy a successful practice he'd been building up with hard work and personal sacrifice.

After he had received Susan Flynn's letter of apology and had become aware of her withdrawing the sexual harassment accusation, he was optimistic that the matter had been put to rest. The incident was just a bump in the road.

Now he was realizing that the issue had developed a tenacious life of its own. It was not simply going away.

Who was feeding these rumors to the crowd? And how could he stem the tide of these devastating storms rushing to destroy him?

Now more than ever he needed Susan Flynn.

He thought he better call Jennifer and find out if she had contacted Susan yet. The statement he had asked of Susan would hopefully put an end to all of this. He would take the matter directly to the highest authorities of the hospital and bypass all the committee meetings and bureaucratic red tape, he would fight the delaying tactics by his adversaries and reveal the identities of those who'd been plotting this conspiracy against him and demand reparation.

If necessary he would take the matter outside this institution to the Department of Health, the highest health care authority of the State of New York. For a moment he even thought of taking legal action against the hospital if his practice suffered from this incident, but the thought of getting lawyers involved made him cringe. The Department of Health would be a good place to go.

His train of thought was broken when his secretary walked in with a bunch of mail she thought he had to see. He asked for two Extra Strength Tylenol tablets and a cup of coffee.

His head was throbbing and he was in bad mood.

The mail was mostly bills, amongst them his quarterly malpractice insurance premium of nineteen thousand dollars, reflecting a fifteen percent increase recently implemented. It was a thorn in his side. With insurance reimbursements continuously decreasing and overhead expenses such as payroll, office rent and supplies costs skyrocketing, the malpractice premium was reaching a critical point. Years ago, the cost of malpractice insurance coverage could be passed on to the patients, but no more. Under Health Maintenance Organization (HMO) contracts he was obligated to accept whatever they paid for office consultations, hospital visits and surgical procedures, and HMO's were unilaterally slashing the reimbursements every year.

Brian was beginning to feel the pinch, despite the fact that he had one of the busiest and most active surgical practices amongst his colleagues. There was no more room to compensate the ever rising costs of the practice by increasing the volume. There were only so many patients he could see or surgical procedures he could perform a day. He was stuck between the proverbial rock and a hard place.

The last letter he opened was from the Office of the Medical Director of the Manhattan Medical Center. *Adding insult to the injury.*

The letter consisted of two parts. He was informed that the next meeting of the Quality Assurance Committee (QA) would be held the following week as usual on Wednesday morning and a number of his cases were up for review by the committee. He was not required to attend, although he could if he chose to.

What the heck is this? They can review my cases without my presence? He was outraged. To make matters worse, there was only a passing reference to the number of cases being reviewed, but no names or medical records numbers.

The second part was more serious and disconcerting. The Administration was deeply concerned about the sexual harassment accusation against him and, despite the fact that the original complaint had been withdrawn there were reasons to believe that an investigation was warranted and therefore the matter will be referred to the Ethics Committee and he will be required to attend.

The letter was signed by the staff secretary on behalf of the Medical Director.

Brian crumbled the letter in his hand and tossed it angrily into the paper basket.

He then picked up the phone and called Dr. Sloan, Chairman of the Department of Surgery.

"Hello Chief. This is Brian."

"Hi, Brian. What's up?"

"Are you aware of the QA Committee meeting agenda for next week?"

"Yes I am. *You* are the agenda. It'll be all about you."

"Damn right. And they tell me I don't even have to be there."

"They wouldn't dare. I told them they cannot do this without your presence and they accepted."

"Not according to this letter they just sent me. They say I don't have to be there but I can attend if I choose to do so."

"I am absolutely furious. These assholes are trying to get you."

"Who ... Chief ... who are they?"

The Chief remained quiet, he wasn't sure if he should give any names to Brian, in case he was wrong in his suspicion. Brian sensed the Chief's hesitation.

"I understand if you don't want to give me names. I am doing my own investigations and there is a strong possibility that within the next few days I will have the names I need to know. I think at least one of them is the Medical Director, but for the life of me I don't understand why he should be after me. Who are the other ones? That's what I want to know. They obviously want to find me at fault with every one of those cases and it is easier for them if I am not there to explain and dispute their conclusions. As a matter of fact, I may exercise the option they have given me and choose not to attend. Then I can protest the whole proceedings as being illegal and unacceptable."

"Calm down, Brian." Dr. Sloan tried to cool him off. "I won't give you names because it will not be fair to you or to them if I am wrong. These matters have to be worked out within the system. You absolutely should attend the meeting and put your arguments and responses on the record."

"I don't even know what cases they're going to discuss."

"They were supposed to send you a list of the patients. Don't tell me they didn't."

"Nope. No names, no numbers, nothing."

"I don't like the sound of this at all. Could you fax me the letter right now?"

"I will"

"Right now, Brian."

"OK, Chief. Have a good day."

Brian hung up the phone and called his secretary.

Moments later the secretary walked in. Brian was missing behind his desk. She looked further in and found him bent over the waste basket. As she watched with amazement he pulled out a small ball of crumbled paper and handed it to the secretary.

"Fax this to Dr. Sloan."

She stared at the crunched paper in the palm of her hand and frowned.

"What is this?" she asked.

"Fax the damn thing." Brian was in no mood to explain.

* * * * *

EIGHTEEN

Susan stepped out of the shower and wrapped her robe around her wet body and anxiously ran into her bedroom to check the clock. It was 5:30 p.m. Ample time to get ready and leave.

She tried to remain calm and relaxed, as if this was to be a casual get together with an old friend, but she knew it was not. Many different thoughts racing in her head were competing for her conscious attention and yet one would jump ahead of the other as she contemplated her approach to Janet Reilly. Should she meet her with a big smile, enthusiastic hand shake and exchange of pleasantries, or should she keep her composure, be a bit cold and frosty expressing her displeasure of the mischievous behavior in the past.

She was well aware of how badly Brian Brinkley was in need of the letter. He was in deep trouble with the hospital authorities and his career was on the line, not to mention the disastrous consequences of a sexual harassment accusation.

This letter alone can save his ass for good. Susan obviously had the upper hand in this exchange and she was determined to play her card well.

She would demand that Dr. Brinkley go full force after Peter Molano and expose him for the devious conspirator he was and see to it that they kicked his ass out of the medical community. *That's what he deserves.*

She planned her timing to eliminate any possibility of being late or missing Janet altogether, in which case she would never find her again. She would leave her apartment at six fifteen, pick up her car from the garage and head for the Lenox Room, a trendy restaurant with a bar and lounge, up at 3rd avenue and 73rd Street. Barring unusual traffic, she would get there by six forty-five, relax at the bar and have a drink before Janet arrives.

By 6 o'clock Susan was all dressed, make-up and hair complete and the letter securely tucked inside her purse. She placed a quick call to Judy Jackson, but had to leave a message for her. *Please Judy, don't miss this opportunity. See you at the Lenox Room. Be there at seven. Bye.*

She heard a knock at her door. That was strange. Perhaps she didn't hear the doorbell while she was talking into the phone. Another knock and the doorknob rattled.
Had to be her neighbor. She often didn't bother to call.

"Wait Barbara, I'll be right there." Susan hollered.
The doorknob was shaking more fiercely and the whole door jolted. *That couldn't be Barbara.* She thought and panic set in. Somebody was trying to force the door open. She noted the security chain was not on. Next she heard a harsh creaking noise. The doorframe cracked and the knob was about to give way. She lunged for the security chain, but it was too late. Another jolt and the door swung open. Susan froze. Standing at the threshold was Dr. Peter Molano.

He was just as surprised to see Susan. He had called several times. No answer. Susan was in the shower. He had rung the doorbell a few times. Susan was on the phone, leaving a message. He was certain she wasn't home. *Good time to search her apartment.* He thought.

Instinctively Susan slammed the door closed, but Peter's foot was through the door and he smashed the door open again and stepped in. He attempted to close the door behind him but the frame was broken and the door would not shut.

Susan lunged for the phone and picked up the receiver.
"Get out … I'm calling the police."

Peter's heavy hand clamped around her wrist and with a quick twist knocked off the receiver and yanked the cord off the wall. The phone went dead.

Susan pulled back to the wall, rubbing her bruised wrist with other hand.

Peter stood at the door and flashed a big smile.

"Susie baby calm down. I'm not here to hurt you."

"You sonofabitch, get out of my apartment, NOW." She shrieked.

"Don't force me to hurt you. C'mon here sit down, I want to talk to you."

"What do you want?"

"I wanna get your job back for you."

"Forget it. I don't need a job."

"OK, then. You be a good girl. Give me the security key you stole from Medical Records and the pictures you took."

"You have no right to be here. Get out of my apartment and I will try to find the key for you."

"No deal baby. Don't play games with me."

Peter's eyes were blazing with anger. His face was flushed and his neck veins were sticking out. A feature Susan had never seen. *The beast is showing his face now.* She reached an antique Chinese cabinet and opened a drawer. She pulled out the Medical Record security key and tossed it towards Peter.

"Take it, you bustard. You'll probably need it when you fuck another girl in there."

Peter caught the key in the air.

"And the pictures?" He asked.

"You stupid ass. You think I keep the pictures in my apartment?"

"Where are they?"

"In a safety deposit box at the bank."

"You're lying to me and you'll pay for this."

Susan took a glance at the clock. 6:45 p.m. She jumped into the kitchen and reached for the knife on the counter.

Peter stood at the door and frowned.

"You step back, all the way back to the door" she demanded.

Peter slowly moved backwards, keeping a sharp gaze at the knife in her hand. Susan jumped and reached the phone on the wall, picked up the receiver and quickly dialed zero and left the receiver hanging in the air. She then shrieked as loudly as she could.

"Help me please; I'm being attacked ..." Her mouth was forcefully shut by Peter's big hand. His arm wrapped around her neck and squeezed. She gasped for air. He jolted her body and tightened the grip around her neck. She dropped the knife. Her chest was heaving for air. She was dizzy and semi-conscious, the room was turning dark, and her vision was blurred. She stretched her arm and tried to reach the counter for anything she could grab. She forced her body backwards, pulling Peter with her. For a second he lost his footing and wobbled. Susan reached the sink and grabbed another knife and exerting every bit of force she could muster, she plunged the knife deep into Peter's groin.

A loud scream followed and he fell on the floor, bending over his thigh trying to pull out the knife.

Susan found herself tumbling into the living room, as she was sucking in as much air as she could into her lungs. Her heart was punching into her ribs.

She managed to regain her balance. Her purse was on top of the antique cabinet. The clock flashed 6:55 p.m.

Peter dragged himself to the kitchen doorway, leaving a trail of blood behind him.

Susan grabbed the purse and ran out of the door, into the hallway. The elevator was nearby but it would take too long. She took the stairway and ran to the first floor, through the lobby and out of the building.

There was a separate entrance to the basement garage, but the door was closed. She ran back into the lobby and down the stairway into the garage and reached her car.

The clock on the dashboard read 7:01 p.m.

Susan revved the engine and pulled out of the parking spot. A loud screeching noise echoed in the air as she pressed the button on the remote control and opened the garage door and rushed into the street.

She had an appointment to keep at all cost. *The hell with Peter and the apartment.*

Peter managed to control the bleeding by wrapping his belt as a tourniquet above the stab wound just below his left groin. He had lost a fair amount of blood by then.

He knew he had to run to an Emergency Room somewhere. The stab wound was on the inner aspect of his left upper thigh, high near the groin, and in the vicinity of a major artery.

He dragged his left foot around the apartment and pulled out every drawer and opened every cabinet he could find looking for pictures. None were found. He was in severe pain.

He reached for the computer. The tower was under the desk. He had no time to search the files. He unplugged the tower, ripped open the side door and pulled out the wide ribbon connected to the motherboard. He disconnected the memory card and took it out.

Susan's computer was just assassinated.

Reaching back into the kitchen he noted the phone receiver dangling on its cord. He picked it up and heard a female voice calling in.

"Hello, are you still there. This is the operator. The police are on the way."

He ripped off the cord and tossed the receiver.

He was dizzy and unsteady on his feet. He went into the hall towards the elevator. As he pushed the button, the door opened. He went in and pushed the basement button. The elevator door opened at the first floor, lobby level. At a glance he saw the police officers talking to the doorman. The elevator door closed again and he exited at the basement level and out the side door into the street and reached his parked car.

As he pulled away, road blocks were being placed by the police, securing the area.

* * * * *

The bartenders were getting ready for the busy night ahead, but the lounge was still quiet. Only a few people were hanging around waiting to be seated at the restaurant.

Jennifer Bradley looked at her watch and shook her head in anger. It was 7:20 p.m. She had vowed to leave at 7:15 if Susan didn't show up.

Jennifer finished her first drink and ordered another one. She knew she couldn't leave just yet.

A well dressed, stylish young lady was pacing the short hall between the lounge and the restaurant and checking her watch frequently. At 7:30 p.m. she kept glancing at Jennifer realizing that she was also looking at her watch frequently. *That has to be Janet Reilly.*

Finally, she couldn't wait anymore. She walked towards Jennifer and caught her attention.

"Excuse me. Looks like you are also waiting for a friend."

"And she is half an hour late. Hi, you must be Miss Judy Jackson." Jennifer responded.

Judy reached for a handshake "And you are Miss Janet Reilly?"

"Yes I am. Nice to meet you, please sit down."

"Susan told me you are a close friend."

"That's right, but not for much longer. She was supposed to be here no later than seven fifteen."

"I'm sure she'll be here soon. There was a lot of traffic on Third Avenue."

"There is always a lot of traffic here. I hope she didn't change her mind."

"Oh, no, actually she left me a message around six o'clock to make sure I'd come."

"So we'll wait for her a bit longer."

"I've called her apartment several times. The phone was busy. She might have left the receiver off the hook." Judy said.

"And I have tried her cell phone several times. No answer." Jennifer responded.

"Susan has been under a lot of stress recently. You know she lost her job?"

"She told me and that's why she wanted to meet with me tonight." Jennifer sounded impatient.

"I don't know why she wanted me to meet you too" Judy inquired.

"She said you two were sharing a common dilemma and she thought

I could help. I don't know what she meant by that."

"Well, I lost my job too."

Jennifer remained quiet for a while. She looked at her watch and glanced at the door a few times.

Judy looked more restless and worried. She opened her cell phone and called Susan's cell. No answer. She left a message.

Ten more minutes went by. They both looked tense and irritated.

Jennifer looked at her watch. It showed 7:50 p.m.

"Listen Judy, I can't wait anymore. Why don't you give me your phone number and we'll get together some other time."

"I'm really sorry, Janet. I'm sure she had a flat tire or something."

Judy gave her cell phone number to Jennifer and stood up to leave.

"When you talk to Susan, tell her not to call me anymore. I'll get in touch with her."

Judy was dismayed by Janet's nastiness. She had no idea that Susan had no way of reaching her.

"I'm sure she has a good explanation for this."

* * * * *

Susan struggled to control the vehicle, despite a sharp piercing pain in her neck and throat, difficulty breathing, blurred vision, pain and swelling on her right wrist, palpitation and extreme anxiety. She could not afford to miss the meeting with Janet. The car veered right and left trying to pass every moving vehicle she could.

She almost side-swiped a few vans and trucks, changing lanes frequently. She reached Third Avenue and headed north. *Every God damn traffic light turns red on me today.* She cursed.

Pedestrians were crossing the road irrespective of the signals. She almost hit a couple of them.

At the intersection with 42nd Street the traffic came to a standstill.

The clock read 7:09 p.m.

She pounded the steering wheel with her fist and screamed. A symphony of blowing horns filled the air. She was at least ten cars behind the traffic light and could not see what was holding up the traffic. Then she heard the sirens of fire trucks and a few police cars.

Five painful minutes passed until traffic started moving again, ever so slowly.

She veered to the middle lane where the cars appeared to be moving faster.

She looked at the clock. 7:14 p.m.

She had no chance to make it in time, unless, hoping against hope, Janet decided to stay longer.

A yellow cab cut her off sharply and almost collided with her car. She was furious and restless. *Typical Manhattan traffic, God damn it!*

As she approached 59th Street the traffic slowed down and stopped again. She was two cars behind the traffic light which was green but the first row of cars would not advance. She couldn't tell what was going on. She kept blowing the horn steadily. *Another thirteen blocks and she would make it there.*

She had no way of knowing that a fatal traffic accident occurred at 59th and Madison. Emergency rescue vehicles were rushing to the area and a single police officer was holding the traffic at 59th and Third. Two cars on her left were allowed to make a left turn and leave. She saw an opening and sharply switched lanes and hit the side of an SUV moving forward but she managed to get ahead of it. The loud bang of the collision shook her up. No way could she get stuck here for a little fender bender. Through the rear view mirror she saw the driver of the SUV getting out of the car. She had to get out of here. Now she found no other cars ahead of her, no traffic through the intersection and the road ahead looked deserted, no cars in sight for several blocks. In an instantaneous urge to get through, she floored the accelerator and the car zoomed forward with a thunderous roar. She had no chance to hear the siren of an approaching ambulance which slammed into the passenger side of her car at eighty five miles an hour.

Her car jumped in the air, rolled over and smashed into the police car parked on 59th Street.

Susan felt the initial impact as her head smashed into the windshield. She uttered a deep howl as the steering wheel pressed into her chest. She felt the sheering crackles of her ribs crushing. The car landed upside down. Her smashed body was dangling by the seat belt. Blood was pouring out of a deep gash on top of her head. She was gasping for air; each breath felt like a stab into her chest, her face turned blue and swelled as the gravity pulled the blood down into her neck and face. Her gaze froze on the pool of blood uddle on the ceiling of the car.

Suddenly she felt no more pain, no more struggle to breathe in, no more rattling sounds of her rolling car, there was eerie silence as her surroundings immersed into eternal darkness. She was at peace with herself. She was gone.

* * * * *

NINETEEN

"American flight 292, you are cleared for take off" the control tower announced.

"American 292. Thank you Sir. We're ready to roll" the Captain responded.

The mighty Boeing 757 started rolling down the runway with a thunderous roar and lifted in the air like a feather riding a gentle wind.

The climb to ten thousand feet was smooth, as the aircraft left Kennedy airport behind, looped around and headed south.

The flight attendant asked the passengers to remain seated until the Captain turned off the Fasten Seat Belt signs. The use of electronic devices was now allowed.

Moments later the Captain's voice came on, welcoming the passengers and announcing the flight plan.

"We shall be cruising at an altitude of thirty eight thousand feet. There are a few pockets of turbulence; otherwise we expect a smooth ride to the Bahamas. Our estimated flight time is two hours fifty eight minutes. Please sit back and enjoy the flight.

Brian gently released his hand from the firm, nervous grip of Jennifer and smiled.

"I can't believe we finally left this God damn city."

"It's about time, Brian. We deserve a vacation." Jennifer grabbed his arm and rested her head on his shoulder. She was happy she'd pushed him to get out of town for few days.

In fact, they had been through many pockets of turbulence within the past two months. They were both still deeply in shock from the tragic death of Susan Flynn one month earlier and Brian still faced an uphill battle against a hostile environment in which he had built up his practice.

Another seemingly unrelated event was the mysterious injury of the chairman of the QA committee, Dr. Peter Molano, who had been hospitalized at New York University Medical Center the same day Susan Flynn was killed in a car accident.

The news of his accident and subsequent surgery at NYU was sketchy and shrouded in mystery. He had declined visitors and did not take any telephone calls. Nevertheless there were rumors whispered around that he had been mugged in downtown Manhattan and stabbed in the groin, severing his femoral artery.

He had undergone major vascular surgery and had run into complications. There was concern that he might lose his leg.

Jennifer, as the manager of the business office at NYU, was privy to some internal information and knew that Peter Molano had been questioned by police several times. Whether this was in relation to the mugging or something else was not clear, but what had puzzled Jennifer was the fact that he was under twenty four hours surveillance by the police guarding his room and isolating him from the public. *Was he a victim or a suspect?*

Dr. Brinkley had received word through the Medical Director's office that the QA Committee meeting had been postponed until further notice. There was no word about the Ethics Committee or Medical Board meeting.

Everything appeared to be quiet for a while. His practice was also slow, which had caused a great deal of concern for him, although he couldn't do anything about it.

The previous week Brian had invited a few of his colleagues, mostly his referring physicians to a dinner. Unexpectedly several of them declined the invitation on grounds of having other engagements. Brian sensed there was clearly a tinge of reluctance in his friends to continue their close association with him in the face of sexual harassment rumors.

Brian was badly damaged already.

Susan Flynn's tragic demise dealt a devastating blow to his hopes of finding out who was behind all these efforts to discredit him and destroy his professional career. In fact he was within minutes of obtaining extremely vital information from Susan. Brian was upset, nervous, moody and restless. It was time for a vacation.

The flight was smooth and landed at Nassau International Airport on time. A private limousine from the Atlantis Resort and Casino was waiting for them. The twenty five minute ride took them through the town, over the bridge and into Paradise Island.

It was a balmy eighty five degrees with a refreshing mild early afternoon breeze.

Jennifer was anxious to hit the beach and dip into the crisp, crystal clear ocean, but they had to check in first.

A luxurious suite at the Royal tower was waiting for them.

Once their luggage was delivered they closed the door and jumped into each other's arms and kissed passionately. For a change they were jovial and even playful like two little kids surrounded by new toys.

Brian made dinner reservation at the Bahamian Club.

They changed into their bathing suits and went to the beach. The ocean was calm and inviting. The water was crystal clear and a bit cool. They swam and played for a little while and then stretched on the warm sands soaking in the sun. After a short nap they went back in the water and washed up.

A long walk along the beach followed as they were consumed in the immense pleasure of being thousands of miles away from the hectic and crazy life of New York.

They left the beach and followed the walkway towards Coral Tower and stopped at Lagoon Bar and Grill. They refreshed with cold beer and Brian lit a cigarette. They relaxed on comfortable chairs and enjoyed the soft afternoon breeze. Brian could not hold off raising the question he was desperately looking for an answer.

"Jenny, what happened to Susan? Why did she die? What made her rush her car through an intersection that was being cleared by police? This could not have been a simple accident."

"It's a mystery Brian. I agree with you" She responded.

"There are a lot of questions in my mind about this accident" Brian followed "I wonder if she was running away from a threat or even being chased by somebody. After all she was coming to you to reveal some names, remember?" Brian took a deep drag and shook his head.

"She had some enemies for sure. Perhaps a breakdown of a close romantic relationship, but, I can't imagine anybody wanted her killed" Jennifer said.

"I think there is a lot more to this accident than meets the eye. Susan was a bright girl and a very good nurse. She was not insane."

"Do we know anything about the police report?" Jenny asked.

"No, but newspaper reports indicated that the police found nothing wrong with the car, and she was not under the influence of alcohol or drugs."

Brian blew smoke in the air and heaved a deep sigh.

"Someday we'll find out a lot more about this. Hope it wouldn't be too late for us." His voice reflecting a deep emotional struggle.

Oh God. I hope he doesn't feel responsible for what happened to Susan. Jennifer pondered. She began to realize that despite Susan's unfair and untrue accusations against Brian, he is deeply saddened by her death and the fact that he's been a party to this tragic event, even though unwillingly, his conscience is overwhelmed with guilt.

She reached and put her arm around his shoulder and looked straight into his eyes.

"What's bothering you, Brian? You are also a victim in this tragedy." She voiced lovingly.

"Victim or not, I had a role in this scenario" Brian lit another cigarette and continued "I am dying to find out who used her and what happened in her personal life when she came to me and apologized. Dammit, we were so close to find everything out."

"Brian, we came here to forget all this for a few days. Remember?" She got up and sat on his lap. "I promise you the truth will come out soon."

The beauty of the surrounding scenery, the chirping of nearby seagulls and the music of the wind finally prevailed to break their grievous conversation.

They went back to their suite and took a warm shower together and enjoyed each other's naked body to the fullest.

After a short rest they dressed up and left the room. Brian was anxious to go to the casino and gamble. Jennifer longed for the shops. They decided they would meet at eight p.m. at the Bahamian Club for dinner.

Jennifer arrived at the restaurant at eight sharp. She paced the hall and kept looking at her watch. Brian was late. She thought if she went to the casino looking for him he might appear here and not find her. Fifteen minutes passed. No Brian. After twenty five minutes she decided to walk towards the casino. As she walked down the hall she spotted him rushing in with a big smile.

"Sorry baby, I was on a roll, couldn't leave the table. You know in black-jack you rarely hit a winning streak. I hit a big one tonight."

He pulled out of his pocket a glittering five thousand dollar chip and put it in Jennifer's hand.

She looked at it and almost let out a cheerful scream.

"You've got to be kidding me. Did you win this?" She gazed at the beautiful chip.

"No. they gave it to me for charity." He said jokingly. They both broke into a loud laughter.

"I'm lucky tonight, baby. Let's go eat." He grabbed her hand and pulled her towards the restaurant.

They dined on the finest steak one could find in the Bahamas, drank a full bottle of Merlot and topped it off with delicious dessert of Crème Brule. They were stuffed.

Jennifer decided to call it a night and go to bed.

Brian was anxious to get back to the table. He promised he would come upstairs no later than midnight. He was lying. All gamblers do.

Jennifer was awakened at 4 a.m. by the sound of the door closing. Brian tip toed in and got undressed and sneaked into the bed.

"What time is it?" she mumbled.

"Not too late baby. I'm sorry I woke you up."

"How did you do?"

"I won again."

"Good, how much?"

He put his arm around her and whispered into her ear "I have three of those chips now"

"Wow ... good."

They kissed and said good night.

The following morning they celebrated their good fortune by ordering room service breakfast shortly after they returned from an hour of working out in the gym.

Their second and third days at the resort were the happiest times they had spent together in a very long time.

Exercise, breakfast and a stroll by the beach in the morning, a quick lunch and then having sex and a short nap in the comfort of their luxurious and cozy suite followed by Jacuzzi and a few laps in the indoor pool in the afternoon, a couple hours of gambling for Brian and shopping for Jenny in the evening, then dinner and back to black-jack tables for Brian until the wee hour of the morning. Jennifer preferred going to bed early, reading a book and falling asleep.

Brian added more to his win column although on the third night he had to struggle to win back some of the money he had lost earlier in the evening.

Altogether, he had won more than twenty thousand dollars in three days.

On the fourth day, all hell broke loose.

* * * * *

Back in New York the Chairman of the Department of Surgery received a most unexpected and unusual visitor.

Dr. Sloan was in his office reviewing a few charts when the secretary stuck her head in and said "Dr. Sloan, there is a gentleman here to see you."

"Who is he?"

"Detective Robert Coleman from the police department."

"Police Department? What does he want?"

The secretary shrugged "He wants to see you."

"OK, send him in"

The plainclothes detective walked in and shook hands with the Chief.

"I apologize for coming in here without advance notice, Dr. Sloan, but we thought it's important to brief you on several issues involving three members of your department."

The Chief couldn't conceal his puzzlement. He frowned and fixed his gaze on the detective whose sharp instincts realized Dr. Sloan's bafflement.

He sank into his chair and nodded the detective to sit down.

"This is only an exchange of information, Doctor," The detective said with a calm and reassuring voice. "But, you may be able to shed some light on a few unsolved issues we have."

"Anything I can do to help" he replied.

"Thank you Sir. I want to discuss the tragic death of Susan Flynn with you. I trust you are familiar with what happened to her."

"Of course I am. What a freaky accident."

"Well, Dr. Sloan, what appeared to be a simple car accident has turned out to be a lot more complicated?"

"Is that right?" the Chief asked with intense interest.

"Yes Sir. We have discovered evidence of criminal activity at her apartment shortly before the time of her death, which means she had fled her apartment fearing for her life."

"And how did you come across this information, if I may ask?" Dr. Sloan inquired.

"We think she was attacked at her apartment by an intruder. She dialed the operator on her phone and left the receiver off the hook. Very smart thing to do. She was heard screaming and the background noise was suggestive of an altercation. The police arrived shortly after she and the intruder had left the apartment. The door frame was broken; a sign of forced entry, and the place was ransacked. We found traces of blood on the kitchen floor, which did not match her blood. Obviously it belonged to the intruder."

"Do you have an ID for the intruder?" Dr. Sloan asked.

"Not positively, but we have come across two names you could call them persons of interest. We are seeking information about these two people."

"Who are they?"

The detective took a glance at his notes in his hand.

"A doctor Brian Brinkley and a woman by the name of Janet Reilly. Do you know these people doctor?"

"I know Dr. Brinkley very well, and for the life of me I can never believe that he had anything to do with this."

"He's not a suspect yet, but his name appears repeatedly in Susan Flynn's diary, the one we found in her apartment."

"He worked with Susan in the operating room. He is a surgeon."

"How about a sexual harassment accusation? You know anything about that?"

"There was a complaint filed by Susan against Dr. Brinkley some time ago and later on she withdrew her complaint."

"We are very much interested in speaking with this doctor. Where could we find him?"

"He is on vacation out of the country. I'll have my secretary give you his office phone number."

The detective was deep in thought. "Out of the country? … Um … Is he planning to come back?"

"Of course. You think he may have *fled* the country?" The Chief asked sarcastically.

"Dr. Sloan. Our job as detectives is to connect the dots. The man has sexually harassed the lady, she files a complaint against him, and he forcibly enters her apartment, they get into a fight, somehow she manages to injure him and leave a deposit of his blood on her kitchen floor, she flees her apartment rushing to keep an important appointment with this other lady, Janet Reilly, and gets killed in a car accident. It's a completely plausible scenario. Don't you think?"

"You can't be serious detective. Your hypothetical scenario is full of holes. To begin with, there is no more sexual harassment complaint against Dr. Brinkley. You have no proof that *he* was the one who forced his way into Susan's apartment. Do you? You have no proof that *his* blood was spilled on the kitchen floor. Do you? Don't you think you are convicting the man before he is accused of anything?"

"We're not convicting anybody. We are only interested to talk to this doctor."

"Good idea, Detective. He is entitled to a presumption of innocence. Please talk to him as soon as he is back from vacation."

The detective paused for a moment organizing his thoughts.

"Dr. Sloan, who is Janet Reilly?"

The Chief sat at the edge of his chair and grunted. *How the hell does he know about Janet reilly?*

"I have heard of that name but, I do not know her personally."

"Does she work in the hospital?"

"I don't believe so."

"How do you know about her?"

The Chief was boiling inside and looked visibly annoyed.

"Am *I* being interrogated now? I heard of that name *somewhere*. I don't know where. How do *you* know about her?" He asked inquisitively.

"Susan's diary." The detective fired back. "That name is all over her diary. She was obsessed with her. She loved her, she hated her, she was desperately looking to find her after she had lost her job, she was fearful of losing her again after she had found her, and guess whom she was frantically rushing to meet the day she was killed.... Janet Reilly!"

Both men remained quiet for a while. The atmosphere was tense. Dr. Sloan felt this was going too far. Very serious legal issues and he was increasingly uncomfortable to say anything that may cause trouble for him. The detective was clearly pushing the envelope.

"Susan had characterized her as an undercover agent of Dr. Brinkley. Yet again, another reason for our interest to see Dr. Brinkley." The detective said calmly.

"Who else did you wanna talk about?" The Chief asked impatiently.

"Do you know Dr. Peter Molano?"

"Of course I do. He's one of our surgeons."

"You know about his accident?"

"Yes I do."

"Do you think he is in any way connected with Susan Flynn's case?"

"I have no reason to think so."

"Neither do we. He claims he was the victim of a mugging incident. Hard to disprove, but we found no evidence of mugging activity at the location he told us, no witnesses, no blood stains on the ground, nothing. On the other hand, we have found his name in Susan's diary and he was stabbed the very same day Susan died. The very same day, Doctor. Too much of a coincidence. Don't you think so?"

"Detective, I don't know what to think anymore."

The Chief was struggling to lie skillfully. He was not a man of deception, trickery and dishonesty, but at that very moment his brilliant mind flashed back to the day he was summoned to the Medical Director's office. Dr. Molano sounded so confident that he could convince Susan to testify against Dr. Brinkley. *Sonofabitch went to her apartment against her will and something happened there.*

"Ok, Dr. Sloan. I'm sorry for the intrusion. I appreciate your assistance in these matters.

Here is my card. Please call me at anytime if you have more information for us."

"I'll do that." The Chief stood up, as if telling the Detective *"Get the hell out of here."*

They shook hands and he left.

The Chief paced the room back and forth a few times and contemplated his next move.

He buzzed his secretary

"Yes Sir?"

"Get me Dr. Brinkley, right away."

"I believe he is on vacation, Sir."

"Find him."

"I have a note here, Sir; he is out of the country."

"Call overseas, get him wherever he is."

"Yes Sir."

* * * * *

TWENTY

Brian left the casino at 6 a.m. He was exhausted and dizzy. A throbbing headache had troubled him all night. Too much drinking. Too many cigarettes. It was not a smooth, pleasant night like the previous three. It was all struggles. One of those roller coaster nights when you just cannot get a good rhythm at the black-jack table. It has always been a mystery why the good hands and bad hands come in streaks, alas mostly bad streaks. Regular black-jack players are keenly aware that quite often, for a period of ten, fifteen or twenty minutes the shoe becomes vicious. No matter what cards you get, you lose. You are sitting on twenty and the dealer draws seven or eight small cards and ends up with twenty one. Every time you double down on ten or eleven against the dealer's small card, you get a deuce or three. Somehow the dealer never breaks, even when he draws on fifteen or sixteen, and that's enough to wreck your nerves. Basic Strategy doesn't work anymore. You feel helpless, defeated, and angry. The dealer is barraged with expletives and insults even though most players know very well that the poor dealer has no decision making power and no control on who gets what card. He is the only punching bag around.

Brian battled through many of these bad streaks, but managed to hold his grounds and not give away much of what he had won the previous nights. The night was more or less a wash, nevertheless bad enough to destroy his short lived jovial mood of last few days.

He went to bed shortly after six a.m. but could not fall asleep. He was careful not to wake up Jennifer. His heart was pounding, his head throbbing and his mind was all over the place. There was flashback after flashback to so many instances when he was so confident of winning with a very good hand and all his hopes and optimism were shattered by the most unlikely combination of cards that materialized in front of the dealer and made him lose. Even when he drew an occasional black-jack, the dealer also had black-jack. *You can't even win with a Goddamn black-jack.* One heartbreak after another. It almost felt like a conspiracy against him, not that he had not faced conspiracy in his short professional life. He could not comprehend the influence of luck and chance on the outcome of his events, as if his expertise and know how didn't matter at all. He recalled a quote from his father, *"gambling mirrors life, but a life on a fast track."* In a very short time one would experience excitement, anticipation, disappointment, luck, success and failure, euphoria and depression, confidence and uncertainty. The world can turn upside down in the blink of an eye.

Brian closed his eyes and fell asleep for a while. His cell phone rang and he almost jumped off the bed. *Who in the world could be calling me now?*

He reached the phone quickly hoping that Jennifer would not wake up.

"Hello."

"Dr. Brinkley?"

"Speaking. Who is this?"

"Sorry to trouble you on your vacation. This is Dr. Sloan's secretary. He wants to talk to you."

"Please tell him I'll call him back in a few minutes. I gotta get to the other phone."

He dragged his tired body out of the bed, stumbled through the bed room into the living area and carefully pulled a retractable divider separating the two rooms. He then picked up his cell phone and dialed the Chief's office in New York.

"Hello chief. What's up?"

"Hi Brian, how's your vacation going?"

"Wonderful. I wish I could stay here forever."

"Maybe you should. Things are getting more complicated here."

"What's happening?" His heart raced.

"This Janet Reilly ... whoever she was, is causing a lot of trouble for you."

"I have told you before I don't know who Janet Reilly is."

"The hospital authorities believe you know her very well." A short pause, waiting for reaction. "They claim they can prove that you used her to undermine the legal proceedings of the hospital, they believe she intimidated Susan Flynn into withdrawing her sexual harassment complaint and despite what's happened to Susan, they are going to convene the Ethics committee to investigate you."

"They can't prove anything, Chief. I'm not a bit concerned about that."

"Well, Brian, this is not why I called you. I had a strange visitor in my office today, looking for you."

Brian frowned. *What is he up to?*

"Who was that?" he asked.

"A detective named Robert Coleman. Ever heard of him?"

"I don't think so. A detective? What did he want?"

"He wanted to talk to you. He thinks you had something to do with Susan's accident."

"Me? ... *I* had something to do with Susan's accident? What in the world is he talking about?" His voice rising with anger.

"Apparently Susan has written a detailed diary, in which your name as well as Janet Reilly's appear frequently. The police have found evidence of foul play at Susan's apartment, shortly before she left to meet Janet Reilly somewhere. She might have been attacked by somebody. They found blood on her kitchen floor which did not match her blood. Somehow the attacker was injured and she freed herself and ran out."

The line remained silent for a while.

"You're still there Brian?"

"Oh yes. I just don't know what to say. This is the first time I heard all this about Susan's apartment. I have never stepped into her apartment."

"That's what you have to prove to Detective Coleman when you come back. He was just as interested to find Janet Reilly."

"It looks to me everybody in the world wants to find Janet Reilly, myself included."

"Damn right, and you better find her fast, Brian. She caused a lot of problems for you in the hospital, and now law enforcement is after you. Detective Coleman didn't like to hear that you were out of the country. He actually asked if you were planning to come back. You know what that means. They are looking at you as a fugitive."

"Fugitive?" He snapped. "What does he think I am running away from?"

"He thinks you were the one who attacked Susan in her apartment. He wants a sample of your blood to check against the one they found on the kitchen floor."

"He can have as much of my blood as I can give him. Why in the world am I a suspect in this?" Brian asked sounding frustrated and helpless.

A soft hissing noise from the bedroom caught his attention. He had tried to avoid waking up Jennifer. Now he wouldn't mind if she heard everything. *Her crazy stunt as Janet Reilly has ruined my life.*

"With all this stuff you can write a thriller or make a movie full of suspense, Brian." The Chief followed. "I don't blame the detective looking at you as a suspect. Here is a young attractive doctor, flirting with and harassing a young nurse with sexual advances. She files a sexual harassment complaint, threatening to destroy his professional life, he resorts to intimidation and pressure her to withdraw her complaint, which she does, maybe with some conditions attached. He forces his way into her apartment and things get out of hand. He is injured as they fight and she escapes in a state of panic, running for her life and sadly losing her life in a driving accident. The doctor flees the country. This is a completely plausible scenario, isn't it?"

"Except that it is all wrong." Brian responded. "I told you Susan had written me a letter of apology. On further conversation with her she confirmed that her sexual harassment complaint was the product of a conspiracy against me in which she had been deceived to take part. She offered to name names and, in fact, she was about to do that when her life was cut short by the car accident."

Peter Molano? The Chief was deep in thought. *He's the one who was injured. The very same day Susan died.*

"Make sure you say all that to the detective when you return to New York."

"I'm not sure what I should or should not say to the Detective. Sounds like he's already accusing me of homicide. I think I should find an attorney."

"I agree with you, Brian. Find an attorney and find Janet Reilly."

"I'll try."

Brian curled up on the couch in the living room as he hung up the phone. He was stone faced, livid, boiling in anger and trembling. He heard Jennifer getting out of bed.

"Janet Reilly" He hollered angrily. "Come on over here, we have to talk."

"I don't like you calling me Janet Reilly. I know what you're getting at." She responded harshly, a preemptive attack to forestall Brian's assault.

"Like it or not I want you to come here and sit down, right on this couch."

She opened the divider and walked over, still in her night gown. She sat on another chair opposite Brian. *I'm not going to walk into your trap.*

"Did you hear any of my conversation with Dr. Sloan?"

"All I heard was Janet Reilly … Janet Reilly. And, something about a detective."

"That's right. A detective is looking for me and Janet Reilly. He thinks we both had something to do with Susan's death."

"Bullshit. She died in a car accident."

"Did you know she was attacked by an intruder in her apartment on the day she died?"

"No."

"I'm sorry Susan died, but I thought my problems with her were over. Apparently that is not so. The hospital is still not giving up on the sexual harassment issue, even though the complaint was withdrawn, and Susan is dead. You know what's keeping the issue alive?" Brian asked with his rising angry voice.

Jennifer shook her head silently.

"Janet Reilly." He barked. "And do you know why the hospital wants to get rid of me?"

Jennifer kept looking at him and shaking his head.

"Janet Reilly." His facial muscles twitching now. "They don't like spooks running around the hospital intimidating the employees." He fixed his gaze on Jennifer.

"And do you know what the detective wants from me?"

Jennifer nodded as if she knew the answer, but said nothing.

"Janet Reilly. You hear me … Janet Reilly." He shouted. "He wants to know why Susan was rushing to see her."

Jennifer finally broke her silence. "Why don't you say what's really on your mind. You're blaming me for all your troubles."

"Damn right Jenny. Don't you see Janet Reilly is ruining my life? Who invented Janet Reilly?"

"Janet Reilly saved your ass by having Susan withdraw her complaint. I think you still don't understand the seriousness of a sexual harassment accusation." Tears started rolling down her face as she spoke. "You could have been in jail by now. Your practice ruined, your reputation and prestige destroyed, and our relationship terminated forever. Would that have been OK with you if Janet Reilly didn't come to rescue?"

"It's no different now." He shouted back. "They're going to take me to the Ethics Committee because they believe Janet Reilly intimidated Susan to withdraw, and they are going to accuse me of sending an undercover agent to interfere with the legal proceedings of the hospital. And now the detective is after me because of Janet Reilly, can't you see what a mess you have created here?"

Susan remained quiet, still shaking her head in disbelief. *Poor Brian is losing his mind.*

She wouldn't take any of this.

"I think we should cool off now. I'm going to take a shower."

Brian didn't move.

They spent rest of the day separate from each other. She went out for a walk by the beach. He chose gambling as a distraction, albeit a very expensive one.

They lunched in different eateries and deep down missed each others' warm and sensual embrace of their afternoon nap. *No sex today.*

Brian had a few drinks throughout the afternoon and evening at the black-jack tables as his luck abandoned him and his fortune shrank. Jennifer had followed him from a distance and had noted his nasty mood and irrational behavior as he was losing large sums of money. He was cursing the dealers, pounding the tables and having non-stop drinks and cigarettes. He staggered from one table to another. He appeared distraught and broken.

By early evening he had given back all the money he had won over the last few days. About twenty thousand dollars was gone. He started drawing from his account with the casino.

They had a dinner reservation at the Italian Restaurant. Jennifer ended up having her dinner alone.

Before retiring to the room she sneaked around the black-jack table area and could not find Brian. She took a walk through the casino. No Brian.

She called the room. No answer.

She called his cell phone. No answer. That of course didn't mean anything. They were in a foreign country. Service was not available all the time. She realized that in most casinos cell phones did not work. *Brian could still be somewhere in the casino.*

The only area she had not checked was the Baccarat Lounge where high stakes black-jack tables also existed. She looked around for the signs and found the lounge far back in the casino. She walked in and immediately spotted Brian at a five hundred dollar minimum bet table. He had asked the pit boss for a marker and was signing the papers for ten thousand dollars from his account.

Jennifer approached his table gingerly. She wanted to grab him and pull him away from the table and take him upstairs. A man's voice echoed in her right ear.

"Excuse me Ma'am. You cannot watch the players in this area. Please leave."

She turned around and saw a well dressed gentleman with a name tag on his lapel.

"I wanna talk to my husband. That's him over there at that table." She pointed towards Brian's table.

"Please stay here." The man walked to the table and whispered to Brian's ear, waited a second and came back.

"Excuse me; he's not your husband. He said he's not married and asked that you leave him alone.

Terribly embarrassed, Jennifer left.

The night dragged on and everything remained gloomy and disastrous for Brian. At around 5 a.m. he ran out of money.

He pointed to the pit boss "Marker please"

"How much Sir?" he asked.

"Ten."

He lost his last bet and had to stay out the rest of the shoe, waiting for the money.

The pit boss checked and re-checked the computer and walked around the table and whispered into Brian's ear.

He responded angrily. "What do you mean I have no more money in my account? I had thirty five grand in there."

"I'm sorry Sir. You've used it all."

"Can't you advance me some money now?"

"I'm afraid not."

He left the table and staggered his way into the VIP lounge and sunk his tired body onto a lush leather sofa. He was served a cup of coffee and a cold-cut sandwich.

What a difference a day makes. He pondered. Only twenty four hours earlier he was enjoying his vacation immensely. New York was a world apart and all his troubles back home were temporarily forgotten. He was being rejuvenated soaking in the sun at the beach and resting his body on a bed of warm, soft sands and taking a dip in the crisp and clear waters of the Atlantic Ocean. His lovely companion peppered him with love and affection. Food was delicious and his forays at the black-jack tables were fruitful.

At this very moment he felt defeated and broke. New York found him in his hiding sanctuary and added another dimension to his miseries. The prospect of a criminal charge by a suspicious detective. His source of moral support and protection became his greatest liability. Jennifer Bradley was replaced by Janet Reilly. His good fortune abandoned him and his bank account at the casino evaporated.

He couldn't stay here much longer and the thought of going back to New York sent shivers down his spine.

He found refuge at exactly where he was. The cozy, dimly lit lounge with the comfort of the soft leather couch. He closed his eyes and fell asleep.

* * * * *

TWENTY ONE

The vascular surgeon rushed into the patient's room, followed with a number of surgical residents and nurses. The patient was restless, agitated and screaming. A nervous nurse was leaning over his bed with both hands on his left groin holding pressure. The existing bandage was soaked with blood and there was blood dripping off the side of the bed.

The vascular surgeon knew right away what had happened. He took a glance at the blood soaked bed sheets and ordered the junior resident to start an IV and ordered two units of blood from blood bank immediately.

He noted that the patient was perspiring profusely. His skin was pale and cold.

He's going into shock. "Get the OR ready right away" he hollered.

A nurse was checking the blood pressure "Seventy systolic, Doctor" she called.

The resident was struggling to get the IV started. The patient's veins were collapsed.

The nurse holding pressure on the groin did not seem to be controlling the hemorrhage effectively. She pointed to another surgical resident, a robust stocky young man in his late twenties, and he took over.

"Keep the pressure on as we move to the OR. If you let go, he will exsanguinate" the surgeon said. The resident understood what he meant; he'll lose all of his blood.

The patient pulled on the surgeon's white coat in extreme anxiety, his chest heaving to get some air in, and struggled to get the words out of his throat "Doc … wha … What's happening?"

"You're bleeding from the wound. Don't worry, everything is under control. We're going to take you to the OR and fix it. Relax now."

The patient calmed down as he felt the warm hand of the surgeon compassionately squeezing his wrist. The surgeon was focused on the patient's pulse rate. *Too fast, he is shocky.*

"Did you get the damn IV started yet?" he hollered at the resident.

"Yes Sir, but only a small twenty two gauge needle, his veins are collapsed." the resident stammered.

"OK, we'll have Anesthesia drop in a central venous line as soon as we get to the OR."

The head nurse was on the phone to the OR, booking the case.

"He's bleeding profusely. They wanna bring him upstairs right away"

"OK, what's the patient's name?"

"Dr. Peter Molano."

"I mean the *patient's* name."

"That *IS* the patient's name. Dr. Peter Molano."

On the way to OR, the resident asked the surgeon "Why is he bleeding so much, Sir?"

The surgeon explained, "His suture line broke. His femoral artery was severed about a month ago, apparently during a mugging incident. We sutured it back together but he developed a wound infection. We had to take him back to the OR once and clean the infected wound. There were no healthy, clean soft tissues to cover the artery. So, here is the artery and the suture line, exposed, at the depths of the infected wound. It popped open today."

"How serious is this complication, Sir?" the resident asked.

"There is a good possibility he'll lose his leg, if we can save his life."

"He'll lose his leg? From where?"

"From the hip. You know what that's called?" the surgeon asked.

Another resident from the back hollered, "Hip disarticulation."

As the group entered the OR the head nurse noted the police officer moving in with them.

"I'm sorry Officer; you can't go beyond this door. This is the Operating Room."

"But he is under police protection. We have to watch him all the time" the cop replied.

The nurse flashed a sarcastic gaze at him "If you can do his surgery come in with us, otherwise stay right here. The man is about to lose his leg. He won't be going anywhere."

Two hours later the patient, Peter Molano, was resting comfortably in the Intensive Care unit. He had received transfusions and his blood pressure was now normal. His leg was barely alive but the surgeon thought there was still a chance that the leg might survive. The artery was repaired again.

Forty eight hours later Peter was delirious, confused and burning in fever. The fowl smell of gangrene filled his surroundings. His nurses were in tears. The residents were working hard to prepare him for the OR. Everybody was somber and overwhelmed with grief. All their efforts of the past four weeks went to waste. It was a poignant scene of a young surgeon victimized by an alleged assailant at a mugging incident and now about to lose his leg if they can save his life.

Late in the evening Peter was taken back to the OR where he underwent a high amputation.

The resident marked in his chart "Left Hip Disarticulation."

* * * * *

The secretary reminded Dr. Sloan for the third time. "They're waiting for you."

"OK… OK, I'll go there right now." He was busy reading a report. He detested the Medical Director for calling these urgent meetings on his own time table.

Get off my back you creep. He wanted to punch him in the nose. He was convinced that Joseph Brown was after Dr. Brinkley. Exactly why and on whose behalf he was not sure, but he was increasingly suspicious of Dr. Peter Molano. He recalled his conversation with Detective Coleman who cast a serious doubt on Dr. Molano's mugging story and remembered Peter's zealous efforts to convince Susan Flynn to testify against Brian Brinkley. He also knew that Susan had apologized to Brian and withdrew her complaint. Slowly but surely a frightening scenario was shaping up in his mind.

Possibly driven by competition or jealousy, the Chief thought, Peter Molano was using Susan Flynn to trap Brian Brinkley into a serious charge of sexual harassment and destroy him. Now it appeared that something had gone wrong somewhere. Coincidentally, albeit hard to believe, exactly on the same day Peter was stabbed on the groin, Susan died in a car accident. *Um ... I wonder.*

Dr. Joseph Brown was clearly shook up when he received the horrible news of Peter's amputation. It was obvious that he would not be back to work anytime soon, if at all, and yet they had a few serious matters at hand.

He called for an urgent meeting of the medical staff leadership.

"I'm sorry I am late" Dr. Sloan said as he walked in. Among the physicians present was Dr. John Elliott, Chairman of the Department of Medicine, who was also serving as the President of the Medical Board, the highest authoritative body of the medical staff affairs.

"Thank you for coming, Mike" Dr. Brown responded. "I'm sorry for such short notice, but you might have heard the horrible news about Dr. Molano" he paused and looked around the room. Nobody seemed to know anything.

"They amputated his leg last evening." A big gasp from the audience and expressions of grief and sadness followed.

"As you know ..." he continued, "we had temporarily postponed the next meeting of the QA committee hoping that Dr. Molano would come back to work soon. This was to be a special meeting to review Dr. Brinkley's complications and Dr. Molano had done a lot of work on that. We can, of course, wait until the Medical Board nominates another Chairman for the QA committee and then have the new Chairman review these cases all over again, but there are other serious issues involving Dr. Brinkley for which the hospital administration is extremely concerned and they would like to see this physician dealt with as expeditiously as possible. Therefore ... "

"Hold on, Joe" Dr Elliott interrupted. "Could you tell us what these other issues are?"

"Glad to" Dr. Brown responded. "More than a month ago, a complaint of sexual harassment was filed against Dr. Brinkley by one of the OR nurses. This is of course a very serious charge which may reflect on the integrity of our hospital and medical staff. Our top people, including some members of the Board of Directors are on pins and needles about this matter. This institution thrives on the moral integrity and reputation of our medical staff and such incidents are not taken lightly. Our plan was to convene the Ethics Committee and deal with this matter ..."

"Sorry to interrupt you, Joe ..." Dr. Sloan jumped in. "But could you also tell our colleagues here that the nurse had subsequently withdrawn her complaint and had apologized to Dr. Brinkley?"

"That is in fact correct" Dr. Brown responded. "But we have reasons to believe that the nurse was coerced and intimidated on behalf of Dr. Brinkley to withdraw her complaint and ..."

"What do you mean *on behalf* of Dr. Brinkley?" another doctor asked.

"A mysterious woman by the name of Janet Reilly visited the nurse, Susan Flynn here and threatened that she would lose her job if she didn't withdraw her complaint."

"And you can prove this?" the doctor asked.

"Yes we can" Dr. Brown continued. "In fact she had agreed to testify against Dr Brinkley at the Ethics committee."

"So, what is the problem here?"

"The problem is that unfortunately Nurse Flynn was killed in a car accident four weeks ago."

Dr. Sloan struggled to control his anger and adhere to civility.

"For cryin' out loud, Joe." He exclaimed "Don't you think you're going overboard with this? The complaint was withdrawn, the apology was issued, the nurse is dead and the issue is moot now. Why don't you let it go?"

"The guys upstairs want to show that we took this matter seriously. They are afraid of adverse publicity and a public relations fiasco."

"I am extremely surprised to hear all this about Dr. Brinkley" Dr.

Elliott intervened. "My colleagues in the Department of Medicine are highly complimentary of him and the quality of his work. I think something is fishy here."

"I agree with you, John." Dr. Sloan responded. "I know Brian very well. I have discussed this issue with him. He strongly believes that there is a conspiracy against him, possibly out of competition or jealousy."

"Let him come and prove it" Dr. Brown declared.

"What else do you have against him?" another physician asked

"There was a trauma case recently. He operated on the patient. After surgery the patient went into shock in the recovery room, bleeding profusely, and Dr. Brinkley was nowhere to be found. Forty five minutes later he showed up and took the patient back to the OR where he died.

It turned out that he had gone to the cafeteria with one of the nurses, spending some intimate time together."

"Hold it, Joe." Dr. Sloan jumped in. "This is another preposterous accusation to which I am certain Dr. Brinkley can respond appropriately."

"That's great" the Medical Director responded. "We would like to give him the opportunity to respond to all of these charges."

He then turned to Dr. Elliott "John, I think in view of the gravity of these charges and the desire of the hospital administration for an expeditious investigation we should bypass both the QA Committee and the Ethics Committee and instead have you call for a special meeting of the Medical Board and bring Dr. Brinkley in for questioning. If the Board is not satisfied with his explanations then we will refer the matter to the Board of Directors."

"That's alright with me if you don't think these matters can be resolved at the other committees" Dr. Elliott responded.

"I think it will take a lot of time to get this through the other committees and at the end they will refer the matter to you."

"Alright then, we shall convene a special meeting of the Medical Board soon" Dr. Elliott responded.

Dr. Brown thanked everybody and the meeting was adjourned.

* * * * *

It was a brief and tense meeting between an inquisitive and suspicious detective and a defiant and frustrated surgeon. Their path inevitably crossed following the tragic death of the nurse, although they were a world apart as to the necessity of this meeting. The surgeon could not fathom why he should be, even remotely, a target of investigation and the detective could not disassociate the surgeon from a tangled web of bizarre events preceding the car accident that took the nurse's life. He had combed through the nurse's diary and within the last few weeks' entries the surgeon's name, as well as two others were all over the place. He had postulated an intriguing scenario of a love-hate relationship fraught with treachery, betrayal and crime. Brian's involvement had gone from the perpetrator of sexual harassment to an innocent victim of a conspiracy, back to the architect of a clandestine operation of intimidation and coercion by the mysterious Janet Reilly and back again to a decent human being and respected professional victimized by a vicious, jealous and invidious competitor named Peter Molano. The detective could not determine which of these characterizations would best fit Brian. To him an alternative scenario appeared completely plausible and more straightforward. A course of events just between the surgeon and the nurse, starting with an act of sexual harassment and ending with a violent confrontation at the nurse's apartment. Not too many dots here to connect. The detective's motto had always been to pursue simple leads and avoid getting tangled in speculative conspiratorial theories. Moreover, he did not intend to discuss Peter Molano's involvement with Brian or even mention his name, since Peter was apparently the subject of a totally unrelated event, allegedly a mugging incident and he wanted to know if Brian would mention or implicate Peter Molano independently and shed light on the scope of his involvement in Susan's fatal accident.

"Detective Coleman … " Brian kept a straight face and said " I have agreed to this meeting only to help you solve the mystery of the tragic death of a young lady, the late Susan Flynn. It is my understanding that I am not the subject of an investigation, as you said, and not a suspect in this matter, otherwise I should not talk to you without the presence of an attorney. So please make it brief and to the point and tell me what is it that I can do for you?"

"I thank you for your time, Dr. Brinkley, and appreciate the opportunity to talk to you. Susan Flynn died in a car accident and initially it did not appear to be any different than many other fatal automobile accidents that happen every day.

However, we have reasons to believe that she was attacked in her apartment by an intruder shortly before she left. Actually, she might have fled her apartment in a state of panic, running for her life which affected her driving ability. We have to find out who the intruder was."

"I can tell you categorically ..." Brian responded firmly "That I have never been in Susan's apartment at any time in the past. I knew nothing about this story until Dr. Sloan mentioned it to me regarding his conversation with you."

"Susan Flynn left a detailed diary" the detective followed "and your name, as well as the names of two other people has been mentioned frequently during the last few weeks of her life. We have not been able to locate or identify one of those two people." He gauged Brian's reaction and followed. "Dr ... . do you know who Miss Janet Reilly is?"

God knows how many more times I have to deny this before I have to admit knowing her.

Brian grunted "I have been asked this question by several people at the hospital, and my answer is always the same. No."

"I respect your position" the detective responded "but, Susan's diary tells us quite a different story."

"I have no knowledge of Susan's diary, Detective. What else do you want to know?" Brian said impatiently. *I don't wanna hear another word about Goddamn Janet Reilly.*

"Do you have any idea who wanted to harm Susan Flynn?" the detective asked.

"None whatsoever" Brian answered quickly.

"We found blood stains in Susan's kitchen. It did not match her blood. It's gotta be the intruder's. Would you be willing to give a sample of your blood for testing?"

"Take as much as you want. That cannot be my blood in her kitchen."

"I appreciate that. We will make arrangements to have your blood sample collected." His instincts told him that would not be necessary.

Brian appeared truthful to him. He better look somewhere else to find the intruder.

They shook hands and he left.

* * * * *

TWENTY TWO

The President of the Medical Board called the meeting to order and checked the attendance to make sure there was a quorum. No problem with that. There was no more room around the gigantic board room table. The attendance was the best they had seen in a long time. Everybody was anxious to know what this special meeting was about. By now, most of them had heard something about Dr. Brinkley's problems through rumors whispered here and there around the hospital. They were going to hear from the horse's mouth today.

The Board consisted of the representatives of each clinical department, usually the Chairpersons. There were also representatives of the nursing department and administration. The Medical Director enjoyed his dual role, both as an administration employee, naturally requiring loyalty to the institution's best interests, and as a physician looking after the rights and interests of his colleagues, the Medical staff. Whenever there was a conflict between the administration and the medical staff, the board was divided between the physicians who had no financial ties to the institution and those who were employed by the hospital, such as representatives of Pathology, Radiology, and even nursing department.

The Medical Board is the highest policy making authority for the medical staff affairs. The unresolved issues are usually referred to the Board of Directors for final decision.

Dr. John Elliott, the President of the Medical Board welcomed the members.

"As you all know," he began "this special meeting is convened to investigate several issues concerning one of our active surgeons, Dr. Brian Brinkley. You have, in the folders in front of you, a brief summary of the issues we shall discuss today. We have invited Dr. Brinkley to explain and respond to any questions you may have. I'll strongly urge you to refrain from confrontational arguments. We prefer dialogue over diatribe. We are not going to force him to accept our opinions just as we are not obligated to accept his. He will be given an opportunity to respond to the allegations brought about by the Medical Director and, after he leaves we shall discuss the issues amongst ourselves and make a final decision."

One of the members raised his hand.

"Mr. President, as I am looking at this brief summary of the allegations against him, it looks to me that most of these issues should have been discussed at other committees and possibly resolved. Why are we bypassing the appropriate committees and rushing these through the Medical Board?"

The President turned to the Medical Director "You wanna respond Joe?"

"Be glad to ..." Dr. Brown answered. "There are nine surgical cases with complications. These were scheduled to be reviewed at the QA Committee. Unfortunately Dr. Molano's tragic accident delayed the committee meeting.

There are also ethical issues that should be addressed as expeditiously as possible otherwise the institution will suffer from adverse publicity. The administration is extremely concerned about this. We decided it was best to hammer out all of these issues at this meeting and send our findings and recommendations to the Board of Directors."

"Thank you, Joe." Dr. Elliott followed "I have already reviewed the nine surgical cases of Dr. Brinkley, from a list provided to me by the Medical Director. These are basically post operative complications."

He then gave a brief summary of each case. There were four cases with infection after surgery; one patient developed blood clots in her leg, which traveled to her lung and killed her. Two cases of ruptured appendicitis in which the surgery could have presumably been done earlier, one case of pediatric hernia repair where the Vas Deferens was accidentally cut and one trauma case with liver injury where the patient died.

Dr. Elliott went on to explain that the ethical issue was a serious charge of sexual harassment filed by one of the nurses against Dr. Brinkley. He acknowledged that the nurse had withdrawn her complaint shortly before her tragic death in a car accident; nevertheless the administration was anxious to pursue the matter for reasons that will be discussed later on.

"Are there any other questions before we call in Dr. Brinkley?" He looked around the table. No questions. Everybody was busy reading the paperwork provided.

The President nodded at the secretary, and she picked up the phone and called her office where Dr. Brinkley was waiting.

Moments later Brian walked in and was greeted by the members. He took his seat.

"Thank you for coming, Dr. Brinkley" the president said. "This special meeting of the Medical Board has been convened upon a request by the administration and Medical Director to review several issues related to your practice of surgery in this hospital ..."

"Mr. President ..." Brian interrupted him as he raised his hand.

"Yes Sir."

"Before we get into any discussions I would like to make a statement."

"Go ahead please."

Brian paused and collected his thoughts. He was not sure how many supporters he had around this table. This was his chance to stem the downfall of his successful practice. He had come to realize that no matter how innocent he might be, he could still fall prey to the vicious forces of his predators empowered by professional rivalry, jealousy and unfair competition. As his gambling debacle in the Bahamas taught him, his life can turn upside down in a fraction of a second by events totally out of his control especially when he places himself in harms way.

His innocent, friendly and witty sexual comments, way back at the time of the kiddy hernia repair, handed him a dangerous accusation of sexual harassment. He had realized that despite his good intentions, in the presence of the people he least suspected to be anything but close friends, he had in fact placed himself in harms way and had given his adversaries an opportunity to attack him. This time he was determined to fight fiercely for his professional life and take control of his own destiny.

He looked around the table and found everybody staring at him with intense interest.

"Thank you Mr. President. I'll be more than happy to respond to any questions you or distinguished members of this committee may have. I'll take responsibility for my actions and this institution has every right to be watchful and concerned about adverse publicity of unprofessional behavior of its members. I would like to appeal to the fair-mindedness of my colleagues here, as we go through this process today, to consider what I strongly believe to be a deliberate conspiracy against me, in order to derail my flourishing and successful career. A conspiracy driven by rivalry and jealousy.

I do not believe any one of the cases or issues that we will discuss today are of such validity and seriousness that would call for a special meeting of this distinguished board. I have no doubt in my mind that the forces behind this conspiracy have compiled a number of individually insignificant cases and anecdotal accounts of unsubstantiated events to fabricate a presumably strong case against me. All I am asking is that you consider this possibility, the conspiracy theory I mean, before you render your final judgment. And, please remember that I have been called here to explain why a very few patients of mine had infection after surgery, as if no other patient in this hospital has had infection, or why an un-fortunate mishap occurred during a pediatric hernia repair, as if there has never been a complication in this hospital, or respond to a sexual harassment accusation against me when, in fact, the accusation has been withdrawn by the accuser who has also apologized to me in writing and the Medical Director has received a copy of that.. Also you should ques-tion why lower level committee meetings in charge of investigating these issues have been bypassed. It is not too difficult to see a pattern here, ladies and gentlemen, a pattern of concerted efforts to push me out of the way of those who have been intimidated by my success."

The Medical Director raised his hand.

"Dr. Brown. Go ahead." The President nodded.

"Mr. President. Dr. Brinkley's statement is nothing but a preemptive effort to distract the attention of this Board from focusing on the seriousness of the charges against him. I urge the members to disregard his concocted conspiracy theory and render their judgment on the basis of the factual evidence of his failures and misconducts."

The chairman of OB-GYN raised his hand.

"Go ahead, Dr. Kaplan." The President said.

"Dr. Brinkley" Dr. Kaplan turned to Brian and flashed a serious gaze. "Your conspiracy theory is a serious accusation against your colleague or colleagues. I suppose you have some evidence for such conspiracy otherwise you would not make such an accusation. Will you be able to prove your point in front of this committee?"

"I think I can, Dr. Kaplan." Brian followed "What constitutes *proof* could be different for different people. I will outline for you all the reasons that have brought me to this conclusion, and then you can make up your own mind, and I appreciate your open-mindedness in this matter as against Dr. Brown who, before asking me for any evidence or proof, has accused me of concocting this theory." He gave a scornful stare at the Medical Director and turned back to Dr. Kaplan. "However, Dr. Kaplan, I think you will have a better grasp at the core and essence of my conspiracy theory if you allow me to explain it to you after I respond to the accusations for which I have been asked to come here."

"I agree with Dr. Brinkley." The President jumped in. "I think we should first discuss the issues at hand and hear Dr. Brinkley's responses. I trust by now you have all looked at the summary of all these cases in your folders. I have reviewed the charts of these patients in detail" He pointed to a stack of nine medical records next to him.

"In my opinion," he continued. "Seven of these nine cases should not have been flagged for investigation. Perhaps the Medical Director can explain why they are here, but first let me ask Dr. Brinkley how many cases he has done in this hospital during last three years."

"Approximately nine hundred." Brian answered.

"Nine hundred … Hmm!" *Impressive*. He thought.

"Here we have four cases of post operative infections." The President paused for a quick calculation, "That's 0.4 percent. One case of fatal pulmonary embolism, that is 0.1 percent and two cases of ruptured appendicitis in which there is no evidence of intentional delay in surgery. Well that's remarkable statistics to me, Joe." He looked at Dr. Brown. "Why were these cases picked for review?"

The Medical Director fingered through a stack of papers in front of him and remained quiet for a while.

"Would you like to answer the question now or later, Joe?" The President asked impatiently. The Medical Director sank further into his chair.

"I don't have a good answer. Dr. Molano had looked through these cases. Unfortunately he is not here today."

"If the committee agrees we shall disregard these cases for now." The President looked around the table. There was no objection. The Medical Director groaned.

"Now, the case of pediatric hernia repair." The President glanced through the patient's chart and followed "The Vas Deferens was cut. Again, this is the only complication he's had out of many such cases …"

"Mr. President …" The Medical Director interrupted as he suddenly sat up in his chair and tried to seize the moment. "Dr. Brinkley has acknowledged that he has done only one kiddy hernia repair. So his complication rate here is one hundred percent." He paused and looked around the table to see the reaction of the members. The room was quiet. "Moreover," he continued "Dr. Gonzalez, who is present today, believes that the injury was bilateral. That means the child has been permanently damaged and will never have a biological child of his own." He looked at Dr. Gonzalez who was nodding in agreement. "And, last but not the least; Dr. Brinkley has refused to inform this kid's parents of this complication. The hospital may suffer seriously if they find out later on and sue the hospital."

The President asked Dr. Brinkley to respond.

"I respectfully disagree with Dr. Brown's statements. Yes, there was a complication. Yes this was the first pediatric hernia repair I did. There is a beginning for everything. But no, I believe the injury was only on the right side. The nurse made a mistake and mixed up the specimens of both sides. With all due respect, there is no way Dr. Gonzalez can be so certain that the injury was on both sides. Again, I believe it was only on the right side and this will have absolutely no adverse effect on this child's future life. He will have children. And, no again, I do not want to destroy his parents' peace of mind and subject them to many years of anxiety and apprehension. There is a human side in this issue that should overshadow the financial concerns of this institution."

Dr. Navarro, Chief of Pediatric Surgery service raised his hand.

"Dr. Brinkley ..." He looked at Brian. "I agree with most of what you said, but you should at least acknowledge your lack of experience in pediatric hernia repair. You are a busy and active surgeon, but when you push yourself to the fringes of the safe practice of surgery the likelihood of something going wrong will be much higher, such as what's happened in this case. I personally believe this case should have been done by a trained pediatric surgeon."

"Dr. Navarro ..." Brian responded "I appreciate your loyalty to your sub-specialty of pediatric surgery, but general surgeons are also trained to perform kiddy hernia repairs. I have done many during my residency training. I am also sure pediatric surgeons have encountered complications such as this. I was unfortunate to have mine with my very first case in private practice."

"OK gentlemen; let's move on to the next case" the President interrupted.

"Dr. Brinkley, you had a trauma case recently when patient went into shock in the recovery room and, according to the nurses notes you were nowhere to be found. Forty five minutes later they found you in the cafeteria spending intimate moments with a nurse. You took the patient back to the OR, but it was too late. Could you tell us what went on with this case?"

"Mr. President," Brian responded, raising his voice a notch. "I take issue with your assertion that I was spending *intimate moments* with a nurse. Knowing you, I am certain this idea was not yours originally. I went for a cup of coffee and the nurse asked if she could talk to me. This was the same nurse who had accused me of sexual harassment and had subsequently apologized. Yes, we had a conversation, sort of making it up to each other and attempting to put this unfortunate incident to rest. I was out of touch with the recovery room because the overhead paging system was not working. This was not my fault."

The Medical Director raised his hand to speak. The President nodded OK.

"Mr. President, we are hearing nothing but denial and denial from Dr. Brinkley. I thought he said he takes responsibility for his actions. A patient died; while he was having a good time in the cafeteria. Dr. Brinkley knows that the overhead paging system is turned off at night so that the patients can get a good night sleep."

Dr. Michael Sloan, Chairman of the Department of Surgery raised his hand. The President looked at him.

"Mr. President, we have done our intra-departmental review of this case. In my opinion this patient had no chance of survival from the moment he was brought into the hospital. He had massive liver injury and the autopsy showed his liver had been ripped off from the Vena Cava which is the largest vein in the body. Retrospectively it did not make any difference whether Dr. Brinkley was in the cafeteria or in recovery room."

Brian darted a glance of appreciation towards him.

"OK, gentlemen." The President called for attention. "We have heard both sides of the argument here. Let's move on."

He then turned to the Medical Director.

"I believe you wanna bring up the sexual harassment issue, Joe. Is that right?"

"That is correct, Sir." Dr. Brown responded. "As I mentioned before, this institution thrives on the integrity and reputation of its staff, and is acutely conscious about the adverse publicity of unethical behavior by its members. We have ample indications that on the day Dr. Brinkley was performing a hernia repair on that kid, ripping off his

Vas Deferens, he was cracking jokes, sexual anecdotes and insulting remarks about the women in the room, mostly directed towards the late Susan Flynn, to the point that she was distracted from her duties and made a serious mistake of mixing up the specimens. She was offended, insulted and humiliated. The other nurses in the room confirmed that after the surgery finished, he pulled Susan to the corner of the room and made remarks about her breasts. *You Goddamn liar. Brian groaned.* She walked away in shame and embarrassment. Later on, she filed a complaint of sexual harassment. The administration decided to refer this matter to the Medical Board, and is requesting that the Board consider expelling Dr. Brinkley from our staff membership."

The eerie silence that followed was heavy and disconcerting. What the members heard was shocking.

They could not believe such unethical behavior from Brian Brinkley.

Moments went by. Nobody talked. Brian was angry and defiant. He shook his head in disbelief. How close he was to having the names of his conspirators in a hand written letter from Susan. *Oh God, why did she die ... where is the letter?*

This was the moment he would crush his accusers and reveal their true identity and intentions and save his career. He would throw the letter into the Medical Director's face and would say *"Read it, you Sonofabitch"*

"I would also like to add ..." the Medical director broke the silence "... that Susan Flynn retracted her complaint against Dr. Brinkley, after she was intimidated by a mysterious person by the name of Janet Reilly, a woman nobody has ever known around here, and yet she presented herself to Susan Flynn as working for Dr. Gonzalez. She was obviously an undercover agent for Dr. Brinkley who convinced Susan that she would lose her job if she did not withdraw her complaint. Perhaps Dr. Brinkley can tell us who Janet Reilly is."

Brian turned to the Medical Director, looking extremely angry and agitated.

"Janet Reilly is a figment of your imagination, Dr. Brown. I do not know such a person, and as you said, nobody around here has ever heard of her."

He then turned to the other members "If you excuse my language, everything Dr. Brown just said is nothing but a bunch of bullshit, and I will not dignify them by providing an answer. I would like to go back to Dr. Kaplan's earlier question of whether I can prove my conspiracy theory. Having heard these ridiculous accusations against me, I trust you now have a sense of whether my behavior was so abhorred or my professional deficiencies so extreme that I deserve to be censured or expelled from the medical staff. What else but a planned conspiracy could pile up nine of my cases for evaluation when in fact the Medical Director who has brought them here cannot explain why seven of these cases are here to begin with? The nurse who filed a sexual harassment complaint against me confessed to me that she had been used by others to play a part in this conspiracy. Dr. Brown has a copy of the letter of apology she wrote to me. Do you wonder why he did not mention a word about that? It is tragic that Susan Flynn is dead; otherwise she would be here in person to confirm what she wrote in her letter. What went on in the OR was nothing more than friendly conversations and a few jokes. And as for Janet Reilly, I have said this before and I will say it again, I have never known a person with this name. I do not have undercover agents and have never attempted to undermine the official proceedings of this institution.

"Thank you Dr. Brinkley" the president said calmly. The room was quiet. "I believe we have gone through all the issues at hand. We shall have a fifteen minute coffee break. After that the Board will review these deliberations and formulate a recommendation to the Board of Directors."

Brian thanked the Board and left.

* * * * *

It was 6:30 a.m. when Brian woke up with a headache. He had stayed up very late the night before, smoking and drinking a lot. The loneliness of his apartment and lack of companionship were devastating. He missed Jenny very badly, but she had stayed away from him since they returned from the Bahamas. It was almost three weeks, the longest they had not seen or talked to each other in years. And for the first time in a long time he felt weak and vulnerable. He had been thrown off the lofty perch of unconditional love and support from Jenny who was badly hurt by Brian's behavior in Bahamas.

Her anger and his ego kept their telephone lines to each other silent.

Later on that morning he called Dr. Sloan to find out what happened after he had left the Medical Board Meeting.

Good news and bad news.

Dr. Sloan told him that in general the members were favorable to his arguments and would have bought his conspiracy theory were it not for the Janet Reilly issue. They were resentful of the Medical Director's aggressive approach and did not consider the medical issues serious enough to call for Brian's censure or dismissal; however the Medical Director kept hammering on the matter of the illusive Janet Reilly. He produced a copy of the letter signed by Brian asking the OR committee to consider firing Susan Flynn. The copy had been allegedly delivered to Susan by Janet Reilly, a tangible evidence of intimidation of the nurse as claimed by the Medical Director. He also produced statements by the receptionist at the Pathology department as well as Dr. Gonzalez' secretary, Janice Turowsky, confirming that Susan Flynn had gone to the Pathology Department asking to see a Janet Reilly.

The members did not believe that Brian knew absolutely nothing about the identity of Janet Reilly and, therefore, with extreme reluctance, they referred the matter to the Board of Directors.

Dr. Sloan expressed serious concern that the Board of Directors would most certainly report Brian to the Department of Health where he would be at risk for losing his license to practice medicine in New York.

Brian's jaw dropped as he hung up the phone.

He had some errands to run before he was due in his office at 2 p.m.

Despite the complexity of his own problems his thoughts drifted to what had happened to Dr. Peter Molano. Although they were never close friends, they were colleagues, working in the same hospital and often seeing each other in the OR, or at various meetings. They were fully aware of an undercurrent of professional rivalry, but on the surface the appearance of civility and professional courtesy was always maintained.

He felt deeply sorry for what had happened to Peter. He lost his leg and, in a sense, lost his professional career as a surgeon for ever. Brian could not feel sorry for himself anymore. His problems paled against Peter's disastrous injury.

He decided to pay him a visit.

* * * * *

TWENTY THREE

The exchange perfectly suited the needs of each party. It was a clandestine exchange, but there was no trace of a guilty conscience on the faces of the man and the woman. No concern for illegality or immorality of the action. They were both convinced of the righteousness of what they were doing.

A thick brown envelope, eight by five inches, was handed over in the dark corner of the vast parking lot where the rendezvous had been arranged, in return for a piece of paper, folded to hide the name, a number and instructions.

The man placed the paper in his pocket and kissed the lady. She crammed the thick envelope into her purse. They were anxious to separate and leave the area. No words were necessary.

They had each other's telephone numbers and they would talk later on if necessary. Usually they preferred not to.

They had done this exchange a few times before. This time the plot was more complicated and, for the lady the task was not yet complete. She could not bring in a special key. The man had to wait for further instructions.

He was tall and thin, early thirties, well dressed, dark hair, brown eyes, cool and confident. He deftly jumped behind the wheel, revved the engine and drove away.

The lady leaned on her car for a minute and smiled. She could not resist checking the envelope after she sat in the car. Packed in the brown envelope was a stack of one hundred dollar bills. She counted twenty. She will get another twenty when the key is delivered and further instructions given.

The man zigzagged his way through uptown streets and avenues, went south on 5th Avenue and found his way onto Park Avenue through 57th street. All along his sharp eyes moved back and forth between the rear view mirror and the road ahead. He was not being followed.

He pulled into the underground parking of his office building, and took the elevator to the 34th floor.

It was shortly after 8 p.m. when Mr. Edgar Lopez, a paralegal in the prestigious Law firm of Weinstein & Rosenberg entered his office building.

The office was quiet. Most of the lawyers had left for the day. A few paralegals and interns were still working. The lights in the library were on. Actually they never went off.

Young lawyers, mostly recent recruits, and a number of paralegals and interns were buried under tons of files, law books and legal pads and deeply consumed in research. They all looked exhausted.

Edgar passed by his own small office, and continued down the hall where the senior partners were housed. He stopped at the office of managing partner of the firm, Douglas Gelfand, and knocked gently.

"Come in."

Edgar nudged the door open enough to stick his head in. The room was dimly lit. Douglas was sitting behind his desk, leaning on his elbows and holding his head in his hands reading something. He looked tired and sleepy, but managed a smile when he saw the head poke through the door.

"Hi Doug" Edgar mumbled. "All is well, you can go home now."

"How much?" he asked.

"Two grand now. Two later."

"It better pay off."

"I'll fill you in tomorrow. This is gonna be in the millions. Go home please."

"See you tomorrow."

Edgar walked back to his office and shed his jacket off and dropped it on a chair. He reached for his pocket and took out the paper and placed it on his desk and sunk in his chair.

What was written on the paper was brief and to the point.

Name: Elliot Silverman. 2 years old.

Medical Records Number: AP236559.

Surgeon: Dr. Brian Brinkley

Problem: Hernia surgery. Damaged permanently. Will never have children.

Get the key from Dr. Peter Molano. Reach him at Rehab Center, NYU. He is a patient there.

We'll meet again in two days. Same place, same time. Bring the envelope and I will tell you how you can retrieve the medical records.

Edgar grinned, folded the paper neatly, placed it in the bottom drawer of his desk and locked it.

* * * * *

The Medical Director was bitching and moaning. He was leaning over his secretary's desk, trashing papers around and looking for his schedule.

"Where the hell is Nancy?" he groaned as he looked at his watch for the tenth time.

Joseph Brown was obsessed with his well established routine. Every detail of his work was predetermined and programmed into his mental acuity. The slightest deviation would drive him crazy.

A true workaholic and captive to his principles of punctuality, he would walk into his office at exactly 7 a.m. every morning.

His desk, a large mahogany colored piece of art was neat and impeccably organized.

Right in front of him, he would find his daily schedule of meetings, appointments and coffee breaks. Nancy would have already collected the appropriate files and medical records he needed to review for his meetings and placed them neatly over the desk. She would do this before going home the previous evening.

Nancy would arrive to work at 9 a.m.

This morning, his desk was clean but nearly empty. No schedule. No files. No medical records.

It was past 9:30 and Nancy had not arrived yet.

The phone rang, and he reluctantly answered it. The Chairman of the Infection Control Committee was looking for him. They'd been waiting since 9 a.m. to get the meeting started.

He asked him to proceed and said he would join them a bit later.

He spent another fifteen minutes messing up the place and looking for his schedule when Nancy Robertson, the staff secretary walked in, huffing and puffing. She looked nervous and was hoping that the medical director had dropped dead that morning and she wouldn't have to face him. She had left her office in an extreme rush the night before to keep an important appointment and this morning she had to get to the bank first thing to make a crucial deposit of two thousand dollars.

"Where is my schedule?" The angry scream shuddered Nancy's eardrums like a horrendous thunder.

His face was inches from hers with his spectacles down to the tip of his nose and lightening flashing out of his angry eyes.

"I'm sorry Joe ..."

"My schedule." He exploded again. "Shut up now. I'm late for the meeting. I have no schedule, no charts, nothing."

Nancy dropped her purse on her desk and ran to her computer. "I'll print one now. I'm awfully sorry ..."

"Just print the damn thing. Don't worry, you're gonna be *really* sorry later on."

Nancy forced the paper out of the printer. He grabbed it and ran out. She collapsed in her chair and broke down.

A few long minutes later she finally got a hold of herself and looked at the schedule. The gorilla would not be back for another hour. She picked up the phone and dialed the number for the rehab center at NYU and asked if she could talk to Dr. Molano.

"Of course, I'll get him for you."

"Thank you."

Nancy cleared her throat. Her voice now more calm and comfortable.

"This is Dr. Molano."

"Hi Peter, this is Nancy. How are you?"

"Tired. These guys take me to physical therapy early in the morning, as if I'm supposed to get ready for climbing Mount Everest."

"They just want to get you back on your feet, Peter."

"Foot, Nancy, my foot, not feet, I have only one now."

Nancy shuddered of the thought of one legged Dr. Molano.

"C'mon now, tiger. You're young and strong. You'll walk again soon."

"Thanks Nancy. You're an angel. What's up now?"

"He'll come to see you today. His name is Edgar Lopez. Have the key ready for him."

"I'll give him the key, if you give me the key to your heart."

You bastard, you never give up. She wanted to say.

"He's already got mine, if you know what I mean."

"I know. I'm disappointed."

"Trust him. He can do the job. Just give him the key. I'll see him tomorrow."

"Will you come to see me soon?"

"I'll try. Gotta go now."

"I love you babe. Bye."

* * * * *

Detective Coleman stopped at the reception desk and asked if Dr. Molano was back from physical therapy.

"Yes he is." The nurse answered. "He was on the phone a few minutes ago. Let me see if he can see you"

She went down the hall and disappeared. The detective followed and stopped for a quick talk with the guard outside Peter's room.

"Mornin' Lieutenant." The guard stood up and dropped the morning paper on the floor.

"Mornin'. How is your prisoner?"

"Not in such a good mood today, he looks tired."

You ain't seen nothin' yet. Wait until I see him. He wanted to say, but decided not to.

"He may be officially charged for murder today."

"Wow, does he know?"

"He will, as soon as I get in there." He nodded towards the door.

"What would I do differently now?"

"I'll let you know later on. For now, no visitors, except his doctors and nurses. Anybody else should be cleared with me in advance."

"Got you, Lieutenant."

The nurse came out and pointed to the detective. "You can go in now."

"Thanks."

He knocked, but didn't wait for response. He went in.

"Mornin' Doc. I need to talk to you and it won't be long."

Peter was in his wheelchair, a blanket on his lap, covering his only leg. He looked pale and tired. A cup of hot coffee and couple hours of morning nap would do. This unexpected visitor was most unwelcome. He was visibly nervous, expecting the bad news.

"Please sit down." He stretched his neck towards the chair.

"I need to ask a few questions, Doc." He pulled the chair close to Peter's and sat down.

"What can I do for you?"

For me? Just be truthful.

"We found blood on the kitchen floor of Susan's apartment which did not match hers."

"And?"

The detective paused, gazing at the front wheels of the wheelchair. Two wheels and one foot. Tapping the floor nervously.

"You didn't wanna ask me Susan who, Dec?"

Peter started shaking.

"Uh yeah, who are you talking about?"

"Susan Flynn. The late Susan Flynn. You knew her."

"Poor Susan. She worked in the OR."

"You know how she died, Doc?"

"Killed in a car accident. This is what they told me"

"Were you close to her?"

"Worked in the OR with her."

"Were you ever in her apartment?"

"No." *Good thing he wasn't hooked to a lie detector.* Nevertheless, his hands were shaking. The detective noticed.

"We found your name all over her diary."

"So?" *She couldn't get enough of me.*

"You could write a romantic novel out of that diary, full of suspense and intrigue, hopes and broken hearts, and a tragic ending."

"What's all that got to do with me?"

"Probably nothing."

Peter tried to hide a deep sigh of relief. His eyes now opened wider and his hands loosened the firm nervous grip on the blanket. His only foot stopped tapping the floor.

"We also found *your* blood on the kitchen floor." The detective looked straight into Peter's eyes, as he delivered the punch line.

No immediate response from Peter. He was mum. His eyes scanned the floor. He knew that the detective knew. No point in faking a surprise reaction. He faked the mugging story. Didn't work.

"You sure it was *my* blood?" One last chance to get out of this jam.

"Yep, perfect match, DNA would not lie."

"I can explain."

"Explain it to the judge. The DA is seeking a murder indictment against you today."

"Not so fast detective. I am the one who got stabbed and she was killed in a car accident. Remember?"

"You attacked her in her apartment. She ran away in absolute panic. She ran for her life. Your actions caused her death."

"I need to talk to my lawyer" Peter replied.

"Sure you do. I just wanted to give you a heads up."

"Get out of here."

The nurse walked in shortly after the detective left.

"Dr. Molano. There is a Mr. Edgar Lopez here to see you, but the guard will not let him in."

"Why?"

"Detective Coleman's orders, you are not allowed to have visitors, unless first cleared by him."

"Tell the fuckin' guard to tell the fuckin' detective that Mr. Lopez is my lawyer's assistant. I have the right to a lawyer, dammit." Peter screamed.

"OK, OK. Watch your language Doctor." She left and slammed the door.

Half an hour later, a knock at the door as it opened slowly and a tall, well dressed, handsome gentleman walked in.

* * * * *

Brian parked his car in the underground parking garage of NYU. As he left his car, he reminisced several years of his residency training when his days started and ended in the very same parking garage. He missed his own designated spot in the Doctor's section. Today he parked in the visitor's section and entered the hospital.

As he walked through the lobby, he was very much tempted to go straight to the business office, find Jennifer, hug her and kiss her all over and tell her he was so sorry and he missed her badly. His big ego knocked him on the head again. The words Janet Reilly echoed in his ears repeatedly and he felt angry at Jennifer all over again.

Forget it. He was there to visit Peter Molano.

He went up to Rehab and stopped at the reception desk.

"May I help you, Sir?" A young nurse asked.

"Hi, I am Dr. Brinkley. I would like to visit Dr. Molano, if possible."

"Unfortunately he's not allowed to have visitors today."

"Oh? … Is he OK?"

"He's fine. He's under police protection because of a mugging incident. They have forbidden him to have visitors."

"I understand, but I am not just any visitor. I'm his friend. We work together. Could you ask him if I could see him for few minutes?"

The girl talked to another older nurse in the back who appeared to recognize Brian from a few years ago and rushed to the reception counter.

"Dr. Brinkley? … Welcome back … So nice to see you."

Brian took a sharp look at her and struggled to remember her name.

"Mrs… Mrs … . Hermes? Is that really you? What a pleasure to see you again. What are you doing in Rehab? You used to work in the OR a few years ago."

"That's right Dr. Brinkley. OR was too hectic for me. I am now a supervisor in this unit."

"Good. I just wanted to say hello to Dr. Molano. You know, we both work at Manhattan Medical Center."

Mrs. Hermes brought her head closer to Brian's and whispered.

"He seems to have some kind of legal problem. He's had a guard at his door since he's been here. They say it's for his protection. I don't believe it."

"I honestly don't know anything about this." Brian said, holding his voice down. "They say he was mugged, stabbed in the groin and lost his leg. I feel so sorry for him. Thought I could cheer him up a little bit."

Mrs. Hermes paused for a moment. "Let me go talk to the guard. He may let you in."

Brian waited at the reception desk, his eyes following Mrs. Hermes down the hall.

She returned with the policeman and introduced Dr. Brinkley to him.

"I'm sorry Doctor. I have to get permission from my superior to let you in."

"Who is your superior and where is he?" Brian asked.

"Detective Robert Coleman. I'll call him now. What was your name again sir?"

"I'm Dr. Brinkley"

The guard went to the phone. Brian was deep in thought. The name sounded very familiar. Detective Robert Coleman. He remembered him. This was the detective who came to his office and questioned him about the events in Susan's apartment shortly before her death. He hated him.

The guard called Brian to the phone. "Lieutenant wants to talk to you, Doc."

Brian took the phone.

"Hello Dr. Brinkley, this is Detective Coleman. Do you remember me?"

"Of course I do. Is my friend under arrest?"

"Not quite yet, Dr. Brinkley, I didn't know you two were friends."

"We are colleagues. We work at the same hospital." As if Detective Coleman didn't know this.

"I was just on my way to the hospital. I was going to call you today. I have something very important to discuss with you. Can you wait there for me?"

"Sure, but I have office hours this afternoon. How long will this take?"

"I'll be there in fifteen minutes. We'll have a private discussion and then you can leave."

"While I am waiting for you to come here, can I visit my friend?"

"No." The response was firm and authoritative.

"Fine, I'll just wait here for you."

"Thanks."

Brian realized that, for whatever reason, Dr. Molano would not be allowed visitors today.

He asked Mrs. Hermes if she would be kind enough to inform Dr. Molano of his coming here to visit him and wish him well. She said she would be delighted to do so.

He loitered around the halls until Detective Coleman arrived.

They got coffee from the nursing station and went to a private lounge and closed the door.

"I'm very surprised Lieutenant, why is he not allowed to have visitors?" Brian was anxious to get this question out of the way.

"He is under suspicion, possibly for murder."

"Wow! Who is the victim and why?"

"The late Susan Flynn."

"Hold on a minute. Didn't she die in a car accident?"

"We have reason to believe that he attacked her in her apartment shortly before she ran out in a state of panic and lost control of her car."

"Reason to believe? ... or proof?"

"You may call it proof. The blood on her kitchen floor that did not match hers, perfectly matched Dr. Molano's. DNA and all" The detective could not keep his eyes off Brian's puzzled facial expressions.

"How in the world did you become suspicious of *this* poor guy? Did you just pick a number out of a hat?"

The detective took a sip of his coffee and smiled. "No, just good detective work, Doc." He was enjoying his bright moment in the sun.

"If you remember ..." Detective Coleman continued, "when I met you in your office I told you about a detailed diary Susan Flynn had left behind." Brian nodded positively. "I also told you of three names we had come across repeatedly during the last few weeks of her life. Your name, a Janet Reilly and a third person I did not name for privacy reasons." Brian listened intently, his eyes bulging out, his mouth hanging open.

"That third person was Dr. Molano. And, it just happened that he had been stabbed in the groin on the very day Susan died. He lied through his teeth and concocted this mugging theory."

"It's unbelievable." Brian kept chewing the edges of his Styrofoam coffee cup, now empty, and remained in deep thought. What in the world was Peter doing in Susan's apartment. Perhaps they had a romantic relationship that went astray. Perhaps the stabbing was accidental, and perhaps the blood test was not accurate. A lot was going through his mind. A passing flash of thought connecting Peter to his own struggles and predicaments crossed his mind but did not take hold. He would not allow himself to go that far.

He threw his chewed-up coffee cup in the trash can and turned to the detective.

"Lieutenant, I don't think you kept me here just to tell me about Dr. Molano. Did you?" Brian asked.

"No I did not. I was planning to see you in your office today."

"For what?"

"When Susan died, her car was taken in for investigation of the cause of the accident. Her personal items were collected. Her purse, cell phone, shoes, watch, jewelry, whatever else she had with her. Nobody has showed up to claim these items. They are kept locked up in the evidence room at the police department. Inside the inner pocket of her purse they found a sealed envelope with your name on it. No address, as if it was being hand delivered to you. In view of what had been discovered in her apartment, I mean the blood in the kitchen and all, they decided to proceed with a criminal investigation in this case and the matter was referred to the District Attorney's office. We know from her diary that she was going to see Janet Reilly that evening. This has brought us back to whatever role the so-called Janet Reilly had played in Susan Flynn's life and maybe even her death. We have to find this Janet Reilly, and we thought maybe, just maybe, you could help us find her. "

Brian had had enough of Janet Reilly. Suddenly his focus was on the envelope, as if he didn't hear what the detective asked about Janet Reilly.

Flash back. He remembered that Susan was going to reveal his enemies names when she was to meet Jennifer … or … darn it, Janet Reilly. He hated the name so much that he couldn't tolerate mentioning it.

"Where is the envelope now?" he asked anxiously.

"At the police precinct"

"When can I have it?"

"Not sure. Since we now know who was in Susan's apartment shortly before her death, you are no more under suspicion; however, we cannot release the letter to you because the criminal investigation is ongoing. If you obtain permission from the District Attorney, you may be able to obtain a copy of the letter."

"Listen Lieutenant, this is a long story. Some people in the hospital where I work had conspired to destroy my career. Competition, jealousy, stupidity, whatever the reason, they used Susan to file a sexual harassment complaint against me.

She soon realized that she had been trapped. She withdrew her complaint and apologized to me. That did not end the matter. The hospital authorities claimed that I had intimidated and coerced her into withdrawing her complaint, and they are still trying hard to kick me off the staff. In the meantime Susan was fired and this enraged her. She decided to blow the whistle on them and promised me that she would reveal the name or the names of the conspirators.

What is written in that letter could save my career, my life, everything. I need to read that letter soon, Lieutenant. How can I get my hands on it?"

"I just told you Doctor. You have to go to the District Attorney's office and claim the letter. Tell them your story, and they may allow you to have a copy of it. The original has to wait until this investigation is over."

The detective was not sure if Brian heard him well. He was suddenly restless, nervously pacing the room, going back and forth to the window looking outside. He could not stay there anymore.

Brian rushed out of the room. The detective jumped to his feet and reached the door and hollered "How about Janet Reilly?"

Brian's response trailed as he rushed away, "Never heard of."

* * * * *

Edgar Lopez closed the door behind him and said hello to Dr. Molano. He took a quick look around the room and stared intensely at Peter. His features reflected uncertainty as to the appropriate manners here. Was he to express sympathy and sadness for what had happened to this young and attractive surgeon and drive him deeper into depression, or was he to ignore the miserable look of this one legged creature confined to a wheelchair and instead try to cheer him up in whatever way he could. There was no background of friendship or acquaintance to exchange pleasantries but Edgar was smart and alert to the subject of their mutual interest and jumped right in.

"Nancy has told me a lot about you, Dr. Molano."

"She's very nice to me but she thinks the world of you."

"We've known each other for quite sometime."

"Personally or professionally?" Peter couldn't help asking the question.

"We've been friends with mutual interests."

"Romantic or otherwise?" Now he was pushing it a bit.

"Both."

The response was quick and final, but Edgar knew he was lying. He was never romantically involved with Nancy, although he had used romance and money to entice her into his well thought out schemes.

As a paralegal by training and with earlier experience as an EMT (Emergency Medical Technician), working with the rescue squads of his neighborhood fire department and riding ambulances, he had been exposed to the facts and fallacies of both worlds.

The medical and the legal system.

While hanging around hospitals, clinics, nursing homes and emergency rooms, he had come across many low level hungry lawyers, the ambulance chasers, passing on their business cards to the injured and the victims' relatives.

He realized that hospitals and the medical profession were treasure troves to the perpetually hungry legal system.

His paralegal training opened his eyes into the immense universe of liability laws, tort system and medical malpractice suits.

He appreciated the interdependence of the two worlds for survival and decided to extend a helping hand, being fully aware and receptive of the lucrative fringe benefits.

"I understand you are working in a law firm as a paralegal." Peter asked.

"Weinstein & Rosenberg. A prestigious law firm in the city."

"How many lawyers in the firm?"

"Fifty six. We cover all areas of law."

"Medical malpractice?"

"Certainly."

"Whom do they mostly defend, the plaintiffs or the defendants."

"Of course the plaintiffs."

"How about criminal law?"

"We have the most aggressive criminal defense attorneys in the country."

"Good. Looks like we're going to need each other's help."

"I'm here to help." Edgar began to like the direction of the conversation.

Peter thought for a moment and moved his wheelchair towards a bedside table and took a glass of water.

"I have been in an unfortunate accident. In addition to losing my leg, I now find myself in legal hot water. I need a very good attorney, but, I don't have the financial means to afford a high priced attorney. I can offer your firm an extremely lucrative medical malpractice case, an open and shut one, with the potential for a multi-million dollars award. I will give you access to the records in exchange for an arrangement for my defense."

"Sounds good to me, but I'll have to run it by our lawyers" Edgar responded happily.

Peter rode his wheelchair to the corner of his room and opened the middle drawer of a small cabinet and retrieved a small box containing a strange looking key. He placed the key in the palm of his hand and fixed his pensive gaze on it. An eerie silence fell upon the room.

Peter remembered that eventful night at the medical records department and how this very key had exchanged hands between Judy Jackson, himself and finally Susan Flynn.

Would this key still work? He questioned himself.

More than likely it would. Peter thought. He knew that this key was only designed to open the door from the inside. The security was not concerned about the lost key since nobody could use it to enter the department, and changing the lock would require dismantling the whole system.

"Here is the key you need to exit the medical records department." He turned towards Edgar and extended his arm. "This is all I can tell you at this time." He continued as Edgar carefully grabbed the key and placed it in his pocket. "Nancy will give you more details on how you can enter the place, find and copy the medical records you need, but first, I expect to see one of your best lawyers right here tomorrow morning with paperwork prepared for me to sign."

"Understand, Doc."

"Take good care of Nancy."

"Will do."

Shortly after Edgar left, a nurse entered the room.

"Hi, Mrs. Hermes. What's for lunch today?" Peter asked.

"Same as yesterday. I came to let you know that Dr. Brinkley came to visit you."

"Dr. Brinkley? He came to kiss my ass?"

"You sound upset. He said you are friends, working at the same hospital."

Peter ignored her.

"But he didn't come in?" Peter asked.

"The detective turned him away. No visitors. He sets the rules around here."

"He can kiss my ass too."

"Dr. Molano! Behave please."

* * * * *

TWENTY FOUR

This time it was a different parking lot. Nancy Robertson had entered the shopping mall three hours earlier. When she had arrived, the parking lot was nearly full. She liked it. She parked the car far out, at a remote corner where there were only a few spots still available.

The mall closed at 9 p.m. and she walked out. It was dark and windy. She surveyed the area for people who could possibly recognize her from work or her neighborhood. None were evident. As she walked across the nearly empty lots she noted the car parked next to hers. The lights were on and the engine was running. She smiled and walked faster.

Edgar reached and opened the passenger door and Nancy dropped in.

The greetings were brief and formal.

"Did you get the key?" Nancy asked.

"I have it."

"Did Dr. Molano explain to you how this key works?"

"No, he was in bad mood."

"Poor guy just lost a leg. What a freaking accident."

"Sounded like he was in deep shit, some kind of a legal problem."

"And you got him a good lawyer, I know."

"They met this morning. All worked out well. I guess he filled you in on that already."

"I would not be here if you guys didn't make the deal with him."

"Indeed, he got a very good deal. Legal defense is not cheap."

"Hey, this is a unique case." She pointed to a bunch of papers she pulled out of her purse. "Could bring you millions, but for now, you have to pitch in."

Edgar pointed to the inner pocket of his jacket and said "I've got it here, let's hear you."

"Ok. The patient's chart is locked in the most secure area of the Medical Records room. It's a potential malpractice suit against the hospital and we don't have access to that chart anymore, otherwise I could get a copy for you.

"Don't worry Nancy, show me the way, and I'll get it out." Edgar said confidently.

Nancy unfolded the papers and pointed to the one on top.

"Here is a sketch of the layout of the Medical Records Department. Forgive my lousy drawings, but it's clear what's what." Her finger pointed to the main entrance and Edgar's gaze followed the finger carefully.

"You enter here; walk through this isle as you turn right. On your left you will see a door to another smaller room. This is the place where the sensitive charts are kept. Practically all the lawsuit charts are there, potential ones or actual. The room is known as the "litigation room", but there is no sign on the door.

"I suppose it's locked."

"Possibly double locked. You've got to open it somehow."

"My few years of working for a locksmith could pay off now." Edgar bragged.

"Inside the room, you'll find many file cabinets, each one locked, but the charts are filed in alphabetical order. There are labels on each cabinet."

Nancy pulled out the second page and placed it on top.

"Here is what else you need to know. Patient's name is Elliott Silverman. In case you find more than one file with the same name, patient's age, date of admission and surgery and the surgeon's name are written here."

Edgar noted that the page was typewritten. *Smart*, he thought.
Nancy put the first page, the sketch, on top again.

"Look here, as you walk down this isle, past the door to the litigation room, directly ahead at the end of the room you'll see a window
with blinds and a door next to it. This is the office of the Director of the
Medical Records. Next to this office there is another room where the doctors dictate their reports and summaries. There are copying machines all
over the place; you can use any one of them. The patient's chart is not
voluminous. He was in the hospital only one day. But, no matter what
the circumstances, you should not take the original chart. The chart is
needed for the defense of the lawsuit your firm is going to bring against
the hospital and the doctor."

Edgar flashed a teasing glance at Nancy "Who do you think you're
talking to, Nancy? I am a paralegal, I understand these things. As a matter of fact, our lawyers have to formally ask the hospital to send them a
copy of the chart once they are retained by the parents of this kid."

Nancy looked puzzled. "Then why the hell are you going through
this to get the chart?" She asked.
Edgar looked at his watch. "Why don't you finish all you have to tell
me and I'll answer that question later.

Nancy pulled out the third page and placed it on top.

"Here is the way I believe you should do this job. I'll explain it to
you, but if you forget the details, it's all written here." Nancy tapped the
paper.
"I'm listening."
"The Medical Records closes at eight p.m. That means all the late
working employees will check out by eight. The Director, however, stays
a bit longer, making her last phone calls. At eight fifteen a security officer
will check in, to make sure everybody has left, and if so, he will close the
door and activate a special security lock. From this moment on, nobody
can get in or out of the room without a special key, and that is the one
you have in your pocket. Don't lose it. Locksmith or not, nobody can trip
that lock"

Edgar instinctively put his hand in his pocket and checked the key. "Go on please." He said.

"You will have to enter the room precisely at ten minutes past eight. I'll make sure the security guard will be tied up with something else between eight and eight fifteen. When you enter, the main lights in the secretarial room are off, but you may notice that the lights in the Director's office are still on. She is there on the phone. You'll have to quietly sneak into the doctors' dictation room and hide there until the Director leaves. You may hear the security guard entering and hollering if anybody is still there. He will ignore the Director. She has her own special key to get out, and bear in mind; she may stay a long time."

"If she's cute I'll have fun with her." Edgar joked.

"Oh, shut up. Something like that happened in there once, and as the result, one person is dead, the Director was fired and another person lost a leg. Disastrous, isn't it?"

Edgar was quiet.

"As a matter of fact, that is why you have that special key in your pocket now."

"Ok, ok Nancy. Continue please."

"When you make sure the Director is gone you'll go to work. Retrieve the chart. Copy it and place it back exactly where you found it. The litigation room door will automatically lock when closed. Then use your special key on the main entrance door and get out."

Nancy stretched her hand holding the papers towards Edgar and said "Envelope please."

Edgar grabbed the papers, folded them and placed them in his pocket and pulled out a small brown envelope and gave it to Nancy. She glanced through and figured there should be approximately twenty of those hundred dollar bills in there.

"Thank you and good luck Edgar." She said with a sweet smile.

"Thank you Nancy. You asked a good question and I should give you the answer. Normally the patients retain a lawyer to bring a malpractice lawsuit against their doctors or hospital. In this case, we are assuming that the patient's parents do not know anything about his injuries, or if they do, they will hire their own lawyer. Our attorneys need to go through this patient's chart, assess the extent of the injury and the merits of the lawsuit and the reward they should ask the court. Then they should somehow take the case to the parents of this kid with concrete evidence in order to convince them to sue the doctor and the hospital. To do all that, they need the chart."

"Ok, you now know how to get it Edgar, good luck." Nancy said as she opened the door and eased out. She got into her car and swiftly drove away.

* * * * *

Brian was in a somber mood. For the past two weeks, since he had met Detective Coleman at the hospital, he had made several attempts to get his hand on Susan's letter at the office of the New York District Attorney. First he was told they had no knowledge of it. He checked with Coleman and was told to be patient. The matter had only recently been referred to the DA's office. These things take time to go through the process. "You know. All the bureaucratic hurtles and what-not."

He went back to the DA's office again a week later.

Yes, they had received the report, but it involved a homicide, under investigation. He had to wait until the investigation was over and it might take weeks or months.

"But the letter is addressed to *me*, Dr. Brian Brinkley. There is important information in there, very crucial for my profession." He said desperately.

"Could we see an ID please?" the clerk responded.

"Sure, what do you want?"

"A picture ID, like a driver's license."

Brian's heart was galloping. His hopes were raised, only to be dashed right away.

The ID was needed only to let him in to see an Assistant District Attorney.

"No Sir" Brian was told "we cannot give you the letter now. Here is a request form. You should fill this out in detail, including your relationship with the deceased. We will then get the ball rolling. A decision will be made in a few weeks whether you should be given a copy of this letter."

Few weeks, my ass. He was fuming.

The office was quiet. Patients were coming in dribs and drabs. Another deep worry was on his mind. The practice was suffering from recent events. Money was only trickling in, and the bills were piling up. The utmost concern on his mind was the rising malpractice premium. Another fifteen percent raise had been announced and now his was at ninety thousand dollars a year. *So unfair, so ridiculously unfair.* He mused.

Oh God, I may have to fire some members of my staff. That's awful. He thought of a few short months ago when his office was sizzling with activity. He didn't have time to relax a minute. Patients were crawling up the walls. He used to go home exhausted. Money was pouring in and all he yearned for was a day off when he could take his boat out to sea. The boat was now up for sale. His beloved boat.

He was down, depressed and desperate, but deep down he knew what he was missing most. Jennifer Bradley, his best companion, his dearest friend, his caring advisor, his true love. Ah, he hated the loneliness, the desperation, the anxiety. He had not seen her for a few weeks. He was wondering if there was any way that Jenny might come back to him and help him out of this miserable situation, and yet, the thought of what Jennifer had done to him in the fictitious character of Janet Reilly made him shudder.

The intercom buzzed and derailed his train of thought. It was his office manager, Helen Hansen. She'd sent the receptionist home earlier. It was a very slow day.

"Dr. Sloan is returning your call. Can you take it now?"
"Sure Helen, what line?"
"On 2729"
"Thank you, I'll take it now" He pushed the extension.

"Hello Chief, how are you"

"I'm fine Brian. What can I do for you?"

"Any news from the Board of Directors?"

"Nope. They meet next month."

"Any idea what they're gonna do with me?"

"I told you before, more than likely they'll refer your case to the Department of Health."

The words "Department of Health" sent shock waves through his body.

"But why?" he asked, his voice trembling. *This was really serious*

"Because this idiot, the Medical Director is pushing for it"

"He is an idiot alright, but why is he so steadfast on getting rid of me?"

"To justify his existence. He is employed by the hospital to keep an eye on the medical staff. He considers himself a medical detective rather than a Medical Director. He is a dangerous man."

Brian paused for a moment as if submitting to his fate.

"What happens after my case is referred to the Department of Health?"

"I don't think your patient care issues such as complications, a couple of infections, or even your mortalities are serious enough to warrant a report to the Department of Health. But, the ethical issue of sexual harassment has not been settled yet and as long as that lady, what's her name … Janet Reilly … remains elusive they're not gonna let you off the hook. You know about OPMC at the Department of Health?"

"You mean Office of Professional Medical Conduct? Yes, I know about that."

"That's where your case will end up."

"In other words they're gonna feed me to the lions. They may revoke my license, Chief."

"That's the danger. You should hire a lawyer if it gets to that point."

"Hire a lawyer? A lawyer? That's a double whammy right there. The Department of Health will take my license away, and the lawyer will rob me of every penny I have."

"Don't get paranoid now, Brian."

"Thank you Chief, I am ever so grateful to you for your understanding and support."

"Keep your spirits high, Brian. These are bad times for our profession. There was a time when the practice of medicine was all pleasure and joy. Patients were so appreciative of doctors saving their lives and relieving their pain. Nowadays, they are ready to go straight for your jugular if they don't like the way you talk to them. No understanding, no appreciation. They expect you to be standing at the ready two o'clock in the morning to run to the ER for symptoms they've had for days and never cared to visit a doctor in the office. Insurance companies are the biggest pain in the ass these days. They pay you peanuts compared to five or ten years ago, when in fact your expenses have quadrupled in that time. Malpractice premium is running the doctors out of practice, not to mention the constant fear of lawsuits if you stay in practice. People don't understand that doctors don't make money anymore. No businessman stays in a profession in which he keeps less than ten cents out of every dollar he makes. It's insane. It is a tragic testimonial to the deterioration of the medical practice when gynecologists do hair removal and gastroenterologists do liposuction. Doctors are pushed to the fringes of medical ethics. They pull the rug out from each other's feet. It's a struggle for survival. You know Brian, whatever happened to those good old times when doctors were almost God? They had prestige, honor and well deserved respect. So we're all in this together. Stand tall and keep on fighting my friend."

"Thank you Dr. Sloan. I understand."

Brian said good bye and hung up. As if he didn't have enough troubles to worry about, now he had one more to add to the list. OPMC.

* * * * *

The phone at the reception desk of the business office at New York University Medical Center rang and the secretary responded.

"Good evening, Business office."

"Hi, this is Ms. Hansen. May I talk to Ms. Jennifer Bradley?"

"She's at a meeting now; would you like to leave a message for her?"

"How long will she be there?"

"Probably another hour."

"Does she have another meeting after that?"

"No, this is her last one for the day. She'll be in her office wrapping up."

"That's better; I wanna catch her when she's not very busy. Just leave a message for her that I called."

"OK, what's your name again?"

"Helen Hansen, she knows me."

"Will do"

One hour later Jennifer returned to her office and saw the message on her desk. She had known Helen as long as she'd known Brian. Helen was in her late fifties, a widow with two grown daughters. She'd been working for Brian from the day he opened his office. She had managed surgical offices all her professional life and her experience was a blessing for Brian. They became very close to each other. Helen found in Brian a son she never had, and he relished the motherly, tender love he had not enjoyed since childhood.

Helen became extremely protective of Brian.

The chemistry was right between them and they became each others' good friend and confidant. Brian's practice flourished rapidly, thanks to Helen's mastery of healthcare issues, HMO organizations and medical economics. She gained the pride and satisfaction of a professional success story, managing Brian's office, and more than that, managing Brian himself. A brilliant, well educated young man with self destructing attributes such as arrogance, impatience, and egotism. Helen's maturity and her influence on Brian brought about significant changes in his attitude and tamed his often aggressive and explosive mood.

Helen was very fond of Jennifer and realized that she played an important role in Brian's life, as a close friend, a good advisor and lover. She and Jenny often worked together behind Brian's back to guide him through his difficulties.

Everything was moving along well until the sexual harassment incident. Helen soon realized that something was wrong with Brian and found him uncharacteristically quiet.

She had the impression that Brian was struggling with something that he could not share with her, contrary to many other problems that he would readily confer with her. Perhaps something he was embarrassed about. Perhaps something below his dignity, or insulting to his ego. She remained quietly watchful.

She noted Brian's frequent phone calls to the Chief of Surgery, Medical Director's office or Medical Records. She noticed Brian changing his surgery schedule frequently, often on a short notice. Cancel tomorrow's. Move Tuesday morning's to the afternoon. I have an *urgent* meeting and cannot go to the hospital this afternoon.

And the day a detective came to the office to see Brian; she knew Brian was in bigger trouble than he'd ever admit.

Helen had to deal with a great deal of disruption to Brian's office and hospital schedule.

She encouraged him to take a vacation and finally succeeded sending him and Jennifer to the Bahamas, alas to find him back in worse shape than when he left. In addition to Brian, she now found Jennifer changed drastically, from the loving, caring and joyful young lady to an extremely angry, unfriendly and distressed woman. She never called the office again and Helen was at a loss what to do.

A few agonizing weeks went bye, and Helen witnessed the continued deterioration of the practice, a sharp decline in referrals, and income.

She decided to call Jennifer.

"Hello, this is Ms. Hansen. I called earlier. Is Ms. Bradley back from her meeting?"

"Oh yes. She's in her office. Hang on, I'll ring her now."

"Helen dear, how are you?" Jennifer's voice was calm and friendly.

"I'm fine darling. Long time no see. Brian is not the only one in this office who loves you." She giggled.

"How is he Helen?"

"Bad, Jenny. Bad … very bad. Everything is bad, he's bad, practice is bad, and I am falling apart. We both need your help."

"You're a strong woman Helen, you don't need my help. He's a bad boy and deserves what's coming to him"

"I don't know what's happened between the two of you, he misses you badly. I can read it in his eyes. He needs you desperately, Jenny. But I also know that he has problems with the hospital. Looks to me his friends have abandoned him. Very few referrals these days. What's going on?"

"It's complicated Helen. He's lucky he has you watching out for him. You know I love him. You know that Helen, don't you?" Jennifer's voice broke. Helen could not see her eyes getting watery.

"I know darling. You're an angel. But, at this time you should love him a little less and help him a little more. Come back to him please. We'll both work together to save him."

"He has a lot of growing up to do, Helen, and it takes time."

"There is a time limit to everything, sweetheart. You young people don't understand this. He may end up closing his office in a month or two. I wish I knew what his problems were. I believe you know and you're the only one who can help him."

"I've been waiting for him to come to his senses and acknowledge his despicable behavior in the Bahamas. I've put up with his nasty attitude many times in the past. This one is different. Believe me Helen, I love him and I miss him too, but I need more time to forgive and maybe forget."

"I'm sure you'll do both. The sooner the better, please."

"I'll try Helen. Thank you for calling me."

When Jennifer hung up, her heart was aching for Helen, but a broad smile appeared on her face. There it was. The first glimpse of Brian's remorsefulness. She had made her silent statement and the impact was now evident. Helen delivered his message of compunction and contrition.

It was time to come to Brian's rescue.

She picked up the phone and called the only person who could possibly shed a light on the mystery of Susan Flynn's death, and perhaps the identity of the person or persons behind Brian's miseries. Judy Jackson.

* * * * *

The meeting took place at the same restaurant they had met the first time, the Lenox Room. This time they both arrived on time, knowing exactly whom they were meeting or at least recognizing each other, even though Judy believed she was to meet Janet Reilly.

But, not for too long. Jennifer was going to be Jennifer tonight. She had had enough of Janet Reilly. Since Janet Reilly had come between her and Brian all hell had broken loose.

She hated Janet Reilly. And, when she heard the voice "Hello Janet." She hated herself.

She struggled to pull herself together.

"Hello Judy, so nice of you to come on such short notice."

"With pleasure." Judy said with a warm smile. "I always wanted to see you again since that eventful night in here."

They were seated and ordered drinks. There was silence at the beginning. Their eyes kept exchanging short glances at each other, not so sure what to expect. Judy recalled Janet Reilly's attitude being somewhat nasty and rude at the first meeting, although her harshness was directed at Susan. *Why did she ask to meet me here this time?* She wondered.

"When I think about our first meeting ..." Jennifer said "I feel ashamed of myself. I was angry at Susan for being late and eventually not showing up, all the while she was losing her life in a car accident. How tragic it was." Jennifer tried to show Judy her true, caring and compassionate side.

Judy was happy to hear this confession.

"Frankly, Janet, I always wanted to know why you were so impatient with her. She was the sweetest sole I knew."

Jennifer took a sip of her drink and cleaned her lips with a napkin. Her eyes appeared misty and her voice reflected her sadness.

"I have a confession to make tonight. There is a lot to be said, and I beg for your understanding. Last time, you came seeking my help. This time I need your help, but first ..." Jennifer paused for a moment, a moment that felt like eons to Judy, who was now restlessly curious.

Jennifer continued "Susan was in fact a beautiful, innocent young lady. She knew me as Janet Reilly, but that is not who I really am. My name is Jennifer Bradley. I am a close friend of Dr. Brian Brinkley. I am the Director of the Business Office at NYU." Her gaze was fixed at the perplexed features of Judy whose frown lines and forehead wrinkles were deepening by the seconds and her jaw half way dropped in astonishment.

"Now, wait a minute …" Judy was incredulous. "You mean you're NOT the real Janet Reilly, the mysterious ghost who had been roaming the halls at the Manhattan Medical Center looking for Susan Flynn?"

"No, there is no real Janet Reilly. There never was one. Susan was in deep trouble, trapped by somebody or some people to create a scandal involving Dr. Brinkley whose adversaries were conspiring to destroy him. He is a successful surgeon and very popular. In three years he trumped his competition and scared a lot of other surgeons. They decided to knock him out and used Susan to file a sexual harassment complaint against him. I alerted Susan of the trap she had fallen into. I had to use an alias otherwise she would find out my closeness to Dr. Brinkley and would reject me as being his agent. She jumped the fence and apologized to Dr. Brinkley and decided to reveal the identity of the conspirators."

"Is that why she was coming here to meet you?" Judy interrupted.

"Exactly. Unfortunately she never made it. And because of that, Brian has had no way of defending himself. The hospital is pushing him out and with the cloud of sexual harassment hanging over his head he is toast."

Judy could not conceal her bafflement.

"No wonder they were dragging him from committee to committee. You know, I was the Director of the Medical Records and a friend of Nancy Robertson, the Medical Director's secretary. I knew what was going on. Every day they were digging into his patients' charts, piling them up and taking them back and forth to committee meetings."

The waitress appeared to take their order.

There was a break in the conversation. They ordered food and more drinks.

Judy remained in deep thought. Knowing the identity of Janet Reilly now, and the troubles of Dr. Brinkley, she was beginning to see a clear picture developing out of an intertwined web of professional rivalry, conspiracy, deceit, sex scandal, jealousy and tragedy.

And suddenly a central figure in this tragic scenario began to take shape, a man who could have easily been behind all this drama. A man who pretended to be her lover while seducing Susan and using her to destroy his nemesis, Dr. Brian Brinkley. *Sonofabitch, he killed Susan.* She wanted to scream.

Jennifer broke the silence. "Who are they, Judy? The people who were after him. The people who wanted him out. Who are they?"

"I hate to erroneously implicate people, but I think I do have answers to your question. But first, let me ask you if Susan ever talked to you about having an affair with one of the surgeons in the hospital?"

"No."

"Did she ever mention to you having pictures of her boyfriend in a sexual act with another woman?"

"Never."

"Did she ever tell you about an incident she was involved with, in the Medical Records Department."

"She did not. Where are you going with these questions?"

"Susan was duped into believing that there was a marriage opportunity for her with her lover, the surgeon, but she had to help him get rid of a formidable rival whose popularity was threatening a number of other surgeons out of practice. She was naïve, young and inexperienced, and went along. Then you came, I mean Janet Reilly came on the scene and shook up her determination. How you did it I don't know. Then, in a most bizarre turn of events she accidentally witnessed her lover being sexually involved with another woman and her hopes and aspirations for the future went up in smoke."

Jennifer interrupted her "Was that the incident in Medical Records, you mentioned before?"

Judy took a deep sigh, and grudgingly nodded.

"And how did you find out about it?"

Judy did not respond. Jennifer noted tears running down her cheeks and got the picture.

"I'm sorry Judy" she said apologetically.

Judy dabbed her eyes with her napkin and continued.

"Anyway, Susan became hostile to the surgeon and decided to reveal his identity. She was distraught when she lost her job. I lost mine too. We were both victimized by the same person. He sure deserves what's happened to him.

"Judy, you're killing me. Who're you talking about?"

"You should know him Jennifer. He's been a patient at your hospital. He lost a leg, after he was stabbed in a mugging accident."

Jennifer was beside herself. The revelation was huge. She could now connect the dots. Peter Molano deceived Susan to fabricate a sexual harassment incident against Brian. At the same time he betrayed Susan and got sexually involved with Judy. Susan found out and revolted against him and possibly threatened to reveal everything. Susan died in a car accident on the same day Peter was stabbed. *Exactly the same day!* Jennifer knew Dr. Molano was under the watchful eyes of law enforcement officials. Perhaps the legitimacy of the mugging incident was in question.

"You're talking about Dr. Peter Molano. Aren't you?"

"Exactly. He is the most devious person I've ever known."

"I tell you Judy, There are many rumors at our hospital questioning the authenticity of this mugging accident. He has a guard at his door all the time. They are treating him more like a suspect than a victim."

"Knowing the man, I wouldn't be surprised if he went after Susan fearing she would show the pictures around.

"What pictures?"

"She had told him that she took pictures when he was in my office, you know what I mean?"

"Did she?"

"I'm not so sure; she told me she made it up to threaten him. But, I've been deeply worried about that too"

"You have nothing to worry about. Susan is dead. Peter Molano is crippled and may even go to jail. Perhaps we can rescue Dr. Brinkley from losing his license to practice medicine."

They had hardly touched their dinner, and the waitress was there to take dessert orders.

Coffee was all they could stomach.

Jennifer was anxious to ask one final question.

"Are there others, Judy?"

"Yes. The one you should fear most now is the Medical Director, Dr. Joseph Brown. He is the worst son of a bitch I've known. You should let Nancy Robertson tell you about him."

"Who is Nancy Robertson?"

"His secretary. She's pissed off at him big time. The man is a nasty prick. Gives her no respect. Treats her like a piece of shit. I always wondered why she stayed with him. But Nancy is a bit mysterious herself. I have a feeling there is something in it for her to stay. Once she told me she was secretly recording the jerk's conversations. She said Peter Molano was always in his office and they had long conversations on many different issues related to the medical staff. No doubt they were in this together on Dr. Brinkley's issues."

"Did you say she recorded their conversations?" Jennifer asked anxiously.

"That's what she told me"

Hmm, that's good. Jennifer pondered.

She wrote the names on a napkin and placed it in her purse.

She then smiled and said "I guess Janet Reilly should pay them a visit."

* * * * *

TWENTY FIVE

The fall foliage along the Pennsylvania highways and back roads exhibit a fascinating masterpiece of nature's revolving sceneries. As the leaves change color, from green to yellow and all shades in between, every turn of the road brings up a new montage of colorful Oak and Maple tree branches and leaves as they dance with the soft breezes of the valleys and hillsides.

The views are breathtaking, exhilarating and relaxing.

Occasionally, a couple of deer can be spotted frolicking moments before they notice a passing car.

The black Mercedes cruised along the winding roads quietly and leisurely. The radio played Kenny Gee's exhilarating soft melodies. The world had suddenly slowed down, inviting relaxation and pleasure. Brian Brinkley was pensive and preoccupied with unsettling thoughts of doom and gloom. He was losing control of his life and, deep down, he was happy to run away from it all.

As the evening sun began to sink behind the tree tops, a pleasant atmosphere of serenity and calmness pervaded the air. Everything was tranquil and peaceful.

He wished he could live his whole life in these few short minutes of emotional revival, free of stress, anxiety, expectations and often the horrors of real life. He deserved a break.

The upheavals of the last few months had derailed his promising personal and professional life. He was becoming increasingly frustrated and discouraged. It looked as though his life was being run by everybody else but him. He needed to escape from everything and everybody.

The Bahamas trip was a disaster. His girlfriend left him. His colleagues started to walk away from him. His business faltered and his beloved boat was auctioned.

He needed a shoulder to cry on, and he knew where to find it.

As he approached Tannersville, he made a left turn, passed by the Crossings outlet stores complex and headed uphill through the winding roads. He noted the Brewery was open and crowded. The parking lot was almost full.

The car roared ahead as darkness began falling on the road. Two sharp uphill turns and then he saw the big sign on the left side. "The Chateau". The silhouette of the big hotel appeared in the background.

He realized that since the old man would not appreciate an unexpected knock at his door this late in the evening he would spend the night at the Chateau.

As he walked into the warm, inviting lobby, he became nostalgic. There, by the flaming fireplace he remembered so many evenings, coming down the ski slopes, he and Jenny would collapse on the posh couches, taking their boots off and holding their freezing feet against the fire to warm up. They would drink a hot cup of coffee served in the lobby, light a cigarette and dream about moments later when they would go to their suite and take a hot shower together.

He reminisced about those ski trips they used to take together. Camelback Ski Resort in the Pocono Mountains was two hours drive from Manhattan, ideal for a day trip or weekend getaway. For more adventure and fun they would fly to Vail or Aspen, Colorado and they would forget that the rest of the world existed as they immersed themselves in a few days and nights of romantic fantasy.

He checked in and went right to the bar. "Grey Goose on the rocks please, Thank you. Make it a double."

The loneliness was torture. His stomach was grumbling but he chose to ignore it. As he gulped the vodka, he felt warm all over. Another double, please. He was offered some mixed nuts, and he munched on a few.

He pretended to watch the TV on the opposite wall. There were two other couples at the bar cozying up to each other. Seeing them reminded him of his loneliness.

He paid the bill and went to his room. It was cold and boring. He stretched on the bed for a while under the dim lights and remembered the intimate moments in the past he used to hold Jenny in his arms and kiss her all over.

This was totally intolerable. His stomach still growling, he decided to get out.

Back in the car, pulled out the CD and tried a different tune for a change of pace, as he rolled out of the parking lot. Beyond the resort area the roads were dark and winding. Two double vodkas on an empty stomach made him dizzy and he had a hard time focusing his eyes on the road.

Barely navigating the two steep downhill turns Brian finally, safely reached the Brewery.

The Barley Creek Brewery of Tannersville was a famous gathering place for skiers, hikers, vacationers and locals.

Inside, the atmosphere was warm and jolly with crowds of young and old chatting loudly, laughing and embracing affectionately.

The bar was crowded and noisy.

He did not notice the young blonde girl sitting next to him until after he ordered the drink.

Brian ordered a pint of Guinness and a double Grey Goose on the rocks and asked if food was served at the bar.

"Of course you can order here, Sir" the bartender responded. "Here's the Menu."

Brian took a brief look at the menu and ordered food.

He lit a cigarette and blew the smoke straight up toward the high cathedral ceiling.

The drinks arrived. He gulped the vodka down right away and washed it off with the beer. He always liked a beer chaser.

He tapped the bar with his index finger and the bartender got the message. Another round, please.

As the warm, delicious vapor rose from the hot dish served before him, Brian heard her voice.

"Looks delicious"

"Thank you. Wanna share it with me?"

"It's tempting, but no thanks."

He took a long drag and blew out, as he turned to see her face. She was young, blonde and beautiful.

"What's a gorgeous girl like you doing here at the bar?" he asked.

"Chasing the handsome men like you" she laughed.

"Watch out, you're asking for trouble young lady."

"I deal with my troubles all the time. And you?"

"You don't wanna know about my troubles. I've come here to forget them all."

He ordered another round of drinks for both of them and insisted that she take a bite of his chicken. She took his fork, picked up a juicy piece of chicken and flirtatiously put it in her mouth and licked her luscious lips as she fixed her sensual gaze on his eyes.

"Umm … delicious."

There was a flash of deep desire bouncing back and forth between them.

He felt her soft and warm hand as he took his fork back.

"You've got to eat something now. Excuse me; can I have a menu for the young lady?"

"Yes Sir, right away."

Her food arrived and they enjoyed dining together, chatting, joking, laughing and flirting.

She washed down her last bite with a sip of her wine and leaned on his shoulder.

"A beauty like you should have a beautiful name."

"I do."

"And that is?"

"Jennifer, you can call me Jenny"

The loud bang of silverware crashing on china caught the attention of most patrons. . As he moved quickly to catch the fork he tipped his drink over and wet her skirt.

"Jennifer?" Brian stammered "what a beautiful name. I'm awfully sorry. I spilled my drink on you."

He jumped off the chair but was wobbly and unstable on his feet, the room was cloudy and the ceiling was spinning around.

Jennifer realized he had had one too many. She stepped down and grabbed his arm.

"Let's go out get some fresh air."

He placed a hundred dollar bill on the counter. "Keep the change, my man."

"Thank you Sir." The bartender winked at the girl as they walked away from the bar.

Outside the air was misty and cool. They walked toward the parking lot.

"Tell me, are you staying around here?" he asked.

"Yep, up there at the Chateau."

"Gotta be kidding me. I just checked in there myself. Nice place."

"I better give you a ride up there. The roads are wet now and slippery."

"Ok, Jenny. You take me there and I'll take it *from* there. Will you have a drink with me? They have a nice cozy bar there."

There was one drink after another. Brian had a ball with his newly found Jennifer.

They joked and laughed and fooled around. A short stretch on the couch at the fireplace in the lobby, kissing passionately, then up in his suite fervently undressing each other and pushing to bed.

The sex was rough, fiery, and passionate, although mostly one sided. Her feminine instincts realized that he was calling, caressing and kissing another Jennifer, the one who had shared in his past romantic life, the one who was the object of his dreams and fascinations, and the one he had tragically lost recently.

As the fire cooled off, he fell asleep.

When he woke up the sun was peeking through the shades, and he was alone in bed.

What a nice dream it was last night. Or was it real?

He began to remember everything.

Where is the girl? He jumped off the bed and ran into the bathroom. The room was warm and misty, the towel was wet and she was gone.

Brian looked all over the place. No trace of her. No notes.

He collapsed back on his bed and pushed his face into her pillow and enjoyed the scent of a woman named Jennifer.

Two hours later Brian woke up again, took a hot shower and cleared his head.

He remembered that he left his car at the Brewery the night before. It would be a good half hour walk and he needed it. He put his warm-up suit and sneakers on and got on the road.

The air was cool and crisp. The pleasant morning sunlight was reflecting off the waves of water running down the rocky creek carrying fallen autumn leaves. The birds chirped and squirrels ran up and down the trees. He envied the people who lived their lives there, so serene, so beautiful.

An hour later Brian checked out of the hotel and drove north, deeper into the higher elevations of the Pocono Mountains. He passed the Camelback Ski Resort area. The slopes were barren and sad, waiting for the snow season. He drove the sharp uphill road until he reached his destination. A small condominium complex with a sign at the entrance: North Hills.

Brian rang the door bell twice and waited anxiously until he heard strong footsteps coming down the stairs. He held onto the railing and tried hard to hide his anxiety. As the door opened and the old man appeared at the threshold Brian managed a smile.

"Hi Dad."

"Brian? Is that you? Son of a gun. Good to see you."

The embrace was warm and deeply emotional.

* * * * *

Nancy Robertson entered the lobby of the Manhattan Medical Center exactly at 8 p.m. She went to the switchboard and saw her friend Joanne at the console.

"Hi Nancy, what're you doing here?"

"I left my cell phone in my office. Could you call Security for me to open the door?"

"Sure hon', hang on there for a moment."

"Thanks."

Nancy stepped back from the counter and took a glance around the lobby.

She saw him at the far corner, sitting on a couch. His face covered by a newspaper in his hand. She anxiously looked at her watch again, hoping the Security would call back right away. There was only a ten minute window of opportunity for him to enter the Record Room. At 8:15 Security would lock the door and that would be the end of it.

"He's on the line Nancy, what should I tell him?"

"Oh good, tell him to meet me at the Medical Director's office."

"OK."

"Thank you Joanne, see you tomorrow."

She rushed to the next hall, down the stairway and entered the basement halls. It was quiet. Very few staff members passed by.

She reached her office and waited in the hall. *C'mon, C'mon. It's getting late.* She mumbled.

Another glance at her watch. 8:09 p.m.

She recognized Edgar passing by her despite his fake mustache and baseball cap pulled down to his eyebrows. He was heading in the right direction, and she smiled.

"Hello Ms. Robertson, What can I do for you?"

"Oh, hello Joe, I'm sorry to trouble you, I left my cell phone in my office, could you open it please?"

"Sure, but be quick, I gotta lock the Record Room now."

The door opened and Nancy entered. She turned the lights on and went to her desk.

"I tell you what," the guard called in "I'm gonna walk down the hall and lock the Record Room while you look for your cell phone. Be back in a minute."

"Oh no Joe, I'll be outa here in a second." She looked at the clock on the wall. 8:13 p.m.

"These locks are time sensitive, gotta go" the guard's voice trailed as he walked away.

Edgar reached the record room at 8:10 p.m. As he approached, the door opened and an employee walked out. He walked past the door and paused at the corner to the next hall and waited a minute. As he started heading back toward the door, he saw the same employee running back. They both reached the door at the same time. She opened the door, reached inside and turned the lights off, closed the door and left. It was 8:13 p.m.

He could almost hear the footsteps of the guard approaching when he quickly entered the dark room and gently closed the door behind him. As expected the Director's office was lit at the end of the large main room. He took his shoes off and tiptoed through the center isle and quietly entered the doctors' dictation room.

Moments later he could hear the security guard hollering through the main entrance if anybody was still there. He then heard the door shut. Instinctively he checked his pocket for the key without which he would be trapped in there.

The light in the Director's office stayed on for another hour and Edgar was losing patience. He opened his cell phone and called Nancy.

"How long is this fuckin' lady gonna stay here?" He whispered, while muffling his voice by cupping his hand around his mouth.

"How the hell would I know, man? I told you she often stays long hours. Be patient."

Another half an hour passed and then he heard her footsteps leaving her office. Her lights went off. She walked quickly in the dark room, used her special key, opened the door and left.

It was time to move. He sneaked out of the room and used a small flashlight and located the door to the litigation room. From his pocket he pulled out his special key chain, investigated the door lock and worked it with different keys until he heard the click. He gently turned the knob and opened the door. He stepped in and closed the door behind him. The room was cold and pitch black. No windows. He felt comfortable and turned on the lights.

Within a few minutes he had Elliot Silverman's chart in his hand.

A copying machine at the end of the room came in handy. Eleven pages were copied quickly. He folded the papers and placed them in his pocket. The chart went back where it belonged.

Back in the main room, he found his way to the entrance in the dark. Behind the door he used his flashlight and located the security lock. He was now perspiring and a bit nervous. He held the flashlight in his mouth and removed the security key from his pocket.

The key slid easily into the key hole. He paused for a moment and placed his ear on the door listening for footsteps or voices. He heard nothing. This was the time to get out of here.

He pushed the key to turn. It didn't. Tried again. Nothing moved. Pushed in the opposite direction. No good.

Shit, I don't need this now.

One more time he tried to turn the key with more force. No luck. The other way. Nope.

Nervously he pulled the key out and looked at it under the flashlight. It looked the same.

He shook the door gently hoping to realign the lock. Placed the key back in and tried again. Nothing.

Sweat was now dripping off the tip of his nose. His hands were shaking and he had no clue what to do next. The clock near the door read 9:30 p.m.

He tried all of his special keys, none would work.

Desperate and worried, he returned to the doctor's dictation room and sat down. He opened his cell phone and called Nancy.

It rang several times. No answer. He left an urgent message, then closed his eyes, took a few deep breaths and tried to calm down.

The room was dark and cold. He cast his flashlight all around the room. No other doors, no windows.

He felt like a death row inmate in an isolation room the night before execution.

* * * * *

Judy Jackson was all dressed up ready to go out for an evening engagement when her phone rang.

"Hello Judy, this is Jennifer Bradley."

"Oh, hi Jennifer. How are you?"

"Just fine, Hope I didn't catch you at a bad time?"

"Not really, I was just getting ready to go out. What's up?"

"You gave me the name of Dr. Brown's secretary the other night. I know I wrote it on a napkin. Was that Robertson or Peterson?"

"Robertson… Nancy Robertson."

"Right. I wonder if you can give me her telephone number. I need to talk to her."

"Sure Jenny. Hang on; I'll get it for you."

"Super. As I understood you too are good friends."

"I know her well, but good friends? I'm not sure."

"You don't seem to think too highly of her, do you?"

"She is a bit strange. Sometimes extremely secretive and other times very open and friendly. She despises her boss, and yet she takes all the flack from him and says nothing."

"You told me she recorded private conversations in Dr. Brown's office, right?"

"That's what she told me, as if she intended to use them against him, when time comes."

"Well, she can have her wish if you put me in touch with her."

"You want me to call her?"

"If you don't mind. Just give her an idea who I am and what I want. I'll then call her and take it from there."

"No problem, Jenny. Whom should I tell her to expect a call from? Jennifer Bradley or Janet Reilly."

"Janet Reilly, of course" she laughed.

"When would you call her?"

"After you give her a call."

"That's fine with me. Here's her telephone number."

* * * * *

Nancy Robertson answered the phone and had a long conversation with Judy Jackson. They exchanged pleasantries and reminisced those good old days when Judy was Director of the Medical Records and they used to see each other frequently. They enjoyed exchanging hospital gossip and secrets.

Nancy often told Judy about her frequent quarrels with the Medical Director. Nancy hated his guts. He was arrogant, abrasive and nasty. His obsession with punctuality, neatness and discipline drove her crazy. He would bark at her in front of other people and enjoyed humiliating her just to remind her who the boss was. Not so infrequently she would run to Judy and cry. Nancy was ready for revenge.

Nancy knew something about the Record Room incident. She knew of Judy and Dr. Peter Molano's relationship and their break-up since the incident.

She used to see Dr. Molano frequently when he visited the Medical Director. She also noted that Peter started showing up in her office more frequently after Judy was fired. She would greet him with a nice smile and pretended to be receptive to his flirtatious nuances.

She had overheard the conversations between Dr. Molano and Dr. Brown and was smart enough to connect certain dots as she heard certain names and words frequently brought up. Susan Flynn, Dr. Brinkley, Janet Reilly, sexual harassment, etc. She started recording these conversations secretly and now had a formidable weapon in her hand to use against the Medical Director when the time was right.

"Seriously Nancy, did you actually record those conversations?" Judy asked.

"Sure I did."

"And you have the tapes?"

"Yep."

"I'm sure he has many enemies who'd love to get their hands on those tapes."

"That's why I made them"

"Let's say, for the sake of argument, if I listened to those tapes, what would I get out of it?

"It would prove to you that this guy is a monster. He doesn't give a shit about his colleagues, I mean the medical doctors on the staff. He is working for the Administration. See what he's doing to Dr. Brinkley? The poor guy has been battered in committee after committee for nothing. I know exactly what these guys were doing. I mean Molano and Brown. You remember how often Dr. Brown would send me to you for a number of Dr. Brinkley's patient records? They were digging dirt. And now, the poor guy's fate is in the hands of the Department of Health."

"You know who had accused him of sexual harassment?" Judy asked, pretending she knew nothing about it."

"Of course I know. I take the notes at all the committee meetings and prepare the minutes. Poor Susan Flynn lost her life over this matter."

"So, you should know that she had retracted her accusation and apologized to Dr. Brinkley."

"That's what Brinkley said to the OR committee."

"So why did the Medical Director pursue the matter so vehemently?"

"For his ego and arrogance and also to show the Administration that he was doing a good job. Moreover, I believe Dr. Molano was constantly badgering him. I think he wanted Brinkley out at all costs. Even now, with his accident and loss of a leg and all Dr. Molano is still pushing the issue. He's on the phone with the Medical Director five times a day."

Judy paused for a moment and prepared for her next question. The one she'd been anxious to bring up.

"I assume you also know about a lady named Janet Reilly."

"Oh yeah, the Ghost. The mysterious figure everybody is looking for. I don't know if she is real or not."

"Well, Nancy. I have news for you. Not only she is real, she will give you anything you want for a copy of those tapes."

"Oh really?" Where is she?"

"She's around. I know her well. She was a dear friend of Susan Flynn and she strongly believes that Brown and Molano were directly responsible for Susan's death. She wants revenge and she needs evidence. What could be better than those tapes? Here's your chance Nancy."

There was silence on the line.

"Are you there Nancy?"
"I'm sorry, I drifted away. How do I get to see this lady?"
"You don't have to do anything. She will find you. Remember, she is a Ghost."

* * * * *

TWENTY SIX

They held on to each other firmly. The embrace was warm and deeply emotional. One of those few precious moments the father and son dreamed of. Their lives were intertwined since Brian was born thirty four years ago. A deep emotional bond had held them together for years.

The old man had endured a tumultuous life in the military, and had failed to reach the ranks his ambitions demanded. He had lost his wife, the only love of his life, when his son was only eight years old. A second marriage was disastrous and ended in divorce. He made the upbringing and education of his son, the only child, the focal point of his life and the only accomplishment that would give true meaning to his existence. He placed the boy under intense scrutiny and applied to him a military style discipline. He demanded hard work, dedication and superior results. He wanted to bring up a highly educated and successful man out of his little boy, and in doing so; he was often harsh and unforgiving.

Young Brian lost his loving mother at age eight and endured the wrath of a jealous, mean and ruthless step-mother until his late teens. The only glare of love and affection he could enjoy was from his father, and that, only when he would bring in good grades from school. He needed to keep the old man happy in order to get a taste of happiness himself, and he did a superb job on that. They became deeply dependent on each other.

After retirement from the military and divorce from his second wife, Lieutenant Colonel George Brinkley chose a life in seclusion in the beautiful Pocono Mountains of northeastern Pennsylvania. He was running away from the evils of urban life and resorting to a life of relaxation, peace of mind and enjoyment from the endless beauty of nature.

Still a relatively young and quite a healthy man in his late sixties, he loved the tremendous variety of diversions and outdoor adventures, skiing, canoeing, the natural scenic beauty and numerous lakes and quaint historical towns that the four county areas of the Pocono Mountains had to offer.

"What a pleasant surprise my boy? I missed you."

"I missed you too Dad. Sorry I didn't call."

"C'mon in. I'll make the coffee."

The living room had large windows on three sides, offering a spectacular panoramic view of the surrounding hills and valleys.

"You live on top of the world, Dad." Brian said as he sunk into a posh convertible sofa and rested his feet on the coffee table. He was emotionally drained and cherished the atmosphere of safety and security he always enjoyed in the presence of his father.

George placed the hot coffee on the table, opened a small window and lit a Cuban cigar and sat down.

"How come you're alone? Where is Jennifer?" he asked

"Oh, she couldn't take time off from work."

"And how is professional life treating you? Are you the Chief of Surgery yet?"

"I've been in practice a little over three years, Dad. You don't become chief in such a short time."

"But you can. I know you can. Don't under estimate your potential."

Oh my God. He never gives up.

"I've been quite successful in such a short time, in fact so successful that I am beginning to have some enemies."

"Don't let them frighten you. Every successful man has to deal with his jealous adversaries."

The coffee was refreshing. Brian picked up his cup and started walking around the room. He glanced at the pictures hanging on the walls. His childhood photos with his younger Dad and his beloved mother. His heart was pounding and his facial muscles tightened. There he was riding his bike for the first time and Dad was running behind him to make sure he kept his balance. And the one with his mother spoon feeding him, as he is splashing juice all over the place. His first school bus ride to kindergarten. And there he was on the ski slopes skidding downhill. The most intriguing one was the piggyback on his Dad's shoulder holding on to his head. He was riding on the shoulder of his giant; he had never felt more secure.

"Brian, I was getting ready to go for my morning walk. You wanna come with me?"

"Sure Dad. Where are we going?"

"Up the hill. There is a nice half an hour walk to the top where you can see the ski slopes on the other side. It's a good cardiovascular exercise."

On the way up the hill he admired his Dad's strength and endurance. A typical military man. He was moving along the uphill road pacing strong and steady. Brian was forcing himself to move, huffing and puffing and hoping every curve ahead would be the last one to the top. *Gotta quit smoking.*

On the way back, Brian was perspiring and wobbly. George noticed but was quiet.

"How would you like a cold beer at the Brewery, Brian?

"Love it Dad. Let's go."

"Should we walk?"

"Oh no, Dad. It's a long way. I'll drive us there."

George shook his head.

They lunched on fried chicken and cold dark beer at the Brewery and relaxed on the outdoor bench. George enjoyed his favorite Angler Black Lager, a dark brew, and Brian tried a stronger one, Atlas Ale, which was high in flavor and alcohol.

"Are you happy living here?" Brian asked.

"Depends on what you mean by "happy". I'm comfortable. I live healthy here. The air is clean; the nature invites physical activity, walking up and down the hill keeps my heart strong and my muscles sturdy."

"How do you cope with loneliness?"

"When you're my age, you enjoy loneliness. You'll find your own space that used to be invaded by everybody around you. The freedom of doing what *you* would like to do is precious. I get out of bed when I like to get up, eat what I want and when I want to, I choose my own hobbies, pleasures and companions. I have no enemies here. I have a few friends around here, all at my stage of life. Some days I walk all the way down to Rudy's village store, just to say hello and have a chat and a cup of coffee. That energizes me and I walk uphill all the way back home. Life is pleasant here. I read a lot and keep my memories alive.

"It's a beautiful country." Brian mumbled while in deep thought.

"You ain't seen nothing yet, kid. Would you like to go for a ride along the countryside?"

"I sure do. Show me the way."

They spent most of the afternoon sightseeing, along the roads through the wooded hills and valleys and by the sparkling lakes and rushing streams and rivers and spectacular waterfalls. The scenery was captivating. They stopped frequently for short walks along the streams. The afternoon sun was peeking through the heavily wooded hill tops.

George was cheerfully upbeat, clearly enjoying the company of his unexpected visitor, his beloved son.

Brian could hardly hide his depressed mood. He was mostly quiet and to himself, something that did not escape George's attention.

George talked about the numerous small communities of only a thousand or less populations and sarcastically reminded Brian that while big cities are saturated with doctors and specialists, these poor people have to travel long distances to seek medical help, especially in the midst of the cold season when the roads are often impassable.

"Don't you think these people deserve good doctors like you around here?"

"Everybody deserves the best of everything, but hardly anybody gets exactly what they want" Brian answered.

"But you educated and sophisticated intellectuals wouldn't give up the gleam and glitter of the urban life for the quiet and peace of rural areas. Would you?"

"I don't think so, Dad. You don't go through most of your young age, the best years of your life, sacrificing everything for the sake of education and specialization, only to live in small communities where you cannot practice your specialty anyhow."

"Uh-huh, you mean to say you're too good for these people?"

"No Dad. You know what I mean. There are doctors and there are doctors. There are general medical doctors who can sit behind the desk and write prescriptions. Doctors like me are highly specialized. We need medical facilities that don't exist in small communities. We need fully equipped operating rooms, we need CAT scans, MRI's, intensive care units, rehab facilities. If I lived here all my education would go to waste."

"But there are so many like you in large cities and so few good doctors around here. And that ain't fair."

Brian appeared to lose his patience with this line of conversation.

"Well, Dad, if you are so concerned about these people not receiving proper health care, you should not have pushed me to higher levels of education. You wanted me to specialize. You wanted me to become famous. It's too late now."

George understood the sensitivity of the matter and cooled it off.

On the way back home they made a short stop at the Barley Creek Brewery again for a couple of beers.

Tired and thirsty, they both opted for a much stronger beer, the Renovator Stout, a full-bodied and very dark brown beer, styled after an Irish Stout. Soon they were cool and relaxed.

They returned home and George prepared for a lavish dinner, as he was eager to show Brian his culinary talent. They dined on filet of salmon, wild mushroom risotto and an assortment of grilled vegetables. George opened a bottle of table red wine, followed by a second one, a 1990 Brunello Di Montalcino he had saved for a special occasion.

They washed the dishes together, cracking jokes and laughing loud.

George lit a candle and dimmed the lights, sunk into his leather recliner and lit his cigar.

Brian relaxed on the couch and borrowed Dad's lighter for his Dunhill International.

George allowed a few minutes of silence until he found the right moment for the question he was itching to ask all day.

"Brian, I think it's time for you to tell me the truth. Why are you here?"

Brian feigned surprise and was lost for words for a moment.

"I came to see you Dad. It's been a while."

"Don't bullshit me kiddo, I knew something was wrong the moment I saw you this morning. Parental instinct, you may call it. You always called me days before you came to visit and rarely came here without Jennifer. I find you uncharacteristically quiet, almost depressed, somehow short tempered and distraught. If you don't want to share with me that's fine, but I can tell something is not right with you. Is it a break up with Jenny? Or did you kill a patient, or what?"

Brian took a long drag and puffed up into the air. He paused and glared at his surroundings and collected his thoughts. He was also looking for an opening.

"Let me ask you a question, Dad. Have there been times in your life when things were going bad and you could not get a handle on the situation? You know what I mean? You had no control on the events. I mean a freefall, really."

"Somethin' close to that, yep. But I am a military man and you are a doctor. We look at our situations differently. In military losing control is tantamount to death."

"Well, the reality is that within the last couple of months my life has turned upside down, I am tumbling and falling fast, and you're right Dad, I have come here for some inspiration, encouragement and advice as you have always been the greatest source of them for me."

George frowned, arched one eyebrow and remained silent and pensive. He suddenly felt empty inside. In fact Brian was always a source of pride and happiness for him. A reminder that all did not go to waste in his turbulent life. He could always point to his only son and say 'see; this is what I have accomplished in my life' ... and now ...

"So, what's the story?" he asked anxiously.

"The story is one of rapid rise to fame and success, sending shock waves through the community of your peers, competitors and adversaries, and then falling prey to an intriguing web of jealousy, conspiracy and back stabbing from six different angles."

"I get the picture, Brian. Would you like to be more specific?"

"Would you believe me if I told you everything?"

"It has to be everything or nothing, if you expect me to put my two cents in."

As hard as it was, Brian brought himself to explain everything that had happened, from the sexual harassment event to surgical complications, to Susan's death and Jennifer's sincere, although questionably unwise, efforts to stem the tide of his downfall. Efforts which have somehow backfired on him. He reassured his father that the sexual harassment accusation was fabricated and he was very close to finding out who was behind it. And, he emphasized that his surgical complications were nothing out of the accepted range and the lawsuits he's been named in are all frivolous and will be dismissed. Nevertheless, his adversaries are using all of these events collectively to make a serious case against him, and if he is unable to stop this roller coaster, he will be losing all of his assets to lawsuits, and he will lose his license to practice surgery, he will lose his office, his patients, his staff, and most likely the love of his life, Jennifer.

George asked what he had done so far to defend himself.

"I've gone through every investigative committee of the hospital and emphatically denied the allegations against me, but, it looks to me there are forces behind the scene working to derail my progress, and no matter how convincingly I have defended myself, my case has been handed to one level higher and is now in the hand of the Board of Directors. They will then refer my case to the Department of Health and that's where they can take my license away. It is very, very serious."

"Serious and dangerous." George roared in anger as he started pacing the room. He was livid. Couldn't believe all he was hearing.

"Brian" He uttered furiously as he turned to his son, his arm stretched out pointing towards the window "looks like the whole world is working in concert to knock you down; are you prepared for the battle of your life?"

"I've been fighting all along, Dad. What else can I do?"

"You cannot win a battle without a good strategy, and strategy means you sort out your friends and foes. You muster support from your friends, and weaken your enemies by attracting their followers to your camp, you collect all the ammunition you can get and organize your supporters to firm up your defense. A good strategy also requires good intelligence. You need to infiltrate the enemy camp and collect information. Then you'll be able to act preemptively. It looks to me you've been fighting this battle alone. If you are truly innocent, as I believe you are, there have to be some among your friends and colleagues who can come to your defense. You have to aggressively search for the people who planned this conspiracy against you. Don't be naïve. They could be among your closest friends, colleagues, competitors, people who smile in your face and stab you in the back. And again, a good strategy requires offense as well as defense. So far you've been going to these cockamamie committees and defending yourself. That's not enough. You have to attack your enemies. Find them, weaken them and go for the kill, Brian. Don't look for the voice of reason. Don't expect justice to be handed to you. People are victimized right and left in this world. It's a jungle out there. I look at you and I see desperation, hopelessness and weakness. This ain't no way to fight. I have always admired the way you excelled in your education. I am proud of your steady progress, your success, your fame. But, as you said, and to your credit, you moved up the ladder too fast and you scared the shit out of your competitors. What the hell did you expect them to do? Rush to kiss your ass? Throw in the towel and disappear?"

He wiped the foam from his mouth with his sleeve and kept roaring.

"Brian, the world is not all pleasure and peace. Forget about justice and fairness. Who said life is fair? There is not a minute in this life that you can put your guard down. You cannot sit on your ass and protect your assets. You have to be aggressive and strong. And yes, you may lose some battles, and you may have to retreat for a while, but don't you ever despair or lose your confidence. You will prevail only if you keep your chin up and maintain your optimism. I'm sure you've heard the idiom that says when the going gets tough, the tough gets going. So toughen up my man, you've got a big fight on your hand, but failure is not an option."

"**Toughen up my man**, toughen up … toughen up" Brian woke up in cold sweat, jumped up and sat at the edge of his bed. His father's strong words echoed in his head. The conversation had gone on, back and forth way past midnight. He went to bed but could not sleep. He thought of a strategy, a plan of action, gathering information and calling upon friends to help him, and once again he deeply missed his beloved Jennifer at his side. He realized he was too tough on her, especially at a time when he needed her most.

Before the dawn broke he heard footsteps coming from the kitchen, downstairs, and noticed the lights were on. The old man could not sleep either. The kettle whistled and he couldn't resist the aroma of fresh coffee.

"I'm sorry I upset you last night, Dad" he said as he walked downstairs.

"It wasn't the first time kid." They both laughed hilariously.

"I thank you for your advice, Dad, I feel like a new man today. I feel I am charged and filled with new energy."

In fact he could hardly wait to get beck to New York.

The sun was coming up, and the early morning air was refreshing.

Brian placed his bag in the trunk of his car. George walked out fully dressed.

"Where are you going, Dad?"

"Up there, on the hill. I don't miss my morning walk. When I get up there and watch the majesty of nature, I realize how pitiful we human beings really are. I submit myself to the grandeur of this universe and feel great.

They hugged firmly and said good bye.

* * * * *

Nancy Robertson was getting ready to go to bed at around 10 p.m. when her cell phone rang.

"Hello"

"Where the fuck have you been Nancy, I called you twice and left messages."

"Edgar? Is that you? What's the matter?"

"This fuckin' shit, the key didn't open the door, Nancy. I'm trapped here. You and your fucker Doctor Molano got all the money and gave me a fake key. What am I gonna do now?"

"Oh my God, Edgar. Calm down. Where are you now?"

"Hiding in the doctor's dictation room. You've gotta get me outta here Nancy."

"I'm awfully sorry, Edgar. Security probably changed the lock. Don't panic. I promise you I'll get you outta there. Let me see what I can do and I'll call you back in a minute."

"You better keep your phone handy. I'll be waiting."

Nancy jumped off the bed and started pacing the room. If Edgar got caught, she would end up in jail. She looked at the clock on the night table. 10:20 p.m. No way she could go to the hospital at this time and make another excuse. She knew there was no other exit from the record room. She lit a cigarette, sat at the edge of her bed and held her head in her hands. *What the hell do I do now?*

Fifteen minutes later she rang Edgar's cell phone.

"You're taking too much time lady. I'm going crazy here."

"Relax Edgar and listen to me. I'll get you outta there safe and sound, but you'll be a guest of the record room for tonight."

"A guest? My ass. What the fuck are you talking about? I ain't gonna stay here all night."

"Yes you are. Shut up now and listen."

Nancy laid out a detailed plan to rescue Edgar but he had to wait until 6:30 a.m.

"Now, I want you to pick up a whole lot of patient's records and place them on the desk of the director. You know where her office is."

"I guess you wanna keep me busy here. Should I redecorate this fucking place for you?"

"You wanna get outa there or not?" Nance raised her voice.

"Where do I get the charts from?"

"From the cabinets along the wall. Don't pick up anything from the employees' desks. They're working on those charts."

"OK, and then what."

"Do whatever you want. Don't make noise and make sure you're awake at six a.m."

Nancy stayed up most of the night. Her plan was time sensitive and had to be executed perfectly. At 5:30 a.m. she took a hot shower, got dressed and had a cup of coffee. She called Edgar's cell phone to make sure he was awake.

He was.

"Are the charts on the Director's desk?"

"They are."

"How many of them?"

"About twenty."

"OK, any questions about the plan?"

"I don't think so. I'm already sitting under the desk in the first cubicle next to the main entrance."

"OK, good luck."

Nancy drove the ten minutes ride to the hospital and approached the switchboard operator at the reception desk at 6:15 a.m. Her friend Joanne, still on duty, looked surprised.

"Morning Nancy. Why are you so early today?"

"I'm in deep trouble, Joanne. My boss is gonna kill me today. I need to get into my office right away. Could you page Security for me, please?"

"Sure, hon. I'll get him right now."

"I'm going down. Have him come to the Medical Director's office."

Nancy rushed down the hall, went downstairs and waited.

Ten minutes later the security officer arrived. His face was puffy and eyes were red.

"Hello Joe. Were you up all night? You look tired."

"One of those nights, Ms. Robertson. What else did you forget?"

"I completely forgot my boss has a very early meeting this morning. I was supposed to prepare a lot of patient charts for him. Oh, he's gonna kill me."

"You wanna work in your office now?"

"I have to, Joe."

"OK, I'll open the door for you. You know it's against the rules to open the offices before 7 a.m."

"I know darling. Just let me in, and you can lock the door behind me if you have to."

The guard opened the door. Nancy smiled, gave the old man a sensual glance and planted a kiss on his cheek. He blushed and looked embarrassed.

"I really appreciate your help Joe. God bless you."

"Not a problem. I'll leave the door unlocked. Be careful."

Nancy turned the lights on, reached her desk, and as the guard was walking away she screamed.

"Oh my god, I forgot, I forgot."

Joe walked back in a rush. "What's the matter honey?"

"The charts I need are in Medical Records. Would you let me in there please, Joe? I'm gonna be fired today for sure.

"OK, let's go." *Another kiss would be lovely*. He thought.

Nancy looked at the clock on the wall. 6:35 am. Some medical records employees would arrive in half an hour.

They walked down the hall, and Joe unlocked the Medical Records door.

"Get your charts quickly Ms. Robertson. I'll stay here."

Nancy entered the room and closed the door behind her. She turned the lights on and quickly reached the first cubicle and saw Edgar under the desk.

"The guard is behind the door. Don't move yet." She whispered."

"OK."

"I'm gonna try to have him come in with me and take him to the Director's office. You'll have a few seconds to sneak out."

She ran back and opened the door.

"You've got to give me a hand Joe. I can't find an empty cart."

The guard groaned under his lip and reluctantly walked in. Nancy walked down the middle isle and said "Come with me, the charts are in the Director's office."

Edgar crawled on the floor and reached the entrance to the cubicle. He saw Nancy pass by and waited for the guard to follow her. He lagged behind for twenty paces or so. He heard Nancy hollering from the Director's office "Are you coming in, Joe?"

"Be there a second" he answered.

Edgar thought he heard a click, but wasn't sure. The guard passed by, reached the end of the room and entered the Director's office.

Edgar quickly moved out, reached the door and turned the knob gently and pulled. Nothing moved. The security lock had been turned on from inside. *I'm gonna kill this motherfucker.* But he had no time. He jumped back into the cubicle, under the desk.

"Do me a favor Joe; I can't carry all these charts. Can you pick half of them and bring them for me?"

"I'll try, Ms. Robertson."

"Nancy. Please call me Nancy."

They picked up the charts and walked back to the door. Joe placed the charts on a nearby desk.

"Oh no, Joe. I wanted you to bring them to my office."

"I know, Nancy. I locked the door when I walked in. This door should be locked until 7 a.m. I can't leave it open."

Nancy realized what had happened. Edgar's still in there.

The guard unlocked the door.

"You take your charts to your office, Nancy, and come back here. I'll wait for you."

Nancy's heart was racing. She had to think of something quickly, otherwise Edgar would remain trapped here. She had to send the guard away from the door.

"But I shut my office door when we walked out. It should be automatically locked again, Joe."

"Dammit, you're right. I'm tired of this crazy system."

Nancy placed her charts on the desk and took a deep breath.

"These damn charts are heavy. Why don't you take your charts to my office and come back. We'll take the rest of them together. I'll wait here for you."

The guard looked at the clock. 6:50 a.m. In ten minutes his shift would be over. He had to be in the Security office to give his report. What the heck. He unlocked the door, picked up his charts and reluctantly walked out.

"Nobody should get in here before 7 a.m., Nancy. Watch the door for me." His voice trailed as he walked down the hall.

Nancy ran to the first cubicle and hollered "Get out now."

Edgar jumped out, kissed Nancy and vanished.

* * * * *

TWENTY SEVEN

Attorney Douglas Gelfand flashed a wide smile as he finished reading the file. He went back and forth through the file and shook his head in delight.

This is great. He mused.

He buzzed Edgar's office.

"Get your ass over here, now."

Edgar walked in and closed the door behind him.

"This is juicy, man. I told you it's worth four grand" he said as he sat down.

"How did you get your hands on this?"

"I have my contacts, but this one wasn't easy. I almost got trapped."

"Don't give me names, but your contact obviously has access to the inner workings of the hospital administration."

"She's a great source. She sits at every committee meeting where the most hidden secrets are discussed. She knows all the mishaps, accidents, errors, wrong doings, and all the garbage they push under the rug, every thing. She takes notes and prepares the minutes."

"Good for you, keep her happy."

Douglas handed Edgar a clip board and a blank piece of paper.

"Write these down. We need additional information. First and foremost I want you to research this surgeon, what's his name … Brian Brinkley. I wanna know everything about him, personal and professional;

I wanna know how long he's been in practice, where he was trained and how many malpractice actions have been filed against him.

Second, I wanna know who this kid's parents are. His father's occupation, business, whatever, and we need to have an idea how we can approach him. We don't know how much he knows, if any. You can't tell from these records if the surgeon informed him of his son's injury. I think you should return to your contact and get information from the discussions at the committee meetings. There have to be minutes and documents. Lastly, I wanna know what firm represents this hospital, and who the CEO is, and who is their insurance carrier."

Edgar finished taking notes and ripped off the paper from the clip board.

"In the mean time" Douglas continued "I'll run this by our medical expert. Somebody will need to testify against this doctor.

"How about Dr. Molano?" Edgar jumped in "We can get a lot of information from him. He knows Brinkley very well. Actually he gave us this case in exchange for defending him in his legal problems. He wants this guy knocked out"

Douglas leaned back on his chair and said "We can get information from him, but legally we cannot use him as an expert witness. He and Brinkley worked at the same hospital, they know each other well and he is obviously biased against him."

"Then who's gonna testify against him?" Edgar asked.

"We have a few experts."

"Doctors?"

"Obviously. In every medical malpractice case a physician should testify for the plaintiff."

"Why would a physician testify against another physician?"

"Money, Edgar, money. Like in any other profession, there are ones who are willing to sell their soul if the price is right."

"Then how come they blame the lawyers for all these lawsuits?"

"Because we make it happen. It doesn't matter if the case has merit or not. The doctors have deep pockets. They have insurance and are covered for millions of dollars. The jury has no medical expertise. They are lay people. They are carpenters, plumbers, store owners, teachers, and mechanics. They're not doctors. We appeal to their emotions and sentiments. We present to them a patient victimized by the doctors' carelessness and negligence. Our medical experts testify against them. The jury eats it up. The verdict goes for the plaintiff. Patient is happy. Family is happy. We are happy. End of the story.

"But I read somewhere having a complication is not necessarily grounds for malpractice. You have to prove negligence" Edgar asked curiously.

"Oh, man. Don't be so naïve. Not everything is black and white. You can spin and twist the truth and influence the jury as much as you want. Imagine in this case you point out to the jury that the surgeon had no experience fixing kiddy hernias, the specimen was not handled properly, and he covered up every thing, lied to the parents and mentioned nothing about the injury, and the hospital authorities did the same thing protecting the doctor, and then you emotionalize the fact that this kid can never have children of his own, and his poor parents will never enjoy having grandchildren, there is no chance that the jury will acquit the doctor. We'll get millions from the doctor's insurance company, millions from the hospital, and we will also get compensation for the parents."

"And for us?"

"Don't worry, no matter how you cut it our share will be in the millions as well."

Edgar made additional notes on his paper.

"I'll do the research and get back to you in a day or two. I'll also try to get my contact to spill some more beans. She actually records the conversations at committee meetings, but, it may cost you another grand or two. She's greedy."

"It's OK, Edgar. Milk as much info as you can out of her. This is a big case."

Edgar spent most of the day at the library and on his computer, searching Google for whatever information he could collect on Dr. Brian Brinkley. He checked the New York State Department of Health website and clicked on Physician Profile.

There it was; whatever he wanted to know about Dr. Brinkley's education, practice and legal actions against him. Also he gathered information on Manhattan Medical Center, the hospital's malpractice insurance carrier, and finally all he wanted to know about Mr. Robert Silverman, Elliot's Dad, his business and financial profile.

He rubbed his eyes and decided it was time to pay a visit to Mr. Silverman. He talked to Douglas Gelfand who concurred with the plan.

* * * * *

Nancy was visibly nervous. Sitting at her desk, she kept looking back and forth to the door, expecting a significant visitor. Her face was flushed and her palms were wet with perspiration. The clock was ticking towards 9:30 a.m.

Her boss was in his office, on the phone, yelling and screaming at someone. This was not the way she wanted to see him this morning. She was hoping to find him calm and receptive since the big storm was yet to come and unless everything went according to the plan, it would hit herself just as hard.

For a moment she thought about calling the visitor to cancel the plan for now, but it was too late. The door swung open and she walked in with a big smile. She looked elegant, calm and confident.

This was not the way she had found Janet Reilly when they met few nights earlier. Then, they were both uneasy with each other at their very first meeting, and an arduous give and take struggle failed to result in a mutually acceptable deal. Finally, a second meeting with the presence of their mutual friend, Judy Jackson, brought the deal to a satisfactory conclusion. Nancy was convinced that her job will not be in jeopardy and financial rewards were substantial. In return, she delivered the most damning evidence of a colossal conspiracy that would shake the foundations of a major organization such as Manhattan Medical Center that had based its reputation on high moral standards in a competitive health care environment.

The Medical Director had just hung up the phone when Nancy entered the room.

"They had no right to cancel the committee meeting without my knowledge." He shouted.

Nancy shrugged and threw her hands in the air "I didn't know either." She responded.

"You give these sons of bitches a position and they think they're ruling the world. Don't they know who's running this place?"

Nancy kept staring, as if saying I'm innocent.
After a short pause he barked again.

"What do you want?
"There is a lady here who wants to see you."
"She has an appointment with me?"
"No."
"What's her name?"

Nancy approached the desk and lowered her voice "Janet Reilly."

"Say that again." His eyes opened wide and his spectacle slipped down to the tip of his nose as he jerked his head up and his jaw dropped.

"Janet Reilly."
"You're sure?"
"That's what she says."

He jumped off his chair, stepped away from the desk and started pacing around the room nervously. Nancy's gaze followed him wondering what he was doing.

"Ok, ok, I want you to alert the Security. If she is the real Janet Reilly I'll have her arrested today. Tell her I'm on the phone, I'm busy. Wait five minutes and send her in."

It was the longest five minutes for Dr. Joseph Brown. Janet Reilly had appeared on the scene again, quite unexpectedly, and he was struggling to make sense out of her presence. He put his brain into high gear trying to analyze the events of the past couple of months. He had always been eager to find this Janet Reilly, since her role as an undercover agent for Dr. Brinkley would vindicate his efforts to pursue the investigation and eventual dismissal of Dr. Brinkley. This was the moment he was waiting for.

A knock at the door.

"Come in please."

The door opened and Janet Reilly walked in and closed the door.

Her impeccable beauty and radiance along with her enticingly gorgeous smile, her tall and imposing figure shrunk the Medical Director to a feeble, weak and unimpressive opponent in the impending and most crucial fight of his professional life where his reputation, authority and power were hanging in the balance.

Jennifer Bradley, known as Janet Reilly in this arena, realized immediately that she had attained the upper hand before the very first words were uttered.

"Good morning Dr. Brown, how are you?"

The Medical Director forced a fictitious smile and rose on his trembling legs and stretched his arm for a handshake.

"I'm fine ... Miss ... ?"

"Reilly... Janet Reilly."

"Please sit down." He pointed to the chair on the other side of his desk and sank into his chair.

"What a surprise Ms. Reilly. We've been very anxious to meet you."

"So have I, Dr. Brown. I should therefore assume you know why I am here."

"Not exactly. We've been curious about your identity. Your name has been floating around here a lot, but nobody seems to know who you are. You obviously don't work in this hospital and yet, your appearance and actions have caused a great deal of turmoil around here."

"Is that right?" Jennifer looked straight into the Director's eyes. "I didn't know I had such influence on this institution. Perhaps you can elaborate."

"We have reasons to believe that you have acted as an imposter in support of a disgraced member of our medical staff, attempting to interfere with the legal proceedings of this hospital. We would like to hear your side of the story. Otherwise, for what you have done here, we can have you arrested."

"Hold on just a minute, Dr. Brown. Before you have me arrested and sent to jail there is a lot you and I have to talk about. Let's start with the tragic death of Susan Flynn."

The Medical Director frowned and leaned forward on the edge of his desk.

"What about Susan Flynn's death?" he asked.

"Susan was a very dear friend of mine. She had no family, no relatives. Only a few close friends and I was one of them. I know every thing about the concocted sexual harassment incident. Poor Susan. She was lonely, in need of love and affection, and she fell into a trap you and Dr. Molano set for her."

Dr. Brown jumped up on his feet and roared. "You better be careful about making false accusations, I had nothing to do with Susan Flynn, let alone her death."

"You haven't heard everything yet, Dr. Brown. Now you sit down and listen." Jennifer fired back.

The Medical Director groaned as he lowered himself back into the chair again.

"I know everything about the conspiracy that you and Dr. Molano cooked up to destroy the reputation of an aspiring, popular and successful surgeon, Dr. Brinkley. Susan told me all about it after she accidentally witnessed the lewd act, right here within the premises of the hospital, between her friend and lover, Dr. Molano, and another female member of this hospital. Susan was devastated and distraught. I know about every conversation that has taken place between you and Dr. Molano in this very office. I believe you two are directly responsible for her death. I was no imposter, Dr. Brown. I was trying to save my dear friend from a catastrophe. I helped her to see the true picture, the trap, the deep hole she was falling into. She came to her senses, and decided to reveal the truth to me. She apologized to Dr. Brinkley. She broke up with Dr. Molano, and yet, he attacked her in her apartment. Are you with me Dr. Brown? You two killed Susan and you have the audacity to accuse *me* of being an imposter?"

"These are all a bunch of lies, lady." The director shouted back. "I don't have to sit here and listen to this bullshit." He was fuming and shaking.

He roared and groaned. Stood up and sat down again. Perspiration was building up on his forehead. He went on "you better get out of my office before I kick you out of here."

"Did you forget Dr. Brown? You were going to arrest me. Take a deep breath and sit down; I'm not finished with you yet. Let's now talk about the disgraced member of your medical staff, Dr. Brinkley."

"We're dealing with Dr. Brinkley, his problems and his behavior, and we don't need advice from you."

"I know every detail of your plans for Dr. Brinkley. I know the exact times and dates when you and Dr. Molano conspired to push your agenda against him through the committee meetings and have him knocked off the staff. Both of you had interest in his downfall, Molano as a jealous competitor and you to strengthen your position of authority and power. You were blinded by Dr. Brinkley's success and popularity. You chose to ignore that Susan had withdrawn her complaint, and pursued the sexual harassment charge against him, even though Susan had died, you subjected him to the humiliation of having his patient's records reviewed and criticized, you have instilled doubt in the minds of his medical colleagues and supporters and have made them withdraw their support of him, you have already damaged his practice, and you are not giving up yet. You are taking the case to the Board of Directors and from there to the Department of Health. Are you listening to me, Dr. Brown? If nobody else understands that all of this is nothing but a carefully planned conspiracy against him, I do and I know everything."

"Enough is enough, lady; I've heard enough nonsense from you and you cannot prove any of this. Before I call Security, perhaps you can tell me why you are here and what do you want from me."

"Now you're talking, Dr. Brown." Jennifer opened her purse and pulled out a sleek mini-tape recorder and placed it on the desk.

"You want proof? It's all in here." She pointed to the device. "Would you like to hear it?"

"What's this now?" The Medical Director frowned and fixed his gaze on the recorder. He was now pale and shaking.

"Just listen for a second." Jennifer gently pushed the play button.

There it was, undeniably his own voice and that of Dr. Molano talking about Dr. Brinkley. "We're going to drag his ass into every committee meeting, scrutinize every minor complication he's had, and hold him responsible for damaging the reputation of this hospital and stick with the sexual harassment charge. He'll be gone in no time"

Jennifer shut the recorder off quickly. "You wanna hear more?" She sneered.

The Medical Director was stunned, numb, and confused. Jennifer remained silent to give him a chance to recover.

He leaned on his elbows over the edge of the desk, held his head in his hands and closed his eyes for a moment.

"How did you make this tape?" he asked with his eyes still closed.

"With a tape recorder, of course" Jennifer replied sarcastically"

He pounded the desk with his fist and yelled "I mean how the hell did you record our conversations here, that's a crime."

"Only if you have me arrested. But, you won't."

"Don't be so sure of that."

"I don't think you want this all over the newspapers tomorrow."

"They won't believe any of this."

"They will, from me. I work for them."

"You work for a news paper?"

"I'm an investigative reporter. It's my job to expose crooks and criminals like you."

"But you have no right to tap my phone or wire my office?"

"Cut the bullshit Doctor. You asked me why I am here. You want an answer?"

He shook his head, rocked his chair and uttered in low voice "Whattya want?"

"First and foremost, I want you to undo the damage you've inflicted on Dr. Brinkley. You'll write him a letter of apology. Then you'll send a memo to all the doctors in this hospital, along with a copy of your letter to Dr. Brinkley, explaining that he had been a target of conspiracy and character assassination and that the sexual harassment charges were fabricated. Are you listening to me Dr. Brown?"

He nodded and remained silent.

"Next, you will stop any investigation of Dr. Brinkley. His case should never reach the Board of Directors."

"I'm afraid it is a bit too late" He muttered.

"Too late? What do you mean by that?"

"The Board of Directors has received and reviewed the case and referred the matter to the Department of Health. They had no choice."

"Then you go to the Board and tell them the truth and ask them to stop the process any way they can."

"I'm not sure it can be done."

"Then they'll be reading about this in the morning paper."

"I'll try something."

"Finally … you have two weeks to hand in your resignation and disappear. So you know your agenda for the last few days you work here, the letter of apology, the Memo and your letter of resignation."

If he had a gun he would shoot the lady right on the spot. The encounter had crushed him. He felt the devastating blow in the pit of his stomach. He wanted to throw up. He was perspiring and his chest was tight.

Jennifer stood up and stared at the man who had been reduced to a lump of dead meat, barely holding himself straight on his chair.

She stretched her arm for a handshake. He did not move.

"I'll be in touch, Dr. Brown. Have a nice day. Perhaps you should go out for a walk. It's a gorgeous day out there.

As she walked towards the door, he felt the foundation of this prestigious institution shaking. He felt a big jolt and suddenly came to the realization that if she walked out of the door there would be no way he could reach her, negotiate with her or get a handle on the situation. He suddenly stood up and hollered "Wait, Ms. Reilly, wait."

Jennifer turned back and took a step towards the desk.

"What?"

"Please sit down. Let me explain a few things."

"My time is running out. You better be quick." She sat down, took out the tape recorder and placed it on the desk and pushed the record button.

"You may talk now."

Dr. Brown rubbed his face, fixed his spectacles and took a deep breath.

"Ms. Reilly. I am not going to argue with your perception that I was party to a conspiracy against Dr. Brinkley. I understand how you could come to that conclusion by listening to certain parts of the conversations you have recorded. Perhaps I was overzealous pursuing this investigation against Dr. Brinkley, but I was only doing my job. I was pushed hard by Dr. Molano, I admit, who was in charge of our Quality Assurance committee. His uncle is on the Board of Directors. They were both leaning hard on me to pursue this issue. I had absolutely nothing to do with Susan Flynn's death. I promise you I'll do my best to right whatever we've done wrong in here, but, I have to remain in this job to do what you want me to do. If you publicize this scandal, this prestigious institution will collapse. People trust this organization. We save a lot of lives here everyday. I'm now beginning to understand how things have gone wrong and by whose hand. Dr. Molano's career has already ended. He has lost a leg and he has serious legal problems to deal with. Give me a chance and allow me to pick up the pieces and put this house in order again."

Jennifer fixed her gaze on the Medical Director and shook her head in disdain.

"You're at it again, Dr. Brown. You're not going to get off the hook so easy. For now, don't forget my conditions. The letter of apology, the memo and your letter of resignation. You have two weeks." She picked up the recorder and left.

* * * * *

TWENTY EIGHT

There appeared to be some sort of commotion in the manager's office. Employees had noted the noises behind the closed door since Robert had been summoned in.

The gigantic furniture store occupied a whole block of Third Avenue on the Upper East Side, with wide window displays of modern and traditional furniture.

A shipment of imports from Italy had been delayed and the manager was furious. Delivery commitments could not be met and several large orders were about to be cancelled.

Robert had failed to inform the customers in advance and now, he was being reamed out for his inaction. As the Assistant Manager, Robert was responsible for the orderly processing of business transactions. Customer satisfaction was the paramount goal of the enterprise. Galaxy Furniture was a big name in the industry, a large franchise with stores in twenty states.

Robert had worked as a salesman for more than ten years, living from day to day on a meager commission until a year ago when he was promoted to assistant manager.

Now, a more secure employment and fixed salary carried with it the burden of management responsibilities. That meant being the target of criticism, reprimand and all the flak the higher ups would dump on him. Life was tough. His aspirations of someday having his own independent business had not materialized. He lived in Brooklyn, in a small two bedroom apartment with his wife and two year old son. The dream of someday having a small house, a new car in the garage, a big backyard with a swing, a pool and a built in barbeque seemed very distant.

When the door finally swung open, Robert dashed out and went straight into his small office. He was pale. He'd been humiliated and insulted by his boss, a shrewd young man few years his junior.

"Mr. Silverman" a secretary's voice stopped him as he was getting behind his desk.

"What?" He responded, his voice harsh and angry.

"You had a call from a Mr. Edgar Lopez. He said he'll call you back in ten minutes.

"Who the hell is he? A customer?"

"No Sir, He said it was a personal call."

"I don't take personal calls today. I don't know who he is. Tell him to get lost."

"Will do."

Ten minutes later, it was the secretary again.

"Mr. Silverman, the guy is calling you again. He says it's very important."

He tossed a bunch of papers on the desk and picked up the phone.

"Mr. Silverman here."

"Hello Mr. Silverman. This is Mr. Edgar Lopez, from the Law firm of Weinstein and Rosenberg."

"Law firm? What's this about?"

"There's a matter we need to discuss with you. I wonder if I can meet you at your convenience."

"I think you should call the manager. I don't handle legal matters."

"Oh no, Mr. Silverman. This has nothing to do with Galaxy. It's a personal matter."

"Personal matter? I'm not aware of a legal problem. I've paid my rent, all my taxes, bills and traffic tickets."

"Mr. Silverman. Please listen to me. This is not a prank call. I have very good news for you, but I can only discuss it in person and in private. When can I come and see you, Sir?"

"I don't have time today. I'm very busy. If this is about a promotional prize or something, send it to me in writing."

"Mr. Silverman. This is about a serious legal matter that can only have significant financial benefits for you. I need to meet with you and soon."

The lunch break happened to be good for both of them. Robert needed to get some fresh air. They agreed to meet at the restaurant across the street.

Robert was stirring the milk and sugar in his coffee when a tall gentleman approached his table and introduced himself.

"Nice to meet you Mr. Silverman. I appreciate your time."
"Please sit down Mr. Lopez. You want coffee?"
"Sounds good. No sugar please, Thank you."

The pleasantries were exchanged. Robert was anxious and extremely curious. *What the hell is this about?*

"Mr. Silverman. Weinstein and Rosenberg is a large law firm. I work there as a Paralegal." He handed him a business card. "The firm specializes in medical malpractice issues."

"I don't have any medical problems, Mr. Lopez."

"Edgar, please call me Edgar. I'm glad you are healthy. But, our firm has come across a serious medical problem related to your son."

Robert cringed. "What's wrong with my son?" He kept looking at the business card.

"Please don't panic. He's OK. We know he had a hernia surgery recently."

"How in the world do you know about my son's surgery? Is there no more privacy left?"

"That's an issue we can discuss later. How we know about it should not be your concern now. *What* we know about it is important.

Robert paused for a moment, as if expecting bad news. He sipped his coffee and asked cautiously "What is it that you know about my son's surgery."

Edgar pulled out a piece of paper, opened it and placed it on the table.

"This is a copy of an admission paper to the hospital. Your son's name is Elliot. Correct?"

"Yes."

"He's two years old. He had a hernia on the right side. Here's the date of the surgery, the name of the hospital, the doctor, the discharge diagnosis, everything." He handed the paper to Mr. Silverman. Robert looked at the paper, his hand shaking visibly.

"Correct?" Edgar asked.

"That's right."

"Mr. Silverman. Did the doctor tell you of a complication that happened at surgery?"

"What complication?" Robert's voice trembled.

Edgar frowned "You don't know anythying about it?"

"No, what?"

"A serious one, which will affect his ability to have children when he is grown up. Let me draw a picture for you here."

Edgar turned the paper over. Pulled out his pen and drew a neat picture he had practiced many times.

When he finished a detailed illustration of anatomy and description of the serious mishap at Elliot's surgery, Robert was holding his head in his hands and questioning what kind of a day he was having.

Still in disbelief, he remained in denial.

"But the doctor told me repeatedly everything went well."

"They lie all the time Mr. Silverman. They are masters of deception. They hide the facts and push the dirt under the rug."

"What's going to happen to my kid, Edgar?"

"He's going to grow up, looking happy and healthy, but …"

"But what?"

Edgar waited a few second. Then in a calm and confident voice he said "He'll never have children of his own. I'm sorry to say so."

Robert felt the tears rolling down his cheeks. He was shaking. He wiped his eyes with a napkin and said "I'm sorry."

Edgar noticed that they had waived the waitress away several times as she had approached to take the orders.

"Why don't we take a break, order lunch and we will talk more." He tried to calm Robert.

"I have no appetite. You order."

During lunch Edgar remained inquisitive. He wanted to know where Mr. Silverman lived, asked about his family, his finances, his employment, and all.

Robert remained suspicious of him and was very cautious with his answers. Somehow he hoped this whole thing was a hoax.

"Mr. Lopez" He asked calmly. "Please forgive me, but how would I know what you're telling me is true."

"All you have to do is ask your questions and we will prove it to you. We have a full copy of your son's hospital record. There is a pathology report that shows they cut the tube, it's called Vas Deferens. We also have copies of the conversations at different committee meetings where this case was discussed. We have concrete proof that the doctor was fully aware of the damage he had caused your son, we have opinion expressed by the chief of pathology that the damage was on both sides, meaning that your son will never be able to have children of his own. We can prove that the hospital authorities were fully aware of this and yet they failed to inform you. They are protecting the doctor and the hospital at all cost. They don't care about you and your family. It doesn't matter to them if you can never enjoy the pleasure of having grandchildren. We have it all Mr. Silverman."

Robert was dazed. His mind was floating all over the place. *I'm gonna kill the sonofabitch. The surgeon.*

He picked up the admission paper again and looked at it front and back, and Edgar realized that Mr. Silverman needed a boost now.

"Now, there is a bit of good news for you in this." He said in a reassuring tone.

"What?"

"Money. And I mean lots of money. Much more than you can ever imagine."

"What're you talkin' about?"

"I'm talkin' about a law suit, Mr. Silverman. I'm talking about dragging these guys' asses to the court and making them pay for their crimes. These doctors have deep pockets. They make tons of money off people like me and you. They live in mansions and drive Mercedes and BMW's. They have multi-million dollar medical malpractice insurance. The hospital has a lot more money. We will sue their asses off and make them pay. I'm talking about millions and millions, Mr. Silverman."

This was a real eye opener for Robert. He was now realizing why this man was there.

"Millions of dollars? Are you sure?

"Of course I am. This is what we do in our firm all the time. We go after patient's rights."

"I would still wanna talk to the doctor. I wanna hear from him what happened to my boy. We talked to him in recovery room. He said everything went well. A week later we were in his office. He checked the kid and said he was fine. I can't believe he was lying to me all that time."

"Mr. Silverman, listen to me. If you decide to sue this doctor, it is not advisable to talk to him. Let your lawyer talk to his lawyer."

"I cannot afford a lawyer. I have no money, Edgar."

"You need not to worry about that. Our lawyers take these cases on contingency plans."

"What does that mean?"

"It means the lawsuit will cost you absolutely nothing. No matter how long it takes, you pay nothing. I'm sure when you meet with our lawyers they'll explain it to you."

"How do they get paid?"

"If you win the case, and believe me this is a slam dunk, they will take their share."

Robert appeared to be relieved somehow. *Millions of dollars. Wow! He would kick his manager's ass and get out of there.*

"When can I see the lawyer?" He asked

"I will arrange it for you."

Edgar paid the bill.

* * * * *

There was an urgent call for Mr. Edward Molano, the prominent member of the Board of Directors at the Manhattan Medical Center.

Dr. Joseph Brown was looking for him urgently.

They located him at the headquarters of his real estate corporation, Molano Realty Inc. LLC, a subsidiary of his financial conglomerate, Molano Investments, Inc.

Edward Molano was a successful businessman with a keen interest in community affairs. This had earned him considerable reputation and power. He was involved with many charitable organizations, community development projects and was a heavyweight in the political arena. He had made a sizable donation to cancer research at Manhattan Medical Center and when the institution was in need of improving its community relations he was invited to join the Board of Directors.

Mr. Molano was a no-nonsense disciplinarian and serious executive. He believed in order to improve the reputation and prestige of the hospital, the clean up should start from within.

He brought in Dr. Joseph Brown, another workaholic zealot and charged him with the supervision of medical staff, patient-doctor relationship and medical ethics.

He helped his nephew, Dr. Peter Molano to obtain staff privileges and soon assigned him as the Chairman of the Quality Assurance committee.

He took the call.

"Hello Joe, how are you doing?"

"I'm fine Ed. I need to see you urgently."

"I'm not going to the hospital until next Thursday"

"As a matter of fact I prefer to see you outside the hospital. There is a very sensitive issue I wanna discuss with you. I'll come to your office."

"That's just fine. I'll be here all afternoon. Come over at one o'clock. We'll have lunch together."

"Will be there, Ed. Thank you.

Since the tumultuous events in his office two days earlier, when Janet Reilly's unexpected arrival came crashing down on him like an avalanche, the Medical Director had gone through two sleepless nights and many hours of agitation and restlessness, trying to figure out how to deal with this crisis. In a short few days the story of a huge scandal at the Manhattan Medical Center along with his picture and that of deceased Susan Flynn will be all over the news papers.

His initial impulse was to confess everything to his patron, Mr. Edward Molano and accept responsibility for having fallen prey to Dr. Peter Molano's unwavering determination to knock out his nemesis, Dr. Brinkley.

An admission of complicity in such an unethical plot would mean professional suicide.

In fact, he sincerely believed that he was innocent in this whole scandal. He never had any personal animosity towards Dr. Brinkley. An allegation of sexual harassment within the hospital was serious enough to be investigated. He pursued the matter as vigorously as possible. He was just doing his job. He was under tremendous pressure by Dr. Molano and he simply went along.

He thought of a few scenarios by which he could do considerable damage control and possibly save his own job and reputation.

He found a very important piece of paper he had hidden in a locked cabinet in his office. A letter that would have exonerated Dr. Brinkley early on had it been presented to the committee meetings and yet, again under tremendous pressure from Dr. Molano he chose to ignore it. Now he would use the letter to save his own neck.

He laid out a detailed scenario, reviewed it repeatedly and called Mr. Edward Molano.

The office of the CEO at the headquarters of Molano Realty Inc was an impeccable display of modern furniture, artwork and antiques. A large mahogany desk and a posh leather chair at one end and a sleek conference table with chairs at the other end.

Edward Molano, 65 years old, was an imposing figure at six foot four, sharply dressed and polished.

He welcomed Dr. Brown and ordered coffee for him. A young secretary handed them a lunch menu and took their orders.

"We'll have a working lunch right here Joe, make yourself comfortable" he said.

They sat at the conference table and coffee was served.

"You look tired Joe. What's up?"

"I would like to talk to you about Dr. Brinkley."

"Oh, that sexual predator sonofabitch? The Board sent the case to DOH. He's gonna get his ass whipped over there. I thought we're done with him."

"So did we, however something new has come up that could totally vindicate Dr. Brinkley."

"Vindicate? How could that be Joe? The report you gave to the Board of directors was so incriminating that it left us with no doubt to refer the matter to the Department of Health (DOH) and we did it." Edward was puzzled.

"I understand Ed. I reported the conclusion of several investigations and committee meetings."

"And you told us that it was the unanimous opinion of the committee members. Is that true?"

"That's correct."

"So, what's changed?"

The Medical Director fixed his glasses on his nose and pulled out a letter from his pocket and handed it to Mr. Molano.

"This is a copy of a letter the accuser had sent to Dr. Brinkley, apologizing and confessing that the sexual harassment accusation had been fabricated. Unbeknownst to us, this copy had been sent to the attention of the OR Committee before Dr. Brinkley had been called in for questioning but for some strange reason the letter had been lost."

Edward patiently read the letter and shook his head.

"You mean to tell me that this whole sexual harassment scandal was a farce and we didn't know it? Didn't Dr. Brinkley talk about this letter at the meeting?"

"He did. Nobody believed him."

"How do we know this letter is authentic?"

"Unfortunately the accuser has died in a car accident. We found the letter misfiled in our office and compared the handwriting with the late Susan Flynn's. They matched perfectly."

"How about the other problems with Dr. Brinkley? They were part of your report as well. His complications, mortalities, etc?"

"That's a whole another story, Ed. If I may beg for your understanding, I believe these reports were highly beefed up and exaggerated by the chairman of the QA Committee."

"And who was that?"

Dr. Brown paused. His head was down and his gaze was fixed on his shaking hands.

"Who was the chairman, Joe?" Edward asked again.

"Edward ..." he answered cautiously. "I understand your kinship and affections towards your nephew, Dr. Molano, especially in light of what's happened to him, but the fact of the matter is that he was the chairman of the QA at the time and he was adamantly pushing to pursue the investigation."

"Are you accusing poor Peter of some sort of conspiracy?"

"To be honest with you Ed, I have come to realize that Dr. Molano had an agenda to knock off his competition, Dr. Brinkley. I consider myself guilty of not realizing this earlier, but now I know and we have to undo the damage done to Dr. Brinkley."

Mr. Molano was now roaring in anger. He raised his voice. His face was flushed.

"What a God damn mess you've created, Joe. We've already sent this case to DOH. We can't go there and ask them to disregard it. Our prestige and reputation is on the line. The Office of Professional Medical Conducts, takes these matters very seriously."

Edward got up and started pacing the room, moaning and groaning. His prestige and power on the Board of Directors was in jeopardy. In fact he was in line to be the President of the Board soon. If this scandal broke out, especially with his nephew as the main culprit, he would lose his position immediately. No way could he allow this to happen.

A quick thought made him rush back to the table.

"Why don't you tear up that God damn letter as if it never existed? Let the DOH take care of this matter. We've done our investigation. Let them decide."

Dr. Brown, now in a cold sweat, his heart racing, and his legs shaking, shook his head in despair.

"We can't do that, Ed" he shrugged. "Please sit down. I haven't told you the whole story yet."

Edward frowned. *What else is there? You fuckin' piece of shit.* He wanted to scream and break the chair on the Director's head. He controlled himself and sat down.

There was a knock at the door. The secretary stuck her head in and said the lunch was ready. The atmosphere cooled off a bit.

"Bring it in."

They both needed a cooling off period, neither had an appetite to eat. There was an eerie silence for a while as they pretentiously nibbled on their cold sandwiches.

Edward couldn't wait anymore.

"Talk to me."

"Let me tell you how I came across this letter. I did not know it existed. I found it hidden in my secretary's desk drawer. I have no doubt she intentionally kept it from me. I knew she was very close to Dr. Molano. I mean very close, Ed. Almost certain they had an affair. I've had tons of problems with this secretary. Anyhow, the letter shook me up. I confronted her and threatened to fire her. She told me all about Peter's obsessive animosity towards Dr. Brinkley. He was the one who concocted the sexual harassment issue against Dr. Brinkley. Then it became clear to me why he was digging into Brinkley's cases, picking up every insignificant complication and building up a serious quality of care case against him. I was embarrassed and devastated.

Two days ago, quite unexpectedly, Dr. Brinkley sent an emissary to my office with a frightening message.

His girlfriend is a freelance investigative reporter. If his case reaches

OPMC, he will flood the major newspapers of this city with every piece of dirt he can dig out and will destroy the reputation of this organization. She also claimed they have a letter from the late Susan Flynn in which she has named Dr. Molano as the person behind all these problems, the original conspirator who forced her to fabricate the sexual harassment accusation against Dr. Brinkley. There could be other names in there. Now, imagine Ed, if all this mess gets into newspapers we are toast. It will shake the foundation of our institution like no earthquake can. I think we should mend things with Dr. Brinkley."

Edward was frozen in his seat. His mind was miles away from here. Banner headlines were parading in front of him.
"SEXUAL SCANDAL AT MANHATTAN MEDICAL CENTER"

"MASS RESIGNATION OF THE BOARD OF DIRECTORS"

"EDWARD MOLANO, SHAMED BY KIN'S INDISCRETIONS, RESIGNS.

"WHO KILLED SUSAN FLYNN?"

"So, what do you think Ed?" Dr. Brown broke the silence.
"I have to think about this for a while. I should talk to some people at the DOH. What I really want to know is whether you are being black-mailed by Dr. Brinkley's emissary."

"I don't know if blackmail is the right word." Dr. Brown responded. "I've been given an ultimatum. I have two weeks time to make sure Brinkley's case will not get to OPMC, and I should send him a letter of apology and a memo to the medical staff and admit the errors we've made and attempt to exonerate Dr. Brinkley."

Edward listened in distress. It was obvious he didn't like what he had heard.
"For Heaven's sake Joe, that is a hard pill to swallow. Apology is tan-tamount to admission of guilt. We'll have no credibility left. Why are you taking this emissary so seriously? Is she for real or just an imposter? All we have to do is to call Dr. Brinkley to a
private meeting and straighten out all these convoluted matters. We

will try to take the case back from OPMC."

"Oh no Ed" The Medical Director jumped in. "The threat is real and serious. Moreover, they have demanded that I resign within the next two weeks, no matter what."

Edward Molano, the shrewd business man, was too smart not to realize that Dr. Brown was struggling to save his own neck. By now he had totally lost confidence in him and was questioning how much of what he had heard was true and how much was shameless lies. His instincts told him that the man himself was deeply involved in this scandal. He was too quick to implicate others; too eager to trash his colleague, Dr. Molano and his secretary, and most of all he was fighting for his own job.

The demand for the Medical Director's resignation did not concern him a bit. He knew Dr. Brown's days were numbered.

Edward would save the pleasure for himself to fire him before the two weeks deadline.

"Listen Joe; let's sleep on this a couple of days. This is a very delicate matter to rush into. The hospital's reputation is on the line. Imagine how many doctors, nurses; employees will lose their jobs, their livelihood, everything, if this place goes down the drain?

I've heard enough for today. Let's get back together in a day or two."

* * * * *

TWENTY NINE

They fell into each other's arms and passionately held on as long as they could. And they both cried.

It was a long and painful separation for both of them, but their love for each other prevailed.

Brian returned from a visit to his father fully energized and rejuvenated, eager to fight all those demonic forces that had derailed his practice and his life for the past few months.

Emotionally and strategically he was in dire need of his closest friend, confidant and the only love of his life, Jennifer. He would go on his knees and ask for forgiveness.

Jennifer was ecstatic and blissful of her triumphant assault on Dr. Brown, the Medical Director, and delighted of her newly gained power to unravel the convoluted web of rivalry, treachery and conspiracies that had remained hidden under the fallacious façade of so called credibility and medical ethics at a major healthcare facility. She now needed Brian more than ever to complete the job.

Upon returning from the Poconos, Brian received a letter from the Office of the New York County (Manhattan) District Attorney that his request for a copy of the late Susan Flynn's letter to him had finally been approved. In addition to that he was informed that the investigation into the tragic death of Susan Flynn had been completed and the intruder who broke into her apartment had been identified.

Once he had the letter in his hand he was overwhelmed by mixed emotions. The thrill of finally finding out the identity of the person who was behind all his miseries and agonies of last few months, Dr. Peter Molano, and the sorrow and sadness of the price Peter Molano had paid for his sheer stupidity, jealously and depravity.

He was dying to share this revelation with Jennifer. *Janet Reilly where are you?*

On the other hand, Jennifer was also anxious to share with Brian the revelations about Peter Molano and her own original suspicion of the way Dr. Molano was being treated at the hospital as a patient under police watch, then the conversations with Judy Jackson and finally the tape recordings from the office of the Medical Director.

The news she was anxious to give Brian was phenomenal. They would finally have their life back together. *Brian, you're all forgiven.*

Ironically, they both had called and left messages for each other around the same time. Not so surprisingly the tone and content of the messages were quite similar. They had missed each other profoundly and were deeply apologetic for having brought their loving relationship to a painful separation. Each one had found his or her life, away from the other one, empty and meaningless and promises of caring for each other and appreciating the value of love and affection were abound.

When the moment of reconciliation arrived the pressure was off. All anger, ego, selfishness, and silliness were replaced with love, devotion, selflessness and loyalty.

They simply could not let go of each other. The tears of joy and happiness mixed with resonance of laughter and reverberation of endearment, caressing and sensual embraces. They kissed passionately. Their eyes fixed onto each other's, gazing deeply with emotional nuances and subtle shades of feelings and meanings no words could describe.

Their arms eventually and reluctantly loosened. They wiped the tears off each others face and ran their fingers through each other's hair straightening the tangled and tousled strands.

Jennifer had prepared her apartment quite skillfully for such a romantic occasion. The lights were dimmed. Soft background music was on and a bottle of wine had been left uncorked to breathe. They toasted their reunion and vowed never again to allow the meaningless events of life separate them from each other.

They got the casual conversation out of the way and sat for a sumptuous dinner prepared skillfully by Jennifer. They joked and laughed throughout the meal.

An hour later they were stretched on the couch, enjoying a cigarette and sipping on a delicious after dinner Blueberry Port.

They had some catching up to do on how things had gone in their lives recently.

Brian could hardly hold back anymore to break the news to Jennifer. He reached the pocket of his jacket and pulled out the letter.

"Jenny, here is the letter Susan was bringing to you the night her life was cut short. Now we know everything, everything baby, the conspiracy and the conspirator and all." He said with a wide smile, waving the piece of paper in his hand.

"Imagine ..." Jennifer responded "how different everything would have been if Susan had made it to the Lenox Room?"

"Honey, there is still time for me to turn this thing around."

"Hope so. You wanna give me the name now?"

"How does Peter Molano grab you?"

Jennifer pretended she knew nothing.

"Poor Peter. He was mugged, stabbed and lost a leg. Hard to believe he was the architect of this conspiracy."

"Well, here it is. It's all in this letter." Brian waved the paper again.

"Is this all the proof you have?" Jennifer was now teasing Brian.

"What else you want Jenny? Susan has exposed him in such detail here."

"The letter could be forgery. You need more than that."

"Not so. Hand writing experts will authenticate this letter."

"By the time that takes place, it'll be too late for you. They have already convicted you. They're sending your case to the DOH. You know what it means? In a way they're saying we have problems with this doctor, you take care of him. Brian, you need more than that piece of paper."

Brian was deep in thought, wondering what Jennifer had in mind. He had hung his hopes on this letter for such a long time and had struggled so much to get his hand on it.

"Tell me Jenny. What else could be better than this letter?"

Jennifer enjoyed prolonging Brian's dilemma.

"I believe I have exactly what you need, but, it's going to cost you."
"I know you're teasing me, but this is a serious matter." Brian said.
"You bet it is. But, I have found the ultimate solution to all of your problems. And, it's going to cost you."
"Cost me what?"
"Perhaps you and I can make a trip to Cartier jewelry store." She giggled.
"I still believe you're not serious. But, if you rescue me from this nightmare Cartier will remember us forever."
"I'll show you what I have found, but if it works in your favor you need to thank somebody else, not me."
"You're killing me, baby. Show me what you've got."

Jennifer jumped off the couch, opened a locked cabinet, pulled out a mini-tape recorder and placed it on the coffee table.

"What's this?" Brian asked looking quite puzzled.
"Just listen." She pushed the play button.

For the next ten minutes Brian was kneeling on the floor, leaning his elbows over the coffee table and keeping his ear closer and closer to the tape recorder as he heard the very familiar voices of Joseph Brown and Peter Molano discussing their strategy to drag Brian into every committee, exaggerate every minor complication and keep drumming up the sexual harassment charges, until Jennifer shut the recorder off.

A long silence followed.

Brian kept staring at the tape recorder as if he expected to hear more, oblivious to the off button that was pushed. He was baffled and totally surprised. Soon his astonishment gave way to happiness and exhilaration.

"Unbelievable" he shouted. "Where the hell did you get a hold of this tape, Jenny?"

"I didn't."

"You didn't? Who did?"

"The person who's been trying to help you all along and you never appreciated her."

"Just tell me who. I'll adore her. I'll admire her. I'll worship her. This tape is phenomenal. It's life saving for me. Please Jenny, tell me more about this. Who gave it to you?"

"Janet Reilly."

Brian froze on his knees and was lost for words. Then let out a loud laughter. Jennifer thought he was losing his mind. She just kept staring at him with a wicked smile. Brian managed to get himself back on the couch. He gave an admiring glance at Jennifer and opened his arms.

"Ok, Ms. Reilly. Common here, sit on my lap, I wanna give you my most sincere apology and heartfelt appreciation."

Jennifer took the bait and threw herself into his arms. No words could do what those deeply sensual and passionate kisses did. They held each other tightly and let their misty eyes, racing heartbeats and the warmth of their breath do the talking.

"You know what, Jenny, I'm gonna take this tape to that sonofabitch Medical Director and whip his ass" Brian finally spoke.

Jennifer put her hands on Brian's shoulders, looked into his eyes and said "It's done already."

"What do you mean it's done already?"

"Janet Reilly paid a visit to Dr. Brown."

Brian was breathless. There was no end to his bewilderment.

"Jennifer, my love, I can't take this anymore. You sit over there; I'll sit over here, and please tell me everything at once" he was begging.

And she did. The whole story.

She fully expected that Brian would soon receive a letter of apology and the medical staff would receive a memo and a copy of that letter and this whole matter would be put to rest once and for all. Brian would not be called to appear before OPMC and best of all Dr. Brown would submit his resignation within the next two weeks.

Little did she know how wrong she was.

* * * * *

Mr. Edward Molano requested an emergency meeting of the Board of Directors at the Manhattan Medical Center.

He had spent an agonizing night after meeting with Dr. Brown. The more he thought about his conversation with the Medical Director the more he realized the magnitude of the looming disaster awaiting him and his empire.

If all he had heard from Dr. Brown was correct he could imagine the type of stories that would fill the pages of the major New York newspapers. He knew those hungry reporters salivated for juicy scandalous stories of power struggles, sex, jealousy and crime involving famous people.

Although he had no personal involvement in any of that, he would not have been immune from guilt by association. Once the name Dr. Peter Molano appeared in the papers, the readers would be able to connect the dots. The powerful Mr. Edward Molano forces the hospital administration to give staff privileges to his nephew, even though he had been rejected before on suspicion of forging an exaggerated report of his experience and the number of surgical procedures he had performed at another hospital. Then he would assign him as the Chairman of the Quality Assurance Committee, a seat of power and influence that would give him the opportunity to knock out his competition. Then he would be accused of covering up the sexual escapades of his nephew, and the tragic death of an innocent nurse, by accusing another innocent physician, a popular and successful surgeon, of sexual harassment.

After all, Edward had been brought in to improve the public relations of the hospital, not to destroy it altogether.

He had called Dr. Brown sometime after midnight to find out how he could get in touch with that mystery figure, Dr. Brinkley's so called emissary, and to his amazement he was told that there was no telephone number or address available for her. She will call us. We cannot call her. Her name was Janet Reilly, although Dr. Brown firmly believed that the name was an alias. This infuriated Edward even more.

The following morning he placed several calls for people he knew in the print media organizations. No such investigative journalist with the name of Janet Reilly existed.

There went any chances of peaceful negotiations to resolve this horrendous issue once and for all.

Should a major institution such as Manhattan Medical center capitulate to the threats by a mysterious figure with a possibly alias name of Janet Reilly?

The answer was a resounding NO.

He became convinced that the Medical Director had failed to handle this problem appropriately and now was blaming his nephew, Dr. Molano. He was not aware of the tape recordings held by Janet Reilly.

He thought of calling Dr. Brinkley for a personal meeting and hearing his side of the story, however Brian had been investigated through several committee meetings and Edward could not ignore the decisions that had been made by the members of those committees and if, in fact, the legitimacy of the sexual harassment accusation against Brian was ever in question it would be the responsibility of the committee members and Medical Director to address that, and they did not. The matter was in the hand of the Department of Health.

Nevertheless, Edward remained extremely concerned about the mysterious identity of Janet Reilly. Obviously she had succeeded to shake the pants off the tough guy, the Medical Director, and demand his resignation and the man was caving in. It was unimaginable for him what she could have possibly had up her sleeve to be able to intimidate and bully the man. He knew Michael Brown for a long time. A man of strong conviction and unbending principles. The more he thought about this the more he wanted to find Janet Reilly and the only link he could think of was Dr. Brinkley.

It was time to call him in for a meeting, a private one on one conversation.

He knew the Medical Director was obviously compromised, and possibly had some direct involvement in this scandal.

He phoned his nephew, Dr. Molano several times. He wasn't taking any calls. He was still in rehab, at NYU, under continuous police watch. He was deeply depressed and secluded in his own world. After several attempts he finally agreed to talk to his beloved uncle, not knowing that he was about to get an earful of what a mess he had created of his own life, his profession and the hospital.

"Listen Peter, some serious problems have surfaced here at the hospital and it is believed that you know very much about them. We need information to deal with these problems and I am told that you're the person to go to."

He heard nothing but frozen silence for a while.
Finally a weak voice. "Like what?"

"What do you know about Janet Reilly?"
"Oh, that bitch again? I've never seen her. You should call that mother fucker Brian Brinkley."
"What is Brian's connection with Janet Reilly?"
"Let me tell you what; Brian insulted my beloved girlfriend, Susan Flynn. It was more than an insult, it was sexual harassment, and she formally complained. He then sent this bitch, Janet Reilly as an imposter and threatened Susan and made her withdraw her complaint. He appeased her and practically stole her from me. He made her write a letter of apology and had her name some people including myself as the conspirators behind his sexual harassment scandal. I believe he caused Susan's death and he was getting away with all that so handily until we decided to pursue the matter."

"Hold on Peter. Who are WE?"
"Myself and Dr. Brown."

"Dr. Brown tells me that Dr. Brinkley is completely innocent, and he should not have been investigated and reported to the Department of Health. He is blaming you for pursuing the investigation out of jealousy and rivalry. He claims he did not know about that letter of apology Susan wrote and that is why he was obligated to continue the investigation of Dr. Brinkley. Now, who is telling the truth here, Peter?"

All he heard in response for a while was grunting, moaning and groaning. Then came a ferocious blurt of obscenities. Edward had to keep the phone away from his ear. He was shouting and cursing nonstop and at times he was not quite coherent.

Edward waited for the calm.

"He didn't know about the letter? Fuck the sonofabitch. He had known about the letter even before the first committee meeting. He was hiding it in his office. He was after Brian for his own ambitions. He wanted to catch a big fish and establish his own power.

This was his first test of authority. He claimed he wanted to uphold the hospital's integrity and reputation. He kept asking me to check into Brian's patients' records and find whatever I could to build a case against him. And now he's putting the blame on me? Tell him to go fuck himself."

"OK, Peter. He's gonna get what he deserves. I promise you. You take care of yourself."

He hung up the phone quickly. He was totally disgusted, dismayed and sickened by his nephew, his Medical Director and the whole shameful mess they had created.

Peter was now effectively out of the picture and stuck with his own miserable life or what was left of it.

Neither Peter nor Dr. Brown had been able to deal effectively with Janet Reilly and now the ball was in his court.

A pre-emptive strike against Janet Reilly's assault on the system was called for.

Dr. Brown had to go.

The Board of Directors meeting was convened urgently upon his request.

The members consisted of the representatives of the administration, including the CEO of the Medical Center, and representatives of the medical staff including the President and past President of the Medical Board, the Medical Director and finally representatives of the community, the most prominent of them was Mr. Molano himself.

After the meeting was called to order, he requested that Dr. Brown be excused so that he could freely discuss a serious issue involving the Medical Director and the integrity of the hospital. Dr. Brown objected strongly and demanded to be present. He could see a big storm coming. He prevailed.

Edward briefed the members of the Board of Directors and focused on serious errors that had been committed by Dr. Brown in dealing with Dr. Brinkley. He mentioned Janet Reilly. He mentioned the late Susan Flynn. He mentioned the sexual harassment accusation, the formal complaint and the alleged withdrawal. He criticized Dr. Brown for bypassing the Ethics Committee and Quality assurance committee to expedite his agenda. He mentioned Dr. Brown's report to this very Board a few weeks earlier convicting Dr. Brinkley of unethical and unprofessional behavior and forcing the board to report him to DOH. He mentioned Dr. Brown's urgent visit to his office and the revelations that could have profound effect on the integrity and possibly even the survival of this institution. He mentioned all that with intensity and vigor.

He did not mention a word about Dr. Peter Molano. It was to be a bad mistake.

Dr. Brown burst into a harsh, repulsive and forceful rebuttal. It was a matter of survival.

He found it shocking that Edward had mentioned nothing about his nephew, Dr. Molano, the man he considered the central figure in this scandalous issue. He characterized Dr. Molano as an insecure, corrupt, unethical, sleazy, jealous, incompetent surgeon, a shameless womanizer who spewed nothing but filth and dirt over the otherwise clean medical environment of this hospital.

He reminded the Board that Dr. Molano had lied about his application for staff privileges regarding the extent of his surgical experience and, in fact, he had been rejected initially until his powerful uncle, the eminent Mr. Edward Molano came on the Board and forced his nephew on the hospital medical staff and in a short few months he made him the Chairman of the powerful QA committee. And yes, he found it shocking that Edward mentioned nothing about the connection between Dr. Molano's accident and Susan Flynn's death. And the fact that Dr. Molano was under police watch in the rehab at NYU. He talked about Peter's jealousy and rivalry towards Dr. Brinkley and considered him the sole responsible figure in this scandal.

Dr. Brown alerted the Board that the threat to this institution by Janet Reilly was real and soon they will be reading things about this institution all over the newspapers they could not have envisioned. He could not emphasize enough the seriousness of the inexorable course of events now reaching its critical mass.

He went on to propose a solution, a real eye opener.

"Get rid of Dr. Molano. Fire Mr. Molano and apologize to Dr. Brinkley and request that DOH disregard his case. And do all this in less than a week and I will make sure nothing will appear in the news papers."

By now the Board had heard enough. Dr. Brown was asked to excuse himself. He reluctantly left the room.

Edward was respectfully asked to comment on or respond to Dr. Brown's accusations and he categorically denied all that was said. He utilized his superb communication talents, his undeniable charm, cool headedness and prestige to wipe out any element of suspicion and mistrust Dr. Brown could have instilled into the minds of the Board members.

He appealed to their sense of humanity and compassion towards the tragic accident of his nephew, an aspiring young surgeon who now had lost a leg and was practically finished with his professional career and how unconscionable it was that the despicable Medical Director was blaming him for his own miserable failures. He assured the Board that he would meet with Dr. Brinkley soon and the mystery of Janet Reilly would be resolved once and for all. He reminded the Board of his close connections with the powerful New York media establishment and assured them that nothing of adversarial nature will ever be put to the public view.

In his calm and assertive way he made the members understand how much this institution needed him. Let's get rid of Dr. Brown. And they did.

Dr. Brown was called back in and asked to submit his resignation by the following day.

He was stunned.

The meeting was adjourned.

* * * * *

THIRTY

They arrived early afternoon and checked in. The lovebirds could not simply let go of their newly found happiness and optimism. Their love was strong and they were both convinced that the dark days of treacherous conspiracies, professional foul play and back stabbing against Brian were behind them.

Jennifer was anxiously waiting for the end of the two weeks deadline and the ultimatum she had given Dr. Brown to come clean and vindicate Brian of the sexual harassment accusation against him. She was actually convinced that Dr. Brown had no way out of this. She was ready to make the taped conversations public if needed. The man was doomed one way or another. Dr. Molano was practically finished, and Brian's long nightmare was over.

A special celebration was in order.

Brian had reserved a suite on the top floor of the Borgata Hotel and Casino, in Atlantic City. He used to be a frequent patron with a couple of casino hosts at his command.

Complimentary rooms, food and beverages were provided readily. They would send a stretch limo to pick him up and return him home anytime.

The choice of the location for this celebration did not sit well with Jennifer initially. The Bahamas disastrous trip was still very much on her mind, but Brian convinced her that the purpose of this trip was to celebrate his freedom and their renewed friendship and love and serious gambling was out of the picture.

They arrived early afternoon and checked into their luxurious suite.

They spent the afternoon at the pool, dipping in and out of the jacuzzi, and ordering a light lunch at the poolside. By the early evening they were relaxing in bed and dozing off.

While Jennifer took a nap, Brian made a couple of phone calls from the living room. He called his casino host and reminded her that he wanted everything ready in their suite at exactly 9:30 p.m.

"Don't you worry Dr. Brinkley; we will set the place up exactly the way you requested."

At 7:30 p.m. they went down for a walk in the casino. Brian fought back the temptation to play some blackjack or craps as they watched the high rollers throw money away.

They stopped by the B-Bar, at the center of the casino for drinks. The place was buzzing with music and lively chatter as people gathered in groups relaxing on comfortable seats around the bar.

At eight o'clock their table was ready at the Old Homestead steak house. They warmed up with another round of drinks and ordered food.

Jennifer was anxious for some serious conversation. Brian was immersed in the euphoria of this very special evening and was ecstatic about what the rest of the evening had in store for him. Nothing else mattered.

"How is your steak darling?" he asked.

"Juicy. And yours?"

"Delicious." He swigged his red wine and smacked his lips.

Jennifer could see the glare of jubilation in his face. Certainly she had put his derailed professional life back on track. Soon the news will explode all over the hospital as the doctors on the medical staff receive the memo from the medical director along with the copy of the letter from the late Susan Flynn, exposing the culprits in the ethical fiasco that had tainted Brian's reputation. He had every reason to be overjoyed.

"As soon as the dust settles, Brian, you should arrange some kind of celebration with your close friends, referring physicians, all those guys you used to take out to dinner."

"I have you back honey, that's all I want" he raised his glass.

"So do I, darling. But, your career is just as important. I'm sure your practice has suffered a lot."

"It has." Brian shook his head in despair. "I hardly see new patients these days. I'm doing very few cases in the OR and I've had to let go of some of my office staff. I can recover from this, Jenny, but what has hurt me most in this tragic event is the fact that so many of my close friends turned their backs on me so quickly. No loyalty, no faith, no true friendship. It's so sad to see everything is tied to business and money."

"Unfortunately that is true, but that's exactly my point, Brian. It's the business you should be concerned about. True friendship will show its color independent of your business, reputation, notoriety, or whatever. You should beware of your adversaries more than looking for your friends.

"I am learning that lesson now, Jenny, but tonight I wanna forget about everything and enjoy our time together."

"I'll drink to that." She raised her glass.

Dessert was followed by a couple glasses of Chivas on the rocks. By now they were relaxed, jolly and witty. They started joking, laughing loud and fooling around.

They left the restaurant shortly after 9:30 p.m. and went for a stroll in the casino.

"Jenny, how would you like us to sit at a table together and gamble a little bit?" He struggled to sound serious.

"No chance. You promised me. No gambling tonight."

"I said no serious gambling. We can have fun together."

"I have better ideas for having fun tonight." She pulled his arm and almost dragged him away from the table games area."

Brian wobbled and laughed it off.

"Where are we going now, baby?" he asked.

"Upstairs. It's our bedtime."

The elevator moved up to the top floor.

"What if I put you in bed, tuck you in, kiss you goodnight and go downstairs for a while."

Jennifer was getting irritated now. She was not about to let him go. One bad experience in the Bahamas was enough.

Brian enjoyed his new acting gig.

Jennifer's pace picked up down the hall, signaling her displeasure. She reached their suite first, placed the card in the slot on the door, entered the room and immediately ran out.

"Oops, I'm sorry. This is the wrong room." She looked embarrassed.

Brian caught up with her.

"It's the right one baby. What's the matter?"

They stood behind the door and Brian pushed the door open.

The lights were off, but the room was lit with numerous candles all over the place. The air was filled with soft music and a pleasant aroma. Jennifer stepped in and Brian dimly turned on the lights.

She was speechless, looking around the room. There was a single posh armchair, decorated with a row of fresh flowers on the top and over the arms.

On the coffee table several candles surrounded a bottle of champagne, and two glasses.

This time Brian had to pull Jennifer's arm and push her frozen body towards the chair.

"Sit down here my angel. I have an announcement to make."

Jennifer sank into the chair and began to realize what was going on.

Brian stood in the middle of the room, facing Jennifer. His face was flush and he looked almost bashful for what he was about to do.

"Jenny, I have some things to tell you and something to ask of you. Would you like me to turn off the music?"

"No, it's better with music. Would you sit down, please." She flashed a joyful smile.

Brian pulled another chair over and sat down in front of her.

"My dear love, my dear angel, my dear Jennifer. I have been through many ups and downs in my short life. From my turbulent childhood to the loss of my beloved mother, through the difficult teens and torturous school years, college and medical school, crushing surgical residency training years, and through my short but aggressive and challenging career, you have been the only one who has given me a taste of love and affection. You are the only one who has given me unconditional support, a sense of purpose and a reason for going through this journey of life. You have blessed me with the most joyous moments of my life and you have stood with me through my miseries, struggles, hardships and despair. Once again, and because of you, I am waking up from a long nightmare, and I find my happiness in your beautiful smile, and the glare of joy in your eyes and the warmth of your touch and I tell myself without you my life is meaningless. Every morning that I wake up, I wanna look into your beautiful face, and I wanna start my day with a sweet kiss from your lips. I want you to be with me and I wanna live for you, and that is why I have you here, with me … and in front of me …to ask you a question I have always wanted to ask …"

Brian then eased forward from his seat, went down on one knee in front of Jennifer and produced a small, sleek velvet covered box, handed it to her and said "My dear angel, this question comes from the bottom I my heart. Would you marry me, please?"

His eyes locked onto hers, tears running down.

Jennifer was stunned with this display of love and dependence by Brian, and she knew in her heart that it was genuine and sincere. She forgot about the jewelry box in her hand. She jumped off her chair, went down on her knees, embraced Brian, and with tears running down her face she hollered "Yes … Yes … Yes."

There was no need for words anymore. The glare of joy and happiness in their eyes, the resonance of laughter, the warmth of their touch and passion of their embrace kept them together and time stopped.

Soon they found each other stretched on the couch with Jennifer leaning back and resting her head on Brian's chest. His arms were wrapped around her body while holding a glass of Champagne from which Jennifer kept taking small sips.

She raised the small jewelry box in front of her and playfully rolled the box in her hand.

"Don't you wanna know what's in it? Open it, Jenny."
"Sure I do."
She gently opened the box and screamed "It's beautiful."

The radiance of the stunning 3 carat brilliant cut diamond ring set in platinum was stunning.
As she removed the ring from the box she noticed the inscription on the inside of the box.
"Cartier"

Brian took the ring and placed it on her finger.
She turned her face towards him and landed a kiss on his cheek and said "You kept your promise to Janet Reilly."
He resented the name, but they laughed it off together.

* * * * *

Their night was one for the storybooks, but reality broke through the illusion of ever lasting pleasure and dreams of "happily ever after" when Brian's cell phone rang early in the morning. They'd been up most of the night, consumed in their private festivities.
Brian jumped off the bed, picked up his cell phone and ran into the living room. Jennifer was fast asleep.

"Hello."
"Morning Brian, This is Dr. Sloan."
"Morning Chief, what's up?"
"Sorry to bother you this early. I haven't seen you here these last few days."
"I'm out of town. What's up?" he asked again.
"A lot is happening here and your name is being tossed around again in the inner circle of the hospital authorities."
"Why is it so important that I should know this now?"
"They're looking for you urgently."

"Who are *they*?"

"Do you know a Mr. Edward Molano?"

"Kind of."

"He's a prominent member of the Board of Directors. He wants to meet with you privately, although the Board is also interested in calling you in for questioning."

"They didn't care to talk to me before they sent my case to DOH. What do they want?"

"Don't know Brian. I don't sit on the Board. All I know is that Mr. Molano called me and asked me to find you. I'll give you his private office number, give him a call."

"I'm sure you know he's Doctor Molano's uncle, don't you?" Brian said.

"I do."

"He brought this jerk to this hospital and both of them have damaged my practice and my reputation. Why should I talk to him?"

"I think you should, Brian. He's a very powerful man. And, I believe he's trying to help you. Don't hold me to this, but I've found out through my own sources that he's very upset with the way your case has been handled and he may take the case back from the DOH. That should be very good news for you."

Brian remained silent and deep in thought. How could he trust the man who'd been the main supporter of his tormentor?

Dr. Sloan continued.

"By the way, there was an emergency meeting of the Board of directors the other day and … are you ready for this? Dr. Brown was fired."

"Fired? You mean … he's gone?" Brian was shocked.

"Yep, gone for good. I resented the guy. You knew that."

Another long pause. Brian was trying to absorb the implications of Dr. Brown being fired. What would happen to Jennifer's plan? After all, the Medical Director was supposed to send a memo to the staff and exonerate Brian. He had agreed to do this so that the tape recordings would not be made public and he would not lose his job. Now that he is fired he has no more incentive to do anything favorable to Brian.

Brian's hopes and expectations of an end to his nightmarish predicaments suddenly collapsed. All that celebrations and jubilations were premature and he wondered how he could break this news to Jennifer.

As if this was not disturbing enough to Brian, Dr. Sloan dropped another bombshell on him.

"One other thing, Brian. I thought you should know that Mr. Molano has been asking me and other people about this elusive woman called Janet Reilly. I'm sure he'll question you about her. Just be prepared.

"Well, Chief, you may as well add his name to the long list of other people who've been asking about Janet Reilly." He sounded as if he couldn't care less. For crying out loud he just got engaged to Janet Reilly. He struggled to control himself. He thanked Dr. Sloan and said good bye.

He almost passed out on the couch. Jennifer was still asleep and Brian decided that she would remain in this imaginary bubble of her newly found happiness, and continue to enjoy her triumphant defeat of Dr. Brown for a while longer. He would not break the news to her at this time.

He got dressed and went down to the casino.

At about 10 a.m. Jennifer rolled in bed, rubbed her eyes and stretched her arm to the other side of the bed, expecting to touch Brian. His place was empty.

He must be in the shower. He would certainly appreciate embracing her nude body under the warm shower. She jumped off the bed, dropped her night gown and slowly opened the door to the shower area. He wasn't there. *He probably went out for a walk.*

One hour later she dialed Brian's cell phone. The phone rang loudly a few feet away from her, on the coffee table. She was now worried. He almost never separated from his cell phone. Perhaps he had planned another surprise for her.

Her festive mood of the last twenty four hours would not give way to anxiety and despair. There had to be a good explanation.

She decided to keep herself busy with a few phone calls to close friends and break the good news to them. She was engaged.

Shortly after, she decided to place a call to her friend, Nancy

Robertson, at the office of the Medical Director. She had asked Nancy to let her know if and when the Medical Director would send the memo to the medical staff and she was fully expecting to hear from Nancy around this time.

A strange voice answered the phone.

"Hi, may I talk to Nancy Robertson, please."
"Who is calling?" The voice was serious and cold.
"I'm her friend. Where is she?"
"She does not work here anymore. She was fired."
That Sonofabitch Brown fired Nancy! She mused.

As unexpected and disconcerting the answer was, Jennifer maintained her composure.

"May I speak to Dr. Brown, please?"
"What's your name, Ma'am?"

Jennifer hesitated for a second. Her instantaneous judgment was that without Nancy there was no way for her to get any information except from Dr. Brown himself.

She made the fatal mistake.

"My name is Janet Reilly. Is he there?"
"Oh, Ms. Reilly. Dr. Brown had been anxious to hear from you. Unfortunately he resigned his job and has left. I'm sure he will check in from time to time for leftover business. If you could give me your telephone number I'll have him call you back."

Jennifer slammed down the phone and collapsed on the bed. She realized that in an instant her whole world had turned upside down again.

With Dr. Brown out of the picture, she had lost her bargaining chip. The power to save Brian's professional career. The power to punish the people who had tormented him for months. She still had the tapes to use but, whom she would bargain with?

She was angry, confused and devastated. She broke down.

How could she possibly break the news to Brian? Poor guy had no more than one day to enjoy his salvation. She needed time to reflect on all this. She decided that Brian would remain in his new and conjured universe of freedom, happiness and optimism a while longer. She would soon come up with another plan of action, a new strategy; another frontal assault on the corrupt system. Justice should and would prevail.

She needed a hot shower and strong coffee.

She let the hot water run for a while until the steam filled the room then stepped in. She stood under the shower and cried loudly. Her soft tender skin warmed up and her tense muscles relaxed. The tears were washed off and her face flushed. The big lump in her throat went away. She filled her lungs with warm air and let out a big sigh. The momentary pleasure was immense and almost euphoric. She could see nothing but the cloud of steam swirling around her beautiful body and could hear nothing but the music of water droplets bouncing off her skin. She did not hear the shower door opened. Brian's strong arms wrapped around her and she felt an instant pleasure of security and comfort.

He was back and that's all that mattered. She hung her arms over his shoulders and they kissed intensely.

They wanted to stretch every moment of this dream. Each one had a sad story to reveal and each one was determined to hold it back for a while. Their temporary happiness, elation and comfort were too precious to spoil. Their love and affection for each other was now mixed with empathy and compassion. Neither one had the heart to hurt the other one. Let's give each other some more time. How much time? They would know later.

They dried each other, cuddled and caressed. They kept their smiling faces and showed no expression of distress or concern. Jennifer did not ask Brian why he'd left the room all morning and did not ask if he went gambling. These were all immaterial at this time.

They had to go for breakfast, or perhaps lunch. It was just past noon and the phone rang.

Jennifer answered.

"Hello."

"Dr. Brinkley, please."

Jennifer pointed the receiver towards Brian.

"It's for you."

"Who's that?"

"Don't know."

He got the phone.
"Dr. Brinkley, here."
"Good afternoon, Dr. Brinkley. This is the front desk. You have an urgent call, but the caller will not identify himself. Would you take the call?"
"I guess I have to. Put it through."
"Yes Sir. Just a moment please."

The voice was unfamiliar.
"Dr. Brinkley?"
"Yes, this is Dr. Brinkley. Who is this?"
"Good to know you're there." The phone went dead.

Brian looked into the receiver and frowned.
"What was that about?" Jennifer asked.
Brian shrugged.

* * * * *

One week was all they could manage to hide from each other and keep their own secrets.

Back in New York, Brian pretended to have one emergency call after another every night and evaded any notion of taking his new fiancé out to dinner or spending time with her.

It gave him some comfort that Jennifer would also call and excuse herself before being asked, for unexpected late staff meetings and need to catch up with work.

The announcement of the great news of their engagement was held back, each one expecting the other one to take action, and the longer the phones remained silent and anticipated congratulatory calls from close friends did not materialize, the more they sensed that something was not right. Their mood was subdued and their telephone conversations were short and often abrupt.

Jennifer was feverishly trying to find out what went wrong with Dr.

Brown and how her strategy fell apart. She made several attempts to reach Nancy Robertson by phone. She was nowhere to be found.

Judy Jackson had left a farewell message on her own answering machine that she had accepted a new job somewhere in New Jersey and she would contact her friends as soon as possible.

Jennifer realized that she had reached a dead end. She had no other friends or resources to gather information and, perhaps it would be better to break the news to Brian and join forces with him to continue the battle together.

Brian returned to his office and received the bad news from his office manager Helen Hansen that his only remaining nurse and two medical assistants had threatened to leave because she could not issue their paychecks the previous week.

There were insufficient funds in the business account and income had trickled down to sporadic small payments.

They reviewed the business activity and the picture was bleak. His referring physicians had disappeared and, except for occasional emergency room patients, he had not seen many new patients in the office and had not scheduled major surgery recently. The practice was in free fall.

As humiliating as it was, he contacted a few small community hospitals in the suburbs and solicited work as in-house physician, surgical assistant, or emergency room physician with minimal hourly payments. Moonlighting to the rescue. He accepted a few night time jobs, the only openings available.

The nurse and one medical assistant were let go.
He would run his office with only one medical assistant and Helen.

He sat behind his desk and reminded himself of his father's strong words:

"Brian, the world is not all pleasure and peace. Forget about justice and fairness. Who said life is fair? There is not a minute in this life that you can put your guard down. You cannot sit on your ass and protect your assets. You have

*to be aggressive and strong. And yes, you may lose some battles, and you may have to retreat for a while, but don't you ever despair or lose your confidence. You will prevail only if you keep your chin up and maintain your optimism. I'm sure you've heard the idiom that says when the going gets tough, the tough gets going. So toughen up my man, you've got a big fight on your hand, but failure is not an option." "**Toughen up my man**, toughen up ... toughen up"*

Brian opened his pocket PC telephone book and dialed the number for Edward Molano.

* * * * * *

THIRTY ONE

The meeting with Mr. Molano started cordially and professionally and ended in disaster.

Brian was determined to present himself as a victim of a corrupt system, forcefully defend his reputation and demand retribution. He would hold his high ground and would not be pushed over by the man he believed was indirectly responsible for his miseries.

With the letter from Susan Flynn and the now infamous tape recordings of the conversations between Drs. Brown and Molano in his pocket he felt confident of having the upper hand in this contentious and unfriendly meeting.

He was wrong.

The hand shake was devoid of any expression of friendship or mutual respect. It was just professional courtesy. There was serious business at hand.

"I've been trying to reach you for few days now, Dr. Brinkley. I thought physicians had to be reachable all the times?" Edward initiated the first attack.

"If you were a patient you could have reached me, Mr. Molano. Did you leave message with my service?"

"I don't know. My secretary placed the calls."

"I was out of town for a few days."

"Atlantic City. I know."

How the hell did he know? Brian was puzzled. Perhaps Dr. Sloan had told him. *That was inappropriate.*

"You wanted to see me?" he asked.

"Badly. The hospital atmosphere is now becoming poisonous with rumors, accusations, gossip, unethical behavior and professional misconduct, and from what I have found out, right or wrong, your name is written all over them."

"Obviously, Mr. Molano. Your sources of information are the same people who had planned this conspiracy against me from the very beginning and the committee meetings that had no interest to hear my side of the story, no matter how forcefully I tried to defend myself. If you belong to the same group of people you are wasting your time here."

Edward paused for a second. Brian was too quick to implicate him as a co-conspirator. He felt insulted.

"Dr. Brinkley," His voice now harsh and authoritative. "If you can be truthful and straightforward with me, you will have no difficulty believing in my impartiality."

"I have nothing to hide from you, Sir. What do you want from me?"

"The truth."

"I have been crying foul for the past few months. Nobody's been listening"

"I am listening now. We are going to settle this matter once and for all, right here, right now."

Brian shook his head and let out a sarcastic laughter.

"You've already convicted me and sent me to the executioners, up there at the DOH. Don't you think it's a bit disingenuous to pretend that I am being afforded due process?"

Edward had to ponder a proper response here. Brian was correct.

"I have to confess, Dr. Brinkley, that your case was not handled properly. I recognized it the day this matter was brought to my attention. I'm not saying you were right and they were wrong. I am saying that the investigative process was not followed properly. This was a sexual harassment issue at the beginning. The ethics committee should have been convened immediately and if the complaint was not genuine, the matter would have been put to rest for good. I have reviewed all the committee meetings minutes and it became clear to me that our overzealous Medical Director controlled and influenced the judgment of the members, including the Board of directors. I realized that he was intentionally rushing this matter through the committees, and he bypassed two committees that were basically charged to deal with matters like this, the Ethics and QURC. This is not acceptable and as you know, Dr. Brown has been fired. Nevertheless, your innocence has not been proven..."

Brian raised his arm and interrupted him.

"Whatever happened to being presumed innocent untill proven guilty? The accusation was bogus, fabricated, planned. The conspiracy was carefully orchestrated by your nephew, Dr. Molano and supported by Dr. Brown. I could have provided proof of this if the Board had called me in before referring the matter to DOH..."

Edward cut him off, with his voice raised a few notches.

"Stop it ... stop it right there. You can claim anything you want. At least have the decency not to accuse my nephew. The poor soul has lost his leg, lost his career, his future is bleak, and he is deeply depressed and devastated. You could not have found a weaker and more vulnerable person to use as a scapegoat. I don't know what's happened between you and him, but for God's sake leave him out of this." He had to stop and catch his breath. He was angry and agitated, moisture building up on his forehead.

"Leave him out of this?" Brian fired back with vengeance. "Just because he is your nephew I should leave him out of this? No Sir. He deserved what he got. Either you don't know the details or you're in denial."

Brian's hand was in his pocket, fingering the mini-tape recorder and ready to pull it out and play. He held back as he noted that Edward remained quiet. No immediate rebuttal. The old man wiped his forehead with his handkerchief. Brian's words echoed what Dr. Brown had told him. They both implicated his nephew as the main conspirator.

Brian felt he had delivered the knock out punch and the man was dazed and weak. He felt sorry for him.

Time to get some concessions and claim victory.

A few minutes of silence helped tempers cool off.

"Dr. Brinkley, who is Janet Reilly?" Edward asked calmly.

"Have no idea. Who is she?"

"I believe you know who she is. We've been trying to find this person for quite some time, and if we do, she'll be arrested."

"I've never heard of such person."

Edward groaned and tried hard to keep his cool.

"Dr. Brinkley. Listen to me please. This is a serious matter." Edward's voice was now stern and threatening.

"A lady by the name of Janet Reilly has been prowling the offices in this hospital, befriending some of our staff members, claiming to be the personal secretary of the Chief of Pathology, illegally tape recording some of the sensitive discussions among our officers and interfering with the legal functions of our institution, all in your name and for your defense. She may be an imposter or she may be legit. We have no employee with the name Janet Reilly. We need to find this person soon. I believe you can help us, and if you do, all charges against you will be dropped. I can ask DOH to totally disregard your case. We shall exonerate you and apologize for mishandling your case. We will promote your practice and may consider an administrative position for you, something like Chief of Surgery, chairman of a committee, whatever. Are you with me, Dr. Brinkley? We must find this lady. She has in her possession illegally recorded material that can place our reputation and prestige in jeopardy."

Brian instinctively removed his hand from his pocket. He realized that he could no longer use the tapes here. That would be an outright acknowledgement of knowing who Janet Reilly was. He still had another weapon at his disposal. The letter from Susan Flynn. However, it was kind of obvious to him that Edward had accepted the truth and believed in Brian's innocence and he needed no more to defend himself. All Edward wanted was Janet Reilly and that was out of question for Brian.

"Mr. Molano. I have told you repeatedly. I have no idea who Janet Reilly is."

Edward exploded in anger. He threw his arms in the air, as if in disbelief and raised his voice sharply.

"You are making a bad mistake, Brian. Come to your senses. This is going to cost you."

Brian jumped in. "Mr. Molano. I have not come here to be accused of lying. I have had it with you, your hospital and all the superficial reputation and prestige you're gloating about. Either you undo the damage my practice and reputation have suffered from this hospital or I shall take my case to higher authorities, and you'll not be happy."

Edward blew out steam and shook his head.
"I was hoping it wouldn't come to this, but I guess I have to."

He left the table, went back to his desk, pulled out a drawer and removed a small tape recorder.

"Janet Reilly made the mistake of calling the Medical Director's office a few days ago. If you claim you don't know this person listen to her voice now."

He set the recorder on the table and continued. "We know she visited Dr. Brown a couple of weeks ago and made a few demands and an ultimatum. We knew she would call back and we were ready for her."

He pushed the play button and Jennifer's voice filled the air. Brian tried not to react.

"You recognize this voice?"
"No."
"We traced the call to the Borgata, in Atlantic City."
Brian almost jumped off his chair.
"We called the number and the front desk connected us to the room,

however, this time we asked for you, and there you were. Would you like to hear your voice?"

Brian felt the roof crashing down on his head. His face was flushed. His facial muscles tightened. He broke in cold sweat.

Edward did not wait for an answer.

"I don't intend to humiliate you, Dr. Brinkley. I tried hard to give you an out on this. Now listen and listen carefully. I will give you two weeks to turn Janet Reilly over to us. This lady has stolen secret information from our hospital and should be in jail. If you do so, I will undo whatever you want me to undo. If you don't, you shall hear from the DOH and Office of Professional Medical Misconducts. You will be fired from our medical staff and rest assured that your license to practice medicine and surgery in the state of New York will be revoked."

Brian could not keep his eyes from the tape recorder and could not absorb this reversal of fortune. He had nothing to say and Edward made things easy for him.

"This meeting is now over, Dr. Brinkley. You may leave."

* * * * *

The atmosphere at the business office of the New York University Hospital was gloomy.

The Director was in her office and the door was closed. Upon her arrival the staff had noticed her eyes were red and moist and her face looked washed out and exhausted. She should have been up all night, perhaps crying. What happened to her beautiful, jolly face a few days earlier when she returned from a week-end trip out of town and flashed around the brilliant engagement ring on her finger? Nobody dared to ask. Perhaps somebody died in her family, or she suddenly realized she had made a bad mistake and didn't know how to deal with it.

Jennifer Bradley had never looked so depressed, disheartened and sad. She had a big dilemma how to break the news to Brian that all her sincere efforts to save him from the beasts in his profession had suddenly gone down the drain when Dr. Brown disappeared from the scene, and she had no more recourse and that she had reached the end of the rope.

She had no way of knowing that Brian, now fully aware of all this, had a much more ominous dilemma on his hand. To reveal the identity of Janet Reilly and feed Jennifer to the lions or lose everything he's worked so hard to build up in his professional life. And everything meant everything, his practice, his license, his lifestyle, his friends, and most of all the love of his life, Jenny.

Since returning from Atlantic City, they had only talked to each other on the phone twice. Very brief talks indeed. Jennifer sensed that Brian was avoiding her even though she herself was hiding.

A knock at the door

"Come in please."

"I'm sorry Ms. Bradley." A staff member opened the door slowly and entered. "I know you are preoccupied with something, but I have to give you a bit of bad news."

Jennifer arched her back, sat straight and frowned. *Haven't I had enough bad news recently?*

"What is it Sally?"

"You looked kind of down and sad this morning. I thought you might have heard about Dr. Molano up in rehab. I know you'd been concerned about him. I hate to do this to you, but you always wanted me to keep you up to date on his condition."

"Another surgery? What is it?" Jennifer asked anxiously.

"No. They found him dead in his bed this morning. I'm really sorry."

You're sorry? I'm not. Sonofabitch deserved what he got. Jennifer tried hard to conceal her reaction.

"They found him dead? You mean he's gone? Oh my God, What happened?"

"Apparently suicide. They found two empty bottles of strong narcotics at his bedside."

"How could this happen in the hospital?"

"Looks like he'd been hiding his daily medications. They're going to do an autopsy today."

"Thank you Sally. I'm so sorry to hear that. I know they tried so hard to save his leg and they couldn't." Sadness displayed on her face. "Now he took his own life. It's so sad. I knew him through a close friend of mine who was a nurse and used to work with him. They had a romantic relationship. My poor friend died in a car crash a couple of months ago. He was devastated. Then came this mugging accident and he was stabbed in the groin, cutting the circulation to his leg. One disaster after another. I guess it was too much for him."

Jennifer's voice trailed as she began to ponder the ramifications of Dr. Molano's death.

There went the last hope she had that someday, somewhere, somehow she would use those incriminating tape recordings and restore Brian's good name.

"You can go back to work, Sally. Thank you again."

She better call Brian. This is important news.

For the next two hours she tried repeatedly to reach Brian by phone. His cell phone was not answering. His office was closed in the morning. She left several messages.

Early afternoon she received a call from Helen Hansen, Brian's office manager.

"Hello Jennifer. Congratulations. I can't believe my dreams came true finally. Brian is such a lucky man."

"Thank you Helen. Where is my fiancé?"

"I don't know. He called and cancelled his hours. There was a call from his dad or about his dad. I'm not sure which."

"Is he OK?"

"Don't know. Brian said he may have to go to Pennsylvania."

"He hasn't called me for couple of days, Helen. I'm worried about him."

"Oh, darling, be patient with him please. He's concerned about his practice. Very few patients here. No major surgery for quite sometime.

Income is very low. He had to let a few people go. It was really hard for him to do that. He is beside himself these days. The other day he had an appointment with one of the big shots at the hospital. He went in very excited and eager, but when he came back he was glum and grumpy, I could tell, something did not go well. He's been on the phone with Dr. Sloan every day. I was so happy you two went out of town the other weekend. He needed that. He brought me the good news of your engagement, but since he's come back he is again down and depressed. And now, this thing with his dad. I'm worried about him."

"Ok, Helen. Please have him give me a call. I need to talk to him soon."

"Will do darling. You take care."

* * * * *

THIRTY TWO

Brian isolated himself from the outside world to get a handle on his deteriorating life. During past few months, he had done all he could do to stem the tide of the calamities befalling upon him and his professional life. His disastrous meeting with Mr. Molano wiped out any hope of recovery unless he would acquiesce to the unthinkable demand of revealing the identity of Janet Reilly. His mood, his conscience and his intelligence had gone through the rollercoaster rides of approval and disapproval of what Jennifer, in all good faith and sincerity, had done to help him.

Ultimately it turned out that she could not have hurt him more.

What bothered him most was that she had kept him out of the decision-making process. She never discussed her moves ahead of time with him, never asked for his advice, and never explained her intentions, goals and actions. She carried out her last act of clandestine heroics in the middle of their engagement celebration, calling the Dr. Brown's office from their suite in Atlantic City and causing both of them to fall into a trap brilliantly set for them. Now he could no more deny knowing Janet Reilly, and at the same time, acknowledging her existence was an absolute impossibility.

He was upset and angry with her while he loved her with every shred of his existence.

He was being torn apart with these conflicting emotions, and the two weeks ultimatum he had been given was approaching fast.

What a nightmare this was. He just got engaged to the person who destroyed his life, wiped out his flourishing surgical practice and left him with a badly tainted reputation.

The darkness was deep and crushing, his heart was racing, his chest heaving for fresh air and he was soaked in cold sweat. He could hear something like a phone ringing but could not move a finger. He struggled, rolled in bed, moaned and groaned until his breathing became more and more labored and when he reached the verge of suffocation, his body sucked in a huge amount of air and with a monstrous scream he jumped off the bed and landed on the floor, panting.

The phone was ringing incessantly.

He dragged himself back up to the edge of the bed and picked up the phone.

"Dr. Brinkley?"
"Speaking."
"This is David Schuster calling from Pocono county medical clinic."
"Yes?"
"Sorry to bother you Sir. We have your dad here."
"What's wrong with him? Is he OK?"
"Well, it's a long story."

Brian shouted into the phone "Make it short, damn it. Is he alive?"
"Oh yes Sir, he's alive alright. Actually he's lucky to be alive. They found him lying flat on the road up the hill, soaked in rain and freezing cold. He was conscious. He told his rescuers that while coming down the hill yesterday evening, he first felt a sharp pain above his right groin and he felt a hard tender lump. It started raining. There was a thunder storm and lightening in the area. He started running down hill when he slipped and crashed down tumbling along the road. When he came to a stop, he could not move his right leg and was in severe pain. It was quite dark then and he was stuck there all night."

Brian shook his head and started shivering.

"Can I talk to him now?"
"No Sir, we warmed him up and he fell asleep."

"Did you examine him?"

"Yes Sir, I did."

"And?" Brian's tone clearly showed his impatience.

"His right leg is swollen, his calf is tender and there is an excruciatingly tender lump above his right groin."

"What do you think it is?"

"To be honest with you, Dr. Brinkley, I'm just a medical assistant. I have never seen anything like this."

"Where the hell are the doctors?"

"We have one doctor working this clinic." He then whispered into the phone "He is old and slow."

"Where is he now?"

"There was a rain storm here last night, the roads are flooded. Actually its still pouring rain right now. Some power lines are down. We haven't heard from the doctor."

Brian rubbed his eyes, making sure this was not all a nightmare. It was not.

"By your description, David, the tender lump is most likely a trapped hernia. Ever heard of an incarcerated hernia?"

"Oh yes Sir, but, I've never seen one."

"The tender lump is a piece of his guts that's been pushed out through a weak spot in the muscles and is now trapped under the skin. It's kind of strangulated and if it stays like that a few more hours the piece of bowel will die and then the patient will die. Understand David?"

"Kind of. You are a surgeon, aren't you? Bet you've seen many of these"

"You bet, David. Do you realize you're the only person who could save my father's life now?"

"Oh no, Sir. I'm no surgeon. I can't do anything here."

"Oh yes you can. I'll guide you through it."

"Dr. Brinkley, I can't do surgery. Are you crazy?"

Brian turned the screw a few more notches and raised his voice.

"Shut up, and listen to me. You don't have to do surgery, but you can reduce that hernia."

"Reduce the hernia? What does it mean?"

"Put it back in the belly so that the bowel wouldn't die."
"No, no Sir. I'm not allowed to touch the patient."

Brian grunted harshly and shouted into the phone.

"Then what the fuck are you doing there? Did they hire you to mop the floor and take the garbage out? You better listen to me and listen good. If my father dies there I'll hold you responsible, I'll sue you and you'll go to jail. You have responsibility there and right now you're the highest ranking medical authority in that fuckin' clinic." Brian almost laughed at his rendition of this pathetic young man's job description. *Highest ranking medical authority?*

David broke out in a cold sweat and was shaking.

"Are you still there? Talk to me." Brian screamed.
"Ok, Dr. Brinkley. Could you explain to me what it is that you want me to do?"
"Now you're talking, man. I want you to push that hernia back into his belly."
"Push it back? Dr. Brinkley, this damn thing is so tender he's gonna kill me if I touch it."
"Are you at his bedside David?"
"Not exactly, but I can go there. There is a long cord on this phone."
"Go, man. Go."
Seconds later.
"Ok, I'm there."
"Is he asleep?"
"Looks like it."
"I want you to turn the head of the bed down, you know what I mean? Turn him almost upside down.
"OK, it's done."
"I want you to lift up the sheet, put your hand on the hernia and gently push it in."

Moments later, Brian heard a loud bang followed by a shrill scream and incessant profanities. He knew it was not from his father.

"What's happening, David?"

"He slapped me hard; I have blood on my nose, God dammit."

"You're not going to give up, David. Are you?"

"Well, I'm not touching him again, Doc."

"Tell you what, David. You've got to sedate him. Give him a shot of Morphine, ten milligrams at least."

"Man, I need a shot myself."

"You can get one later. Right now you gotta save this man's life."

The patient calmed down after a while but the shot did not knock him out completely.

"Is there anybody else in the clinic right now?" Brian asked anxiously.

"Yeah, we have an orderly here, John."

"Call John and have him hold the patient as you push the hernia in."

"Good idea, at least *he* gets slapped in the face this time."

"How is my dad doing now?"

"Looks like he is falling asleep. Hey John come over here, hold this man's hands and keep him still."

"Very good David, let's try it again. That clinic needs a hero. This is your chance."

"This clinic needs a surgeon, Sir."

David's sarcastic tone impacted Brian smack into his heart. The words of his father, on Brian's last visit echoed in his head. *"While big cities are saturated with doctors and specialists, these poor people have to travel long distances to seek medical help, especially in the midst of the cold season when the roads are often impassable.*

Don't you think these people deserve good doctors like you around here?"

Brian now had tears in his eyes and a big lump in his throat. He swallowed and took a deep breath and tried to conceal his emotions.

"You ready, David?"

"Think so, tell me what to do."

"I want you to tilt the head of his bed further down as much as possible, almost turn him upside down. This will relax his muscles"

"Good idea, it's done."

"Is John holding him?"

"He is."

"Go ahead, put your hand on the lump, and see if you can grab either side of it by your fingers."

"Ok, I am. But he's pushing against my hand"

"Ignore him, keep pushing."

Brian could hear a commotion going on. "Hold him John, hold him fast." There were loud screams, harsh grunting, screeching noises all mixed with profanities by all.

"It's not going in Doc. He's kicking and jumping."

"Keep pushing, wiggle the damn thing around and push it in"

"He's fighting me."

"Dammit, David, show him who's stronger."

Suddenly, Brian heard a loud bang and the phone went silent, then he heard them as if they were miles away from the phone. *Dammit, he dropped the phone.*

"David, David. What's going on?"

No answer. The phone went dead. No voice, no tone, nothing.

Brian froze at the edge of his bed looking into the receiver.

Five minutes later the phone rang.

"Hello."

He first heard heavy breathing; somebody trying to catch his breath, then a tired voice "Dr. Brinkley, I did it ... I did it."

Brian let out a cheerful scream "You're kidding me, it went in?"

"Yep. Sorry I dropped the phone. I had to use both hands. It popped in and all of a sudden the man calmed down, stopped fighting, really relaxed and took a couple of deep breaths."

"Thank you David, God bless you, I'm proud of you, man." Tears streamed down Brian's face, his voice quivering. "Now let him sleep a while and then get an x-ray of his leg.

"Ok, Dr. Brinkley. I'll call you with the results."

Brian collapsed in bed.

Two hours later he woke up. He was rested and felt a deep sense of excitement and happiness. Something he had not experienced for long time. The surgeon in him was exhilarated. Success is always sweet, more so in life saving situations and he was certain his father would be proud of him when he comprehends what Brian had done. It was a long distance hernia repair. Well, not exactly, the hernia was still there, but it was no longer trapped and no more a threat to his father's life.

The phone rang. David Schuster called. X-Rays of the leg were normal. No broken bone.

He was only concerned about the swelling.

"I think he twisted his leg when he fell." David euphorically expressed a medical opinion.

"I hope that's all there is. I would worry about a blood clot in his leg. Any chance of getting a sonogram?"

"For that he has to be transferred to a hospital forty miles from here. He wants to go home."

"What? He wants to go home? Absolutely not. You should keep him there a few days; He can't handle himself at home."

"We can keep him here overnight but no more. This is only a clinic, Dr. Brinkley"

"How's he feeling?"

"Fine. Just tired. The pain is gone."

"Thanks to you, David. You can come to New York and work with me."

"How about *you* coming here working with us? People around here need a good doctor."

Brian evaded the question. He had already heard an earful from his father on this subject.

"Thanks but no thanks. You think I can talk to him on the phone?"

"He's asleep and I'd rather not wake him up."

"OK. Please tell him I'll come up in a day or two to visit."

Brian was in no mood to hold office hours in the afternoon. He'd had enough excitements for one day. Office was boring if not depressing these days. He called his office and told Helen Hansen to cancel his hours and that he may have to go visit his father.

During the early afternoon his cell phone rang three times. The caller ID indicated Jennifer was calling. He chose not to answer, simply because he'd not made up his mind how to deal with her. Part of him was deeply in love with her and could not do anything to hurt her and part of him was furious and held her responsible for the collapse of his practice and devastation of his personal life. Deep down he was hoping Jennifer herself would find a way out of this dilemma and they would resume their loving relationship in peace and happiness. Just typical of Brian to seek help from Jenny every time he had a big problem on his hand.

Helen Hansen called.

She told him that Jennifer had called the office several times and she had to return her call and that Jenny was looking for him.

"Why are you not returning her calls? She was extremely anxious to talk to you. I think something urgent had come up."

"I was tied up with my dad's accident. I'll call her right now."

Jennifer received the call in her office. They apologized to each other for being out of touch last few days. Each one still trying to walk the very fine line of not hurting the other and yet somehow opening the door to the sad realities they both had to deal with.

"I know, I know, you've been busy Jenny. I had my hands full with lots of problems the last few days; I'll tell you about them later on. My dad had an accident yesterday and almost died. It's a long story. I may have to go up there for few days."

"Hope he'll be alright. Go see him darling, but as soon as possible we should find time for each other. We have matters to discuss." She sounded serious and uninterested in the condition of Brian's father.

Brian found a small opening here and took advantage of it.

"To tell you the truth, I am also anxious for us to sit down and discuss a few matters. I'll call you as soon as I come back."

"Before you leave, I heard sad news about Dr. Molano this morning. They found him dead in his room. An apparent suicide. I don't know if we should be sad or happy about it. The man was a monster and did a lot of bad things in his life and paid for it dearly."

Brian remained silent. The news was shocking to him. Just the way Jennifer had felt, when she received the news, Peter Molano was his last chance to save himself from the perils of false accusations if and when he would get a chance to expose him, his misdeeds and his unethical behavior. Once again the cruel events, totally out of his control, shut the door on him and left him hanging in the breeze. He could not believe how harsh destiny was treating him. He felt victimized again and again. This time, he was totally deprived of his support system. Jennifer was now more of an adversary than an advisor. His father was ill and his friends had all abandoned him.

"Let him go to hell, Jenny. He deserved it."

The conversation ended short and rather cool. They both realized they had to brace for a harsh confrontation with each other soon.

* * * * * *

A few days after the death of Dr. Molano, Dr. Michael Sloan, reviewed the operating room statistics and realized that the number of major surgical procedures performed had dropped significantly within the last few months.

The reason was obvious. Two of their most active surgeons had practically minimal activity recently. Dr. Molano had been in the hospital for a long time and now he was dead.

Dr. Brinkley had been abandoned by his referring physicians since the sexual harassment accusation against him and his case load had dwindled significantly. Nevertheless he was still on the active staff and perhaps he could be helped to resolve his problems and regain his reputation. All along the Chief was convinced that Brian had been victimized by an overly jealous competitor surgeon and an obsessively autocratic Medical Director.

He called Brian in to his office for a chat.

"Nice to see you Brian." The chief struggled to keep a happy face with a fake smile. "I talked to your office manager wondering when you would return from your trip and she gave me very good news. Congratulations on your engagement Brian. I'm so happy for you"

"Thank you Chief. That's the only bright spot in my miserable life these days."

"I understand, Brian, but I strongly believe that the key to solving your problems is in your own hands."

"What do you mean?"

"Listen, Dr. Molano is dead. Dr. Brown is gone. The Department of Surgery is in need of young, active, aggressive surgeons like yourself. You have had a good reputation here and the hospital is willing to exonerate you and support you to build an even bigger and more successful practice. Think about it."

"And what am I supposed to do for all that to happen?" Brian asked cautiously.

Dr. Sloan paused for a moment, collected his thoughts and continued.

"I've had a long discussion with Edward Molano. I know about your meeting with him. You may not believe it but he is upset with the way your case was handled. He believes in your innocence. That's why he kicked Brown's ass out of here, but ..." He swiveled his chair and waved his index finger in the air.

Brian moved to the edge of his chair. "But what?"

"He is deeply disturbed with the issue of Janet Reilly."

Brian leaned back on his chair, cocked his head and gazed at the ceiling. The gesture meant to indicate disgust and frustration.

Dr. Sloan frowned and raised his voice a notch.

"Listen Brian, one way or another you have to face reality. It's either Janet Reilly or the end of your career here. No two ways about it. The man is very serious. He is deeply concerned about Janet Reilly having in her possession some tape recordings and sensitive material that if publicized will badly damage the reputation of this institution. He is hell bent on finding this lady, perhaps even making a deal with her."

The Chief could not sit still anymore. He got up and started pacing the room. Brian remained quiet.

"I have no idea ..." Dr. Sloan threw his arms up in the air as he faced Brian. "What this lady could have with her, so sensitive, so important, that's driving Molano crazy. All I know is that the Medical Director went to him and told him about Janet Reilly and some secret tape recordings. She had threatened that she would publish them if her conditions were not met." He walked toward the opposite wall and suddenly turned back.

"By the way, Brian, is Janet Reilly an investigative reporter?"

Brian scowled. *Go fool yourself*

"When I find Janet Reilly I'll let you know." He responded sarcastically.

"Well, if you wanna save your career, you better find her. I understand Molano gave you two weeks, and time is almost up. I don't wanna lose you Brian. You know, I've been a friend and a supporter. As a friend I am telling you now, this guy Molano is dead serious. Either you make it possible for him to find Janet Reilly, or within the next few days you will be fired from the surgical staff of this hospital, you'll be called by OPMC, Department of health, and you will lose your license to practice in the State of New York. I can have him give you two more weeks, but that's it, Brian, that is it."

A heavy and painful silence filled the air.

Brian struggled to keep his cool and remained respectful of the man who had been caught in the middle of this scandal. He stood up and walked toward Dr. Sloan.

"Don't worry, Chief." He stretched out his arm and shook his hand. "This matter will be resolved very soon. I guess I should go find Janet Reilly."

The Chief's face perked up.

"Good idea, my friend, go find her." He now had a real smile across his face.

Brian walked through the door, turned around and stuck his head in.

"In the meantime, Chief, keep an eye on the newspapers."
He closed the door.

* * * * *

THIRTY THREE

The ride to the Poconos was not an easy one. Before he even left the town Brian hit heavy traffic behind the George Washington Bridge and was stuck there for more than two hours. There was a fatal collision involving an eighteen wheeler somewhere on Route 80 West and only one lane was open. His usual two hour ride barely got him past the GWB.

Brian had talked to his father once since the accident and the problem with his hernia. His old man sounded upbeat, denied any pain over the hernia and wanted to resume his daily walk up the hill. His right leg, however, was a problem. Swelling had persisted and his calf was tense and painful when walking. Brian had begged him to go back to the clinic and try to get a sonogram. He was worried about blood clots.

The old man wouldn't have any of it.

"That sonofabitch David Schuster tortured me. I'm not going anywhere near that Goddamn place."

"But … Dad, he saved your life. Your hernia was trapped. I mean that big painful lump above your groin. He had to push it back in."

"How did you know about that, son?"

"I was on the phone with him the whole time."

"Well, he knew about my swollen leg right then. He didn't do anything about it."

"Dad, there was a horrendous rain storm in the area, the roads were closed, their doctor couldn't come in, David Schuster did a marvelous job saving your life. You couldn't expect more of him."

"You mean to tell me David is not a doctor?" the old man groaned.

"He's a medical assistant."

"I keep telling you son, people here die because there aren't enough doctors and medical facilities here while you big shots build mansions and buy your private boats and airplanes."

Traffic started moving along Route 80 West towards the Delaware Water Gap, into Pennsylvania. Four hours on the road, Brian was dead tired and had a splitting headache. He was sorry he left late in the evening. He had planned to visit his father in the coming weekend. He was already in tremendous emotional turmoil after visiting Dr. Sloan that morning. They had him boxed into choosing between his beloved Jennifer and his career. An absolutely impossible task. He needed somebody to talk to, and who would be better than his father. The man knew how to perk him up and to get his adrenalin going again, cheer him or kick him in the ass, one way or another he was always a source of inspiration.

And suddenly the call came late in the afternoon. It was his father.

"Don't want you to worry son, I felt a sharp pain on the side of my chest this afternoon. Been short of breath a bit, but I am resting now and feeling better. When are you coming up here?"

Oh no. Brian thought. *It must be blood clots from his leg moving up to his lungs. Pulmonary Embolus.*

"Try to get a good night's rest Dad. Don't worry. You must have pulled a muscle. I'll come up tomorrow."

Who was he kidding? No way could he wait until tomorrow. There was no possibility he could get his old man back to the clinic, and what if he could, what would a medical assistant do for him. He decided to get on the road.

Reluctantly he called Jennifer.

"My Dad is not feeling well; I have to go up there tonight."

"Hope he's OK, but Brian, I need to see you soon. We have to get together and clear a few matters. I can't seem to be able to get hold of you."

"If everything is OK with him I'll be back in couple of days. I wanna see you too, I miss you." He wasn't so sure of that.

"I miss you too. Hope all goes well and call me soon."

The conversation was mutually cold and devoid of affection.

Never had he felt the pain and agony of loneliness so deeply, as he struggled to move along the Route 80 into Pennsylvania. Behind him, his shattered life of professional and personal ambitions and aspirations. Ahead of him, another life was hanging by a thread. The life of a man who was now his only source of support and encouragement. This was all he had left for him now. A sick old man somewhere up there, in the darkness of the distant mountains, alone and helpless waiting for his only son to save his life.

Stuck in a slow traffic, his thoughts traveled back in time and, once again, he was immersed in the reminiscences of his bittersweet childhood.

There, was his beloved mother holding him in her arms. And over there was his young Dad running behind his bicycle making sure he would keep his balance.

The memories of his adolescence quelled the sweetness of his childhood recollections. He remembered the difficulties of his teen years, when his beloved mother had been replaced with a notorious stepmother, and his father was tough and demanding. His life was devoid of love and compassion. He recalled days and nights he would lock himself in his own room and rebel the forces of authoritative parents. He could still feel the wetness of his pillowcase when he cried quietly all night and missed his mom.

Then his step-mother vanished and his father showed some compassion as Brian excelled in his education and fed his Dad's insatiable appetite for some semblance of success and achievement in his own turbulent life.

More than five hours into the trip Brian arrived at Tannersville and headed for Camelback. The sky was dark, the rain was coming down hard and the roads were slippery. It was almost 11 p.m.

As he approached The Chateau, he began to question whether it was a good idea to arrive at his Dad's this late at night. The man was most likely asleep and resting. He drove up to the North Hills complex and pulled into the parking lot in front of the condo. The lights were off. The rain was tapping on the windows. Everything inside looked so quiet and serene. Brian was dead tired, drowsy and badly in need of a hot shower and a warm bed.

The Chateau would do for now. Let the man sleep. He would see him in the morning.

He drove back downhill and checked in.

The hot shower relaxed his tense and tired muscles but his mind was restless. No way could he sleep all night not knowing about his Dad's condition. He had to get into the condo somehow and check him out.

He called his Dad. No answer. He had to go there.

He parked the car in front of the condo and glanced at the upstairs windows. He approached the door and rang the bell. No answer. Then he noted that the door was not completely shut.

"Hello, Dad. I'm here." He called cautiously as he stepped up the stairway. No answer.

He fumbled in the dark and turned the lights on. The living room was neat and organized as usual. *That's my Dad.*

He carefully peeked through the bedroom. A night lamp was dimly lit.

There he was, sound asleep. He stepped back and gently closed the door.

Back in the parking lot he picked up his small suitcase and went upstairs.

In the clam and quiet atmosphere of the living room he stretched his legs on the couch for a while, but the eerie silence was killing him.

Is he OK?

No sound from the bedroom. He gingerly walked into the kitchen. Everything was clean and pristine. No sign of Dad having had dinner this evening.

Gotta wake him up.

The bedroom door squeaked.

"Hello, Dad. I'm here." He muttered as he quietly moved in.

The old man was still facing the opposite wall, his head partially covered with the blanket.

Brian gently touched his back, hoping he wouldn't jump off the bed in fear.

"Dad? … " No reaction, no movement.

Brian felt his heart racing and moving up to his throat as a sudden rush of anxiety engulfed him. He lunged to the wall and turned the ceiling lights on.

Dad? … it's me, Brian. Dad?

He pulled back the blanket and exposed his face.

The skin was pale and ashen, the jaw was dropped, the eyes were open and fixed to the wall. No glare, no radiance, no sign of life.

Lieutenant Colonel George Brinkley was dead.

Brian sank on his knees, dropped his shattered body on his father and screamed … Dad … Dad … Dad.

* * * * *

The funeral was small and private. It was attended mostly by George's close friends from the area. His neighbors were there. Rudy from the village store, Andy and Greg from the Brewery and a few of his hiking friends.

Jennifer and Helen Hansen, Brian's secretary, arrived together.

George was eulogized by a number of his close friends who remembered him as a man of character and strength, a true gentleman, a dear friend and a pillar of the community. Since moving to this area he had put his military style convictions behind the betterment of the community, the schools, the roads, the recreation areas and most importantly of all the healthcare facilities. He was loved by everyone.

They remembered he constantly complained that there were not enough physicians and specialists practicing in the area.

Brian could not help noticing that with each comment like this, eyes would turn towards him, as if it was entirely his fault and he should feel guilty. As if he didn't have enough problems in his own life; he was fiercely at the grip of a guilty conscience for the loss of his father. He blamed himself for not acting fast enough. From the night he was at the clinic with an incarcerated hernia, his swollen leg appeared to be a different problem, he knew better, the man fell and bruised his leg and developed blood clots. His life threatening hernia overshadowed everything else. He never received proper treatment for the blood clots in his leg, and for a man who didn't know how to rest, relax and limit his activities, it was inevitable that the clots would move up to his lungs and kill him.

And now, he could read in people's eyes that he was being blamed for the shortage of medical care in their community, or at least he thought so, what was the difference. He was crushed, devastated and confused. Where did he go wrong? The allure of a life of comfort and luxury in a big city? The drive of professional competition and thrill of success? The glamour of rank and prestige? Or just arrogance and indifference?

Where did he go wrong?

When the gathering broke up after the burial, a young man approached him and offered his condolences.

"Dr. Brinkley, I am David Schuster from the clinic."

"Hello David, nice to meet you and thank you for coming."

"I'm so sorry Dr. Brinkley. I was hoping he would be fine after that night. We failed him."

"You should not feel bad David. You are the only one who did him some good; actually you saved his life the other night. I admired your courage."

"You are very kind Dr. Brinkley. I like the medical profession more and more, actually I am planning to go to medical school."

"And then what?" Brian asked, teasing him.

"Perhaps someday I'll come to New York and work with you."

"David ... David, going to medical school is a good idea but if you leave this area, who's gonna fix the incarcerated hernias?"

David shook his head "I understand what you're talking about. It's sad."

People said good bye and left.

Brian, Jennifer and Helen returned to the condo.

The atmosphere was gloomy. The man who used to entertain them and shower them with love and kindness, the generous host who used to cook those sumptuous dinners, the voice of happiness and pleasure suddenly was not there anymore, and it was hard to absorb the vacuum and emptiness.

They could look at each other's teary eyes only so much. The girls tried hard to convince Brian to go back to New York with them. He would not go. It was just not possible for him to walk away as if nothing had happened.

Before the girls left, Brian asked Helen to cancel his office hours for the next two weeks, and perhaps it would be better to ask the only remaining medical assistant to look for another job.

Helen frowned and looked at Brian as if asking him what in the world he was doing.

Brian nodded.

"Don't worry Helen. Nothing much is left of this practice. We will start from the beginning again, Just me and you, like we did the first time.

Jennifer hugged him and said good bye. It was a rather cool farewell.

There remained a lot to be worked out in their relationship, and they both knew it.

* * * * *

A week after the funeral Brian returned to more bad news in his office.

As he walked in he noted a man sitting in the corner of the waiting room reading a magazine. He didn't have office hours.

The man, a process server, jumped on his feet.

"Are you Dr. Brian Brinkley?"

"Yes, can I help you?"

The man handed him a folded document.

"You've just been served, Sir."

Brian glanced at the folded paper and realized what it was. Another lawsuit.

"Thank you."

"Good day Sir." He left.

Helen stuck her head through the reception window, curious what was going on.

"Good morning Brian."

"What's good about it, Helen?" He waved the papers in his hand, walked into his consultation room and slammed it on his desk.

He did not notice two other envelopes on his desk waiting for his immediate attention.

The rest of his mail from the past ten days or so was piled on the side of the desk top, along with a few patient charts.

He took off his jacket and sank into his chair.

Helen walked in cautiously. "Can I get you a cup of coffee?"

"Yes please."

"I signed the return receipts for those two envelopes. I gather they are more important than the rest. I have a few messages for you. Want them now?"

"May as well. Bring them in and add them to this junk, I'll take care of them later on."

He sipped the coffee before he touched the envelopes. They could only be bad news, what else.

The larger envelope spoke for itself. Brian noted the sender. New York State Department of Health, Office of Professional Medical Conduct.

Finally, he had heard from the dreaded OPMC.

The letter was official and brief. In light of multiple allegations of professional misconduct filed with the Department of Health against him by the Manhattan Medical Center, he had been ordered to report in person to the OPMC at a date specified. He did not have to be represented by an attorney although he could choose to have one present.

He threw the letter on the desk and mumbled. *There goes my license to practice in the State of New York.*

He reluctantly glanced at the second envelope and noted it was from the hospital.

Dear Dr. Brinkley

On behalf of the Board of Directors of the Manhattan Medical Center I regret to inform you that your affiliation with this institution as a member of the medical staff at the Department of Surgery is terminated effective immediately.

You have the right to appeal this decision in writing within the next two weeks and request a hearing.

The letter was signed by the newly elected President of the Board of Directors, Mr. Edward Molano.

Although there was no surprise there, he suddenly felt empty, weak, distraught and lost.

He'd been abandoned by his friends, supporters, colleagues, and his beloved fiancée Jennifer. He even felt angry at his departed father. Did he have to leave him at such a critical time of his life?

There was hardly any day that this office was not sizzling in activity. Swarmed by numerous patients, the staff would struggle to get things going in an orderly fashion.

Now, the only sole he would find in the waiting room was a process server, ready to hammer the final nail in the coffin of his professional life.

Oh ... the lawsuit. He almost forgot.

His hands were visibly shaking as he reached for summons. He could not think straight anymore and had no idea who and why.

He lit a cigarette, and took the last sip of his coffee.

The letter was a summons the like of which he had seen before.

Supreme Court of the State of New York Index# 4112-02

- --

Robert Silverman, as custodian for

Elliot Silverman Plaintiff

- against -

Brian Brinkley, M.D.
Manhattan Medical Center Defendants

- --

To the above named defendants:

You are hereby summoned to answer the complaint in this action and to serve a copy of your answer on the plaintiff attorney designated below within twenty days after the service of this summons. In case of your failure to appear or answer, judgment will be taken against you by default for the relief demanded in the complaint.

The summons was signed by Douglas Gelfand, attorney for Plaintiff, from the law firm of Weinstein & Rosenberg

Attached to this letter were four pages outlining the allegations of wrongdoing, negligence and deviation from the community standards of medical care against the defendants.

As the customary tone and design of these allegations dictate, they are repeated numerous times, save for minor changes in wording, in order to fill a few pages and make the matter look much more ominous and menacing than it actually is.

The idea is that the defense attorneys paint a horrendous picture of the accused and depict him or her as the most negligent, careless and heartless physician ever existed who lacks the up-to-date knowledge in medicine.

Brian was not alien to these baseless accusations. He had been named in lawsuits a number of times in the past few years and he had never lost a case.

He took a sharp glance through four pages of mumbo-jumbo and summarized the main points as follows:

The defendant Dr. Brian Brinkley carelessly and negligently failed to:

- Properly render surgical treatment to the plaintiff for treatment of a right inguinal hernia.
- Obtain an informed consent.
- Explain the surgical procedure and potential risk and benefits to the plaintiff's parents.
- Obtain proper consent for an additional incision he made above the opposite groin and failed to alert the parents that such additional incision might be necessary.
- Inform the parents of the injury he had caused and lied to them when he told them that surgery went well.
- Instruct the nurse the proper way of handling the specimens so that the tissues from both sides would not get mixed up.
- The defendant, Dr. Brian Brinkley, by applying poor surgical technique caused transection or severance of the Vas Deferens, a vital passage way for sperms without which the patient is permanently deprived of ever having children of his own.
- The defendant, Dr. Brian Brinkley, has admitted to the investigative committees of the hospital that he had never performed such operation on an infant in his private practice.

On the last page, one line stood out and shook Brian up.
The plaintiff had asked for monetary damages of ten million dollars.

Ten million dollars? For heaven's sake, how did they figure that out?
Moreover, how in the world did the lawyers get their hands on this case?

That was beyond his comprehension. On the other hand, it wouldn't be surprising to him to tie this to the rest of the treacherous acts of conspiracy that had destroyed his life recently.

Consumed in sadness and disbelief Brian sat in silence for a while, his gaze fixed on the three letters lined up on his desk in front of him, pondering if things could get any worse than this. The hospital fired him, OPMC will soon take his license away and the lawsuit will wipe out whatever assets he had. His father was dead and his fiancée was estranged.

A while ago, he dreaded the thought of having to cut his staff and fire a few nurses. Now he had to let his beloved Helen go. *Oh God, how can I do this?*

He leaned forward, resting his elbows on the desk and held his head in his hands. He closed his eyes, as if hiding from the rest of the world. He was in a free fall.

In a moment of quiet solitude it dawned on him that through all this turmoil and upheaval he had desperately sought help from almost everybody, his chief, his colleagues, his girlfriend and now fiancée, his father and his secretary, EXCEPT from Brian Brinkley. He realized that the insecurity of dependency and absence of self motivation had weakened his self confidence and resolve. Nobody could save him from this tragedy, and there was nobody else to turn to but himself.

He felt a rush of energy and excitement and suddenly he had a premonition. The dark clouds of desperation and hopelessness began to clear. Beyond this point he had nothing to lose and everything to gain. He realized that there is always a chance for a new beginning, all by himself.

And now with no hesitation, he suddenly knew what he had to do.

He instructed Helen to inform his medical malpractice insurance company of the summons he had just been served. Somehow in a rage of revenge for ever increasing malpractice insurance premium that had crippled his financial health, he was willing to tell them this lawsuit was their problem and not his. Let them pay the millions.

He dictated a letter to OPMC and advised them that he would vigorously defend himself against unjust treatment he had received by the authorities of the Manhattan Medical Center, and warned them ahead of time that he had in his possession undeniable evidence of corruption and illegal activity going on at that institution.

He then dictated a letter to Mr. Edward Molano, and informed him that he had no right to fire him without due process. He will institute legal action against the hospital and Mr. Molano personally, and he should expect them meeting again, this time in the court of law.

And then he gave the bad news to Helen. He will have to terminate his surgical practice and his office will be closed.

He acknowledged that after many years of their personal and professional working relationship he could not muster the courage to fire her, and therefore he had decided to fire himself from the practice. He would leave all his assets, finances, account receivables, furniture and everything of value to Helen and he would simply walk away.

Helen would turn over his patient's charts to another surgeon he would choose in a day or two. He would give Helen the power of attorney for all these matters.

Finally he made it clear to Helen that he was going to effectively sever his ties with his past life and permanently disappear from the scene.

Before leaving the office, with Helen in tears, he had one more matter to take care of.

A final meeting with Jennifer.

He picked up the phone and dialed.

* * * * * *

THIRTY FOUR

It was the most painful meeting for both of them. And yet, both were anxious to get it over with.

The first problem was the location of the meeting. Each one wanted to have home turf advantage. This was not going to be a cordial, romantic or even friendly meeting. They both knew it very well. It had to be either her or his apartment. No other place would give them the freedom of yelling, shouting, arguing or crying out loud if circumstances called for it.

Brian scored the first point. They would meet at his apartment.

Jennifer had tried several times to reach Helen Hansen to no avail. She was nowhere to be found. Jennifer was anxious to get some first hand information about Brian's mood, and demeanor after the death of his father.

She could hardly keep herself awake after a nearly sleepless night. She skipped work and stayed home drinking one cup of coffee after another and making phone calls. She kept trying for Helen. It was most unusual to call Brian's office and get no answer. Not even his answering service would respond. The whole office from manager to receptionist, secretaries and nurses and the doctor had suddenly vanished. It was ominous.

She called her friend Judy Jackson and received the same recorded message she had heard before. Judy had accepted a new job in New

Jersey and she would call her as soon as she was settled down in her new location. No phone number, no address.

She tried to get a nap in the afternoon, but that was impossible. Her mind was too busy contemplating a strategy for facing Brian.

By now she was certain that Brian was fully aware of the developments in the hospital, of Dr. Brown being fired and of the complete deterioration of her strategy to force Dr. Brown to exonerate Brian of all accusations.

She felt so sorry for him after all that euphoria in Atlantic City, the prospect of life returning to normal and the excitement of their upcoming marriage and future life together. All that was now a shattered dream and a painfully lost opportunity.

Nevertheless, being totally unaware of Brian's meeting with Mr. Molano, she was still optimistic that she could come up with another solution.

By 6 p.m. she was dazed, exhausted and nervous. A hot shower would do wonders.

She stayed under the water and cried. She reminisced the good times when they would wrap their arms around each other, under the shower and enjoy the thrill of ultimate intimacy.

Numerous occasions of his bad behavior didn't matter anymore. She loved him dearly and she knew very well that it could all end this evening.

Brian's behavior, since they returned form Atlantic City, was puzzling her. She had kept all the bad news of Dr. Brown's resignation from Brian because it meant no immediate salvation for him as they had expected and celebrated ahead of time, but she didn't know why Brian was hiding from her. And that's what she was afraid of finding out.

The greeting was nothing like it used to be. A quick peck on the cheek. No embrace.

He offered her a drink and she said "later on."

They both struggled to keep a meaningless smile on their face. They sat as far away from each other as they could.

Brian helped himself to a scotch on the rocks and lit a cigarette. That would help to hide his anger for a while. Jennifer kept quiet and avoided an early confrontation. After all, she thought, the man had lost his beloved father only a few days earlier and needed room to deal with his loss. A large picture of Lieutenant Colonel George Brinkley, in full military dress stared at both of them from the opposite wall.

"I'm so sorry I couldn't see him recently. He was a good man." Jennifer used the sympathy approach to break the ice.

Brian kept looking at the picture and took a long drag and blew the smoke to the ceiling and said nothing.

"I understand how you feel Brian, but life goes on. His memory will live in our hearts forever."

He showed no patience for this line of conversation.

"Let's cut the nonsense Jenny. We're not here to talk about him. We have other matters to discuss." His voice was harsh, and disrespectful. Jennifer was shocked.

"Where do you want to start?" she fired back.

"First, I wanna know if you have any idea what's happened to me and why?"

"Of course I know what's happened to you, I'm not so sure why."

"Then let's start from the beginning. Somebody cooked up a sexual harassment accusation against me. A serious issue, I understand, but as soon as I got my first chance to discredit my accuser, a lady by the name of Janet Reilly appears on the scene, totally out of my knowledge and control. She befriends Susan Flynn and tries to get her to rescind her complaint. Now, all the authorities of the hospital are convinced that I had sent in an undercover agent to disrupt the investigative process. People had a hard time believing my innocence, and I had no choice but to deny knowing who Janet Reilly was.

At the peak of my popularity and reputation I suddenly became a pariah.

The next brilliant move of Janet Reilly was to knock at Dr. Brown's door and threaten him with an ultimatum, again totally without my knowledge and out of my control. Now everybody is searching for this elusive figure named Janet Reilly, believed to be my agent. In the meantime the sexual harassment accusation lingers on, and my friends, supporters and referring physicians begin to distance themselves from me. One thing you may never understand is that in this highly competitive environment of surgical practice it is not good enough to be a very good surgeon. There are a lot of other factors that affect your survival and the most important of them are ethical issues. Imagine if the patients or their families find out that their doctor referred them to a surgeon who is rumored to be a sexual predator.

I could have put an end to this ridiculous accusation in a very short time, but Janet Reilly complicated matters. I lost credibility. I began to slide. Committee after committee I was questioned about Janet Reilly more than the main issue of sexual harassment. By this time my destiny didn't matter anymore. The hospital was concerned about its own reputation in the community. They needed to catch this Janet Reilly and everybody believed I knew the person. I had no choice but to keep denying and denying. Even people like my chief, Dr. Sloan, who believed in my innocence kept questioning me about Janet Reilly. Detective Robert Coleman was looking for Janet Reilly. And, the ones who were working to kick me out of the practice, like Brown and Molano, kept drumming up the issue of Janet Reilly.

When Janet Reilly visited Dr. Brown and confronted him with the secretly recorded conversations and threatened him with going to the media and publish everything, a wave of panic shook up the administrative authorities.

Janet Reilly had to be found at all cost."

Jennifer could not take this any longer. With tears running down her face she shouted "Stop right there Brian, I've heard enough bullshit. Let me talk now."

"I'm not finished yet." Brian objected.

"You'll never finish. This cannot be a one way conversation. Shut up for a little while and listen to me. You can talk again when I'm done."

Brian struggled to control his temper and resorted to another drink and another cigarette.

"I'm listening." he said calmly.

"Let's go back to the beginning again. All this nonsense about you being able to put an end to the sexual harassment accusation early on is just that, nonsense.

Let me remind you of the time when, following the surgery on that kid's hernia, you were devastated and distraught about the events in the OR. Remember you called me to meet you at the Hyatt Regency? Remember how you were helpless and hysterical because you knew this could end your career? I had never seen you so weak, so vulnerable and perhaps confused. You were begging for help. I wanted to believe that the accusation was false, but the woman in me always wanted to know what really happened there. You obviously gave Susan Flynn an opening. A few sexual jokes. A little flirting or perhaps more than that. Did you touch her? Did you pinch her butt? Did you invite her to have sex with you? Whether you were serious or just joking you had to accept some responsibility for what happened. You knew it Brian. You knew how serious the matter was and you needed help. Or, maybe you don't even remember. I practically carried you home that night."

Brian tried to interject and she stopped him cold "Hold off, not yet." She stretched her arm raising the palm of her hand.

"I wanna remind you again of the following night when we had dinner at the Sign of the Dove."

Brian took a long puff and nodded.

"You agreed to write a letter to the OR Committee and accuse Susan Flynn of erroneously mixing up the specimens and ask for her dismissal. Remember? You did it, but not really for the OR committee. You did it so that I could show the letter to Susan and make her rescind her complaint against you. In a sense, you accepted Janet Reilly to be your agent. You drafted the letter, I typed it on your letterhead and showed it to her and it worked. She was scared of losing her job; she wrote to you and apologized. Don't forget how overjoyed you were when you got the letter. You get the picture, Brian? You were part of the team all along. Don't you now dare blame me for Janet Reilly's efforts to save your ass."

Jennifer's face was flush and tense.

Brian tried to talk again and she stopped him. "I'm not done yet, I need to get a drink, and I can help myself." The sarcasm did not sit well with Brian but he kept quiet.

Jennifer fixed a drink and returned to her seat.

"Now, let me tell you about Janet Reilly's visit with that jackass Brown. When I walked into his office I knew I had taken a big risk. I knew everybody was looking for Janet Reilly, and I knew I could be arrested. But I wasn't. You hear me, Brian? I was not arrested. Why is that Brian? As badly as you say the authorities were anxious to get their hands on me, why is it that they did not arrest me? Why Brian? Are you listening to me? That's because the truth was on our side. I had proof that his secretary had secretly tape recorded the meetings he had with Dr. Molano. I paid dearly for those tapes and I got them. I caught the man red-handed. He could not risk the tapes being publicized and that is why he accepted my conditions. And do you remember, Brian, when I told you about this you were ecstatic, jubilant, over the moon? We celebrated together. And now you are shamelessly blaming Janet Reilly for all your troubles. Do you understand how disingenuous you are?

I'm not surprised that you are losing it altogether. I understand the seriousness of your troubles, but you are dead wrong to blame Janet Reilly when all along you have approved, appreciated and participated in the process."

She caught her breath and took a big swig of her drink.
Brian took advantage of the break and jumped in.

"Listen Jenny, my problem is not with what Janet Reilly actually did, but *how* she did it. I never questioned your good intentions but I criticize your judgment.

Why in the world you kept *me* out of the loop when planning all these moves? You never thought I had the right to know what you were doing on my behalf? You kept me in the dark as if I didn't exist and you caused me embarrassment after embarrassment."

"Embarrassment? Like what?" Jennifer fired back.

"I'll tell you what. Your last brilliant adventure took place right under my nose, when we were together in Atlantic City. Right when we were celebrating our engagement and basking in the promise of our newfound happiness. Smack in the middle of that you called Dr. Brown's office from our suite, and gave your name as Janet Reilly. You didn't know that they had set a trap for you and me. I guess you remember that somebody called our room and asked if I was Dr. Brinkley and I said yes and he said good to know that I was there. You actually asked me "what was that about?" and I had no clue. Well, for the first time after I had denied knowing Janet Reilly, and said that repeatedly to everybody, to my chief, to Dr. Brown, the OR committee, the Medical Board committee, and the rest of the world that I knew nothing about Janet Reilly's identity, they skillfully found both of us in the same place, same suite, at the same time, and they recorded it on the tape. Some poetic justice! Tit for tat or better to say tape for tape. As if that was not embarrassment enough, I had my share of shame and humiliation when I met Mr. Molano in his office later on and he confronted me with the tape after I steadfastly denied for the umpteenth times knowing Janet Reilly?"

Jennifer was shook up with this revelation. She could feel Brian's humiliation and disappointment. She inadvertently asked "Why did you have to go see Mr. Molano?"

"Because he had sent for me to meet him. Before you made that call to Dr. Brown's office from Atlantic City, I received a call from my chief, Dr. Sloan, on my cell phone. You were asleep and I called him back from the living room. He informed me that Dr. Brown had been fired. Mr. Molano was very critical of the way my case had been handled and was favorable to my assertion of innocence, but at the same time he was extremely disturbed with the issue of Janet Reilly and was dead serious on finding her one way or another. The news of Dr. Brown's dismissal was devastating to me. I knew all your efforts had gone to waste and our celebration was premature. I could not break the news to you and destroy the extreme happiness we were sharing together. I needed time to think. Dr. Sloan begged me to go see Mr. Molano, hoping that the visit would put an end to all my problems. He didn't want to lose me and I decided to take his advice."

Jennifer wiped the tears off her face and remained in deep thought. Brian fixed himself another drink and ignored Jennifer.

"What was the conclusion of your meeting?" Jennifer asked.

"You don't wanna know this one. I went in to clear this whole mess and I came out with another layer of agony and dilemma added to the ones I already had.

This time it was Molano's turn to hit me with an ultimatum. He offered to clear my name, undo all the wrongdoings of Dr. Brown, re-establish my reputation and revive my dwindling practice, all under one serious condition."

He paused to light up his cigarette. Jennifer couldn't wait.
"What was the condition?"

"Turn over Janet Reilly to him. He said she had stolen secret information from the hospital and she should be in jail."
"You believed him?"
"I believe he could easily put you in jail. He is a very powerful man."
"And what was your decision?"

Brian paused for a moment, took a sip of his drink and a puff of his cigarette.

"What would you have done if you were me?" He asked.
"I'm not you, Brian. Sometimes you have to make your own decision." The insinuation was harsh for Brian to accept. He had already passed that threshold and had taken control of his life.
He shouted in an anguished voice "Would you have turned her over to the wolves, Jennifer. Would you? Answer me."
"I don't have to answer your ridiculous question. This is your problem, deal with it." Jennifer shouted back.

They were tired and tormented. Tempers were flying high. There was no more room for courtesy and good manners.
Brian followed "Oh, no young lady. You created this Janet Reilly. She was your invention. You should decide her fate. What's it gonna be?"

"No chance Brian." Jennifer shouted back. "If the Janet Reilly scenario turned out to be a disaster, you were as much a part of it as I was. I admit to my guilt of loving you blindly and coming to your rescue every time you cried fowl, but I won't allow you to claim complete innocence here. I invented Janet Reilly alright, but you initiated this whole catastrophe by flirting with the nurse, of all places in the middle of a surgical procedure. And you wonder why things went wrong. You deserve to be sued by his parents. You destroyed this kid's life, and you know damn well that this did not sit very well with the hospital authorities. Are you also blaming Janet Reilly for your complications in surgery? The trauma patient who went into shock in the recovery room for forty five minutes and died later when you were cozying up with Susan Flynn in the cafeteria and ignored the pages. Was that also Janet Reilly's fault? At some point in your life, Brian, you should stop blaming others for your mistakes and take charge of your life. Your father is gone. Your friends are nowhere to be seen. I am the only one you have and soon you will have to find me in jail. I'll be no good to you anymore ..."

Jennifer struggled to maintain her composure as her voice cracked and she felt the lump in her throat. She was now pacing the room in all directions. With tears pouring out she was struggling to have an impact on Brian. She took a deep breath and continued "So here you are. For the first time you have to make a big decision all by yourself, Brian. Now, you tell me, what's it gonna be?"

Brian would have none of these accusations and remained totally unaffected by Jennifer's crying. He was now furious and agitated and started shouting back.

"I'm sorry to see that you are no different than all the others. First of all I was not flirting with the nurse in the OR and I resent your saying so. Our conversation was no different than any other day. Some serious talk and a few jokes, as always.

Second, I have not destroyed this kid's life. I am absolutely certain he will have children of his own some day. As for my complications, they have been no more than what is considered acceptable and expected. And, much to your dismay, I was not cozying up with Susan Flynn. She came to me and asked if she could talk to me and I said yes. We had a professional conversation in the cafeteria. Late at night, they shut off the overhead paging system so that the patients can get some sleep. It was not my fault they couldn't find me. Moreover, that patient never had a chance to survive. His liver was shattered. Don't you blame me for his death. What do *you* know about anatomy and trauma?

Finally, the lawsuit you believe I deserved would have materialized whether I deserved it or not. Once the lawyers get their bloody hands on these types of cases they descend on them like vultures. Why do you think I have to pay almost every penny I make towards malpractice insurance? "

Jennifer was frozen cold.

Brian wiped the foam off his mouth and walked to his desk in the corner of the room and picked up a few pieces of paper.

"Indeed Jennifer, I have already made my decision."
He handed a piece of paper to her and said "It's all written in there. Read it."

Jennifer took the paper and sat down. Her hands were shaking. She opened the folded paper and found herself reading the letter from Mr. Molano to Brian. He had been terminated as a member of the surgical staff at Manhattan Medical Center. Suddenly, she realized Brian had sacrificed everything he had; his good name, his reputation, his career, and his big ego and had refused to feed her to the wolves.

Before she had a chance to say a word, Brian handed her another piece of paper.

"Read this one too." he said.

She took the paper and looked at it. Brian had been called to appear before the OPMC. She knew what it meant. Brian would be stripped of his privileges to practice medicine anywhere in the State of New York. Brian had lost everything.

She took her eyes off the paper and saw Brian handing her another bunch of papers clipped together.

"Here, Jenny, look at these. You got your wish." He went back for another drink.

Jennifer recognized a summons. The lawsuit she said would happen. She took her time with it. Read it page by page, her tears raining down on the paper, and when she reached the ten million dollars damages claimed by the plaintiff, she broke down. She threw the papers on the floor and held her face in the palm of her hands and cried loudly.

Brian showed no emotion. He stood leaning against the window and lit another cigarette.

The silence was deafening, for both of them.

There was nothing left to say.

Jennifer wiped her face with a tissue and controlled her emotions. She went to the bathroom and washed up.

Brian was exhausted. He went to his bedroom and collapsed on his bed. He pushed his face into the pillow and broke down. He had tried hard not to cry in front of Jennifer. He was overwhelmed with the load of shattering emotions that crashed down on him. Anger, bewilderment, frustration, a badly bruised ego and a deep seated love that was being torn into pieces. Oh, God, how could he bark like this at his beloved Jennifer, insult her, demean and trivialize her? He was trashing the most valuable asset of his life. How low could he get? This had to be a nightmare.

His pillowcase was soaked.

When he calmed down he washed his face and returned to the living room.

Jennifer was gone.

He sank into his chair and stared into the ceiling for a while. Then fixed his gaze onto his father's picture on the wall. The old man's features were stern, serious and unyielding.

He was a tower of strength and vigor. Brian felt so lonely, weak and fallen.

And now with Jennifer gone, he felt a piece of his heart was ripped out.

He wondered if this gut wrenching meeting was finished.

A strange looking object caught his eyes on the coffee table. Something wrapped in paper. He ripped off the paper and was shocked to see a familiar looking small velvet covered box. He opened the top and saw the glaring, brilliant diamond ring with the Cartier insignia on the inside of the box.

Under the box he saw a small piece of paper with Jennifer's familiar handwriting on it.

"I'm so sorry it had to end this way."

* * * * *

THIRTY FIVE

They all arrived on time and took their seats around the large rectangular conference room table. Each one had a large blank notepad in front of them with the Hyatt Regency name and logo on top. In addition to that, they all placed their personal file of papers and notes in front of them on the table.

Some of them knew each other and some were total strangers. Altogether there were six women and four men.

Jennifer Bradley warmly welcomed each and every one, in person as they arrived, and expressed her thanks and gratitude for responding to her call on such short notice.

She took her seat at the head of the table. Madam Chairperson.

For most of the past six weeks since the breakdown of her relationship and engagement to Dr. Brian Brinkley she lamented the loss of her beloved companion and fiancé and grieved the total collapse of her aspirations and dreams of a happy and prosperous future.

The first few days she locked herself in her apartment and cried day and night. Then there came a glimmer of hope that once Brian got over the shock and distress of the first few days he would call her and they would somehow rekindle their loving relationship. There was never any doubt that their attachment to and love for each other was genuine and would withstand this upheavals.

She sat by the phone and stared at the receiver many long hours, to no avail.

By the end of the second week she mustered the courage to call him. She tried his office hoping she would talk with Helen, but heard an ominous message. "The number you've dialed has been disconnected. No other information is available." After so many years she actually rechecked the number. No errors. It was a fact. Dr. Brian Brinkley's office no longer existed.

She then called his apartment. A strange voice answered. It was his landlord. Brian had vacated the apartment one week ago and he'd left no forwarding address. The phone line would be disconnected the following day.

Brian's cell phone was no help either. "You've dialed a non-working number. Please check the number and dial again."

Finally, a flicker of hope cracked the mysterious puzzle of Brian's disappearance. She found Helen Hansen via her cell phone. She appeared to be stiff lipped at the beginning of the conversation. Jennifer opened the door by volunteering information about her last meeting with Brian, the arguments, the yelling and shouting and mutual exchange of blame and returning of her engagement ring, and, for the first time, disclosed the identity of Janet Reilly to her. Helen was always a mother figure to both Brian and Jenny and she could'nt keep her in the dark anymore. Helen told Jennifer of the last discussions she had with Brian in their office, his unwavering decision to close the practice and his desire to disappear from the scene for a while. Helen assured Jenny that she had no idea where Brian was. He would call Helen when necessary.

By the end of the third week, with all the grieving, depression and anguish cooled off to some extent, Jennifer went back to her usual fighting mode and started the orderly process of analysis, planning and execution.

Janet Reilly was back to work in full force.

Despite what she told Brian in anger and resentment, in her heart of hearts Jennifer always believed in Brian's innocence and favored the conspiracy theory he adhered to all along.

So, she thought, let's go back to the very first day, in the OR, where everything started.

With the help of Judy Jackson, who had finally called her back Jennifer managed to get in touch with a Medical Records employee named Evelyn Hillman and found out who else was present in the OR when Brian performed the now infamous pediatric hernia repair. In addition to the late Susan Flynn there was a second nurse, named Karen Mench and an anesthesiologist named Dr. James Ross.

Jennifer also managed to find Nancy Robertson, a key player in exposing the conspiracies cooked up by the late Dr. Peter Molano and the ex-Medical Director Dr. Joseph Brown.

Over the next couple of weeks she did all the preliminary work to put the team together. All she needed was access to the media. A friend of hers was dating a reporter at the New York Post. Contacts were made and he recommended a freelance investigative reporter very well known for his anti-crime and corruption work.

It was time to get everybody together.

Jennifer opened the meeting by reiterating her appreciation for their cooperation in this endeavor and yet she made everybody understand that every person sitting around this table had a personal interest in disclosing the corrupt practices at Manhattan Medical Center. What they were about to do was in fact a moral duty on the part of the people who were in the thick of things by providing concrete and verifiable information.

"I'm sure some of you know each other well and some don't. Why don't we go around the table so that each of you can introduce yourself to the group and briefly describe your position and what you will contribute to this effort. Then we will go into detail and put the pieces together for a comprehensive report."

She then nodded to the lady on her left side.

"Good morning, everybody. My name is Judy Jackson. I was the Director of the Medical Records Department at the time when many bad things happened at the hospital. I have prepared a detailed account of my observations and will provide each of you with a copy, but briefly, for a period of several weeks we were constantly badgered by the office of Medical Director, Dr. Brown and by the Chairman of QA committee, the late Dr. Molano to compile numerous charts of Dr. Brinkley's patients. They would ask us to flag the charts with even the most minor abnormalities such as a low grade temperature. It was obvious that they were digging up dirt on him. I am also embarrassed to say that I was romantically involved with Dr. Molano not knowing that at the same time he was fooling around with the late Susan Flynn with whom he conspired to land a sexual harassment accusation against Dr. Brinkley. Dr. Molano was a devious, disgusting character who would stop at nothing to knock out his competition, and when his relationship with me and Susan Flynn was no more a secret, he managed to have both of us fired."

"Thank you Judy." Jennifer nodded at the next person.

"Hi, my name is Evelyn Hillman. I currently work in the Medical Records Department. I have been in charge of highly sensitive medical records, the ones with potential lawsuits against the hospital and physicians. These records are kept in a secure area informally known as the litigation room. Like Ms. Jackson I was also subject to considerable pressure from the Medical Director and Dr. Molano to provide them with Dr. Brinkley's patients' records.

No physician had that many of his patients' records designated as highly sensitive. It was obvious that they were building a case against him."

Jennifer turned to the next person.

"Hello, my name is Karen Mench. I am a nurse working in the OR. I used to team up with Susan Flynn quite frequently, and we would alternate between scrubbing in and helping the surgeon during surgery or staying in the back as a circulating nurse in charge of providing medications and surgical material as needed and also preparing specimens and sending it to the pathology lab. I clearly remember Dr. Brinkley's case repairing a kiddy hernia, and the reason I remember it is that I was shocked when I heard the following day that Susan had filed a sexual harassment complaint against Dr. Brinkley. I was there the whole time and I saw nothing close to unethical behavior on the part of Dr. Brinkley. Yes, there was joking, teasing, and humorous conversations, but sexual harassment? No way. This was a fabrication from the very beginning."

Karen nodded to the gentleman sitting next to her.

"My name is James Ross. I am an anesthesiologist. I was with Dr. Brinkley in the OR when he repaired the kid's hernia. I fully agree with Karen's assessment of the situation in the OR. The case was going nice and smooth, everybody was relaxed and in good mood, except Susan Flynn. Towards the end of the case she was uncharacteristically rude to Dr. Brinkley, as if trying to irritate or provoke him. When we wheeled the patient to the Recovery Room, she accused him of unethical behavior and said he was going to pay for it. I was amazed. Her reaction was way out of proportion. It just didn't make sense to me. I knew Brian very well. He was no sexual predator.

"Good morning everybody, I am Helen Hansen, Dr. Brinkley's office manager. I've been with him since he started his surgical practice a few years ago. Our relationship was also kind of mother and son type of thing. He had lost his mother at age eight or nine and was raised by a very authoritative father who pushed him hard. He grew up as a well disciplined, responsible and very ethical person, and when this sexual harassment accusation came up he was totally devastated. Actually he kept it from me for a long time. He was embarrassed to talk about it. Perhaps he was in a state of denial for a while. You would expect him to explode, turn the place upside down and demand an immediate investigation to clear his name. He didn't and this was his weakness. He believed he was innocent and his name would be eventually cleared. Well, as the matter lingered on, his practice suffered. His referring physicians abandoned him and his income disappeared.

This was a devastating blow to his standing in the medical community, his prestige, his reputation and his ego. The way the hospital authorities treated him was nothing short of a travesty."

The next person was sitting across the table and appeared nervous; as if she was not sure she should be there. Everybody was looking at her and she was not talking.

Jennifer realized this and came to her rescue.

"Next is Miss Robertson. Before she talks I would like everybody to know that she is the best ally one could have in a situation like this. She's been extremely helpful to me and she has gracefully accepted to participate in our efforts. Please go ahead Nancy."

"OK, my name is Nancy Robertson. Indeed I have a lot to say. I have them all written down here." She pointed to a large note pad in front of her. "Briefly, I was the staff secretary working in the office of the Medical Director, Dr. Joseph Brown. I attended all the committee meetings and was present at numerous meetings Dr. Brown held in his office. I know exactly what was going on behind the scene and it was ugly and shameful. Dr. Brown was a power hungry egomaniac. He believed he had been brought here to clean up the medical staff and protect the reputation of the hospital. He was a man on a mission. And when the sexual harassment accusation was brought up against Dr. Brinkley he found his target. Perhaps at the beginning he did not know that this horrendous accusation had been fabricated by Dr. Molano, but the fact is that they both worked together in every step of the way to destroy Dr. Brinkley. I know of their conversations and collusion. Dr. Brown was a nasty son of a bitch; excuse my language, who constantly humiliated me. I knew someday, somehow his irrational behavior would be exposed, so I decided to secretly record his meetings and conversations with Dr. Molano. I have it all."

Nancy wiped her wet eyes with a tissue and remained silent. The gentleman next to her started talking.

"Good morning, I am Dr. Michael Sloan, the Chairman of the Department of Surgery. I have accepted Miss. Bradley's invitation because all along I believed in Brian's innocence and I also concur with Miss Robertson's characterization of Dr. Brown. I stood up to him in every committee meeting as well as meetings in his office. He was obviously strongly supported by higher ups and managed to do whatever he wanted to do. As a result of his actions, the hospital has suffered and more specifically, the surgery department has lost one of its most active, knowledgeable and talented surgeons. I will do everything in my power to bring Dr. Brinkley back."

"Thank you very much Dr. Sloan." Jennifer responded. "No doubt that the participation of an authority like yourself will help our cause and lend credibility to our story."

She then looked at the gentleman sitting next to Dr. Sloan.

"Hello everybody, I'm sure most of you do not know me and have never seen me. My name is Robert Coleman. I am a detective. I became involved with the case of the late Susan Flynn. As you know she was killed in a car accident. But most of you may not know that shortly before her fatal accident, Susan was attacked in her apartment by an intruder. She managed to flee after she had dialed the telephone operator, who alerted the police and within minutes the police were at the scene. I was given the case to investigate. The apartment was ransacked and there was blood on the kitchen floor. We found her diary in which she had confessed being trapped by a Dr. Molano to accuse Dr. Brinkley of sexual harassment. Coincidentally, at the same time Dr. Molano had been admitted to NYU with a stab wound that had severed an artery to the leg. Subsequently we found a perfect match between Dr. Molano's blood and the one we'd found on the kitchen floor of Susan's apartment. No question that he was the intruder. We found, in Susan's diary, the story of her romantic relationship with Dr. Molano and the break-down of their relationship when Susan, quite accidentally witnessed a lewd act taking place between Dr. Molano and another woman, late in the evening in the office of the Director of Medical Records... "

The detective paused for a moment. Judy Jackson was visibly uncomfortable, clasping her hands together and staring at her notepad. This did not go unnoticed by most of the people present. The detective continued.

"Susan's diary is a phenomenal story of professional rivalry gone awry, a drama fraught with conspiracy, back stabbing, power grabbing, sex and crime all in a health care institution that thrives on its reputation and credibility. I considered it my moral duty to join this group."

"Thank you Lieutenant Coleman. We appreciate your valued contribution." Jennifer exchanged a nice smile with the Lieutenant.

"Before we give the floor to the next gentleman, I would like to give you a synopsis of my own story. By now you all know who I am. Jennifer Bradley, a close friend of Dr. Brinkley and, actually for a very brief period, his fiancée. Unfortunately a complexity of events has caused a break-up in our relationship. At this time I have no idea where he is and whether or not he will come back to this community. Nevertheless, a colossal injustice has been done to him and I think it is our obligation to expose the corrupt people and the institution that have all but destroyed Dr. Brinkley's professional career and personal life. The sexual harassment accusation devastated Dr. Brinkley. He is a proud, ethical person, and this was clearly too much for him to tolerate. As his closest friend and confidant, I had no choice but to begin my own investigation. This, I had to do without his knowledge otherwise he would not afford me the freedom of action necessary to get to the bottom of this tragedy. Therefore I acted under an assumed name I am sure most of you have heard of with curiosity. Yes, in fact the Janet Reilly you were all looking for is now speaking to you."

Jennifer paused. This was an astounding revelation to the people around the table. Dr. Sloan looked particularly perplexed, shaking his head in disbelief. The detective nodded in concurrence.

"But, Miss Bradley ..." Dr. Sloan turned to Jennifer "I repeatedly asked Brian who Janet Reilly was and he adamantly denied knowing her."

"He was truthful, Dr. Sloan. As I told you Janet Reilly was my creation. He had nothing to do with it. Of course there came a time when I told him all about Janet Reilly, and that was relatively recently."

Dr. Sloan turned to the people around the table "The mystery of Janet Reilly became an extremely sensitive issue for the hospital hierarchy. They wanted to find Janet Reilly so badly that they made an offer to Brian; hand over Janet Reilly and they would clear his record, help him to rebuild his practice and exonerate him fully. He stuck to his denial to the end. Of course I now understand why."

The detective jumped in "We were also looking for Janet Reilly. Her name was all over Susan's diary. On her last day, she was rushing out to meet Janet Reilly. The law enforcement wanted to know if Janet Reilly had anything to do with her death. I specifically questioned Dr. Brinkley and he forcefully denied knowing her."

"OK, gentlemen, let me clear a few things here." Jennifer continued. "At the beginning Brian had no knowledge of Janet Reilly, and if he denied knowing her, he was correct. Later on, I can imagine it would have been extremely difficult or embarrassing for him to change his position, more so that he had no part in what Janet Reilly was doing, none whatsoever.

Towards the end, when he was given a two week ultimatum to turn in Janet Reilly, he had fully appreciated what Janet Reilly had accomplished. He realized that Janet Reilly had broken through the wall of secrecy behind which the most unethical and unprofessional acts had taken place and she was ready to break this open to the outside world. Adhering to his own ethical and professional principles, and perhaps for the love of his closest friend and companion, Brian made the ultimate sacrifice. He decided against revealing the identity of Janet Reilly, and, as a result, he was stripped of his staff privileges. He lost his practice, closed his office and disappeared. He will most likely lose his license to practice medicine in the state of New York, because the hospital has piled up a totally fabricated report of unethical behavior and professional wrongdoing and sent it to the OPMC office at the department of health.

More than likely his malpractice insurance company will also drop him."

Jennifer fought the lump in her throat, cleaned her misty eyes and struggled to remain focused. She took a deep breath and continued.

"As we go over the details later on, I will take you through the efforts of Janet Reilly step by step, but I would like you to know that without Janet Reilly we would not be here today. At this time I would like to introduce to you this gentleman who is sitting next to me. Mr. Peter McLean.

Mr. McLean is a well known investigative reporter who has agreed to hear our story, and help us let the outside world know what goes on in this presumably prestigious institution.

Mr. Mclean I give you the floor now."

"Thank you Miss. Bradley."

"Jennifer. Please call me Jennifer."

"Thank you Jennifer and good mornin' everybody. Frankly, when I was first contacted by Jennifer, I had my doubts if we had a newsworthy story on our hand. As you know, I am an investigative reporter. I have spent many years of my professional life exposing corruption and illegal activities in public service institutions. As I heard more details I decided to look further into this story. I requested this gathering so that I can meet all the people involved. The brief descriptions each one of you gave today have strengthened my belief that we are onto something big. However, I have my own rules and principles; therefore I requested, through Jennifer, that each of you write a detailed description of your account of the events. I shall review these and arrange individual interviews with every one of you. I would also like you to know that outside this group, I have established my own sources of information and I'll do my best to corroborate your stories with my own findings. Within the next few weeks, I will have my full report prepared. At that time I can determine the level of seriousness of this matter and decide if it is worth my professional integrity to make the report public. You know, as the result of such revelations heads will roll, people's careers will collapse, and many lives will change forever. One cannot be more careful and there is no substitution for total accuracy.

At this time I would like you to give me your written accounts and make sure your names and telephone numbers are included. We will handle this with the utmost confidentiality."

People were fingering through their notebooks, making last minute changes.

Jennifer thanked Mr. McLean and rest of the people around the table.

"We shall now get to work." she smiled.

* * * * *

THIRTY SIX

The bombshell dropped and caught everybody by surprise. People were running in and out of the coffee shop grabbing a copy of the newspaper, any of them they could get their hands on. The Times, Post, Daily News, Village Voice, all of them were running shocking headlines.

It was early in the morning. The secretaries were in, the bosses were not. People ran from office to office spreading the word. "Have you seen the papers today?"

The Manhattan Medical Center was hit by a major earthquake.

For some mysterious reason there were copies of newspapers all over the lobby, at the nursing stations, in the waiting rooms and in the OR lounge, where nurses were especially stunned with the headline WHO KILLED SUSAN FLYNN?

Mr. Edward Molano's limousine was standing by to take him to his corporate headquarters. He was not due at the hospital until early in the afternoon for Board of Directors meeting.

He sat at his breakfast table. His wife poured the coffee and placed his favorite toasted bran muffin in front of him. His eyes were searching for the morning paper. A man of his stature, a successful businessman and a powerful community leader would not start his day without a feast of important daily news, economic reports and political events. He took a sip of his coffee and picked up a piece of muffin on a fork as he opened the New York Times and glanced at the front page headlines. His wife almost jumped off her chair with the loud bang of the stainless steel fork crashing on the glass top table as he grabbed and opened the paper with both hands and let out a roaring scream "what the hell is this?"

There it was, in large bold letters the headline read:

"SEXUAL SCANDAL AT MANHATTAN MEDICAL CENTER"

Moments later, as he was trying to control his shaking hands and trembling feet, his cell phone rang. It was his secretary at the hospital.

"Have you seen the papers today, Sir?"

"I just saw the Times, what's going on?" The secretary noticed his shaking voice.

"I think you should come here as soon as possible. This is not good, Sir. The place is in turmoil, all these reports of scandals, awful things they claim happening in here, you should see the headlines. You've got to stop this, Sir. This is bad."

"OK, I'll be there shortly; I want a copy of all the papers on my desk."

By the time he walked into his office he was fuming in rage. He slammed the door shut, took off his jacket and rushed to his desk. He buzzed his secretary.

"Nobody should know I am here. No calls. Need a little time to see what's goin' on."

"Yes Sir. Coffee?"

"Yes."

The papers were lined up in such a way the big headlines stood out.

"SEXUAL SCANDAL AT MANHATTAN MEDICAL CENTER"

"WHO KILLED SUSAN FLYNN?"

"POPULAR SURGEON BANISHED FROM MANHATTAN HOSPITAL"

He slumped over the desk, shuffling the papers, not quite sure where he should start.

He spent the next few hours reading every article in detail. Every line and every paragraph were stabs into his heart. The stories were fraught with illegal and unethical acts of jealousy, rivalry, conspiracy and sexual harassment taking place right under his nose. A wave of horror ran through his body when he reached the depth of his consciousness and some inner feeling told him that this may actually be true. The author of the articles had emphasized that the scandal had passed beyond rumors and innuendoes. It was factual and verifiable. He made references to the availability of recorded conversations and testimonies by the people close to the hospital authorities. Names kept confidential. What was most devastating to Mr. Molano were numerous references to his late nephew, Dr. Peter Molano and his sexual escapades and his role in Susan Flynn's demise and destruction of Dr. Brinkley's practice. The story very clearly indicated that all this tragedy started when Mr. Molano was brought in, as a member of the Board of Directors who immediately admitted his nephew, Dr. Peter Molano, to the medical staff of the hospital, when in fact he had been rejected earlier for having lied on his application.

The secretary knocked and he barked at her.

"Leave me alone. I told you no calls, no visitors, nothing."

She snuck her head in, and he unleashed a barrage of verbal expletives.

"Can't you hear me? Are you deaf? Shut the goddamn door."

She left and the door closed.

Half an hour later, another knock at the door. Before he had a chance to roar and groan again the door opened and two familiar faces walked in. Dr. Michael Sloan, and Dr. John Elliott, Chairman of the Department of Medicine and President of the Medical Board.

"Mornin' Ed. Sorry we had to barge in like this." Dr. Elliott spoke first. "We've been trying to reach you all morning. You don't take calls, you don't accept visitors, the hospital is in chaos and you're hiding behind closed doors." He was a no nonsense man and he was angry.

"I'm not hiding John. I'm trying to get a handle on this situation. Who is this goddamn reporter, Peter McLean? How did he suddenly come out of nowhere and bombard us like this?" He picked up a couple of newspapers and smashed them on the desk. He was visibly shaking.

Dr. Sloan pretended he knew nothing about this guy. "It doesn't matter now who he is. We'll have ample time to find out. We have more immediate problems on our hand. The hospital switchboard is inundated with calls from the media. They want interviews. They're asking all sorts of questions. Is the hospital going to respond to these accusations? Whose heads are going to roll now?"

"OK, gentlemen. Please sit down, let's talk this over." Edward tried to cool things off. "I'll issue a statement to the media. No interviews at this time. We are evaluating the situation, analyzing the reports and will respond accordingly. I'll categorically deny the most heinous parts of these stories and reassure the public that the institution remains committed to its ethical standards. We will buy ourselves some time until I can dig into the source of these reports. Any suggestions?"

"Can I ask you a question Ed?" Dr. Elliott asked.
"Please."
"With all due respect, is it true that recently a lady with the name of Janet Reilly as well as Dr. Brinkley himself had informed Dr. Brown and yourself that they had in their possessions tape recorded conversations that were damaging to the reputation of this institution and they were prepared to go to the media?"
"Yes, that is true." Edward responded with extreme reluctance.
"And yet, you went ahead and fired Dr. Brinkley even though you believed in his innocence?"
"It's a long story, John."
"Sure it is. But you never discussed this with us. Since when have we had a one man rule here? Were you protecting your own reputation in the face of Dr. Molano's scandals? Is it true that he was fucking the ladies in this hospital right and left, right here inside the hospital? Did you know about these?"

Edward was numb and perplexed and could not respond. He was in a cold sweat, shaking his head. Dr. Sloan intervened.
"OK guys. What we don't need now is squabbling between ourselves. Why don't you issue your statement to the media, Ed. Are we going to have a Board meeting today?"
"It was scheduled. Let's do it at 2 p.m. We have major decisions to

make."

* * * * *

There was a flurry of telephone conversations between the members of the group. The excitement and exhilaration of their triumphant coup d'état was hard to conceal. They praised each other's courage and resolve and congratulated themselves for a successful campaign against the forces of corporate corruption.

Three days after the initial media assault on the institution, the headlines were more rewarding.

Jennifer Bradley spread the papers on her desk, pounded the large headline on the front page of the Times with her clenched fist and hollered "This is what I wanted, damn it."

The headline read "MASS RESIGNATION OF THE BOARD OF DIRECTORS"

Judy Jackson called her.

"Hey Jenny, did you see the Daily News today?"
"They brought me the papers just now, haven't seen that one yet."

She quickly shuffled the mound of papers in front of her and screamed in joy as she saw the front page of the Daily.

"EDWARD MOLANO, SHAMED BY KIN'S INDISCRETIONS, RESIGNS."

Judy Jackson could not stop talking. "That sonofabitch paid with his life. His uncle should be punished too."

Later on, Jennifer called Dr. Sloan.
"I just wanted to thank you again, Dr. Sloan. I'm glad there are still some decent people around."
"Thank you Miss. Bradley. Heard anything from Brian?"
"No, nothing. I can't find him. It's been two months since he's disappeared."

"Well, wherever he is he'll probably hear about the developments here. He may call us. Let me know if you find him. There are major changes in the works and I need him badly."

Three days later Jennifer received a call from the reporter, Peter McLean.

"There is going to be a news conference at the hospital, at 2 p.m. today. Thought you may wanna watch. Most of the networks will broadcast. I'll be there to ask questions. Anything you want me to ask?

"Yep, Peter. Ask them if they are going to issue an apology to Dr. Brinkley and redeem his financial losses."

"I was planning to, Jennifer. Make sure you watch."

Jennifer left work early and was glued to the TV at 1:45 p.m.

Promptly at 2 the hospital spokesperson made a few announcements.

The Board of Directors was dismissed and Mr. Edward Molano resigned.

A new Board comprising of the representatives of administration, medical staff, community leaders and clergy was announced.

Jennifer cheered when she heard the next announcement.

Dr. Michael Sloan has been appointed the Executive Director of the hospital and Dr. John Elliott will be the President of the Board.

Both physicians were on the stage near the podium, ready to answer questions.

In response to numerous questions from the reporters regarding Dr. Brinkley, Dr. Sloan reiterated the newspaper accounts of how Dr. Brinkley had been victimized by a jealous and devious competitor and a megalomaniac medical director who sabotaged the legal system of the hospital, bypassing the relevant investigative committees and rushing the case towards the Department of Health and OPMC. He then expressed regret that Dr. Brinkley had not been heard from since he was fired. He addressed Brian directly, in case he was watching the news conference.

"Dr. Brinkley, this institution owes you an apology and not just a verbal one. A great injustice has been done to you and we recognize our obligation to undo the damage. I am formally inviting you back to our family of medical staff. We acknowledge the value of your work and your expertise. I am offering you the position of Chairman of the Department of Surgery. We look forward to hearing from you."

Jennifer could not hold back tears. She found herself on her knees on the floor, crying loudly and praying that Brian was watching.

She almost had no doubt that Lieutenant Colonel George Brinkley was watching down on both of them with a big smile. Brian would finally make Chief.

* * * * *

Brian did not make it to his appointment date with OPMC. He had returned to New York in preparation for the meeting. He called the office to confirm his appointment and was told that his appointment had been put on hold because of developments at the hospital. The Department of Health was investigating the newspaper reports and was following the revelations of events related to Brian with keen interest. He was also given a hint that more than likely his case will be dismissed.

He met with his malpractice attorney in preparation for a deposition in the Silverman lawsuit. They spent hours going over the records. His attorney kept asking sharp, stinging questions. Why this? Why that? Brian was agitated. He hated lawyers. They knew nothing and claimed to know everything about medicine. "They're all crooks and money hungry." He used to say. He wondered if this guy's job was to defend him or offend him.

"Dr. Brinkley, when we go for the deposition, please make sure you'll have on a good looking suit and tie."

"Suit and tie?" Brian asked with disgust.

"Yes Doctor. Appearance is important."

"I see. Like those thugs and criminals they parade into the court room dressed in nice looking suits and ties they've never put on in their lifetimes."

The lawyer ignored the comment.

"We've done our internal review of this case, Dr. Brinkley. Our in-house expert thinks this case cannot be defended and we're better off settling it."

"I don't wanna hear about settlement. I've paid your company bundles for times like this. Your job is to defend me. I have done nothing wrong. Who's gonna be our expert witness?" Brian sounded quite angry.

"I cannot give you the name, but he's an experienced retired surgeon. He is reviewing the case as we speak. I'll let you know what he thinks."

"Can I discuss the case with him?"

"Absolutely not. You're not supposed to know his name either. Granted, our expert witness will argue the case in our favor, but in theory, he's supposed to be completely independent."

"I won't give these guys a penny. I took good care of the kid and he's going to be OK in the future." Brian was steadfastly defiant.

"I understand Dr. Brinkley. You have every right to defend yourself. But economic realities dictate differently. They're asking for ten million dollars in damages. Your insurance covers you for one point three. If the jury awards the plaintiff a few million dollars your assets, whatever they are, will be wiped out.

"I believe in my work and trust the legal system will protect my innocence. I know the plaintiff's attorney will turn and twist the facts and play every trick under the sun to deceive the jury. They have no shame to what extent they go to undermine the justice system. They lie, they hide the facts, and they play with the juror's emotions to make the plaintiff look victimized and mistreated. Nevertheless, I believe in my innocence and I stand behind it. Don't talk to me about settling the case."

A date was set for deposition. The trial may not take place for another three to five years.

Before leaving New York for good, he spent a few days in town. The only person he made contact with was the surgeon who took over the care of his existing patients and made sure they were in good hands.

During the day he took long walks in Central Park and reminisced when he would go jogging early in the morning.

At this time, towards the end of the fall, the park atmosphere was gloomy and depressing. The air was thick with humidity and trees were bare and shaking with gusts of harsh winds. He felt nature was sympathizing with his downfall. He liked the company.

At nighttime he went around the town, bar hopping and reminiscing those wonderful years of his restless adolescence and many endless nights when life was so simple and pleasant. His friends and buddies from school, his many girlfriends and most important of
all his loving relationship with Jennifer left him with lasting, sweet memories.

As much as Manhattan had been his home, he no longer felt at peace here. He would now leave all this behind and attempt to rise again from the ashes of his destroyed professional and personal life and start anew somewhere else.

The temptation of calling Jennifer and inviting her for a quick drink crossed his mind several times and he let it pass.

He knew about the developments at the hospital, the new administration and the call for him to come back.

He couldn't care less.

On his last day in the city, he went to the post office where he had set a P.O. Box number and collected his mail.

There was a letter from his malpractice insurance company. He had been regretfully informed that his insurance policy would not be renewed.

He knew what it meant. Without malpractice insurance he could not practice.

A bitter smile on his solemn face revealed what was on his mind. They just hammered in the last nail on his coffin.

Farewell New York.

* * * * *

THIRTY SEVEN

The winds of autumn gave way to the blizzards of winter. This was an unusually harsh winter in New York. Day after day snow piled over snow and froze at night. The city had a slow pulse and most of the usually vibrant hot spots for night life were in hibernation.

Likewise, Jennifer Bradley's feverish efforts to find Brian gradually cooled off and gave way to despair and hopelessness.

Initially, after Brian disappeared, she used to spend many hours on the phone with Helen Hansen or Dr. Sloan or anybody who might possibly receive a call from Brian. She shed many tears on the phone and was desperate for a hint as to where he could have gone.

Before the snow storms, she made two trips to the Poconos. The late George Brinkley's apartment was locked and appeared lifeless. The neighbors had not seen anybody coming or going for weeks. She stayed at the Chateau and asked around. She stopped by the village store and talked to Rudy. She had meals at the Barley Creek Brewery and sipped dark beer, while keeping an eye on the crowd. She came back home more disturbed, disappointed and lost.

She started having nightmares. She would see Brian jumping off the George Washington Bridge. In absolute horror she would reach down grabbing his hand but could not hold firm. Finger after finger the hand would slip away and he was gone. She would wake up screaming.

She spent many hours looking at her picture albums. All those wonderful years of a loving relationship with Brian would come back to her in vivid color. The trips to the Hamptons, taking the boat out, jumping into the chilly water and then those romantic moments in the cozy quarter under the deck. She was still bitter that their last trip out there was spoiled by the urgent call from the hospital. That was when this whole disaster started.

She remembered the trips to the Bahamas or Atlantic City. Every one of them a roller coaster of good times at the beach, in the privacy of their luxurious suites, the spa, the Jacuzzi and most intimate moments in bed and then the chaos and mayhem of his irrational behavior in the casino. How hard she would try to tame his passion for gambling.

It was not unusual for her to actively engage herself in problem solving efforts on behalf of Brian, hence the saga of Janet Reilly.

This was, however, the first time that a series of complex events rendered her efforts counterproductive, at times, and caused frequent bickering between them.

But Jennifer was the one who would not succumb to adversity. She was a fighter and adversity would only strengthen her motivation and resolve. So she pushed relentlessly, harder and harder, all on her own, no matter what the risk.

What was most heart wrenching for Jennifer was the fact that Brian had disappeared before Janet Reilly's ultimate triumph. Had he been around, Jennifer would have been totally vindicated and her loving relationship with Brian would be back on track.

Endless days of hope and expectation brought her nothing but long nights of despair. She wandered through the libraries, shopping centers, book stores, museums and any place where Brian had visited with interest. She frequented the restaurants, bars, movie theatres and places Brian used to take her.

As winter took hold and her enthusiasm chilled out her sadness gave way to self-incrimination and guilt. Certainly, she found ample reasons to blame herself.

She realized that her creation of Janet Reilly without input from Brian was wrong and brought him nothing but embarrassment and humiliation. He was forced to lie and repeatedly deny any knowledge of Janet Reilly. Perhaps they could have devised a different version of Janet Reilly scenario together.

Finally she became sorely regretful of returning her engagement ring. She began to realize that after a cooling off period, the ring would most likely bring Brian back to her. How tragically she had cut off the lifeline of their long relationship. The nightmares were now in reverse. She would find herself falling off a cliff, begging Brian to stretch out his arm and save her but he would stand there motionless and emotionless. She would wake up screaming.

The long, harsh winter spilled over into the spring. The leaves did not open till late May and blossoms were delayed and short lived. Nature had lost part of her majestic beauty and vitality.

Jennifer had lost everything for which she had lived for last few years. Although she had not lost hope completely, reality was beginning to sink in and she was allowing herself to accept her destiny. Life without Brian was hard to imagine but more and more it looked inevitable. Increasingly she kept busy with her job and kept in touch with the very few friends she had.

Peter McLean, the reporter, advised her to start writing the story of her relationship with Brian and the events surrounding his professional career and perhaps someday he would help her to put it into a book. She remembered the comments of Detective Coleman on the diary of the late Susan Flynn. There, he had found all the ingredients for a thriller novel fraught with conspiracy, rivalry, sex and crime. Lieutenant Coleman promised he would get her a copy of the diary.

She liked the idea and went right to work. The first step was collecting material and documents. With the help of Judy Jackson, and Evelyn Hillman she obtained copies of the medical records of two of Dr. Brinkley's now infamous patients. The kid whose hernia was repaired and the trauma patient who died in the OR.

Nancy Robertson had not worked in the hospital since she'd been fired, but she did have copies of all the committee meeting minutes in which Dr. Brinkley's case was discussed.

Jennifer had in her own possession copies of two letters from the late Susan Flynn addressed to Dr. Brinkley. One was the letter of apology and the other one was to reveal the names of the people who had conspired to destroy Dr. Brinkley's practice. This one had traveled a long distance from Susan Flynn to the scene of her fatal accident to the police department to the District Attorney's office and finally a copy to Brian.

She also had the most damning evidence against Dr. Brown and Dr. Molano; the tape recordings of their meetings and personal conversations.

In addition to these, there was an abundance of newspaper reports, the shocking headlines, the editorials and other articles.

As the documents and references piled up, Jennifer became increasingly enthusiastic about her new literary endeavor. Again, the "Janet Reilly" in her advised her to do the work methodically by going through the steps of research, planning and execution.

She reckoned the work would be emotionally difficult. It was hard for her to remain unbiased, but she was committed to it and would do her very best.

She thought she would title the book "Janet Reilly."

Somehow she felt that writing her story would keep her focused on finding Brian. Perhaps someday the book would catch his eye as he browsed around in a book store. Certainly the name Janet Reilly would get his attention like a bomb blast.

She also envisioned that, as work moved along, she might actually have a chance to write the last chapter of her own destiny exactly as she would like it to be.

Summer arrived early. The city woke up from a long freezing winter and a short subdued spring. Activities picked up speed and energy levels soared.

Jennifer was increasingly excited about her project however her enthusiasm was often tempered with difficulties she encountered along the way.

Her story had such depth and dimension she could hardly move it forward without having to frequently revise and rewrite, add, delete, refashion the words, sentences and paragraphs.

Soon she realized that the progress was painfully slow, as the recollection of events would crush her emotionally, slow her down and make her quit writing for days.

Deep down she wanted the story to linger on. That would keep the flames of her love for Brian alive. Weeks and months had gone by and her life was empty.

Her love was the only precious thing she had left.

That, she would not lose.

* * * * *

THIRTY EIGHT

FIVE YEARS LATER

The plaintiff's attorney was quite pleased. Defense counsel readily accepted the deal. Brian was originally opposed to settling the case, but he realized that his options were limited. A ten million dollars malpractice law suit was hanging around his neck like an albatross and would surely follow him wherever he went. For the past five years he'd done his best to break ties with his turbulent past. He had reached the height of his frustration and dismay when his professional world crashed around him and he needed to wipe the slate clean for a fresh start. This lawsuit was a great distraction.

In the past he had fervently fought every malpractice suit filed against him. Most of them were frivolous and insulting to his honor and prestige. His lawyers knew from the very beginning that "settling" was not in his vocabulary. Settling a lawsuit was tantamount to an admission of guilt, he argued, and that was unacceptable. He knew the insurance company couldn't care less for his reputation and professional integrity. Theirs was a calculated effort to save money and Brian would argue that he had paid hefty premiums for times like this and it was the obligation of the insurance company to defend him at all cost.

He fought and won every single case.

This time Brian had ample reasons to settle the case and be done with it. His ardent efforts of the past five years to build himself a new practice and a new professional and personal life were just about coming to fruition. He was enthusiastic about the prospects of his new professional endeavors and he had big and ambitious plans in mind. Lieutenant Colonel George Brinkley would be proud of him.

The outcome of this law suit would have no effect on his new job. He knew he would never go back to New York. He decided to swallow his pride and let the insurance company pay the plaintiff and his hungry lawyers the maximum amount he had coverage for. One point three million dollars. A court battle would take another few years of his time and energy and was likely to drag him back and forth to New York.

Deep in his heart he knew there was another reason he was resisting trips back to New York.

No matter how hard he had tried to bury all his memories of the past there was one that he'd not been able to completely free himself from.

That was a piece of his heart he had left behind in New York, perhaps forever, a part of his existence that could never be without the comforting companionship and support of a genuine love in Jennifer Bradley.

When in rage over Janet Reilly debacles, he would run away from Jennifer, only to be dragged back by the force of love and dependence.

Since leaving New York, he'd tried hard to resist any temptation of going back to her. He'd forced himself to suppress the boiling desire of contacting her again. He kept busy with his new work, new plans, new ideas, far reaching goals, working day and night and even pushing himself into new romances and pretentious love which would last no more than a fleeting instance of self deception only to realize that a genuine love could not be killed.

Nevertheless, he was still in deep pain and could not give up the belief that Jennifer had something to do with that.

Or, was it Janet Reilly?

Brian signed the papers, said farewell to his attorney, and insurance company for that matter, and left New York in a hurry.

He had a big event waiting for him.

* * * * *

The dedication ceremony had been planned in such a way that it would send shock waves not only to the local communities, townships and counties, but all across the state and perhaps nation.

The brand new medical facility in the heart of long forgotten, remote areas of the Pocono Mountains was in many ways a miracle of thoughtful planning, financing, constructing and commencing full operation in the shortest period of time in the history of Pennsylvania.

The ceremony had been arranged outdoors because of an anticipated high attendance. The building was surrounded by sprawling natural greenery as far as the eyes could see. Far back a shade of blue from a nearby lake stretched to the distant horizon. The front yard had been cleared of bushes, trees and foliage of all kinds and adorned with artistically designed flower beds with finely manicured hedges. Part of the large parking lot in front was now lined with many rows of chairs and benches to accommodate some five hundred invited guests. The front row seats were reserved for dignitaries. The Governor and some members of the assembly and state senate were attending.

Two brand new ambulances were strategically parked at either side of the parking lot, each one decorated with flags and ribbons.

The façade of the building was decorated with balloons and flowers.

Above the main entrance the name of the new facility was covered with a large decorative curtain waiting to be unveiled.

A podium had been set in front of the main entrance, complete with microphone and high tech speakers mounted on the tall stands on either side.

The area was surrounded by a large number of reporters and TV crews from the statewide media establishments.

The guests arrived mostly on time and took their seats.

A band of musicians seated on the west side of the front yard filled the air with cheerful music. A soft breeze from the lake mingled with the dancing leaves and branches.

The atmosphere was jolly. People greeting each other with triumphant smiles and handshakes as if they could hardly hold back hollering "we did it".

The Governor and his entourage including the State Commissioner of Health arrived at five p.m. and were welcomed by the staff.

The ceremony started by a popular vocalist from the area singing "God Bless America."

Once everybody was seated a handsome young physician in a long white coat stepped behind the podium.

"Good evening ladies and gentlemen. My name is Dr. David Schuster."

A loud cheerful applause broke out from a large number of guests in the audience who had known David for many years as a dedicated medical assistant keeping the doors of the old clinic open and attending to the desperately ill patients who could manage to travel the dirt roads and potholes in rain or snow and seek medical care.

"Thank you, thank you." David was all smiles as he addressed the guests. "It is my privilege to welcome you all to the dedication ceremony of our revolutionary medical facility. An entity that, we hope, will serve as a gold standard for modern concepts of health care delivery. And you shall hear from our distinguished medical director and architect of this marvel of modern health care services all the details you would like to know. At this time I would like to invite the honorable Richard Hardy, Governor of the great State of Pennsylvania to come up here for unveiling the name of our new facility."

The Governor stepped up to the joyful applause from the audience.

The band started playing themes from America the Beautiful.

David Schuster directed the Governor to the right side of the main entrance where a long, shiny silk rope connected to the curtain.

The photographers were scrambling back and forth to record the historic moment everybody was waiting for. Some focused on the anxious features of the audience from whom the new name of the facility had been kept secret.

The curtain opened slowly and the place roared with cheers and loud incessant applause.

Above the main entrance shined the glittering words mounted on a mosaic of multicolored ceramic tiles.

It read: **Lieutenant Colonel George Brinkley People's Clinic.**

The crowd was on their feet applauding. Some, overwhelmed with emotion, hugged each other with tears running down. There was hardly anybody who did not know George Brinkley and his dedicated contributions to the betterment of the lives of the people in this area.

At this time the staff started distributing the program for this event. In the spirit of maintaining secrecy and an element of surprise they had not distributed the program earlier.

The Governor made a brief speech, expressing admiration for the hard work and dedication of the people involved in this project with specific recognition of the Director of the clinic who undertook a remarkable endeavor almost without substantial assistance from the government. The only contribution of the local and state governments was improving the access roads to the clinic, which in itself was a major undertaking and the work was still in progress.

The Commissioner of Health spoke next and admired the innovative plans for providing health care and medical assistance to the area.

After a short break David Schuster appeared at the podium and the crowd went silent in anticipation of the next speaker.

"Ladies and Gentlemen, It is time for us to hear from the man who's been the driving force behind this remarkable project, the man to whom I am personally and deeply indebted. Almost five years ago I thought I had reached the peak of my professional career. I was a medical assistant working in our old clinic. Thanks to the support and encouragement of this remarkable man, I am now a fully trained physician. I cherish the opportunity to work with him and, knowing him, I am certain he will not leave me alone until I further expand my horizons, become a more knowledgeable, more capable and reliable physician.

Ladies and Gentlemen, it is my distinct privilege and honor to present to you our distinguished Medical Director, my dear friend and mentor Dr. Brian Brinkley."

The crowd roared again with cheers and applause as Brian walked up and embraced Dr. David Schuster and positioned himself behind the podium.

People in the front rows could clearly see the gleam of excitement and happiness in his face. His wide smile radiated with thrill and ecstasy of success and achievement. He almost looked bewildered with the thunderous reception he was receiving from the rank and file, the ordinary people who mattered to him a lot more than the authorities and politicians.

He threw his arms in the air waving for the audience to sit down as he repeatedly uttered thank you, thank you. The applause trickled down slowly and silence prevailed.

"Good evening my dear friends and welcome to the dedication ceremony of this modern medical facility which is truly yours. You paid for it, you supported it and you made it possible. And here you are … it's all yours."

Another round of applause broke out and lasted a few minutes.

"Thank you David for your most generous introduction. I would like to thank our honorable Governor Richard Hardy of Pennsylvania and Commissioner of Health, Mr. Bill Richardson as well as the distinguished members of the assembly and state senate for their unwavering support and cooperation.

Five years ago, in the middle of a stormy night a very special patient was brought to this clinic, a man who was known as a community leader here, a man who had dedicated many years of his life in retirement to the improvement of life in this community. With a distinguished military career behind him, he had applied the same principles of hard work and discipline to his efforts here and had brought about significant improvements in the living conditions of this area. Unfortunately this clinic failed him.

There was no physician on the premises at the time, and the burden of caring for a critically ill patient fell on the shoulder of a courageous young man, the medical assistant David Schuster."

Another round of applause.

Brian went on to explain how David Schuster managed to get help and guidance from the patient's son, a surgeon, on the phone and relieve his trapped hernia which was an immediate threat to his life. David had also realized that something was wrong with the patient's leg but unfortunately a lack of proper diagnostic modalities left a very critical condition of blood clots in his leg undiagnosed and untreated. A week later the patient was found dead from a pulmonary embolism.

Brian then revealed the patient's identity, his beloved late father, Lieutenant Colonel George Brinkley.

Applause and cheers.

"The facility was practically worthless" he continued. "And one can imagine if a dedicated leader of the community could not get sufficient medical care here, what could a regular person expect?"

Brian explained how frequently his father had questioned him as to why people of these communities should be deprived of well trained specialists and why they should suffer from lack of medical facilities and good physicians.

"After his death ..." Brian held back tears and continued "his words kept ringing in my ear, calling me to come here and complete his unfinished mission."

Brian further explained how he explored, investigated and analyzed the roots of the problem. He realized that the poor living conditions made it unattractive for well trained young physicians to move to this area, work and raise a family. Among others, the government bureaucracy and lack of financial incentives stood out. He also realized that the real solution rested with the people. He organized volunteers to approach the general public for a nominal contribution. With almost three million people living in the vast area of the Pocono Mountains, a few dollars from each would add up to a small fortune. Brian held town hall meetings, knocked on doors and amassed a formidable grass roots support for the project.

He then applied his own concept of health care delivery. A one stop shop, you might say, complete with diagnostic facilities, medication supply and laboratory.

To this, he added his outreach programs, to take the health care to the patient, whenever it was needed.

"We have it all in here now." He pointed to the building.
The crowd went wild with cheers and applause.

"This establishment is going to set the example for other rural areas in the state and across the country. This is the people's clinic. Our
people paid for it, built it and now will use it to their advantage. You
can no longer expect the government to provide you with everything
you need. The true power is with the people. The people who helped us
build this place have also pledged to repeat their few dollars contribution every year. That will make it possible for us to deliver free health
care to the needy and perhaps expand our operations in other areas. At
this medical facility we remain committed to take responsibility for the
care of whoever walks through these doors. We realize that this is not a
hospital. If we cannot completely cure a patient here, we consider it our
own responsibility to get the patient to another facility where he or she
can receive the level of care they may need. Lieutenant Colonel George
Brinkley would not have been sent home from this clinic without a de-
finitive diagnosis of blood clots in his leg and treatment with blood thin-
ners. He would have been alive today."

Brian went on to briefly describe the layout of the clinic, the members
of the staff, and the availability of modern diagnostic equipment such as
X-ray, Sonography and CT scan, an operating room for minor surgery,
holding rooms for overnight stay and educational booklets, pamphlets,
brochures, video and audio tapes. There was also an array of communication modalities to facilitate contacts between the clinic and people,
such as e-mail, fax, phone lines, and monitoring devices that would elec-
tronically transmit information from patient to clinic.

At the end of his speech, Brian expressed hope that someday similar
clinics will flourish all over the state and his model of health care delivery will be adopted by other communities.

He received a standing ovation and was showered with congratulatory remarks and complements. It was a long time since he had truly
enjoyed the fruit of his hard work and basked in the joy and gratification
of success, popularity and fame.

Once again, he was where he wanted to be, or … was it where George Brinkley wanted him to be? He glanced above the main entrance. The name was shining and he was sure his father was watching over him from above.

The Governor cut the ribbon and the main entrance opened to the visitors.

A tour of the facility was followed by a reception.

The following day, almost every major newspaper across the state of Pennsylvania had front page reports of the event. This triggered extensive editorial dialogue on health care problems in the nation and arguments about too much dependence on the government to solve the problems. Brian was interviewed by print media and television. His picture was printed and broadcast repeatedly. Praise for the founders of the "Lieutenant Colonel George Brinkley People's Clinic" spilled from local media to the statewide outlets and national press.

One paper with a picture of Brian on front page found its way to the desk of the Director of Business Office at the New York University Hospital.

* * * * *

THIRTY NINE

The fall foliage once again was displaying a magnificent show of breathtaking multicolor scenery along the winding road which snaked its way uphill on the back side of the Camelback ski slopes, ending at the very top of the hill where a large parking lot had been built for the tourists and visitors who would stop for a walk through the state park and for viewing the spectacular sunset.

The cool evening air was refreshing, especially for the hikers who would make it to the top, soaked in perspiration, and would relax on the benches facing the ski slopes and base lodge way down in the background. A few patches of fluffy white clouds moved majestically across the sky and, way back above the far away hills, the reflection of the sinking sunlight sliced through the clouds and fanned out on the vast expanse of the horizon.

Brian would prefer to drive up there every evening and spend a relaxing hour or two contemplating the magnificent display of nature. He was no hiker and clearly remembered the times he would struggle his way up there on foot when he accompanied his father. This was George Brinkley's mountain.

Once or twice a week Brian would make the walk for George, but this time he had another reason to drive up there instead of walking. His little companion was barely four years old, too young to hike these hills.

The hill top restaurant was closed, but the view from the bench where Brian was sitting revived many sweet and bitter memories of the past. The brick and wood structure was sitting on top of the expert rated ski slopes. He remembered the snow covered hills, trees and ski slopes of a few distant winters of his younger ages when he and Jennifer would ski off the chair as it reached the top station and cruise right into the restaurant area. The boots would click free from the mounting brackets and the skis would stand vertically, pushed deep into the mound of snow on the sides. Often the harsh and punishing wind of the mountain top in the winter would push them faster into the restaurant where the warm air and the aroma of coffee and food immersed them in the ultimate pleasure of ski season. They would take a table behind the window, take off their hats, gloves and jackets and start with a hot cup of soup and relax in the warmth of the sunshine pouring in through the glass window.

It all appeared like a pleasant dream. The cold, dark structure of the vacant restaurant brought Brian back to reality.

Just below the restaurant the view from the expert ski slopes would make him shudder.

The memory of a disastrous day just a few years ago was so unbearable he could not keep his gaze on the slopes. This was a nightmare he would never wake up from.

He stretched on the bench, relaxed and closed his eyes for a moment. Nostalgia set in and a parade of distant memories carried him back to a past life he had left behind in New York. The hectic life of a surgeon so consumed in his work that would never let him face the loneliness, the way he was experiencing now.

The wind was picking up and the sun was now behind the hills. Only a glow of red and yellow painted the rim of the distant horizon. A shade of darkness was moving over the peaks and valleys. The parking lot was dimly lit with a few scattered lights.

A car entered the parking lot and parked exactly opposite where Brian was sitting. He quickly turned around looking for the boy. He was riding his small bike under the light post far away from the car. He was safe.

He turned back for a last glance at the western horizon.

He ignored the sounds of the car door opening and closing. Moments later he heard the foot steps coming in his direction. He turned around again and his face was lit with the nearby light. He squinted and struggled to make out the feminine silhouette of a tall, shapely woman walking towards him.

Still in the shadow of darkness, the voice came in unquestionably clear and familiar.

"Dr. Brinkley?"

Brian jumped off the bench, turned around and stood in disbelief.

"Jenny? Is that you?"

"Still remember me?" this time the voice was trembling.

"Oh my God, that *is* you."

He rushed forward and right there, in the middle of the parking lot, they stood face to face.

There was a moment of uncertainty. Just a fleeting moment that did not last. Almost simultaneously they threw themselves forward and once again they were in each other's arms. Jennifer broke down and cried loudly. Brian held her tight to his chest and buried his face into her beautiful hair struggling to hold back tears. Her arms moved up to his shoulder and her hands softly caressed the back of his neck. He could hardly make out the broken words she was muttering under her breath. "I missed you darling, I missed you … I missed you."

"Oh my God, is this a dream or what? I missed you too baby." Brian's voice breaking.

He swung his arm around her waist and walked her slowly back to his bench and sat her down, still holding each other tight.

"I'm so sorry." Jennifer sniffed and wiped her face with a small handkerchief.

"What in the world are you doing here Jenny?"

She rested her head on his shoulder and said "I don't know."

"Have you forgiven me yet?"

"I'm not sure. I wanna spank you." She giggled.

"I deserve more punishment than that. I was a bad boy, a very bad boy. How you put up with me all those years, I don't know."

"I was equally guilty, Brian. I'm sorry we both failed each other."

The cool breeze calmed her down. Tears stopped and she sucked the fresh air into her chest deeply.

Still holding hands, they talked to each other calmly. Jennifer briefly explained to him what had gone on after he had disappeared. The decisive attack she organized against the hospital authorities through the print media and caused the collapse of the institution's hierarchy.

She told him of the new administration calling for his return and offering him the position of the Chief of Surgery. Some of these took Brian by surprise, but at this time he had no regret for what he'd done.

Brian explained to her his new profession at the clinic, his tireless efforts to bring meaningful changes and the success of his project.

He described the triumphant dedication ceremony in detail and how he was praised by the governor and authorities of the state and worshipped by the people.

"I read it all in the paper darling. It made me so proud of you."

He went on to make Jenny understand that he is truly happy here. Life is not that complicated. People are simple, pure and friendly. The atmosphere is always pleasant and inviting. Here in the heart of nature people are healthier, live longer and enjoy life free of hassles and stress.

They had a lot to catch up with, but the night was settling in and time was short.

With the tears gone and faces now radiant with the joy of renewed friendship, alas a very short one, they embraced each other passionately and kissed.

"Stay here I have something for you in the car." Jennifer took off and returned with a gift wrapped package. Brian took it and weighed it in his hand. It was heavy.

"Is it a book?" he asked with a nice smile.
"You have to open it."

Before Brian had a chance to open the package, the boy jumped off his bike behind their bench, ran around and dropped himself onto Brian's lap and said "Let's go home dad."

Jennifer didn't realize what hit her. She felt life was sucked out of her as her whole body chilled. She was pale and confused. She pulled herself back and struggled to keep her composure. She looked at the boy totally baffled and bewildered. *Dad?*

The boy looked at her with a beautiful smile and said "Hi."
Her gaze jumped back and forth from Brian to the boy and the similarity was astounding.
Her chest was tight and she struggled to take a deep breath.

"Is he ... is he your son?" She asked, her voice trembling and hoping for a different explanation. Her eyes wide open and pushing out.
Brian nodded but could not utter a word.

"Hello young man. What's your name?" She turned to the boy.
The boy looked at his father for approval and turned to Jennifer "George."
"Oh, that's a nice name. How old are you."

The boy stuck his head into Brian's chest, raised his hand and flashed four fingers.
"Four? Wow you're a big boy."
"That's my bike" he pointed behind the bench.
"You've been riding, are you tired?"
"Yes."
"Time to go to bed?"
"Yes."
"You're right, it's getting late. I gotta go too." She stood up to leave, looking back and forth between the two boys and her car.

Brian asked George to ride around for a few more minutes so the grown ups could finish talking. Then he turned to Jennifer.

"Jenny, please. Try to understand." Brian understood her shocked reaction. "There's a lot I need to tell you."
"It's not important. I just wanted you to read the book." Jennifer quietly replied, doing her best to hold off the flood of tears building up.

"But you don't know everything. Give me a chance to explain."

Jennifer looked up with glossy eyes and suddenly started ranting. "I... I...I don't know what I was thinking. Of course you have a family. It's been five long years since I've seen you. Five years since that dreaded day I made the biggest mistake of my life. I never should have broken off our engagement, I regret that moment every day of my life. I've barely managed to get on with my life, but I see you've picked right up and moved on."

Jennifer took a breath. She was bordering on anger and didn't want to end the conversation that way. She looked at Brian deeply and said, "If you're happy, I'm happy for you. Please, read the book and then forget I ever came here. I'm so sorry to disrupt your life like this."

She quickly spun around and walked towards her car
The car made a screeching U-turn and disappeared.

Brian collapsed on the bench. Suddenly his mind was so cloudy and confused. Did this really happen or was it just a fleeting flare of imagination?

Oh, no, it was so real, the aroma of her soft and fluffy hair, the warmth and softness of her skin, the glitter of her eyes, her desire filled glances, the fire of her passionate kisses, the strength of her embrace, and the gentleness of her caressing touches, they were all
hers, they were really hers, those beautiful hands, her fingers, her shiny nails, the way she walked, the way she moved, the nuances of her voice, her piercing gaze, her luscious lips with a shade of beautiful smile, and the ocean of her love and affection, they were all real, he felt them, absorbed them, and it all came back to him, the thrill and ecstasy of having his beloved Jennifer in his arms again.

His gaze moved to the ski slope again. It was dark and ominous looking. It was right on that slope some three years ago when the girl he had married out of loneliness and desperation smashed her head into a tree and died instantly. George was one year old.

He looked back towards the parking lot, as if looking for Jennifer and hoping she would return and give him a chance to explain it all.

There was only darkness and a huge void.

With tears running down his face he ripped off the gift wrap and found a brand new, hard cover book in his hand.

He glanced at the cover. There, set against a background of a hospital operating room with people in gowns and masks and gloves hovering over a patient under the drapes, the title was written in bold and dark letters. **Janet Reilly's Crusade.**

* * * * *

Days went bye, weeks passed and his desperate efforts to reach Jennifer failed. She would not return his calls and he was told by her co-workers that she was taking some time off and they were not sure if she would ever return. She simply vanished.

He read the book over and over again, with keen interest in every detail. He was amazed at Jenny's ability to remain so unbiased. She never claimed innocence for things gone wrong. She did not blame Brian's behavior for the downfall of his practice. She expressed regret for unleashing Janet Reilly without Brian's knowledge; however, at the end she credited the role of Janet Reilly with the ultimate triumph of bringing down the house of corruption, discrimination, conspiracy, rivalry, jealousy and crime.

The final chapter dealt with Jenny's destiny. Having lost Brian, presumably for ever, she had accepted her fate of living the rest of her life without the man who was in many ways the centerpiece of her life.

And now, even with what he observed on that fateful night at the top of the hill, Brian refused to believe he'd lost the love of his life not once but twice.

* * * * *

THE FINAL CHAPTER

FIFTEEN YEARS LATER

"Good night dad, I'm going out." George waved at his father and walked to his step-mother for her customary good night kiss.

He was nineteen and looked awfully handsome. Back from college, he was spending the summer at home. His twelve year old sister, Rachel, was playing a video game on a hand held gadget while her mom was gently combing her long blond hair.

Brian was relaxing on the couch, his feet up on the coffee table while reading the New York Times.

He glanced over the rim of his glasses and flashed a wide smile at the sight of his second wife hugging George so lovingly. The painful memories of his own poignant and miserable relationship with his stepmother still lingered on. That was the reason he'd hesitated for a long time to marry again, but now, looking at his gorgeous daughter and his smashingly beautiful wife he knew it was all worth it.

"Don't be too late young man and drive carefully."

"Don't·worry Dad."

Soft classical music filled the air adding to the pleasure of a restful evening.

On a small table next to the couch there was a stack of mail and some papers Brian had brought home to work on. Glancing through his mail one envelope caught his eye. It was postmarked from New York. The sender's name on the upper left hand corner stood out. Robert Silverman

The name struck Brian with many unpleasant memories of his turbulent past in New York and he flinched.

Rachel called her Dad twice. He was deep in thought, staring at the envelope front and back.

"Dad, can't you hear me? My video needs a new battery."

"Oh, I'm sorry sweetheart. I was distracted. Give me a minute."

Brian opened the envelope and pulled out a two page letter addressed to him as "Dear Dr. Brinkley." He anxiously surveyed the two pages front and back, as a wave of nervous curiosity stiffened the muscles in his hands.

"I hope this letter will find you well and happy. I trust you still remember me and my son, Elliot, from the years past when you were a practicing surgeon here in New York.

The purpose of this letter is to share with you the most delightful news, actually nothing short of a miracle, that has blessed our family with the arrival of our first grandchild, Elliot's beautiful son we've named Brian, after you."

For a second or two Brian's gaze moved back and forth through this sentence, to make sure it was not an illusion. When reality set in, he leaned back, took a deep breath and exhaled a deep sigh of relief.

"Honey look at this" Brian called on his wife, extremely excited.

"What's that, darling?" she said, gently sliding the comb through the tangled strands of Rachel's hair.

"Elliot Silverman had a child."

"Who?" She asked … her eyes still on the tangled hair.

"Elliot Silverman, sweetheart." He voiced surprise.

"So what?"

"So what? I've been waiting for this news for twenty years."

"Who was he again?"

Brian missed the question. He was consumed in excitement and was reading the letter again. He'd finally been vindicated.

The letter went on to explain how badly Mr. Silverman and his wife had suffered emotionally through almost twenty years believing that their precious son had been so tragically damaged at surgery and deprived of ever having children of his own, and now that their long nightmare is over, they wish they had never been told of the mishap at surgery.

He explained how this matter was brought to his attention by hungry lawyers who made him initiate the lawsuit, prevented him from talking to Dr. Brinkley and, at the end, took a large chunk of the money they'd received through the settlement.

The rest of the letter was all expression of apology and regret that the lawsuit had caused emotional and financial damages to Dr. Brinkley. He asked for Brian's forgiveness because he was approaching his golden ages and could see the sunset of his life over the horizon. He needed to clear his conscience.

"How could you not know who Elliot Silverman is? Brian turned to his wife waving the letter in his hand.

"Oh, you mean the boy … the kiddie hernia ?

"Yep … that's the one"

"No kiddin', he had a child?"

"I told everybody from the day one that this kid's going to grow up and have children."

He raised his head, glanced at his wife over the rim of his glasses and said

"Remember that?"

* * * * *

ABOUT THE AUTHOR

Dr. Hormoz Mansouri has been in the practice of General and Vascular surgery in New York since 1972. He was born in Iran, to a family highly dedicated to education and culture. Dr. Mansouri started writing poetry and short stories as a child. He immigrated to the United States in 1966.

Over the past thirty years, he has contributed numerous articles, in Persian (Farsi) and English, to Persian magazines published in the United States. In 1998 he published a collection of his poems in Farsi. He has also published many articles on Astronomy and Cosmology, an area of his intense interest since childhood.

In addition to his literary interests, Dr. Mansouri writes, composes and plays Persian music. He is an avid reader and enjoys discussing social and cultural issues. He has long been a guest speaker in Iranian cultural societies.

Dr. Mansouri lives with his wife of forty years, Vida, on Long Island, New York.

Their three grown children practice in the fields of Finance, Law and Medicine.

* * * * *

ISBN 1425180639

9 781425 180638